Severance Package

Severance Package

Eric Nilsson

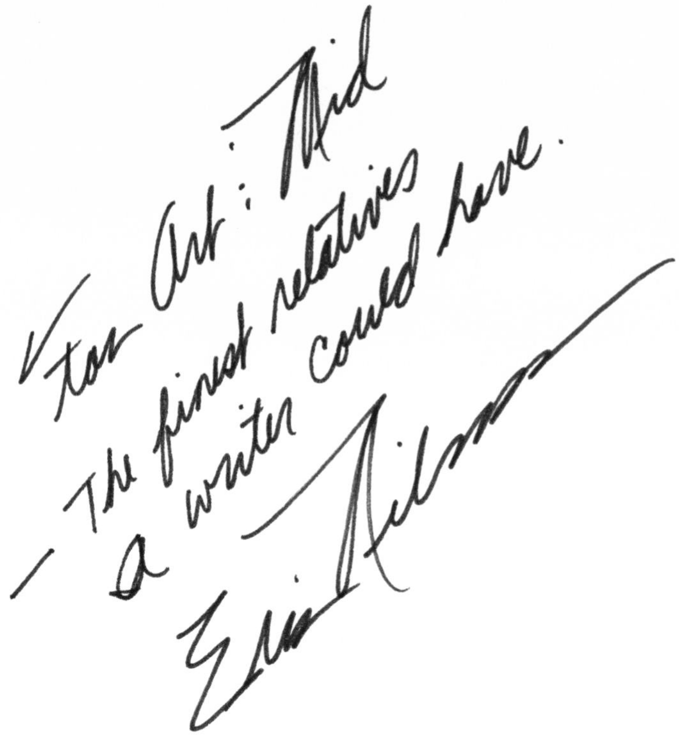

Third Option Publishers, LLC
MINNEAPOLIS, MINNESOTA

This book is a work of fiction. Names, characters, places and incidents are either products of the author's imagination or are used fictitiously. Any resemblance to actual events, locales or persons, living or dead, is entirely coincidental and not intended by the author.

THIRD OPTION PUBLISHERS, LLC
1400 AT&T Tower
901 Marquette Ave. So.
Minneapolis, MN 55402-2859

First edition
10 9 8 7 6 5 4 3 2 1

ISBN: 0-9677444-0-7

Library of Congress Catalog Card Number: 99-98266
Printed in the United States of America

Acknowledgements

If in conceptualizing this book I had known what it would take to publish it, I never would have forged beyond the first page. So it is with many achievements in life: our naïveté protects us from reality until our commitment is irreversible. As it turned out, many people were necessary for the successful production of this novel. I am deeply grateful to them—corporate soldiers across America who shared their stories with me; reporters with *The Wall Street Journal* for the daily stream of "material"; friends and family for their indefatigable support and encouragement; author Vince Flynn for his guidance and inspiration; Paul Kielb for his quality work on the cover design; Jeff LeClerc for his technical advice regarding the hunting scene; all the people at Third Option Publishers, LLC for their backing, enthusiasm and editing assistance; Don Leeper at Stanton Publication Services, Inc. for his advice, expertise and integrity; and Minnesota author and humorist Bill Holm for having prompted me (quite unwittingly) to write this book, when he remarked on a cold December day in 1997, "not since Kafka has anyone written about the office." Finally, I must acknowledge that if life had not imitated art—that is, if I had not been surprised with a *real* severance package in the middle of October 1999—I would not have found time to see this project through. *Writing* the book was the easy part.

For the good people I have managed (or mismanaged)
during my years as a corporate middle manager.

When it comes to money, all men are of the same religion.

—VOLTAIRE

Severance Package

♦ CHAPTER ONE ♦

A Banker's Lot

JOHN ANCHOR, AN ORDINARY GUY among forty-five hundred vice presidents—give or take—at HeartBank before the merger, was an unlikely person to gain dominion over the bank's chairman and CEO, Max Brinkman. A year-long chain of events, however, crowned by an alimentary disturbance of urgent proportions, led John to a time and place favored by fate. With the help of his lover, John seized chance, contrived a plan, imposed terms and held sway. Despite lawyers' dueling and the size of the deal, closing took just forty-four minutes: Brinkman was ordered to be done with it quickly, and he held no leverage; he could not afford for anyone to learn what John and his lover knew.

$ $ $ $

The chain of events began with a phone call to John, just before noon on a hot day in August. "John Anchor," he said with his business voice.

"What are you doing for lunch?" the caller asked. John recognized the voice of Steve Torseth, John's best friend—to the extent that John had friends. The men had met years ago at Lake Bank, one of HeartBank's local rivals. Steve still worked there.

"In fact," said John, "I was going to walk down to the tobacco shop at Ninth and Marquette to buy a Powerball ticket."

"What?" Steve's voice expressed disapproval as well as surprise. "I didn't know you were a gambling man."

"I'm not," said John, "but whenever the Powerball pot hits $10 million, I buy a ticket, just one ticket."

"That's throwing a buck away."

"But if I don't buy a ticket, Steve, I don't even have the theoretical chance of winning."

"Face it," said Steve. "Some of us are luckier than others."

"What do you mean?" John asked.

"I mean, today I got very lucky, and it didn't involve buying a lottery ticket. I'll tell you over lunch at Betty's, noon sharp. If you leave your office now, you'll have a chance to buy your theo*re-ti-cal* chance on the way to lunch," Steve said, mockingly. "What do you say?" Steve definitely had something up his sleeve. Intrigued, John broke out of his slouch, said "sure" and "goodbye" and kicked into gear.

On the way down Nicollet Mall, which he'd follow to Ninth Street before cutting over one block to Marquette, John tried to fantasize about winning the lottery. However, his admittedly infinitesimal odds led him to dwell more on how his life had wound up in a cul-de-sac—or rather, why it had never left the cul-de-sac. Other than by winning the lottery, there was no way he, John Anchor, Mr. HeartBank Vice President, Mr. Middle Manager, Mr. Midwestern-Middle-Class, Mr. Middle-of-the-Road, would be anything but stalled out. At the intersection of Fourth and Nicollet, John stopped and waited for the light to change, even though the approaching cross-traffic was a safe distance away. While he waited, he thought that to be something other than the schmo that he was, a person had to fall into one of four categories—(1) athletes and Hollywood entertainers; (2) Nobel prize winners and other distinguished professionals—brain surgeons and high-powered lawyers; (3) entrepreneurs; and (4) senior executives of Fortune 500 companies. A graduate of the University of Minnesota with a B.S. in Business Administration, John was neither entertainer nor brain surgeon, and he knew it. At forty-two, he was far too cautious to be an entrepreneur, and, just as a long, black limousine accelerated through the intersection to beat the yellow light, John acknowledged to himself that he had neither the temperament nor the desire to become some big shot exec. Besides, in a throwback to his Scandinavian heritage, John sported a bushy red mustache, which he wasn't about to sacrifice, and how many execs with facial hair did one find at HeartBank or, for that matter, at any other bank?

Throngs of lunchtime sun seekers strolled down the Mall, their eyes hidden behind sunglasses and their chins pointing high to maximize exposure. John wondered where they all worked, but judging by their attire and slow pace, he figured a good third were middle management and below. Another third were techies—he could tell by the pagers riding on their belts. The remaining third, he decided, were legal secretaries, paralegals, associates and junior partners from the many downtown Minneapolis law firms. Missing were senior executives and senior partners. Surely it was too nice a day for them not to be golfing.

Beginning at Eighth Street, John slowed his pace to prevent his underarms from overheating. Golf, he thought. That's why I'm not going anywhere—I don't play golf. But he had no regrets. Club memberships were obscenely expensive, and the clothes and equipment, he imagined, were costly too. Not as expensive, perhaps, as all the hunting gear he had acquired over the years, but hunting was real sport, and besides, you didn't have to belong to an exclusive club to do it. You just needed a dad with some acreage up north.

At Ninth, he turned off Nicollet, and with his suitcoat hooked on his finger and draped over his shoulder, he walked toward Marquette. On the way, he saw a man in filthy jeans, a badly soiled denim jacket and a dull green stocking cap bearing the lettering, Green Bay Packers. The air was much too hot for such an outfit, and to boot, the man labored under a large, dirty pack, which bulged with what John assumed were the man's worldly possessions. The vagabond's weathered face was creased with age and framed by an off-white matted beard. John wondered how a guy like that had fallen to such depths, and in his curiosity, John stole a second glance at the man's face. For an instant, their eyes met, and the man's steel blue pupils gave John the chills, despite the heat. Penetrating and intelligent, the grubby man's eyes were like . . . like his father's. His father, who had made a nice living until . . . .

John's thoughts turned from wealth to mere security. With all the merger activity and reorganizations these days, banks no longer offered job security. Though he had never talked to his wife Sandy about it—better not to worry her and their two girls—he knew he had to take charge of his career, not in a way that would make him rich, just in a way that would make him secure. It was something to talk to Steve about.

At the tobacco shop, John bought a lottery ticket and stuck it into his wallet. It was not a winner, but it would be weeks before John got around to discarding it, along with a dozen ATM receipts and VISA slips.

Three blocks farther on, John arrived at Betty's Place, tucked away in an ancient brick building a healthy distance from the central business district of Minneapolis. He and Steve considered it a safe haven—far enough from their respective offices to attract few colleagues, and noisy enough to hide conversation from neighboring tables. Already on hand was Steve Torseth, tall and lanky, with dark curly hair, expressive eyebrows and glasses that slid down his nose. Witty and always good for an amusing story, he gave John a lift, no matter how gray the day. They greeted each other and stepped up to the flimsy metal stand that held a sign reading, Please Wait to be Seated.

"So what's the word?" John asked Steve, as the hostess craned her neck to spot an empty table.

"Big news," said Steve. "You'll be too envious to take it standing up. Let's wait until we've got a table." Steve had a keen sense of timing and a knack for the theatrical.

The hostess gestured for them to follow her to a booth in the far rear of the long but narrow eating establishment. They sat down and ignored the menu. "You know, of course," Steve started out, "that for quite awhile now, I've seen the handwriting on the wall for my group at the bank. There's been lots of consolidation going on for months to reduce expenses, increase earnings and jack up the bank stock, which is great for my 401(k) but not so hot for my current employment."

"You guys in line for a takeover?" asked John.

"Hell John, you know that every goddamn bank in this country is in line for a takeover—either as the devourer or as the devouree. But yes, in the case of my bank, it looks like it will happen sooner rather than later."

"So what does all this mean for you?"

"Me?" Steve answered, pointing to himself, as if John might have someone else in mind. "My job ends as of next Monday—no big surprise—so my résumé is out on the street, here in Minnesota and other parts of the country too."

"Wait a sec," said John, pushing his unopened menu aside, as if it were obstructing the conversation. "I thought the reason we're here is so you could tell me how lucky you got today. Losing your job doesn't strike me as being particularly lucky."

"Hey," Steve said with an overtone of cockiness, "I did get lucky. I got a *v-e-e-r-y* nice package."

"Let me guess. A six-month severance package." John said.

"Try a whole goddamn nine months. Plus, I get outplacement services. And you know that with my credentials, I can land a job in no time flat," said Steve.

"You're terrible," John laughed. "You're now free as can be, with dinero in your pocket and time on your hands to figure out what you really want to do when you grow up. Me? I'm stuck in the same old rut. No such deal in sight for me."

"Wait a minute, pal." Steve said. "You too can qualify for a severance package. Hire me as your agent, and I'll set you up just fine, believe me. I'll take ten percent of the cash portion of your package and you'll think it's a helluva deal. What do you say?" Steve turned the drinking glasses up and poured ice water from the carafe on the table.

"It would be hard to guess you lost your job, Steve. This is the most upbeat I've seen you in ages."

"You got that right. Enough Fake Bank bullshit for me." Steve used the nickname that he and John had assigned to Lake Bank years ago. "Someone said the job losses are hitting middle managers over forty—most of whom are white males—the hardest and there's talk of a class action age discrimination suit. Me, I'm ready to leave, even if the guy who's telling me I have to leave is a pipsqueak barely thirty-five—imagine that, John. My boss was only a fifth grader when I graduated from high school. But it doesn't matter. Just pay me my severance package and I'll sign anything that says I won't sue the bank for age discrimination. Banks are fast becoming dinosaurs. They're in the final stage of extinction, and with all the competition for food, they're eating their own. I'd say Fake Bank—the toothless T-rex—is doing me a huge favor to send me packing before I'm forty-five and really over the hill. But hey, let's talk about you."

"What about me?"

"Your severance package. Let's talk about your severance package." Their usual waitress, Louise, whisked by, interrupting with assurances that she'd be right with them. "Here's what you do. You go into Heckler's office and tell him how you can jack up earnings simply by eliminating your position, provided he gives you a decent package. At your level, hell, you ought to get a good six to nine months, unless, of course, you want to hire me as your agent."

"Yeah, right," said John. "I'd hire you to get myself fired, not to get myself a severance package." Through conversations with John over the past five years, Steve was well-acquainted with John's boss, Dennis Heckler.

"Suit yourself, but I'm telling you, you'd come out smelling roses if you'd allow me to help you through the negotiations."

"Okay, Mr. Severance Package, I'm curious how you think I'm going to swing a severance package out of Heckler, " said John.

"Am I hired?" Steve's eyes widened as his eyebrows rose in feigned delight. Just then, Louise reappeared.

"So what'll it be for my friendly bankers today?" Louise asked, from her signature stance—a leftward lean, with her foot pointing up the aisle.

"He'll have the severance package with broccoli on the side and a diet of Coke," Steve said, "and I'll have the hot Cajun chicken on a bun, with water to put the fire out."

"Huh?" Louise answered, wrinkling her nose. "Have you gone totally loon-brained or what?"

"Sorry, Louise. Inside joke," Steve said, winking at John. The two bankers placed their orders.

"Okay," John continued his conversation with Steve. "I'm not saying you can run my negotiations. In fact, you won't. But I'm curious how you think I'm going to dupe Heckler, of all people, into giving me a hefty severance package."

"It's easy," said Steve. "You simply go to him with a sweet proposal to eliminate your job." John took a sip of water and peered at Steve over the top of his glass.

"Not a hard proposition, I've got to admit," said John. "God knows I've been wallowing in that job for all too long. Heckler doesn't need me—he doesn't need anyone in that spot, and probably won't for a long time."

"Exactly. Tell him he'll not only save your salary and benefits—which are what in your case, twenty-five to thirty percent of salary?—but also occupancy and overhead allocations based on employee count, which, if they're anything like ours at Fake Bank, are at least another fifteen percent of your salary. And then there's all the computer and technology bullshit, which has to be five grand, at least. All told, you've got to be saving him—what are you making?"

"Ninety-three grand."

"Okay, take ninety-three thou, plus thirty percent for insurance and retirement benefits, that's just a hundred bucks short of a 121 Gs, plus ten percent for overhead allocations, that's another 12,090 bucks. What are we up to now, ten clams short of 133,000? Add another five grand for the computer, and we're up to the whopping sum of $137,990, call it 138, just to keep it simple. Over five years with annual raises, you save him over seven hundred thousand big ones, which is real money. I say your settlement value is somewhere between nine and twelve months' worth of severance." John wondered how many thirty-something banker hot-shots—if there were any hot-shots left in the banking world—could wrestle numbers without a calculator the way Steve could.

"With that kind of lead time, I could find what I really want to do for a living." John thought out loud. "I'm telling you, I'm sure not good for sticking with that place or any big company for more than a year or two anyway. Why not get a jump on it now?"

"Precisely," said Steve. "Guys like you and me, John, we don't belong in the corporate world. I mean, look what's going on out there. Corporations all across the country are consolidating like there's no tomorrow. We're going to be squeezed out by technological advances, expense takeouts and constant reorganizing." It was about time for Steve to push his glasses back up his nose. "At our level, we're stuck. Unless you're a gunner, willing to stomp on people, kiss butt, stab backs, play the big corporate game and adopt a single-minded purpose in life, you're never going to advance, my friend. And eventually, you'll wake up fired or retired, but either way, you'll look back on your career at HeartBank or any other big company and ask, 'Why the hell did I waste my life on that institution?' John, we're just a bunch of pawns like all the other slugs, let's face it."

"You'd have a hard time convincing some of the people in my group that I'm a slug when they're making less than half what I'm making." When Steve got carried away with himself, John loved to break his momentum. "I might be a pawn, but I'm not a slug. Slugs are lower down on the corporate food chain. Maybe they can pull themselves up to my level, maybe they can't, but geez, Steve, don't confuse pawns with slugs." John smiled.

"I stand corrected," said Steve. It's reassuring to know that however much you're being exploited by the top guys, who are making a mint, there's always someone below you."

"But however you want to look at it, Steve, there's more to this life than working inside a goddamn bank." John's tone turned serious, just as the food arrived. "You're lucky. You got a package and can figure out your next step. I don't have a package, and I'm not sure I can get one. Besides, I don't know how Sandy and the girls would react to my trying."

John worried about Sandy's reaction. They never talked about work. Sandy knew that John worked at HeartBank, but, if asked, she couldn't describe much about what he actually did there. She assumed that whatever it was, it was paying well enough and would keep right on paying well enough until . . . John retired. He wasn't sure how to broach the subject with her.

"They shouldn't worry, John. They'll be just fine because you'll do just fine."

"We'll see."

The two men turned to their meals and moved on to other subjects—their kids, plans for the upcoming weekend and the doings of mutual acquaintances. When the bill came, Steve grabbed it with a flourish of confidence. Steve had every reason to be confident about his prospects of finding employment, John thought. The economy hadn't tanked yet, despite the latest news out of Russia, and warnings by the Fed had failed to shake the current rally on Wall Street. Steve would do just fine.

The two friends left Betty's Place, and while Steve slid a toothpick into his mouth, John chomped into a piece of cherry DentDream. With their hands in their pockets, they walked slowly back toward the skyscraper district. Steve pulled his toothpick from his mouth and said, "Hey, I've got this great joke." Steve was always good for some humor, by way of either an amusing story or one of his original jokes. "What's the smartest muscle in the body?"

"I give."

"The sphincter."

"The sphincter?" John let out a laugh.

"The sphincter."

"How's that?"

"It knows the difference between a gas, a solid and a liquid."

John laughed and kept cachinnating all the way back. As he and Steve stopped at the corner opposite the HeartBank Tower, Steve slapped him on the back and said, "You can't go in there laughing yourself silly or you'll be severed without a package. Now straighten up and be a banker for the rest of the afternoon." John liked Steve's sense of humor and smiled broadly in return. Why couldn't more people inside that tall, cold corporate tower be as open, funny and original as Steve? But then again, Steve was leaving the banking world. He'd had enough. He had a package and time to find himself. John shook hands with his friend, wishing him all the best, and the two parted ways.

"Keep me posted," said John.

"Will do."

With both hands, John gripped the mighty handle of one of the imposing, burnished steel-plated doors on the west side of the HeartBank Tower and pulled with all the might of his 170 pounds on a six-foot frame. The fifteen-foot-high doors weighed so much and their hinges turned so tightly, that if you didn't put all your weight into the pull (or push, in exiting), you would lose your momentum and have to stop to position yourself for increased leverage. John knew the ponderous doors had been designed specially to symbolize HeartBank's awesome, irresistible power—the unassailable, unequivocal, unrivaled strength of this formidable $115 billion corporation, the eleventh largest bank holding company in America, a far-flung empire of commercial and retail banks, trust, investment and insurance services, electronic banking, finance companies, mortgage banks, venture capital subsidiaries and other financial services. Perhaps out-of-town visitors were impressed by the vault-like doors, but everyone else John knew—customers, fellow employees and others—loathed the struggle for ingress and egress.

After man-handling his way through the doorway, John strode across the wide vestibule and faced one of the dozen sets of heavy revolving doors that offered entry to the cold, cavernous lobby. The people who hated the outside doors were downright offended when it came to the revolving doors, which dragged about as easily as monoliths anchored to concrete. However, as a former football player—he had played with moderate success in high school and had been a regular starter at St. Olaf—John enjoyed taking on the revolving doors into the HeartBank lobby. He imagined the dozen sets as linemen on an opposing team and further imagined them as characters at HeartBank. His favorite was Max Brinkman himself. John had never met the CEO and had only caught glimpses of him from a distance, but John imagined that Brinkman was a good six-four in height and a solid two hundred pounds. Like anyone who had worked at HeartBank for more than a couple of weeks, John had heard plenty of colorful stories about the big cheese—his force, brashness and intimidating style. As he stepped into the opening of a set of revolving doors, John would lock his hands together, lower his left shoulder and grunt as he blocked Brinkman and shoved him back from the line of scrimmage.

The HeartBank lobby projected a heartless image. Enormous slabs of white marble rose imposingly from a rough granite floor, and between the seven banks of elevators that whisked people to all levels of power inside the seventy-story tower, hung gargantuan tiered light fixtures, suspended from cables the size of ocean liner anchor chains. The inhospitable lobby echoed like a medieval cathedral in the middle of the week and gave John the chills. The power suits, cell phone ears and high-end laptop cases that moved through the lobby didn't exactly warm up the place. Normally a walker with a relaxed pace, John shifted into a much higher gear between the line of scrimmage and the elevator.

John marched all the way to the east end of the lobby, to the elevator bank marked, Floors 3 – 14. At one time, his department—National Real Estate Financial Services of HeartBank, National Association, flagship bank of HeartBank Holding Company—had enjoyed considerable favor with Brinkman and resided on the relatively prestigious thirtieth floor. However, after various reorganizations, National Real Estate had fallen from favor, dropping its quarters to the fifth floor. Ever since Brinkman had ascended to the throne six years back, he signaled his like or dislike of a department or an individual minion by ordering a move up or down within the tower. Pursuant to what people jokingly referred to as the "down and out" policy, severance packages tended to be passed out more frequently to managers who had first migrated down a few floors.

John stepped onto the elevator and heard Steve Torseth's advice over lunch echoing in his ears. The reverberations continued with the quiet rise of the car, which carried half a dozen people, all facing the front, all with eyes trained on the light that illuminated the numbers above the doors. Who among these, John wondered, will someday qualify for a severance package? He imagined the elevator as a lottery. The higher the number you punched, the lower the likelihood of a severance package. His fellow passengers all hit floor buttons higher than his. My odds are best—at least among this lot, he told himself.

He stepped off on his floor, passed by the receptionist station, which had been abandoned several years ago pursuant to one of Brinkman's cost-cutting edicts, when HeartBank stock was temporarily depressed, and used his security ID card to gain entry to his department. Long rows of colorless cubicles stretched down the length of the floor to John's section, the Special Assets Section of National Real Estate Financial Services.

Special Assets was a euphemism for workouts—commercial real estate loans that were downgraded or non-performing assets ("NPAs" in bank parlance). Bankers on the loan origination side of the department, people who made loans to real estate developers, contractors and others, referred to John's group as the "Special *Asses.*" The two groups—loan originators and workout specialists—never got along very well. In the late eighties and early nineties, the workout people had plenty to do and thrived while the lenders sat and twiddled their thumbs or received the boot and a severance package. Now things had changed. John's group retained its "Special Asses" reputation, but the demand for workout services was greatly diminished. To keep his group intact, John sought and accepted odd assignments and deals that related in some fashion to real estate but that couldn't find a home anywhere else in the bank. His group had achieved moderate success in obtaining profitable work to offset the cost associated with maintaining workout expertise in an economic environment that produced very few bad deals. Nevertheless, his heart was no longer in the game. He went through the motions of being a manager, but the days when sparks flew were in the distant past.

John's office abutted an interior wall. He was one of ten managers besides Heckler who had an office, albeit a small one. At least it had a door. Inside, the furniture was standard issue for John's level of management—nicer than what his direct reports, his subordinates had, with an extra long credenza thrown in, but a few grades below and smaller than what Heckler had. On the wall was a *Trophy Buck at the Salt Lick* print, signed by Les Kouba, and atop the credenza stood various framed photos of Sandy and the girls and a picture of John and his dad in full hunting gear, kneeling next to their quarry. He hung up his suitcoat on the back of the door and sat down at his desk to check the e-mail that had accumulated over the lunch hour.

No fewer than fifteen new messages popped up. He scrolled down and deleted eight of them. John knew by the sender names that they would be irrelevant or unintelligible gibberish. He then checked the remaining seven to see what required an immediate response and what could wait.

One came from a woman he didn't know, a Doris Hohlinger from the HeartBank West branch in Reno, Nevada. John pulled up the text of the message.

> **I tried calling you but you were out. I have a customer with a deal you might be interested in. Call me at (702) 555-2387 and I'll explain.**

John pulled out a tablet from the clutter that covered his desk and located a pen by the flat-palm pat method of spreading his fingers apart, palms down, and patting the shuffled papers that lay atop his desk. He then phoned Doris.

"HeartBank West, Doris Hohlinger speaking," the woman answered with the voice of someone in her late fifties.

"Hi Doris. This is John Anchor from National Real Estate in Minneapolis."

"Oh, hi John. Thanks for calling back. I'm with private banking out here in Reno, and I have a customer with some needs I don't feel I'm able to handle. I phoned a few people in Minneapolis and finally talked to Byron Caldwell in Master Trust and Custody who said your group might be interested."

"You can try us. What do you have?"

"My client is Walden Financial, an agent for a large trust based in Hawaii. They're a really good customer, really nice people. They've opened several accounts with me here in Reno and have been with us for over a month now." The words "large trust" and "Hawaii," not to mention the Reno connection, raised some suspicions in John's mind, but he listened politely to Doris, whose naïve voice reminded him of Miss Blomquist, his fourth grade teacher and the target of innumerable childish pranks.

"Uh-huh."

"Today the President of Walden–David Prachna–and their CFO came in and asked me if we could set up a real estate funding account for the trust."

"A real estate funding account? What's it for?"

"Do you have any real estate funding accounts in your area?" asked Doris.

"Uh, not exactly, Doris. I'm not sure what they mean by real estate funding account."

"Well, as I understand it—and I have some documents they said I could look over—this is a very big trust, a trust with assets totaling over $5 billion. The people at Walden said that I'd recognize the names behind the trust, but they can't tell us because the names I'd recognize want to maintain their privacy—that's why they've hired Walden Financial as their agent. Anyway, the trust wants to invest about $500 million in various commercial real estate projects around the country, and they want to set up a funding account for acquiring properties that Walden identifies for them."

"I see," said John. He was willing to let Doris Blomquist Hohlinger finish her explanation.

"David Prachna says the money would sit uninvested until Walden certifies that a closing on a real estate purchase has been scheduled. Then we'd wire the funds to the closing. The trust would continually replenish the account until the real estate portion of the trust reaches about $1 billion. Mr. Prachna said the average balance in the account will be over $400 million for the first year. He said if this works out, they'd like to use us for other funding accounts as well."

"You're talking huge dollar amounts," said John, without revealing his skepticism about the whole deal.

"Yes we are—and imagine what the bank would earn on the uninvested cash—what's our internal investment pricing, five point four percent?—times an average balance of $400 million." The voice of Miss Blomquist reincarnated assumed the tone of a commissioned salesperson calculating her take.

"Why would they leave that kind of money uninvested?"

"I asked Mr. Prachna that, and he said the trust wants to have plenty of cash immediately available for buying opportunities, plus, the trust instrument limits the percentage of total funds that can be in any sort of securities or money market accounts—I couldn't really understand it all—he said the permissible investments under the trust instrument were very complicated, the whole trust is very complicated, but he said he wouldn't expect us to charge any fees because we would be getting the benefit of the cash not being invested."

John estimated that the interest income that the bank would earn from $400 million to $500 million sitting around uninvested would be about $20 million to $25 million—enough to knock the socks off his boss,

Heckler, and Heckler's boss, Jack Dunn. Something that big would even earn kudos from Brinkman himself. But John quickly came to his senses. He had encountered a number of scams during his years at the bank, and one feature was a dead giveaway: If the revenues associated with a prospective deal are too good to be true, then the deal is probably a scam. There's no such thing as a free lunch.

"I don't know, Doris," John said. He couldn't extinguish the image of Miss Blomquist in his mind and wasn't as assertive as he would have been with someone younger and less sweet-sounding. "I question what you've got here. I'm not sure this is a legitimate deal."

"I had to ask myself that too, John, but I checked out Walden and they're legitimate. They have a Website and everything. They're out of Toronto and they gave me several references, which checked out, and they've been a very good customer. Mr. Prachna is a very nice man. He even had flowers sent to me when he heard my cat died."

"But Doris, how does a trust based in Hawaii hire a financial advisor based in Toronto, Ontario, who comes into a HeartBank West branch in Reno, Nevada?"

"Oh, I didn't tell you. Walden just opened an office here. They have a number of clients here in the Tahoe area—very wealthy clients—and through one of their contacts here, they got the Hawaii trust referral."

"I see," John lied. He didn't see it and he didn't buy it. He owed it to Doris to dash her naïveté before it got her and the bank into trouble. "Well, Doris, I'd be very cautious about this, and to tell you the truth—" Doris cut him off.

"John, I'd really like to help the customer. What if I fax you what I have, and then you can look it over and we can talk some more?" John agreed. He figured he'd get the fax, confirm his suspicions, call Doris back and be done with it. Little did he know that his conversation with Doris, a relatively low-level private banker in a faraway branch, a woman he could only guess about and would never meet, would one day lead him to the right place at the right time.

He hung up. The call had suppressed his pondering about a severance package, and a series of interruptions—members of his group dropping by to complain about one thing or another, from "Why can't Jan get off her fat ass and get me the such and such report?" to "Why hasn't my promotion gone through yet?"—effectively distracted John from any further thoughts about a severance package. He was in a rut, a ditch, and as much as he could move to the left or to the right, he couldn't move out. John spent the rest of his workday treading water, as had become his routine. He volleyed e-mail back and forth, plowed his way through unintelligible computer printouts reporting transactions of one sort or another, jabbered with others in the office and took in the latest gossip. John also stared at *Trophy Buck at the Salt Lick,* mined his nose and wallowed in thoughts about his job. A job that had become like his recliner in the den at home—soft and comfortable but old, ugly and not going anywhere, except maybe to Goodwill.

There were a couple of letters he needed to send out, items that had been on his To Do list for several days, but it wasn't until about four-thirty that John remembered. One of them had to go out before day's end. Recently, a clever borrower, whose business was on the ropes, had tried to manipulate John into discounting the guy's building loan of $450,000. After a couple of meetings with John, the borrower had sent him a letter of distortions. "Pursuant to our recent conversations in which you indicated the bank would be willing to discount the principal owing on my loan," the unscrupulous borrower had written—John had said nothing about any discount—"I propose payment of $100,000 in full satisfaction of the loan. Unless I hear from you to the contrary by the end of business, Tuesday August 22, I will assume you accept this proposal and will rely on your acceptance in connection with inventory purchases I plan to make on Wednesday August 23."

John knew the deadbeat's scheme wouldn't hold up in court, or could it? This particular borrower had a litigious reputation, and a written rejection, faxed out today, was an advisable caution. Accordingly, John scrambled to draft the appropriate response. Most people in the department sent out their own letters, but John still relied on his administrative assistant, Diana, to format a letter and to print it onto HeartBank letterhead. Between Diana's mistakes and her lack of speed, the letter barely went out by half past five.

♦ CHAPTER TWO ♦

The Home Front

DONE FOR THE DAY, JOHN LEFT THE OFFICE. As he merged into traffic crawling westward out of the city on I-394, John noticed the hint of fall in the air. Here and there, a maple revealed a tinge of red, and the sun, declining earlier by the day, was swinging closer to the end of the highway. In less than a month, on the fall equinox, it would be smack dab in his eyes at this time of day, and then gradually, it would drift south of the east-west highway and signal the onset of winter.

Ever since his first deer hunting trip with his father and grandfather, John's favorite season was autumn. It brought invigorating air down from Canada and an excuse to escape to the wilds of northern Wisconsin, far from the static and commotion of life at the bank and away from family demands. His wife understood it as a male thing, and failed to grasp its full significance to John. His daughters knew it only as a time when their father disappeared into the woods.

John daydreamed about the hunting season ahead. Just he and his father. Just the two of them, so they could talk about life, about work, about John's struggle to find vocational purpose. His daydreaming turned to fantasy, as he imagined himself and Sandy, after the girls left for college, living in a small community up north, where he could rid his life of stress and corporate nonsense and make a tidy income doing something like carving hunting decoys, a hobby at which he dabbled now and again. With a severance package, he thought, perhaps he could accelerate the timetable or lay the foundation, and set up a decoy carving business in his very own basement. But how to secure the severance package? He wished he had the gumption of his friend Steve. Would Heckler really react favorably to such a plan?

As John exited the freeway onto Rose Briar Road, he imagined himself sitting in Heckler's office, the paunchy Heckler strutting back and forth, black eyes bulging, hair greased straight back over a rapidly expanding bald spot, hands pulling on his obnoxious suspenders—the ones with the dollar signs—his big, round, shiny cufflinks flashing beams about the room. Mr. Flash-and-Dash would not be an easy audience. For the next mile to John's neighborhood, the car proceeded robotically after years over the same daily route. "Dennis," John began aloud his imaginary script, "I have an idea that can save you lots of money," only to see Heckler spin around and flash his oversized, intimidating eyes. It was as far as John could imagine without feeling a lump of fear in his throat.

John turned down his street and followed it to his house at the end of the cul-de-sac. Although his family had lived there for eight years, they knew few of the neighbors. Everyone was far too busy to get acquainted. Not the most expensive homes in Minnetonka by a very long shot, they did bear impressive facades. It was amazing how much better vinyl soffits and shutters looked today than they did fifteen years ago, when John and Sandy had bought their first house, a rambler in the low rent district of the same suburb. John assumed that his neighbors enjoyed successful and fulfilling careers. He doubted that any of them worried about how to negotiate a severance package.

He parked his Ford Explorer next to Sandy's mini-van in the garage and followed the routine of dragging his briefcase and suitcoat out of the SUV and himself into the house. The family was already at the kitchen table, halfway into their dinner. "We figured you were going to be late, so we went ahead without you," said Sandy. Her tone reflected the usual disappointment when John failed to appear by 5:30 sharp.

"An emergency came up at work. I had to deal with it." John's characterization of his procrastination-turned-to-urgency failed to elicit any sympathy or interest. "Hi kids," he added. The television on the kitchen counter held their attention. "I said *'Hi kids!'*"

"Oh, hi, Dad," sixteen-year-old Jessica mumbled, as she speared a piece of lettuce from her salad. Jessica looked like her mother's younger sister, with distant blue eyes, light brown hair that brushed her shoulders and a pleasing figure.

"Hi," added her year-younger sister, Linnea. Linnea more closely resembled John, with her reddish hair and blue eyes that always sparkled ahead of her smile when she greeted a friend. Less intense than her mother or sister, she shared her father's love of nature and stayed apart from the crowd.

"So how was everyone's day?" John tried to give the slip to his thoughts about work. Over her daughters' protests, Sandy rose to turn off the television. The conversation went nowhere, however, and soon the girls were off while their parents exchanged information.

"Your dad called today, John. He wants to talk about your Thanksgiving vacation deer hunting trip. He and your mom are expecting you."

"What about you and the kids?"

"Remember? My folks are expecting Jessica and me down in Phoenix that whole week. Linnea is going with you," said Sandy. "By the way, I'll have to work the weekend before Thanksgiving." To bring in some extra cash, Sandy worked part-time as an arranger at a floral shop. A former teacher like John's mother, Sandy had quit when the girls were young and had never gone back. For the past five years, she'd worked at the shop and acquired a respectable reputation as a floral arranger. John didn't appreciate all that went into it, but he thought it might form the basis for a business. A nice severance package would go a long way toward getting it off the ground.

"Remember Steve Torseth?" John changed the subject.

"Yeah. What about him?"

"I had lunch with him today. He got the ax at Lake Bank and walked out with a nine-month severance package."

"What's he going to do for a job?" The liberal severance package made no impression on Sandy, who was a very pragmatic person and always looked at total and long-term solutions, not temporary remedies.

"Don't know, but I'm sure he'll do just fine. He's already got his résumé out to a bunch of places. He should land something good fairly quickly."

"Hope so for his sake," said Sandy. Her voice said she wasn't convinced. Although John and Steve were long-standing friends, they had done very little together outside the workplace, and Sandy had met Steve only a few times. She possessed little interest in his prospects.

"Actually, Steve tried to talk me into asking Heckler for a severance package myself."

"I hope he didn't succeed."

"Since you raised the question, I have to say, 'Yes.' I've been thinking about it."

Sandy looked up and shot a look of disapproval at John. "Why would you want to do a thing like that? Your job isn't on the line is it? I mean you've never said anything about it being on the line." If she had ever worried about the family's main source of income, she had never let on to John.

"No, my job isn't on the line," said John. He saw his trial balloon plunge.

"Whew," said Sandy, feigning relief. "You had me worried." She stood up, cleared her plate and drinking glass from the table and moved toward the kitchen sink. "John, I have to run some errands this evening. Target and the grocery store, and I promised Cindy I'd swing by the shop to finish off an arrangement that's going out first thing tomorrow. Do you mind cleaning up?"

"No, uh, fine." John answered.

"Jessica and Linnea are going over to Soderberg's—they should be home by ten. The house is yours, but you probably want to get the lawn mowed. It's supposed to rain tomorrow."

John felt the door of his vocational cage slam shut. How could he explain to Sandy his frustration with his daily routine, his desire to try something new and different? Steve had spurred John to think about taking a bold first step. Now Sandy, in her inimitably pragmatic way, had yanked John back to reality.

However, Sandy's pragmatism worked only when she was present to enforce it. By the time she and the girls were gone and John was behind the lawn mower, his thoughts had found their way back to the lock on his cage and how he might jimmy it open. Later that evening, he repaired to the den, sank into the Lazy-Boy and pulled *The Wall Street Journal* from his briefcase. He opened the *Market* section and turned to the ads under the *Business Opportunities* banner. Some caught his attention:

Tired of the Corporate Routine?
Run your own arbitration service
call 1-800-555-3443 for introductory kit

and

Equipment Leasing Broker
Clear $100K -1st 12 mo.
Work from home
We provide funding sources
www.eqleasbrok.com
1-800-555-8712

Other ads, like "Be in the dough—be a donut hole franchisee," made his present circumstances seem downright desirable. He folded up the paper, tossed it into the recycling pile in the garage and realized he'd forgotten to return his father's call.

"Hello?"

"Hi Dad. It's me."

"John. You got my message. Time to think about deer, even though it isn't deer time yet, what do you think?" Marv Anchor's rich, confident voice hid the disappointments of his life.

"I can't wait, Dad. Especially this year. I can't wait to get away."

"Everything okay?"

"Yeah, sure, everything's fine, Dad."

"Can it wait until we go huntin'?" It was hard for John to fool his dad, even when John wasn't trying to fool him. On the other hand, John's father wasn't one to pry, and he had plenty of patience.

"Sure, Dad." John acknowledged there was something to talk about, but it pained him to think that by talking about work, he might reopen his father's wounds. For an instant, John recalled how his father—himself a bank vice president—had lost his job.

"Okay, then. 'Bye now."

"'Bye, Dad." In the silence that followed, John returned to his recollection of that dark period in his youth. John was a freshman at St. Olaf College when the blow had struck, just before Christmas. After twenty-seven years of loyal service at First Metropolitan Bank—an institution that had long since disappeared in successive waves of bank mergers and acquisitions—John's father had been given the boot. Back then, in the late seventies, they didn't hand out severance packages unless you were at the very top. John's dad got two weeks' notice and six weeks' pay after that—a generous package by the standards of the day.

John gazed out at the backyard and pondered how at fifty-two, his father had been too old to find another job at equal pay and too young to retire securely. He had become a consultant but found it rough sledding. John's mother, a former teacher, had found work as a substitute, but the family's income had never fully recovered. John had been forced to transfer to the U of M, and both he and his younger sister had worked hard to cover the cost of education. He didn't want his own kids to go through what he had experienced.

◆ CHAPTER THREE ◆

The Scam

SEVERAL WEEKS PASSED, and little changed at work, except for the deal from hell—the deal that Doris Hohlinger had innocently unloaded on John. When John resisted taking it, Heckler caught wind of it and stormed into John's office.

"I hear you turned down a $25 million piece of business. You sure are getting crotchety in your old age. What the hell are you thinking about, anyway?"

"It was a piece of crap, Dennis, of the scam variety. You're lucky I turned it down."

"Piece of crap, my ass. Twenty-five million bucks dropping to the bottom line is not a piece of crap, at least the last time I checked our stock price."

"Dennis, it's a scam, and it works like this." Heckler hadn't stormed out of John's office yet, which gave John some hope he could explain things. "These con-men establish contact with a friendly, naïve banker out in Nevada. They open a few diddly accounts to establish a relationship and a reference, someone who will vouch for them. When they have the poor banker eating out of their greasy palms, they lay the big one on her.

"She's in over her head, which they're counting on, so she calls someone out here—eventually gets to me. I turn the deal down, but then these sly characters ask me to explain what it is I don't like about the deal."

"And what exactly is it that you don't like about twenty-five million bucks?" Heckler said, reproachfully.

"Dennis, there's no such thing as a free lunch, first of all, and second, since when do hush-hush Hawaiian trusts hire a fly-by-night, so-called financial agent to set up a real estate funding account with half a billion bucks of uninvested cash in a Minnesota bank?"

"So? We do all kinds of oddball deals. That's our game. Besides, my friend, you know as well as me—oddball deals are what give us job security around here. We start accepting deals *they* can understand," Heckler referred to the execs on the seventieth floor by pointing at the ceiling, "and before we know it, we're dispensable. Besides, 'odd' doesn't mean the deal is a scam. Where's the scam?"

John saw where the discussion was going, but he tried to pull Heckler back. "The scam is where you can't see it. Somewhere along the way—before they ever deposit half a billion bucks or even half of one buck, they'll get you when you aren't looking. There'll be a request for something—an advance for some legal fees, something like that. There'll be some fabricated snafu in getting the funds wired in from Liberia. Geez, Dennis, I don't know, but believe me, this is not a real deal. At best, it's laundered money, how's that for you? Laundered money that's going to be used by Afram Safram and Bin Sinbad to buy nuclear missiles for terrorists, I don't know. Just let this one go, Dennis."

"Okay, okay. Maybe you're right, but maybe you're not. Here's what I'm willing to do. I want you to call these guys back and give 'em a little more slack. These guys aren't in workout, you know. Just make damn sure they aren't legit, and by no means do I want to be getting calls from upstairs—I mean *way* upstairs—asking me why we turned down $25 million in bottom line money. Understood?" Heckler thrust at John a message slip with the phone number for Dave Prachna at Walden and walked out without waiting for John's reply.

Heckler was dangerous. How he had managed to survive as long as he had, surprised John and most others in the department. However, Heckler was the King of Bamboozlement, and he had kept auditors and external bank examiners at bay for a respectable number of years. Heckler ran his department as a personal fiefdom. Either by design (Heckler was no dummy) or by accident, he had created such a hydra-headed group of computer systems, accounting complexities, obfuscated businesses and reporting entanglements, that he effectively kept everyone off balance—both the legions below him and the senior executives above. True, Brinkman had kicked Dennis' department down many floors of the tower, but the odds seemed to favor Dennis' avoiding exile or execution. People were afraid of him, and certainly none of the people on the seventieth floor had a clue about his business, except that it involved real estate.

John steamed and felt his face swell with anger. He resolved to shut down the Walden swindle. He also resolved to ask for a severance package. To hell with Heckler, thought John, and to hell with HeartBank, whether Sandy thinks leaving the bank is good idea or not. Besides, how would she ever understand what an utter zoo this place is? It would be far easier to ask forgiveness than to obtain permission.

But first things first. John phoned Prachna, got voice mail and left a message. Within minutes, the scam artist called back. Judging by the background noise, John guessed that Prachna was calling from a cell phone in a bar, not from a legitimate office.

"Hello." John could coat his voice with ice when he disliked someone.

"Mr. Anchor, I'm so pleased you phoned. I can certainly understand your reticence—you sound like a very intelligent guy, exactly the kind of banker I want to do business with. What I'd like to do is send you some documents and some background on us at Walden. We represent a large number of offshore companies, trusts and wealthy individuals who want to protect their privacy. You'd be impressed by the list of famous people who use us. Walden was formed five years ago by a group of former investment bankers to take advantage of a huge market out there. Anyway, let me send you some stuff, take a look at it and we can go from there."

John had "no" on his tongue, but to his surprise, "okay" rolled off and over the phone. He concluded the conversation as if he'd just stepped in a dog turd on the sidewalk. "Damn it!" he yelled, as he slammed the receiver down.

Later that day, Diana walked in with a lengthy fax from Prachna. John leafed through the papers, which included a cover letter; three pages of marketing materials, including quotations by satisfied but unidentified "clients"; a two-page draft agreement, which struck John as having a little too much legalese and too little substance to have been written by a legitimate lawyer. By the way, John asked himself, where *are* the lawyers? Since when did anyone in this country do a half billion-dollar deal without a bevy of lawyers? He'd forgotten to mention *that* to Heckler. An article by a Professor Simpkins from the *Journal of International Economics* made up the rest of the fax. Based on the section headings, the article seemed to concern arcana about foreign exchange and the electronic transfer of money internationally.

John went back to the cover letter.

> Dear Mr. Anchor,
>
> Thank you for your interest in doing business with Walden Financial, as agent for various private trusts, foundations and individuals. We look forward to a long-standing, mutually rewarding relationship. Pursuant to our phone conversation this afternoon, please mark up the enclosed draft agreement and return it at your earliest convenience. We will then put it into final form for signature.
>
> Sincerely,
> /s/
> David Prachna
> CEO and President

John saw red. Prachna was a liar and a cheat. Time to shut down the crook's maneuvering, once and for all, but try as he might, he couldn't reach him by phone, and nothing would go through on the fax.

♦ CHAPTER FOUR ♦

A Prospect

TWO WEEKS LATER, John entered Betty's Place and scanned the tables and booths for Steve Torseth. The two hadn't seen each other since their previous lunch at Betty's. John found him in a booth at the far end of the room.

"Good to see you, Steve."

"Yeah, likewise. How goes it? How goes that severance package?" The sparkle was gone from Steve's eyes, but in his inimitable way, he put on a smile.

"I'm finally going to do something about it."

"You mean you don't have one yet? Geez you move slow." Steve's old spunk was making a comeback.

"But you, Steve. How are you doing?" Before he could answer, Louise slid up to their booth.

"Burgers for bankers today?" she said.

"I'll have the burger, he's still the banker," said Steve.

"Huh?" Louise gave him one of her "I don't understand, but you're not going to make me feel dumb" looks. In return, they gave their orders.

"I'm facing a dilemma, John." Steve assumed a serious countenance again. "AmBanCo in Charlotte has all but given me an offer—an attractive one, too. They want to fly Beth and me out there next week to talk salary, have a look at houses, schools, the whole shebang."

"I thought you'd left corporate life, not to mention the banking world," said John. Steve winced. "Sorry. What's the job?"

"Eastern Regional Sales Manager for Institutional Investment Products."

"Sounds great." John lied. It sounded incredibly boring.

"Except neither of us wants to uproot the kids and move to North Carolina. Can you imagine moving there?"

"No, I can't, but what other prospects do you have right now?"

"That's really the only sure thing. The headhunter who called me about it is really pushing it, of course, but I'd like to generate some offers here in the Twin Cities before I leap at the first opportunity. I've got to explore some other angles." They turned to other subjects. The usual. When the check came, John noticed Steve did not reach for it, as he usually did, to figure his share. To test Steve's confidence in his job and financial prospects, John let the check rest next to an ice cube that had escaped from the water carafe. The ice cube melted into a pond the size of a half dollar and soaked the check. Steve never did pick it up, and John paid for both of them.

As they exited Betty's, Steve stopped. "I'm parked down this way," he said, as he pointed away from the central business district of Minneapolis. Parking's cheaper."

"So I'm on my own back to the high rent district?" said John.

"High rent and high stress."

"Not once I get my severance package."

"The operative words there," Steve said, pointing his finger into John's face, "are 'once I get.' If you don't get on the stick, you'll wind up at Heart-Bank for life—like the banker who was so stressed out, his doctor said, 'You're about to have the big one.'"

"As in heart attack?" John smiled at the prospect of a joke.

"Yeah. There was this banker, see, who'd worked his way up the organization, was really successful, made tons of money and had a thousand people under him. Only problem was, he was stressed out. I mean so stressed out he had to go to his doctor. His doctor says, 'You're in serious trouble, man. You're nanoseconds away from the Big One. The ol' ticker can't handle any more stress. You're going to have to back way off; take time off from work, relax, not lift a finger around the house—and I really mean that—your wife should do everything for you, you know the routine . . . I stand corrected. You probably *don't* know the routine. In fact, I want your wife to come in so I can talk to her.'" Steve pulled the toothpick from his mouth and smiled at John.

"So, the wife comes in and the doctor tells her pretty much the same thing, only he stresses the need for her to wait on the guy hand and foot.

'You've got to do everything for him—not only meals, laundry, that sort of thing, but getting the newspaper every morning, taking care of the dog—everything. If you don't do all these things for him, he is very likely to die of a heart attack.' Okay, so the wife returns home and her husband asks her, 'So, what did the doctor tell you?' And the wife goes, 'He says you're gonna die!'"

The two friends gave each other the high five. "Good one," said John.

"Moral of the story, John, is don't get stressed out at HeartBank or your wife will let you have a heart attack. Good luck with the severance package," said Steve, as he gestured farewell with his hand and backed away from John.

"Thanks and good luck." John noticed that Steve had not offered to negotiate John's package, but fine, whatever Steve was feeling about severance now, John knew that he himself had reached the end of his rope with Heckler and HeartBank.

◆ CHAPTER FIVE ◆

Worse than Foiled

A WEEK LATER, JOHN MET WITH HECKLER. John had purposely scheduled the session late in the day so that regardless of the outcome, he could exit the office gracefully. For the past several days, all his thoughts, all his energies had focused on the big meeting with his boss. Over and over, behind the closed door of his office, in the car to and from work, on his daily three-mile jog, in bed at two in the morning, John had rehearsed his pitch to Heckler. Except for Steve Torseth, no one knew, not even John's wife, Sandy. "Come on in," Heckler said, effusively. Good, thought John. The asshole's in a good mood. "You here to tell me we're taking that $25 million deal after all?" Heckler laughed, as he pulled his dollar sign suspenders and let them snap against the sides of his paunch.

"No, I'm here on something else." The two took seats opposite each other at the round conference table in Heckler's well-appointed office. A few streams of sunshine slipped through neighboring office buildings and lit up a section of Heckler's corner lair. Tombstones locked in Lucite cubes announcing HeartBank deals lined the shelf that extended along the bottom of the entire line of windows. On the walls were large photographs of famous golf holes around the country. Off to the side of the office opposite the conference table was an office putting green, which Heckler often used when negotiating with someone. If Heckler picked up his putter and moved toward the green, you knew he was prepared to wheel and deal.

"Shoot."

"Well, Dennis, with the economy going strong and our default rate holding steady, I've been thinking. My job . . . you see, you really don't need the position anymore. I mean, you could easily consolidate my group with Risk Management and eliminate the expense of my position—"

"You know what, Anchor?" Heckler interrupted, as he rose from his chair, lifted his right leg and pulled at his crotch to free up a bind in his underwear. "You've got to give me lots of credit."

"How's that, Dennis?" Heckler moved to the window with his back to John. He hooked his thumbs around the base of his suspenders and assumed the stance of Napoleon surveying conquered lands, though far less real estate could be viewed from his fifth floor window than from his former perch on the thirtieth floor. It worried John that Heckler had not moved toward the putting green.

"I had the very same idea." Heckler was famous for claiming credit for other people's ideas. "I was just waiting to see how long it would take you to realize this on your own." Before John could utter another word, Heckler spun around and continued, "I've got another job for you, Anchor." John had to give Heckler credit for thinking on the fly, but he saw his plans for a severance package evaporating into the hot air of Heckler's office. "Our collateral control area needs some management. I'm going to create a new unit and I want you to run it. We'll move your office down to the end there by the file room, where you can keep an eye on your new charges." John opened his mouth, but his tongue wouldn't move. "I'll have to take it to Dunn or forge his signature on the approval form, one way or the other, depending on his schedule, get an announcement together, you know, that sort of thing, but we should be able to roll by month's end."

Shock swept over John as he realized his plan had blown up in his face. He felt sick, weak, diminished and completely without control of his destiny. What remained to salvage? John switched to damage control mode. "How much of a pay increase will I get from this, Dennis?"

Heckler's mouth shifted to a contemptuous angle. "Pay increase? Oh yeah, pay increase." He said, as he stepped around the end of his oversized desk and sank into his chair. With hands clasped together behind his greasy head, Heckler leaned back and propped his oversized wing tips up on the corner of the desk. "If you do a good job, I think you'll qualify for a significant pay bump in April."

"April?" John's heart sank. "Dennis, that's half a year away."

"Wait a minute, Anchor." Heckler, who could never hold a stance or position for more than a few seconds, removed his feet from the desktop and leaned forward. "As I recall, you came in here saying you'd worked your position to a point it should be eliminated. I agreed, and now I've given you a new life, a new job, and you demand a pay raise? Anchor, I never thought of you as a money grubber. You disappoint me."

John stood flabbergasted, as his collar tightened and perspiration soaked the armpits of his shirt. He panicked. He caved. "Sorry, Dennis."

"It's okay, John." Heckler parked himself on the corner of his desk and crossed his hands over his half lap. "By the way, there's a particular part of the job I'm counting on you to take care of right away."

"What's that?"

"You know this guy Will or Willy or Billy or whatever the hell Franklin? Been here almost a year now?"

"The black guy back there in the cube next to the office by the file room? I think he goes by 'William.'"

"Yeah, whatever. Anyway, HR foisted him on us as part of their brilliant Hire an Incompetent Minority program. He supposedly graduated from college somewhere—down South somewhere—but he just isn't cutting the mustard. Not that that comes as a surprise. Name me one black guy that can do anything besides run, catch or dribble a ball. Not only that but your friend William there is probably gay—I saw him hug a man once, and it wasn't on a basketball court. It was right here in the office. Floyd back there—his current boss—has always complained about Franklin, so there you go. I want Franklin out of here." Once Heckler knocked you down, he liked to kick you senseless, just for good measure. "I'll count it toward your bonus, if he's gone by the first of the year. It won't be easy with all the HR bullshit you have to go through to get rid of a minority."

John wanted to dash for the door, scramble outside and never come back. At a minimum, he realized, he had to leave Heckler's office before Heckler's choke hold got any tighter. "I've got to leave for an appointment," John said.

"Fine." Heckler basked in victory, but he wasn't through yet. "But before you go, there's one more thing."

"There is?" The door handle felt cool against John's sweaty palm, as he pressed the metal. Heckler's words struck John's ears like the clank of a dead bolt lock on the other side of the door.

"Dunn has been after me to appoint someone to represent our department on the Corporate Diversity Council. Since you're a liberal with that walrus mustache and all, I figured you'd be a good choice." John didn't consider himself a liberal or a conservative or much of anything politically. He just happened to have a heavy mustache, that was all. "There's a meeting coming up. I'll tell Dunn's secretary you've volunteered, and someone will call you." Heckler's phone rang, and as Heckler picked up the receiver, John slipped out, free at last.

$ $ $ $

John didn't tell Sandy the whole story, only that he had a new job. "How much more does it pay?" she asked, as she cleared the dishes from the kitchen table.

"Uh, it'll be more, but I don't know exactly how much yet."

"What? Heckler gave you a new job, and you don't know what it pays?" Sandy had a way of getting right to the point, and she was making fast progress in the case at hand.

"Actually, you see, well, Heckler will give me a nice pay hike in April."

"Why not now? The job starts now, doesn't it?"

"Sandy, look, it's complicated. Switching jobs doesn't necessarily mean a pay increase right off the bat."

"It doesn't?" Sandy's tone conveyed skepticism. Whenever John had changed jobs or had been promoted in the past, her first and usually only question related to pay. In her mind, you didn't change jobs unless the change brought expanded financial benefits. Now John had worked himself into a jam. He couldn't very well explain the whole story. He'd figured that with a generous severance package in hand, he could have mollified Sandy. He could have persuaded her of his need to take a vocational breather. As things stood, he had completely miscalculated the outcome of his encounter with Heckler. Were she granted full knowledge of the facts, Sandy would likely blow a fuse and berate John mercilessly. In withholding the facts, John left Sandy perplexed. A vast gap existed in their relationship to begin with. John's predicament at work only widened their differences. John would never be able to communicate his concerns to Sandy, and Sandy would never understand by any other means. She wanted no part of John's vocational frustrations, only the bread that his biweekly paycheck put on the table.

"The girls went to the mall, and I want to get to some arrangements before the weekend rush." Sandy was in her own world of flowers. She'd never even set foot in John's office, and in fact, John couldn't remember a time she'd been inside HeartBank Tower. With the house to himself, John paced between the kitchen and the family room and replayed in his mind the disastrous scene with Heckler. Not a gambling man, John felt as though he'd made one big bet and lost. Worse than lost. He felt as though he'd lost the bet and won a bizarre set of booby prizes that would shackle him until he was old and broken. He understood, more clearly than ever, what had happened to his father, whom he loved. His father, however, had at least achieved some sense of freedom, albeit not from financial worries.

◆ CHAPTER SIX ◆

A Raw Deal

WHEN JOHN BROKE THE NEWS to his staff, faces fell. Compared to other managers in the department, Debra Tarwinski, "the Police Woman"; Pete Cunningham, "Mr. Blow Hard"; Skip Schuneman, "Sycophant"; and Brian Post, "the Invisible Man" (most of the time out of town abusing his expense account and a man of no words when he was present), to name a few, John was reasonably well-liked. He never screamed at his people, allowed them ample slack when appropriate and rose to their defense when unfounded accusations, innuendoes and other forms of malevolence swept the department. Their new boss, the humorless Police Woman, was a control freak, and everyone knew their work lives would change radically. In John's relatively democratic world, people enjoyed First Amendment rights. In the Police Woman's police state, people learned to keep reasonable requests, good ideas and constructive criticism under wraps or face severe sanctions, threats and abuse.

Heckler tolerated the Police Woman. In fact, he needed her. In her role as head of Risk Management, she projected an image of control. Her hair was always pulled back and tied so tight it hurt to look at it. Her hollow cheeks, razor-thin eyebrows, down-turned mouth and otherwise unattractive face sold well at meetings with the credit folks, auditors and examiners, all of whom viewed most revenue-generating activity as gunpowder near an open flame. It was all for show. Heckler kept the Police Woman on a short leash whenever she threatened to impose any meaningful controls on his business.

Having said farewell to his old crew, John next turned to meet his new people, including William Franklin, the guy Heckler wanted fired. They were generally a bunch of misfits. People who had bounced around the department from one dead end job to another. The under-achievers.

With the exception of Franklin, Heckler hated to let people go. HeartBank's Human Resources Department, which wielded considerable power at the bank, assigned high importance to employee turnover rates. If a manager showed low employee turnover in a tight job market, HR would look the other way if the manager fell behind in advancing certain HR initiatives. Heckler avoided or evaded most HR initiatives anyway, but he effectively hid many of his HR sins behind his department's artificially low turnover. He cajoled, threatened and outmaneuvered people—as he had done with John—to keep them chained and quiet, and departures infrequent. Thus, the misfits, like John's new people, and the people with ability, like John himself, who should have been promoted or moved on years ago, labored on in Heckler's realm.

However, Heckler, a native of Stergus, Wisconsin, a blue-collar, beer-sloshing suburb of Milwaukee, flat out didn't like African Americans. He considered them dumb, lazy and dangerous. Franklin had slipped through the gate, and with John now in place to perform the dirty work, Heckler would be free of the one African American among his six hundred employees.

John's inquiry into Franklin's performance revealed, in fact, some serious issues. Barely out of college, William Franklin came from a place a million miles from HeartBank Tower. Born and raised in rural Mississippi, William had scratched his way out of poverty and attended Clark University in Atlanta. To draw more African Americans to white Minnesota, HR recruited actively at schools like Clark, Tuskegee and Howard. William was one of five recent Clark graduates to have accepted offers at HeartBank. Over six feet tall, with unadulterated black skin and the physique of a body builder, William stood out among his co-workers. Taciturn even among his friends and relatives back in subtropical Mississippi, William must have felt excruciatingly introverted among snowbound Minnesotans. If William had a friend in the Twin Cities, John thought, it wasn't anyone at HeartBank. Even if William worked hard, his lack of confidence and inability to fit in would doom him to failure.

Early on in his new role as collateral control manager, John called William into his office for the difficult conversation that Heckler had ordered. John knew the voluminous "HR Manual for Managers" contained all sorts of convoluted procedures for the dismissal of employees—he had recently reviewed them in connection with his quest for a severance package. He also knew that he was about to violate most of the rules. However, he didn't want to prolong William's agony with all kinds of letters, warnings and bureaucratic obscurantism that would eventually lead to the same announcement—"William Franklin is seeking other opportunities."

"Thanks for coming in, William."

"Yes, sir."

"You can call me John, William. Have a chair." John gestured toward one of the chairs facing John's desk. "Tell me about yourself, William. What possessed you to come up to this godforsaken part of the world?"

William's large, sincere eyes widened further. It was the first time in over a year, he explained, that anyone had expressed the slightest interest in how and why he had come to HeartBank.

"Well, sir—I mean John." William shifted in his chair and cleared his throat. "HeartBank was recruiting on campus—at Clark U in Atlanta—that's where I went to school, and the folks who interviewed me said this would be a great place to work, with lots of opportunity, you know, that sort of thing. It sounded real good, you know, and well, I checked it out—you know, I read the material and interviewed with a couple of people from the HR department and you know, they seemed like really nice people and wanted me to come up here to work." William cleared his throat again and gave John a chance to interrupt.

"Did they bring you up here for any interviews?"

"Yeah, uh, they did, as a matter of fact."

"What time of year?"

"Uh, I believe it was in May last year."

"Was it nice out?"

"Yeah, uh, real nice, you know, warm—real warm. I said, you know, this ain't bad. This Minnesota ain't bad at all." William laughed through his nose as he shook his head. "Little did I know it gets to be r-r-r-e-e-e-a-l cold here come October, November and stays cold until May again." John echoed William's laugh. You had to live in Minnesota for a full year to appreciate the length as well as the depth of its winters.

"So what did they tell you when you signed on—I mean what kind of job did they tell you you'd have?"

"Well, as I understood it, HR was going to find me something, you know, get me placed somewhere, and then it would be up to whoever hired me to put together a plan. They kept talking about the plan, you know, that the people who hired me would put together a plan for moving up." William no longer cleared his throat after every statement.

"Did anyone ever develop a plan?"

"No sir. No plan. No one to ask about it either. Those HR folks weren't around anymore, and I sure as heck wasn't going to ask nobody else." By now, John felt sorry for the young black man in front of him. All for appearances and at a deceivingly nice time of year, the bank had snookered William into a job at a big name company—and then abandoned him. John didn't know any blacks, and throughout his education and career, he had met so few, seen so few he held no strong opinions about them one way or another. However shallow his understanding of the plight of blacks in America, John found William's story disturbing. As a lifelong Minnesotan, he felt a twinge of shame. He also felt the uncomfortable weight of William's trust.

John knew it was the wrong thing to say. He knew HR would be all over him for saying it, but the words escaped, "Sounds to me like you got a raw deal, William." Once the words were out, they were out, and they pulled out more words behind them that John knew should not be heard.

"Uh-huh. Yes, sir. I mean that's it, a raw deal."

"Well, William, I'm sorry. There's plenty wrong with this place, and, well, I'm sorry, but I'm not sure this is the right place for you."

"Yeah," William cleared his throat, "I *know* this ain't the place for me."

"You seem like a nice guy, William, a deserving guy, and I want to make this as easy as I can for you, but I think we need to look ahead and work out a way that you can find another position." John felt the moisture breaking out on his forehead, under his collar, under his sleeves.

"Yes sir. How much time do I have?"

"I think I can give you till the end of the year to find something, William."

"Okay sir. That would be good, I mean, I'm not sure what I'm going to do, but that gives me a little time."

"I'll have to talk to HR to see what else we can do, William, but for now, let's plan on the end of the year." As John rose from his chair, his shirt stuck to his back. He felt miserable for surely having made William miserable. He extended his hand to William, who graciously responded, and the two men looked each other in the eye as they shook hands. William thanked John and walked out. John plopped back down into his chair and pushed his head into his hands. For all the wrong reasons, he thought, Heckler was right—William Franklin didn't belong at HeartBank.

♦ CHAPTER SEVEN ♦

The Tar Baby

"JOHN," ERICA, HIS NEW ASSISTANT, said from the doorway of his office, "there's a David Prachna on the phone. Do you want to talk to him?" Erica swept her curly, dark-red hair back over her shoulder as she chomped on her gum and awaited John's reply.

"The scam artist from hell is back," John said.

"Whatever. So what do you want me to tell the guy?"

"Send him through. I'll take it." Erica returned to her desk and John swore under his breath. A moment later, the call came through to John's phone.

"Hello?"

"Mr. Anchor. This is David Prachna. How are you today? Got any snow up there in Minnesota yet?" John could imagine gold chains around the guy's neck. He wanted to yank them tight and strangle the crook with them.

"No, actually, we've been lucky so far. It'll come soon enough though." John disappointed himself with his tame response, but it was hard to be overtly vexatious out of the chute, when someone—even a crook—uttered a pleasantry.

"Say John, I'm calling to see if you've had a chance to read the materials I sent you awhile back."

"Uh, yes, I have, and as a matter of fact, David, I tried to reach you but the numbers you gave me didn't work. I had no way of reaching you."

"Yes, I know. I'm sorry, my fault. We've changed offices—same building, just different offices. Our phone lines got all screwed up. Sorry about that. So what did you think of our materials? Are there any questions I can answer for you?" John wanted to call the guy a liar and hang up, but he counseled himself against reacting in a fashion he'd later regret.

"No, David, I don't have any questions, and I know that we just don't want to do this transaction, that's all there is to it. And by the way." John suddenly remembered Prachna's cover letter replete with distortions, which suggested a commitment on the part of HeartBank. "I took issue with your cover letter." John's back cracked audibly as he straightened up in his chair.

"Wait a second, John. First of all, can you help me understand just what it is about the transaction that you have a problem with?" Prachna's question put John on alert. Doubtless the con-man was fishing for hints as to how the scam could be made more credible.

"No, David, we simply don't want to do this deal, and your attempt to portray our previous phone conversation as somehow committing to the deal was completely inaccurate. The deal simply doesn't comply with our acceptance guidelines."

"John can you help me understand what your acceptance guidelines are and how we might adjust the terms of the deal so it does fit your guidelines?" The Police Woman had created a major campaign around "acceptance guidelines" and insisted that every deal the department took on fit within certain pre-approved guidelines, unless specially approved by the head of the department—Heckler. Her three-volume "Acceptance Guidelines" manual was the most cumbersome thing imaginable. However, no one cared, since Heckler signed off on just about any deal you put in front of his face, as long as the promise of revenue was there, whether or not it complied with the guidelines. Here, finally, was an instance where acceptance guidelines figured conveniently in John's attempt to squelch the scam.

"I'm sorry, David," John said, as he cautioned himself not to get steamed but to be Minnesota nice. "Our acceptance guidelines are proprietary. I'm not at liberty to go into it with you."

"Well, John, I guess we don't have much else to talk about then. I'm really sorry you're taking this position. Your bank stands to lose a very large opportunity here." John's visceral dislike of the scam artist won out over Minnesota nice.

"Look." John's tone changed abruptly. "We're not doing the deal, all right? End of discussion."

"Mr. Anchor, I'm surprised by your reaction, especially in light of your earlier commitment—" The word "commitment" rankled John.

"Wait a second, mister." John's voice filled with steam. "I never made anything close to a commitment—"

"Oh no? Geez, that's not how I viewed it."

"Well, you viewed it wrong."

"I'm not going to argue about what you said or didn't say." Prachna maintained his calm, which only raised John's blood pressure. "We obviously have a communication problem and have gotten off the track. I think what really needs to happen is I need to speak with your superiors." Prachna was as persistent as he was slimy.

"Wrong. What needs to happen is you need to drop it. HeartBank is not going to do this deal. Have a nice day." John finally slammed down the phone, as he knew he should have done after his first talk with Prachna.

Not more than five minutes later, Erica reappeared in the doorway to John's office. "What now?" he said, his voice still sharp from his encounter with Prachna.

"Don't kill the messenger," Erica said, as her gum popped. "It sounds like some black dude. He says it's really urgent."

Puzzlement displaced John's irritation. "Huh?"

"What should I tell him?"

"Patch him through." A black guy? What black guy would be calling John at the bank? The only black guy he knew was William Franklin, who presumably was in his cubicle.

"Hello, John Anchor here."

"Hi, Mr. Anchor. This is Calvin Maynard with Walden Financial, how you doin' today, sir?" Erica was right. The caller was definitely a dude. Exasperated, John slouched in his chair and rolled his eyes.

"Good grief," he said, with no attempt to hide his displeasure. John's vituperative exchange with Prachna was having a lasting effect. "I told your boss or cohort or whoever the hell he is that I didn't want to deal with you anymore. How many ways can you spell the word 'no'?"

"Well, sir, I can understand your frustration. This is an unusual deal, but just let me explain. You see, we've put together an impressive team of financial experts that seeks out those opportunities that are niche opportunities and especially lu-cra-tive." Mr. Maynard certainly had his script down, and John wondered why guys like Maynard and Prachna turned to con games. If they applied equal effort, persistence and sales skills to legitimate business, they could be hugely successful.

"Mr. Maynard, I'm going to say it one more time, and then I don't ever want to talk to you or Prachna or anyone else associated with Walden—ever again, is that clear? And I don't want to hear that you've called anyone else at HeartBank either, is *that* clear?"

"Yes, very clear. I'm just sorry you don't want to take advantage of a very significant opportunity."

"Goodbye!" John's volume and the hard impact of plastic on plastic, as John slammed down the phone, drew Erica back to his doorway.

"Something wrong, boss?"

"No, no, I mean, look, would you please screen my calls for the rest of the day? If a Calvin Maynard or a David Prachna or anyone else associated with a Walden Financial calls, tell them I'm not here."

"Sure."

"And don't give out any other numbers, okay?"

"You got it."

$ $ $ $

Four days later, Heckler stormed into John's office. Startled, John flinched. Heckler's neck looked especially thick, a sign he was on the rampage again. His eyes bulged more than usual, and in fact, Heckler's irises floated free of his eyelids. John recalled what his sister Maia had told him about people whose irises did that. "It's a sign of poor health," she'd said authoritatively, "and in Japan, they won't do business with you if your irises don't touch your eyelids—it's a sign you're not a good risk, that you might not be long for this world."

Heckler thrust a piece of paper onto John's messy desk. "This is exactly what I didn't want to happen," he said to John, who had been poring over the *Business Opportunities* section of *The Wall Street Journal*.

Close on the tail of Heckler's invective was the distinct odor of garlic. "What's this?" said John, as he made his abrupt re-entry into reality.

"It's a goddamn nasty-gram from the customer who was intent on enabling us to make a lousy $25 million, Anchor." John wondered if he'd call 9-1-1 or just look the other way if Heckler ever had a heart attack.

"Well, wait a minute. Can I read it?" John asked.

Heckler began pacing back and forth in front of John's desk, his lips curled inward and his piercing gaze trained on John, as John read the scathing letter.

Dear Mr. Brinkman,

As a major customer of your bank, we thought you might want to know about the shoddy treatment we've been subjected to by one of your employees, John Anchor of the National Real Estate Financial Services Department.

We serve as financial agent for large private trusts, foundations and wealthy individuals. Lately we brought a major piece of business (we estimated the value of the transaction to your bank would have been somewhere between $20 million and $25 million) to HeartBank (Doris Hohlinger of your Reno branch) and were referred to Mr. Anchor. At first, Mr. Anchor was very accommodating, and after receiving a commitment from Mr. Anchor we thanked him by way of the enclosed letter.

However, when we next talked with Mr. Anchor, he changed his tune completely and said he wouldn't do any business with us. He wouldn't explain why, but used very unprofessional language and was very abusive. We don't know why he went back on his commitment (which we assumed he had the authority to make) but he reversed himself after my partner, Mr. Calvin Maynard (an African American), got involved.

As a result of Mr. Anchor's turning us down, we face losing a major transaction and a major client. We are trying desperately to avoid losses, but no assurances can be made.

Sincerely yours,
/s/
David Prachna
CEO and President
Walden Financial

Stapled to the letter was a memo from Brinkman's secretary to Heckler's boss, Jack Dunn, which stated simply, "Please take care of this." On any given day of the week, Brinkman's office probably received a dozen written customer complaints, some legitimate, many utterly ridiculous, blown out of proportion or otherwise meritless. Attached atop the memo to Dunn was another memo from Dunn's office to Heckler, which contained the directive, "Let me know when this is taken care of" and bore the initials, "J.D." In John's mind, Heckler was far too nervous about Walden. A "nasty-gram" didn't justify making a federal case of the matter.

"For crying out loud," John said, as he flipped the pages back and forth.

"Now do you care to explain to me what the hell you've done to piss these guys off so much they write to Brinkman?"

"First of all, the letter is a pack of lies," said John. His own stress produced heat and sweat under the collar. "Second, there was never $25 million of business out there for us, I promise you, Dennis. Third, we leave these guys alone and never talk to them again. They're bad actors, I'm telling you, Dennis. Talking to them is like walking through a patch of sand burrs—they stick to your clothes and hurt to pull off."

"Okay smarty pants. We're never going to see the $25 million of earnings. You've done a great job of making sure that doesn't happen. But now I want you to clean up the mess you've created and tell Dunn you've done so." With that, Heckler exhaled steam and stomped out of John's stuffy office.

The Walden matter reminded John of the Tar Baby in the *Brer Rabbit* tales he had read to his daughters when they were young. In one last attempt to rid himself of the Tar Baby, John wrote under Dunn's directive, "Taken care of," followed by the date, and signed it. He then handed it to Erica and instructed her to return it to Dunn's office, with a copy to Heckler.

Although John's instincts regarding Walden were accurate, he had failed to discern the exact nature of Prachna's scheme and had therefore underestimated the magnitude of the attempted fraud. Not that anyone else at the bank could have discerned the objective. Despite the memos coming down the bank hierarchy, senior management was, in truth, oblivious. Heckler, dollar signs in his eyes, saw no risk, except to his reputation for having lost an opportunity to add $25 million to his bottom line. The Police Woman, who, within the department, technically had the job of managing such matters as Walden, was too busy berating people for picayune infractions of her petty rules. Yet, Walden would soon become the bane of the bank. It would also put John in the right place at the right time to exercise total control of his destiny.

◆ CHAPTER EIGHT ◆

Deposal

MOST DEPARTMENTS WITHIN THE BANK observed fairly conventional hierarchical structures, depicted by a chart with the head honcho in the top box, his personal secretary or assistant in a box off to the side, the honcho's five to nine "direct reports" in boxes lined up in a row below, and rows and columns of direct reports of direct reports below the first row and so on. Heckler's "org" chart, however, differed radically from the norm. You couldn't readily decide who was a direct report, who was some kind of glorified adjutant and who was an afterthought. Heckler was the master of dotted-line reporting, and consequently, no one knew exactly who was superior and who was subordinate.

Although Heckler scheduled a direct reports meeting for every Wednesday at 9:00, he canceled most of them. When they did occur, they were free-for-alls. The mere assembly process prevented any of his meetings from starting on time. People entered the conference room, poured some coffee, left for their desks and returned a few minutes later for refills and exited again, until Heckler himself strode in—at least fifteen minutes behind schedule. After a minute or two of bantering, he'd say, "Okay troops—time for show and tell."

Heckler's usual format for conducting a direct reports meeting was to go around the table and ask people to talk about what was going on in each of their respective "worlds," as divisions or groups were called. John wasn't sure if anyone else noticed that Heckler always started with a person seated next to John and continued in the opposite direction so that John would be the last to be called on. Invariably, before this system reached John, the unorganized assembly had exhausted Heckler's patience for verbal flatulence. Before John could clear his throat to utter a terse update or, more often than not, "I have nothing to report," people were already pushing away from the conference table and Heckler was using a crumpled paper cup to shoot a three-pointer at the refuse container. John found most of these meetings to be insufferable, as people either droned on interminably about operational snafus, systems upgrades and bureaucratic mumbo jumbo or engaged in patently self-serving puffery about their dubious achievements and the "great opportunities" with "huge potential" that they had uncovered in the "marketplace."

The people whom Heckler's secretary—presumably on Heckler's orders—invited to his directs meetings were a motley crew, and half the attendees changed every month. Besides John, Jenny Jacobson (John's closest friend in the department and the source for all nicknames) and the Police Woman, the other regulars were Pete "Blowhard" Cunningham and Skip "Sycophant" Schuneman. Blowhard, who managed the department's loan participation division, invariably picked a chair at one end of the conference room table. A physically large man with a premature paunch and thick, black hair and bushy eyebrows, he possessed dark, hairy forearms, which for some strange reason, he thought everyone should see. John wondered if Blowhard's shirt-sleeves were ever not rolled up. Blowhard always brought a fresh tablet of white paper, which he dropped onto the table with an audible *'slap'* to announce his presence. He never actually used the tablet, except to show off his black, Mont Blanc pen—the HeartBank's Finest award he'd won for having exceeded his sandbagged plan several years before. Blowhard owned an opinionated voice, which he projected from an oversized mouth to overpower everyone else in the room. A self-appointed expert on all subjects, he slashed Heckler to shreds (behind Heckler's back, of course) and was convinced he would succeed his boss on the day Jack Dunn got wise and sent Heckler "in search of other opportunities."

Blowhard's competition for Heckler's job was Sycophant, head of the Sales and Marketing Division. He was a man in his late thirties who reached for six feet of height by lifting his chin higher than it needed to be and viewing the world from atop the slope of his nose. His gold-rimmed glasses were not so much for vision, John thought, as for visual effect—Sycophant habitually pulled them on and off whenever someone else was talking. It gave Sycophant an air of superiority. Coincidentally, Sycophant happened to wind up next to Heckler at nearly every meeting. He accomplished this by precise orchestration. As the meeting time approached, he'd hover around Heckler's office, intercept him on the way to the conference room and fabricate a question that couldn't be answered until the two gentlemen had entered the room, habitually poured themselves coffee and found a couple of seats—next to each other. Throughout the meeting, the Sycophant would bob his head in agreement with everything that came out of Heckler's mouth. This practice put Sycophant in an awkward position on the odd occasion when Heckler expressly agreed with one of Blowhard's heartfelt opinions. A terrible judge of character, Sycophant ignorantly assumed that Heckler would gain a promotion some day and nominate his chief sycophant as his successor.

Every once in awhile, however, Heckler's meetings revealed some interesting developments. One such gathering occurred in early November. Just before Heckler quieted things down with his "show and tell" signal, Blowhard boomed across the room, "What do you know about Dunn getting the boot, Dennis?" The rumor stopped the crowd cold. Blowhard was showing off and trying to scare Sycophant. However, there had been rumblings lately that some senior heads were about to roll. Not wishing to be upstaged by Blowhard, Heckler instinctively shifted into denial.

"I don't think so, Cunningham. You'd better check your sources next time." Smuggly, Sycophant nodded in agreement, and Heckler, visibly shocked by the rumor, tried to put it aside as quickly as possible. "Okay, Skip, what's going on in your world?"

"Everything's running real smoothly," he lied. Behind the scenes, John knew, Sycophant's minions were about to riot over cramped working conditions, system failures and pay inequities. "We're real close to implementing our new call reporting system,"—another lie—"and otherwise, we're just happy to be optimizing shareholder value." In John's mind, Sycophant never optimized anything of value.

Shaken by Blowhard's remark, Heckler moved around the table more quickly than usual. When the Police Woman issued her typical public indictments of various peers, Heckler asked her to "take those problems off line." When a new sales manager showed too much exuberance for "new market opportunities," Heckler shook his head in feigned happy disbelief and said, "Really? You know, I'd like to hear about that at length. In fact, why don't you schedule time with my secretary?"

Immediately following the meeting, rumors of Dunn's demise spread across the department like a cloud of bad gas. Heckler, of course, hauled

Blowhard straight into his office, but only after the others—except for Sycophant, who never missed a thing, and John, who, through fortuitous circumstances, often observed things others missed—had dispersed and couldn't witness the two together. In a lame attempt to lose Sycophant, Heckler tried a shallow ruse. "Say Pete," Heckler said for Sycophant's ears, "I need to talk to you about that participation deal with Wells Fargo that's scheduled to close on Friday—" It didn't work. Sycophant was beside himself over the fact that Blowhard had upstaged him and won the inside track, however briefly.

"Say, I've got a question about that too," Sycophant said to weasel his way into what was sure to be a conversation replete with interesting disclosures by Blowhard. John wound up behind the trio and reached Heckler's office just as Sycophant closed the door to outsiders. Sycophant happened to make eye contact with John and flashed a cold, toothy grin—the kind that looks like a nervous tic—as if to say, "Sorry pal. You're not in the inner circle like me, and in case you're wondering, someday you'll be reporting to me, so get used to my face looking down at yours." John didn't care. He knew he was not a contender, and moreover, he knew that Sycophant and Blowhard didn't view him as a contender either. It was much easier that way. He didn't have to worry about being ambushed or stabbed in the back. John needed to worry only about being steamrollered or suffocated by the ambition that swirled around him.

Safely behind the closed door of his office, Heckler changed to the real subject at hand. "What the hell is this about Dunn?"

"O'Gara phoned to tell me Dunn has been axed," said Blowhard, authoritatively.

"No shit!" Heckler said with a forced smirk, which quickly turned into genuine concern. "But why would O'Gara be calling you?" It was next to torture for a guy like Heckler to know that Mike O'Gara, Dunn's peer and archrival for the position of first-among-equals, would be calling one of Heckler's underlings directly.

"He was returning the phone call you told me to make to Dunn about calling on one of our prospects," said Blowhard.

"I see," Heckler said, regretting, no doubt, that he had allowed Blowhard to phone Dunn in the first place. "This is really big shit." Not often short on words, Heckler remained stunned by the news from the sixty-ninth floor and not a little peeved that the news had traveled first to one of his underlings. "You know," Heckler tried to recover his stature, "I've suspected this for a long time. Dunn just wasn't a player. You could see it coming. Of course he was just too plain dumb to get out of the way." If Blowhard's information was correct, and Heckler possessed no reason to doubt it, it was safe to malign his boss right out in the open. In fact, it was advantageous to do so. The smart thing to do in an organization like HeartBank was to distance yourself as quickly as possible from anyone who got booted out.

Ever desirous of appearing to be like one of the big boys, Sycophant cleared his throat in an artificially deep, authoritative manner and said, "This makes you one of Brinkman's direct reports, Dennis."

Heckler grinned, first at Sycophant, then at Blowhard and said, "Of course, I knew this would happen eventually." Stretching to reduce his paunch as he tugged at the top of his trousers, Heckler stepped toward the windows overlooking Third Street below and offered his explanation for his boss' demise. "Dunn was simply getting too big for his britches. His big mistake was to make a run for National Credit Cards, O'Gara's pet department. The power grab didn't sit well with O'Gara, who's hated Dunn's guts for the past three years."

"You could see it coming," Sycophant said, even though he hadn't seen a thing coming.

"You know what really happened?" Blowhard asked, as if he knew. "O'Gara leveled a threat at Brinkman to the effect that if Dunn wasn't gone by the end of the year, O'Gara would leave. Brinkman can't afford to lose O'Gara, so he had to let Dunn go."

"How well do you know O'Gara, Dennis?" asked Sycophant, with furrows of worry across his forehead.

"O'Gara? He's a helluva lot smarter than Dunn." Heckler's confident response was based on nothing more than the fact that Dunn was out and O'Gara wasn't and that Heckler had never gotten along with his aloof boss. "Dunn simply wasn't a long termer in this organization. I mean, look at the guy, stiff and dumb. Tried to steal part of O'Gara's empire right out from under his nose. You don't go far pulling a stunt like that." Heckler himself, of course, had made a career of stealing business away from his own set of rivals.

"I wonder what kind of package he got," said Sycophant.

"I'm sure he's getting a sweet deal," Heckler said.

"Usually at that level they get half a million or more in cash, plus the equivalent of whatever options they had coming this year," Blowhard said, in pure speculation.

Just then, Heckler's phone rang. "Heckler," he answered. ". . . Danny!" It was Heckler's sometime friend, Dan Berquist, head of Small Business Loans, who also reported to Dunn. Sycophant and Blowhard paced slowly around Heckler's office as Heckler gossiped with Berquist about Dunn's departure. Heckler's subordinates hoped that he would elevate their status by putting Berquist on the speaker phone. Instead, he demoted their egos with gestures toward the door of his office.

As an outsider, John resorted to other sources to obtain the story behind Dunn's ouster. He called Paul Dahl, an accountant in the bank's Finance Department, whom John had gotten to know over the years. Like John, Paul was pretty well locked into his current job level for life, or at least until a reorganization or "right sizing" eliminated his position. The two men weren't close friends or associates, but John trusted Paul, who had no axes to grind. Moreover, though Paul was no muckety-muck, he was a highly regarded "numbers cruncher" who had access to high-level financial information and was often asked to attend finance meetings among the highest senior executives, or "business team captains," as they were called at HeartBank. Quiet, short, thin and pale, Paul went unnoticed as he sat behind his boss, who sat among the captains. From this prime vantage point, Paul had access to corporate intelligence that climbers like Blowhard and Sycophant—not to mention a stock analyst or two—would kill for.

"Hello, Paul. John Anchor here."

"Hello, John," Paul spoke with such a quiet voice, John froze in position to hear better. "Say, Paul, what is this I hear about Dunn getting canned?"

"It's true. Collingwood's numbers were looking pretty bad for fourth quarter." Paul referred to the head of the Corporate Banking Department, Wayne Collingwood, a peer of Dunn and O'Gara. "He then struck a deal with O'Gara—each would take half of Dunn's world, effective immediately, but Collingwood would agree to take the lion's share of the one-time expenses associated with the reorganization. That way Collingwood can hide the fact he's behind plan. Instead of looking *pretty* bad, he'll look *really* bad and explain it away as reorg expenses. They got Brinkman to sign off on it yesterday."

"So who will Heckler wind up reporting to?"

"Hard to say. Between you and me, John, no one wants Heckler. He's kind of a laughing stock up on the captains' floor. I think O'Gara's agreed to take him till the end of the year, but who knows after that."

John wanted to speculate further about the implications of the shake-up, which would be announced officially later in the day, but customarily, Paul refused to speculate about things if he had only a limited foundation. They exchanged some idle chat and signed off.

John sank back into his chair, amused by the thought of Heckler, Blowhard and Sycophant conjuring up how and why Dunn had been deposed and how they would take advantage of the opportunity. If they only knew.

♦ CHAPTER NINE ♦

The Faded Prospect

WITH A SMILE, JOHN PICKED UP THE PHONE and called Steve Torseth at his friend's outplacement services office.

"Executive offices," the receptionist answered. John snickered at the euphemism for "outplacement offices," which, in turn, was a euphemism for the non-cash portion of any respectable severance package—"the place a person's former employer pays for, where the person is given a phone, a desk and a tiny office for the purpose of lining up a new job."

"Can I have Steve Torseth?"

"One moment please." John wondered what it was like for the receptionist to be the employed and all the office occupants to be the *un*employed.

"Hello, Steve Torseth." He sounded much too serious.

"Steve, John."

"John? It's great to hear your voice." John himself felt better for the sudden buoyancy in Steve's voice.

"How's it going? How was your trip to Charlotte?" A second or two passed before Steve responded.

"Okay, I guess."

"What kind of an answer is that? Did you take the job or not?"

"Well, I haven't exactly decided yet." Steve's responses weren't quick enough. John knew it was time for lunch again.

"How about lunch tomorrow, Steve?"

"Yeah, that would be good." Steve needed to talk, and John always seemed to connect with the need.

"Betty's at 11:30 to get ahead of the crowd."

"I'll see you there."

$ $ $ $

The next day brought cold, windy weather, and after he buttoned his suitcoat and pulled the collar up around his neck, John barreled his way through the revolving door, gathered steam through the vestibule and lowered his shoulder to shove his way out of the HeartBank Tower and onto the sidewalk. On windy days, downdrafts created by the Tower forced passersby to clutch their clothes, purses and briefcases and resist the pressure to fly off the sidewalk right into traffic. The flashing Don't Walk sign at the intersection where John exited the Tower beckoned, "Run fast before the light turns red." He made a run for it, like a receiver out for a pass, he imagined. Safely across, John kept running, partly to defy the cold, partly because he was late, all the way to the end zone called Betty's Place. His nose ran like an open tap, and his thick, sandy hair was so tousled, John winced when he ran his comb through it.

Barely inside, John immediately spotted Steve seated in a booth. With his eyebrows miming disapproval, Steve shoved his wrist out of his sleeve and conspicuously viewed his watch. "I was wondering when Mr. Important, Mr. Quasi Vice President was going to make it." Steve said, as John rushed up to the booth, removed his suitcoat and hung it on the clothes peg that stuck out from the booth divider.

"Geez, I'm sorry, Steve. Time got away from me."

"Time flies when you're employed."

"Ooo. What's that supposed to mean?" John was taken aback and briefly stopped his slide across the bench on his side of the table. He knew exactly what Steve meant, but Steve's hint of bitterness surprised him. Wasn't Steve the more enviable of the two of them? Hadn't he escaped from Fake Bank with a rich severance package and now—just two months later—with an attractive job offer, albeit out of state? What was wrong?

"Sorry, John." Steve's face showed strain. "Some days just aren't so great. Maybe it's the weather, the thought of winter, I don't know. Maybe I'm just getting impatient."

"Something tells me Charlotte didn't go so well. Tell me about it." John said, as Louise pulled up with her order pad.

"What'll it be today for my favorite money men? Can I interest you in the daily special—our cold weather keeps-you-warm soup and tuna hot dish?" She pronounced "hot dish" in true Minnesotan—"hot *deesh.*" Louise was born for her job. She stood on top of her game. It was enough to arouse jealousy in any self-respecting middle manager in search of his calling.

"No thanks, Louise," said John. Tuna hot dish made him feel over the hill, a codger. "I'll have the grilled cheese with a salad—make it French dressing—and Steve here will have . . . what do you want, Steve?"

"I'll go for the grilled chicken sandwich, Louise—it reminds me of me."

"Huh?"

"With Coke for a diet—I mean, a Diet Coke." Even when he was down, Steve never lost entirely his sense of humor.

"Okay, Steve, tell me about Charlotte," John asked, earnestly.

"Well, we flew out there on a Sunday, late afternoon, and got there in time for dinner. We were supposed to meet this guy Salentino, the guy who'd be hiring me, but something came up and he wasn't able to make it. So Beth and I went out to dinner on our own and kind of walked around downtown Charlotte. Nothing going on there on a Sunday evening." Steve lifted his water glass to his mouth and took a long sip. The power of suggestion made John thirsty too.

Steve continued. "I left Beth on her own Monday morning and met Salentino at his office. It was really weird, John."

"What do you mean?"

"Well, he just seemed lukewarm about the whole thing. I couldn't tell exactly what it was. I mean, am I that goofy looking that my appearance worked against me?" Steve wasn't your standard-issue banker, John thought, and if Steve's glasses slipped too far down his nose, he assumed somewhat of a Poindexter look. However, in front of people he had to impress, Steve was fully presentable. John assumed that under the circumstances, Steve had worn his best suit, tucked his shirt in, checked his tie and fixed his glasses firmly to the bridge of his nose before he met Salentino.

"No, absolutely not." John said.

"Well, anyway, he introduced me, to a couple of his direct reports, as one of the candidates for the Eastern Regional Sales Manager position. And I'm thinking, *one* of? John, I thought I was the *only* one. Then he takes me into his office. Wow, what an office! They don't give out offices like that to bankers out here. Not even executive vice presidents out here get offices like Salentino's, and he's just a lowly senior vice president. My God, John! It was the size of my house, with sofas, coffee tables, paintings, bookcases, a putting green—"

"Heckler has a putting green."

"Yeah, but Salentino can probably actually golf. John, this was an amazing office, and I'm thinking, this guy has some pull. His desk was big enough to park a car on, and except for a desk pad, pen-and-pencil set and telephone—in a cherry wood box, no less—there wasn't *nothin'* on that desktop.

"So, he offers me a chair—one of those thick, formal leather types—in front of his desk and sits down in *his* chair. Geez, that sucker must have cost five thousand bucks—leather with a real high back, eighteen inches higher than the top of his head—and John, this guy was no shrimp. He was real tall, dark hair, with every strand in place. Except when he talked—and when he did, he reminded me of some kind of anchorman—he kept his mouth closed so tight his lips looked like they were in pain. His eyes were steely blue, clear as the sky in Minnesota when it's thirty below. He wore a dark blue power suit, pressed by a steam roller, a silk handkerchief poking out of the suitcoat pocket and a matching fancy red tie that must have cost more than my entire suit. Are you getting the picture, John?"

"Sounds like a guy to impress."

"He wore one of those dual-colored shirts, you know, blue with white cuffs and collar, starched like the kind priests wear backwards. He had monogrammed cufflinks, as well as monogrammed cuffs. I'm thinking, They don't dress up like this back in Minnesota."

"Okay, so he's surprised you with the indirect bomb that you've got competition and he's Mr. Power Banker, but how did the interview go?"

"Well, like I said, he wasn't exactly bubbling with enthusiasm. He was just cold and matter-of-fact. He explained how they were organized, what their growth strategy is, you know, that kind of thing, but really didn't seem too interested in me." Steve hesitated. "Then all hell broke loose."

Just then, Louise arrived. "Here's your lunch, guys," she said, as she slid the thick china plates onto the table and plopped down Steve's Diet Coke. At the same time, she juggled sundry plates, bowls and tumblers that were headed for adjacent booths. She looked like an octopus lady, John thought, the way she managed all that breakable china and sloshing liquid, without so much as losing the articulated fry that dangled precariously over the edge of one plate. Definitely a woman on top of her game.

"You left me hanging," said John, turning his eyes back to Steve. "So what kind of hell broke loose?" John was intrigued by Steve's adventures thus far, even though they appeared to have produced a dubious outcome.

"He had one of those noses you see on ancient statues," said Steve, as he picked a piece of wilted lettuce out of his salad. "You know, perfectly shaped, strong and fairly thin, like the prow of a destroyer. All of a sudden, a booger appeared. A big white one, sort of hanging out like a car backing out of a garage. I couldn't believe it. Every time he inhaled, the car drove back in. When he exhaled, it backed out again. After half a dozen cycles of this, I lost all concentration. I mean, what do you do, stop right in the middle of the conversation and say, 'Sorry, but you have a big honker booger sticking out of your nose?' No, of course not. So instead, I have to sit there and look at it or try not to look at it. Then his secretary walks in, this gorgeous woman, to hand him some sort of message, and stands there and looks right at him while he's looking over the piece of paper. She turned to me, flared her lovely nostrils and winked. Can you believe it? And you know what happened then?"

"No," said John. He couldn't suppress a laugh.

"I burst out laughing. Jesus Christ, John, I just couldn't believe myself. I mean, here I am in Mr. Power Banker's office in the middle of a serious interview when I'm unemployed and looking for a decent job and a booger—a lousy, goddamned booger, not in my nose but in Mr. Perfect's nose—makes me laugh. How absolutely stupid and inappropriate." Steve's voice betrayed disappointment on top of anger, but the absurdity of the occasion prompted a laugh from Steve nonetheless.

It took awhile for the two men to get over the humor. Finally, John said, "Well, Steve, you can't leave me hanging. What happened next?"

"Well, as you might imagine, Salentino didn't see what was so funny, and his Italian eyebrows told me I'd better shut up and behave myself if I had any hope of being reimbursed for the expense of flying out to Charlotte. He continued the interview, talked about the position, salary, their bonus program, benefits. He asked me about my job at Fake Bank—"

"You didn't call it that, I hope."

"No, John, from that point forward I was on my best behavior. I told him about the reorg at Lake Bank, how I'd been pushed out, blah, blah,

blah. Salentino kind of went through my résumé, asked a few questions and the deal was over."

"So did you get an offer or what?"

"I'm still waiting. They said it would be a couple of weeks, and with the holidays coming up, Thanksgiving, then Christmas, it might even be stretched out into January before I hear. At least they didn't say, 'Scram! You laughed at a senior vice president, we don't want to see your face again,' although there's no telling what they really thought of me. Everyone I met there—except the secretary who winked at me—was so darned buttoned down and serious. They're all transplants from American National, which came out on top of the merger with Banco. I think Salentino runs a tight ship, and I'm not sure I want to work for an outfit like that."

"What does Beth think about the whole thing?"

"She thought the guy we went out to dinner with that night was a stiff in a stuffed shirt, but she didn't think Charlotte was such a bad place. The only thing is she's all worried about the kids making the adjustment and being so far from her folks. On balance, she'd go if I said 'Let's go,' but I don't think she's all that excited about it."

"So what are you doing in the meantime?"

"With the holidays coming up, it's kind of hard to get appointments scheduled. People are busy with getting year-end stuff closed, office parties, who knows what all. Plus, people are concerned about year-end financial performance, and before they make any key hiring decisions, they want to see how the end of the quarter shakes out. It's just not a good time to be interviewing."

"Geez, Steve, you'd think that with your background and the tight job market, there'd be a number of firms interested in talking to you, at least." John wanted to be supportive.

"You thought wrong." Steve's reply stung John.

"I'm sorry. I was just trying to be helpful." A long pause followed as they chewed quietly at their sandwiches.

"So how are you doing, John?" Steve asked the question as an apology for having snapped at his friend.

"The usual crap. Only worse. I tried out the severance package idea on Heckler."

"A-a-nd?" Steve knew, of course, that John hadn't gotten one.

"I got a new job before I could even float the concept of a severance package."

"Oh?" Now it was Steve's turn to be jealous of John, but when John explained his circumstances, the grounds for Steve's jealousy dissipated.

"Once a schmo, always a schmo. I think that's the moral of the story for us guys. You know, John, when I hear stuff like that, I think to myself, It ain't so bad being unemployed for awhile."

The men turned in earnest to their food, and conversation diminished to a vacuous exchange about the weather and the Timberwolves. It was a challenge to talk with your mouth full, especially if you were, after all, just a schmo. John popped for the check when it came. He didn't need to put Steve through the test again. The two friends parted ways, and John jogged through the cold, back to the Tower.

♦ CHAPTER TEN ♦

The Diversity Council

A WEEK LATER, JOHN STEPPED OFF THE ELEVATOR at the forty-second floor of the Tower and entered the HR world of HeartBank. Welcome to Human Resources! shouted the sign across the top of the wall in front of the elevators. It was one of the few places at the bank, John noted, where *Human Resources* was spelled out. Years ago, it was called *personnel,* but then some genius came up with the warmer, fuzzier term *Human Resources,* to trick schlep-employees into thinking they were more important than mere *personnel.* How ironic, thought John, that nearly everyone in corporate America had long since reduced *Human Resources* simply to *HR,* which was far less warm and fuzzy than the old-fashioned *personnel.*

Around the corner from the elevators, large, upholstered, soothing mauve chairs were arranged in a horseshoe formation around an expansive coffee table covered with an assortment of magazines and newspapers. Large potted plants, an immoderate poster boasting the HeartBank logo (a stylized heart superimposed on a map of the continental U.S.), framed poster-sized photographs by Craig Block featuring scenes of the four seasons in Minnesota and low volume, easy listening music gave the reception area a relaxing ambiance. If only real offices were so pleasant, John thought, until he turned his eyes to the two-inch thick window in front of the receptionist, a black woman. The bulletproof glass offers great protection against disgruntled employees turned violent, he said to himself.

"May I help you?" She spoke into a microphone, and her voice came through a speaker just under the window, as if she were talking to John's knees.

"Yes. I'm here for the Diversity Council meeting at 8:30."

"It's in conference room A, straight back." As she spoke, a buzzer went off, and John pulled open the security door to the left of the receptionist window. Upon entering the conference room John felt as though he had left HeartBank of Minnesota and landed in the heart of New York, L.A. or Chicago. Four of the eight people already present were non-Caucasian, in contrast to HeartBank's overall minority population of less than ten percent. One of the Caucasians, a woman, sat in a wheelchair. Another, a man, who boasted carefully managed and sculpted hair, sat with his back arched and leaned his chin atop the backs of his fingers, with tips barely touching, while his elbows rested on the conference table. It occurred to John that the man might be gay. That left one other Caucasian man who looked like roughly half the employees at HeartBank—middle-aged men of northern European descent. Susan, a senior HR person and co-chair of the Diversity Council, greeted John cordially, despite her severe appearance. About forty-five years old, judging by the pronounced crows' feet next to her eyes, she maximized her medium height by standing straight and looking thin. She had dark, close-cropped hair and wore black-rimmed glasses to match her dark, penetrating eyes. A small metal chain, attached to the bows of her glasses, hung down and around the back of her neck. John figured that lots of things in her life—including people—were kept on a short leash. If ever there was someone you'd address *Ms.*, thought John, this woman was it.

"You must be John," she said, energetically. John guessed she was well-caffeinated.

"That's right."

"Why don't you help yourself to the rolls and beverages and we'll make introductions." She gestured toward a long credenza, which was laden with jelly rolls, gourmet coffee and juice bottles. John did as she suggested and found a chair at the table. "Well everyone," Ms. Miller said, calling the meeting to order, "it looks like we can get underway. First off, I'd like you to meet our newest member, John Anchor from National Real Estate Financial Services. I thought to make things interesting, we could go around the table for introductions. To get just a little better-acquainted, why don't we tell what we're doing for Thanksgiving, which is right around the corner—hard to believe, isn't it?"

"Hi John and welcome aboard," said a dark-skinned woman on Ms. Miller's immediate right. She spoke with an accent. "I'm Kamala Sindriwali from Equipment Leasing. My brother and his wife and their children are coming out from New York and we'll be having a big turkey dinner at my house."

I'll never remember a name like that, John worried. Not only was this New York and L.A., but it was Mumbai and Beijing, as well. To someone with a Scandinavian background, born and bred in Minnesota, this meeting group looked singularly exotic. The introductions that followed included an African American man, an Hispanic woman, the white woman in the wheelchair, an Asian woman, the man who John was certain was gay, the white man who John assumed was straight and Ms. Miller. John worried that the group would think he was unacceptably illiberal if they discovered he planned to go deer hunting in northern Wisconsin over the long Thanksgiving weekend. He thought it best to say, "Dinner with the family and my parents."

"Good, good," Ms. Miller closed off the pleasantries. "Ann and I have a number of things we'd like you to consider," she said, referring to her co-chair seated next to her, the African American woman, whose progressively drooping eyelids over the course of the meeting would give John the impression she was under-caffeinated, drowsy and not a morning person. "First of all is the matter of our survey results and what we're going to do with them," Ms. Miller continued, as she passed a stack of papers down her side of the table. "I think we have some really interesting results."

"When was the survey conducted?" John asked.

"About three months ago," Ms. Miller said, as she removed her glasses and gave John a look that signaled he had asked a very dumb question. The survey had been circulated among HeartBank employees with considerable fanfare. Not only John but most of his colleagues in Real Estate Financial Services ignored initiatives like the diversity survey. Ms. Miller's glare, combined with odd looks from the rest of the Council members, jogged John's memory. He now vaguely remembered Heckler's having mentioned the survey (as all managers had been urged to do) at one of his direct reports meetings, and further remembered having tossed the twelve-page survey form one day when he uncovered it during one of his periodic office cleanings and saw that the deadline was two weeks' past. John could feel his body heat rush to his ears. He was not in the habit of participating out loud in Heckler's meetings. Why should his tongue wag in this meeting? A loud inner voice told him to keep his mouth closed for the duration of the session.

Ms. Miller returned her glasses to her face and walked the group through the survey, question by question, response by response, and sliced and diced the results by percentages in five or six categories of gender, race, sexual orientation, title and various combinations of the foregoing. Attached to the statistics were several pages of conclusions prepared by Ms. Miller, none of which was challenged by anyone in the group. John wanted to dispute things, but his inner voice renewed its earlier command to stay quiet. He reviewed some of the questions and wondered how anything meaningful or in the slightest way reliable could be drawn from the responses. "Do you think you are valued by your supervisor?" for example. What did it mean that the average score among the five gay African Americans who responded to the question was 1.9 on a five-point scale, one being the low end? And so it was with the vast majority of the fuzzily worded eighty-five questions.

The wheelchair-bound woman, whose name John had by now forgotten, remarked stridently that to "keep the momentum going" on diversity, it was essential that "the Council follow through on the survey. Otherwise, people will think we're not really interested in their concerns about diversity." John watched as the others around the table nodded in agreement and avowed themselves, one after another, in support of the wheelchair woman's axiomatic declaration. He hated Heckler for having put him in the meeting at hand, and his mind drifted to the encounter in Heckler's office that day when John had planned to get a severance package. Son of a bitch! John yelled silently at a mental image of his boss.

"You're quite right," Ms. Miller said. However, as a leading proponent of diversity awareness at HeartBank, despite the fad's having slipped from vogue over the past year, she was well-prepared. "I'll pass out a letter I've written for Mr. Brinkman to sign. I'd be interested in your comments. What I'd like to do is show it to him at our meeting with him. As you can see, the Brinkman meeting is the next item on the agenda. The business team captains have agreed to meet with us over lunch to discuss diversity at HeartBank. Mr. Brinkman himself has agreed to be there."

"How did you manage that?" asked the wheelchair woman.

"I spoke to Hillary Fohrmplatz, the senior liaison director for HR, who believes very strongly in our Council, and she spoke to Mr. Brinkman's assistant. We then got a campaign going among all the HR reps for the captains. We said something has to be done or all the efforts of the last several years will be lost." Again, all in the choir nodded and took turns affirming the self-evident truth in Ms. Miller's statement. By this time, John was throwing imaginary darts at Heckler.

"The meeting is scheduled for Wednesday, December 6, from 11:30 to 1:00 at the Metropolitan Club down on Marquette and Tenth. I told Barb—that's Mr. Brinkman's assistant—that we'd give a little background on the Diversity Council and then hopefully have a chance to talk to the captains about diversity at HeartBank. She was the one, actually, who suggested lunch, so I said, 'Great!'"

"I'll prepare a little outline and send it around by e-mail. If you have any comments, please get them to me by this time next week."

The meeting droned on with talk about the upcoming Brightness Festival to be sponsored by the Diversity Council and celebrated in the cavernous, stony lobby of HeartBank Tower. Staged to "break down the barriers set by tradition," according to publicity flyers, it promised to be a bland mixture of Kwanzaa, Chanukah, Christmas and pagan obscurantism. When the meeting adjourned, John felt as though he were being released from eighth grade detention.

♦ CHAPTER ELEVEN ♦

Severance

EVERY DAY, LIKE A RECURRING SYMPTOM of a chronic disease, the same feeling of despair washed over John's thoughts as he made the transition from work world to private world. Another day wasted. Another day closer to the end of his life and not a thing to show for it except for agenda-less meetings, several dozen e-mail messages and various encounters by phone and in person, some scheduled, some not, all of which theoretically related to earnings per share, but little of which made any sense and none of which bestowed on John any sense of benefit or purpose in life. If she had bothered to look, Sandy would have noticed the weariness in John's eyes and the weight that bore down on the corners of his mouth as he entered the kitchen. He mumbled a "hello," pulled a plate from the cupboard and helped himself to spaghetti and sauce from the stovetop pots. By the time he joined the rest of his family at the supper table, they were using the last remnants of their French bread to mop up what Ragu sauce remained on their plates. "So how was your day?" Sandy said, with an uninterested tone.

"I have to leave now," Jessica said, before John could respond.

"Where are you off to?" John turned to his older daughter, just as the younger one, Linnea, rose from her chair.

"Me too," said Linnea. "Basketball practice. See you later, Dad." John offered no resistance. His daughters were well past the point of being hauled back, questioned, controlled.

John knew his wife had asked him something just a moment before the sudden flurry, but he couldn't remember what it was. Sandy didn't seem to remember that she had asked a question.

"I've got some arrangements to work on before Jessica and I leave for

Arizona tomorrow," she said when the girls were barely gone. Some weeks before, John and Sandy had agreed that she and Jessica would fly to Arizona to be with her folks for Thanksgiving while John and Linnea would drive up north to be with his parents. "You'll have the house to yourself. I'd better get going. You want to clean up? Thanks." As Sandy crumpled up her napkin and dropped it onto her plate, John suddenly remembered what she had asked him. He wanted to tell her exactly how rotten his day had been. For once, he felt a strong need to dump work woes at her feet and heap them so deep she'd have to stop and listen.

"Sandy, you want to know how my day was?" he said, just as she grasped the sides of her chair to shift it out from the table. A puzzled look crossed her face. She had forgotten altogether that she had asked him that very question less than half a minute before.

"Well, what do you mean? Yeah, I guess. What about it?" She glanced down at her watch and looked up again and signaled with her shifting eyes and furrowed forehead that she was not allotting much time to John's answer.

"I can see you're real interested." John's sarcasm pulled the corner of his mouth back and hardened his gaze.

"What's that supposed to mean?" Sandy had long ago grown weary of John's glumness about work. She didn't want to hear about work woes, not when it was past the dinner hour and she needed to leave the house. Her impatience transformed to contempt, which John readily discerned in her voice and face. "Look, we all have bad days, okay? Be glad you have a good job. Sometimes I just don't understand you."

"*Good* job?"

"Look, if you want to talk about something, fine. Let's talk later. Right now, you're tired, I'm busy and I need to go." With that, Sandy carried her plate to the kitchen sink, rinsed her hands and dried them, and left the kitchen. Moments later, she was out of the house. John finished what was on his plate, but he tasted nothing of it.

Alone, John shoved his plate forward, put his elbows up on the table and pressed the palms of his hands against his closed eyes and forehead. He felt trapped, derailed, cut off from all meaning in life. Five minutes or more passed before he summoned the energy to leave the kitchen and head upstairs to change out of his suit.

Jeans, a sweatshirt and running shoes gave him a lift. As he descended the staircase, a radical thought entered his head. Why not go out? Why not drive to Cedardale and check out the latest hunting gear at Sportsmen's Paradise and get mentally ready for deer hunting with his father over the coming weekend? Before he knew it, John was on the road, headed for the large shopping center ten minutes from home.

John lost all track of time in the sprawling store, browsing through the merchandise on all three levels. The décor—mounted game, whole birches and pine and all kinds of antique (or imitation antique) hunting and outdoors equipment—lined the half-log walls throughout the store and was dispersed among the racks and rows of merchandise. He imagined working in such a place and further imagined living in the real environment that set designers had so accurately mimicked. But how would he ever do such a thing? How could he ever pay off his debts, finance his daughters' education and have enough left over to retire at a decent age? Without a severance package and time to figure things out, he told himself, it was only idle dreaming to think he could ever achieve happiness as he defined it.

He exited the store at just past eight-thirty, and rather than turn left and head immediately back to the car, he hesitated. The image of a cup of hot mocha entered his mind, and the imaginary steam rising from the imaginary cup triggered the thought that he deserved a splurging, a treat. A coffee shop bustled with business just down the mall to his right, so he proceeded in that direction. He joined half a dozen other people in line. Recorded guitar music emanated from hidden speakers, while frenetic servers behind the counter took orders and relaxed patrons sat around tables, sipped and chatted. John looked around at the crowd of strangers and noticed how contented they appeared to be. Suddenly, he felt as if his senses had left him. There in the corner, he saw Sandy, seated with a man, elbows on the table, their hands clasped together over steaming cappuccinos. After what seemed like minutes of suspended animation, John excused himself from the line and stepped back several steps to the entrance of the crowded shop. He felt hot and nauseated.

John staggered to a bench near a cluster of potted, ornamental trees just down the corridor from the coffee shop. Anger, disappointment, sadness, anxiety, confusion and feelings of betrayal and defeat all swirled around in John's head, as all other thoughts and visual and aural perceptions fled his brain. Gradually, he regained his senses and recovered his composure. As he looked through the trees and watched the entrance to the coffee shop, John realized he hadn't observed or couldn't remember a single physical characteristic of the man except that he wore a sweater. Who could it be? Where had they met? How long had they been seeing each other? What did it all mean for John? For the girls?

After another twenty minutes or so, the couple stepped out of the coffee shop and into the corridor. They pulled on their jackets and with their backs facing John, walked arm in arm toward the exit to the parking lot. Again, John caught only a fleeting glimpse of Sandy's partner, but the man's build and hair were revealed, at least. He looked about five-nine and 165 pounds, though it was hard to say what was weight and what was sweater and parka. His blond hair was cut very short, and from what John had seen of his face, the mystery man appeared to be on the junior side of forty. His gait was not particularly athletic and his knees leaned inward. John followed the couple out of the mall and into the cold, late November air. They walked slowly down a long row of cars to Sandy's vehicle, where Sandy turned and initiated a long embrace with the Man. Silhouetted in the night, they kissed—no, they slobbered all over each other's lips—and kept on slobbering all too long, even for legitimate lovers in the parking lot of a shopping mall.

John dashed to his SUV several rows over, and as his heart pumped, he debated between driving straight home to confront Sandy when she arrived, and following the Man to see where he lived and to confront him. By the time he reached his vehicle and inserted the key into the ignition, he realized it was all for naught. His marriage to Sandy was over. To a very large extent, he realized, his life was over. It was now officially a failure, and he would just have to learn to live with the fact that it was—that he himself was a failure. He drove to a dark house, helped himself to a beer from the refrigerator and sank into his den chair. John expected Sandy to arrive just behind him, but his daughters turned up first, shortly after he had opened his beer. It was nearly eleven o'clock when Sandy finally returned. Who knew what had taken her so long from the parking lot? John didn't want to speculate.

By convention, John was certainly within his behavioral rights to hurl his emotions at Sandy's face, but he thought of the girls and how they would react to an unconfined explosion on his part. He was determined to retain what little dignity remained in his life. When Sandy reached the stairs at the end of the hallway near the den, John called out to her. She appeared in the doorway.

"You're up late," she said, with an inflection that made it sound like a criticism.

"Who is he?" said John.

"Huh?" Sandy drew her head back with a look of perturbed confusion. She looked as though it had yet to dawn on her that John might know something about her affair.

"Who is he? The man I saw you with this evening?"

"Have you been following me around?" Sandy said with a mix of indignation and genuine worry.

"I saw you, Sandy. At the coffee shop at Cedardale. I went out tonight on a whim and just happened to see you there. I know you're in love with the guy, but who is he?"

Sandy was smart enough, John knew, to realize there existed no room for denial or explanation. In fact, there was nothing to deny or explain except that she loved Stu and wanted a divorce from John. "John, I'm sorry, I wanted to tell you, but I wanted to wait until the holidays were over—you know, for the girls and all."

"The girls and all?" John stood up as his emotions surfaced. "What about me? Why couldn't you level with *me*? Do you realize what you've done? Do you realize what you've done with our lives?" For a fraction of a moment, John thought of Heckler and all his manipulations and maneuvering. John intuitively reacted to injustice whenever it arose before him. Heckler, and now Sandy, had committed gross injustices, and their infractions by themselves seemed to weigh more on John than the personal harm that resulted.

Except for the final hearing in their divorce proceedings, just before the judge would sign the order granting their divorce, this was the last time Sandy and John would see each other as husband and wife. Despite the injustice of it all, John would choose not to fight the division of property. Concerned for his daughters' welfare, John would put their interests ahead of his own. Accordingly, in addition to making child support payments, he would agree to relinquish the house on very favorable terms for Sandy, and he would kick in more than his fair share of the rest of their modest net worth, mostly in the form of retirement accounts and college savings. All in all, a tidy severance package for Sandy. Stu, as it turned out, worked at the floral shop as a designer. He didn't make much and never would.

♦ CHAPTER TWELVE ♦

Wisdom

JUST BEFORE DAWN THE NEXT MORNING, John awoke from his fitful sleep on the downstairs sofa and grappled with the cold reality of his breakup with Sandy. There he was, down on his luck at work, stuck in a deep, dark rut, when *wham*! His marriage blows up in his face and leaves him scorched and shell-shocked. In coming days, weeks and months, John knew, he'd be in for rough sledding. What he couldn't fully anticipate was that a heavy sense of rejection and failure would push him to the edge of emotional stability—and even off the edge, if you counted his breakdown at work one afternoon two weeks after the divorce was final.

Fortunately, no one would see it. He would be in his office with the door closed. The weight of his entire predicament would press down so hard, he would suddenly burst out crying—something that had not happened to him since early childhood. It would scare him. He would jump to his feet, grab his suitcoat and flee from his office to the elevators and straight out of HeartBank Tower and into the chill of winter. He would walk aimlessly from one block to the next, his eyes flooded with tears of pain and anger. John would ignore the Don't Walk signs along the way, and it would take the angry horn blast of a delivery van to jolt him back to his senses. He would take it as a sign to pick himself up and get on with his life.

That emotional crisis and turnaround were weeks away. In the meantime, before daylight seeped into the room on the morning after the big breakup, John sat up on the sofa and inhaled deeply. How to tell the girls about all this? And at a time like this, when in a couple of hours, Sandy and Jessica would be aboard a flight bound for Arizona and he and Linnea would be well on their way up north. In keeping with his Scandinavian heritage, John stuffed his emotions, his fear, shock, anger and humiliation, into a vault within his heart and slammed the door shut. It would remain shut until after the long Thanksgiving weekend. As if nothing were amiss, he stole upstairs and awoke Linnea. "We want to get going to beat the traffic," he whispered in her ear. He realized how ridiculous that sounded. Traffic? On the way to Wisconsin on a Wednesday morning? But what did it matter? Anything to get underway before an awkward encounter with Sandy in front of the kids. After a quick shower, John slipped into the bedroom that he would never again share with Sandy. She lay still, either asleep or pretending to be, and John avoided looking at her. He groped in his dresser and the closet, pulled out some clothes, crammed them into a duffel bag and exited the room. If Sandy had any sense at all, she would stay in bed until he and Linnea were out of the house. Sense or not, Sandy didn't appear, and John exhaled with relief when, twenty minutes later, he and Linnea stepped out of the house and into the garage.

Honest to goodness calm settled over John, as he and Linnea turned onto the highway and headed to his parents' home in northwestern Wisconsin, about three hours from the Twin Cities. The bright morning sun melted the early morning frost and warmed up the yellows and browns of the countryside. The harvest was in, the hay stored, and all was ready for the onslaught of winter. It usually came by now, and John could not remember a Thanksgiving when there wasn't snow on the ground, for at least part of the long weekend. Every year at Thanksgiving, John had traveled to his parents' cabin on Petty Lake for dual attractions—the turkey dinner with his parents and sister's family, and deer hunting with his father.

For years, Sandy had tolerated the trip. She hated the crowded quarters of the cozy cabin that John's father had repaired, restored and improved, one project at a time over the years. Sandy also hated everything related to deer hunting. She thought it was cruel and primitive, particularly the part when John and his father hung the eviscerated deer from the big oak tree behind the cabin. In recent years, Sandy had established her own tradition of taking at least one of the girls to her parents' home in Phoenix. It was far more civilized down there, and besides, it offered a warm respite from early winter. This year, she expanded the tradition to include Stu, her boyfriend, who no doubt also thought deer hunting was cruel and primitive.

John realized Linnea had not uttered a word since they had entered the countryside, and he glanced to see if she was awake. The headphones were on—who knew what kind of music kids listened to these days, he thought, and who cared, as long as they confined it to their headphones—but her eyes were closed and her head, turned slightly toward him, lay still against the headrest. John checked the road ahead and peered back at Linnea. Her mouth was open but still, and the CD player rested in her motionless hands atop her lap. She was definitely asleep. Excused from having to engage in conversation, John cast his thoughts ahead to the drive's destination and back to its origins.

John's dad had purchased the place up on Petty Lake, back when land was cheap and he was doing well at First Metro. Built back in the twenties by a craftsman from Sweden, the cabin had fallen into disrepair, and the asking price, which included 160 acres of surrounding woodlands, was too good to pass up. John smiled at the thought of how Marv Anchor had paid cash on the barrelhead for the entire package. Nothing like owning real estate free and clear from the get go. John thought about all the mortgage loans he had closed—and *fore*closed—over the years, and how highly leveraged real estate was in this country.

As one farm after another drifted by, John recalled the past before his own—the stories about how Grandpa and Grandma Anchor, Great Uncle Niels and his cheerful wife Bertha had come over from Denmark in search of land and a new life. It amused him to think that his job in the real estate department at HeartBank had its roots in his ancestors' quest for land. The connection had never occurred to him before. They came to America in 1910 and immediately headed west to Minnesota, where so many of their farming countrymen had preceded them. Before John's father bought the cabin, the family had routinely visited Uncle Niels and Bertha on their farm near Tracy, about two hours southwest of Minneapolis. Niels and Bertha *Olsen*. John always marveled at how his grandfather, Isaak *Anchor*, had wound up with a different last name from his grandfather's brother Niels. According to Grandpa, Niels, being the older brother, had led the way through the registration line at Ellis Island. Niels just happened to be the last individual to be registered before the immigration officer went off duty. That particular officer followed the practice of changing every *Olessen*—Ole's son, in Danish, and at that time, it seemed that every other Dane was Ole's son—to the more practical *Olsen*. The officer who then came on duty took a different approach. He replaced *Olessen* with a name plucked out of the air. He started with A and progressed alphabetically, just as they do in naming hurricanes. In Isaak's case, the officer said, "Anchor." Thus, the two brothers, ever as close as brothers could be, stepped ashore as the brothers *Olessen* and headed west as the brothers *Olsen* and *Anchor.*

John's thoughts found their way back to the cabin on Petty Lake. The family used it as a summer retreat for the first few years, but eventually, financial pressures caused John's parents to adopt the place as their permanent residence. John's mother, Gladys, found part-time work in Hayward, eight miles away, and Marv himself took up a job at the lumberyard in town, which afforded him discounts on materials for improving the cabin. The log abode remained modest in size, but its warm and inviting rusticity rearranged John's priorities whenever he visited.

$ $ $ $

The tradition had been set nearly twenty years ago. On Thanksgiving Day, everyone would partake in the feast, take a walk down the long drive, watch football on television, and eat turkey sandwiches and play board games until around eight o'clock. Then John and Marv would marshal their gear for the hunt the next day. On Friday, John and Marv would rise before dawn, down some coffee and homemade donuts and quietly leave the house before the others stirred. The first day of hunting was for hiking through the woods and learning how the deer would likely move, given the season's wind and precipitation or lack thereof. There was also the unspoken understanding that the first day was for talking, father and son, friend to friend, and not for shooting. Only on Saturday would the two get down to serious business and bag a couple of deer.

They never ventured off Marv's 160 acres. In the first place, there were plenty of deer within the boundaries. More important, however, was the fact that this was Marv's land, free and clear. It was his domain, he liked to remind John—his corner of the earth that no one could take away from him, no matter what happened in the greater world of mergers and acquisitions, down-sizing and right-sizing, economic booms and busts. It gave him a sense of security and control to go out once a year and kill meat without having to leave his *manse.* John understood, now more than ever before.

John looked over again at Linnea. In her sleep, she had turned her head the other way, but she was still out. He could hear her deep, steady breathing. She would be out for miles to come. As the car descended into the St. Croix River gorge at Taylor's Falls, John thought about Sandy, Sandy's affair, the impending divorce, the girls, the house, his finances. He thought about work, Heckler, William Franklin and Walden; about Steve, a severance package, hunting, his walk in the woods with his father.

$ $ $ $

All went according to plan and tradition, and just beyond daybreak on Friday, John and Marv Anchor started down the trail that led into the woods behind the cabin. The air was crisp but not cold, and John took a deep breath of air through his nostrils to smell the leaves that covered the ground. Once the sun rose, the mercury would rise too, maybe into the fifties. In summer, the foliage in these woods blocked his sight beyond thirty yards or so, but now, with all the leaves down, John could see for a hundred yards or more. During this interlude between the splendor of fall colors and the great white blanket of winter, the land revealed itself, much like a beautiful woman who, in changing from dinner dress to bathrobe, reveals her sensuous curves.

The two men walked in silence, and though it was John's father who led the trek, John knew exactly where they were going. At a bend in the trail, where a fallen giant of the forest lay under a blanket of moss, Marv would enter the undulating woodlands and lead toward a stand of towering white pine. Too small to have interested the lumbermen who pillaged the forest a century before, these sentries of Marv's woods had been allowed to grow into their present full magnificence. John and his father would stop there to gaze upward at the windswept boughs and admire the wild beauty that soared above the lesser trees. The pines were a landmark, which led to another—a solitary white pine—and beyond that, a hill dominated by mature poplars. John and Marv would admire those trees too and the pointed limbs, which, unlike pine boughs, reached vertically to scratch the sky. In due course, the two men would hike over the hill to a bog full of jack pine, skirt around the west side and continue straight over two small ridges to a third, dubbed Deer Ridge, which overlooked a meandering creek. Depending on the wind direction, overall weather conditions and the time of day, Deer Ridge could turn out to be the best place for spotting deer.

At the base of a sturdy white oak at the mid-point of Deer Ridge, they laid down their gear, pulled out their cushions and found a comfortable spot on which to sit down and rest. After John and his father acknowledged to each other the splendor of the day, Marv got down to the business of asking how things were.

With some effort at first, followed by a torrent of feelings, contemplations and explanations, John poured forth. For a long while, John's father said nothing but simply listened. That was his way. As long as John could remember, his father had been a good listener, an honest and open listener, who waited to pass judgment, to respond, to advise, until John had finished with all he had to say. It was not unusual either, for John's father to lay a light hand on his back and to say with that gesture, "I hear you, son."

When John finished this time, his father picked up a small stick and tossed it lightly with no particular aim. "Your troubles will pass, John, believe me. They always do, and you know, you'll always have your mother's and my support."

"Thanks, Dad," John said, as he emulated his father's toss of a stick.

They talked at length about the impending divorce, John, Sandy and the girls, until the sun moved the hunters to shed their jackets and loosen their shirts. John's father pulled the thermos from their pack and poured two cups of coffee.

"You wanting to talk about work, too?" John's father asked. John marveled at him. There seemed to be no end to the man's willingness to listen, to share John's burdens. Perhaps it was because Marv himself had struggled mightily but largely quietly with many things in his life. His own struggles had made him more understanding, more patient, more capable of helping others who floundered. The question about work drew the two men into a long discussion about the bank and business in general.

"Not much has changed in a quarter of a century," said John's father, "except the same old things happen faster and more often, thanks to voice-mail, e-mail and the bombardment of information. Frankly, I don't know how you guys today put up with it all. They push you too far and the whole engine of commerce is likely to freeze up. I mean, they have everyone running around like there was no tomorrow, and no one gets to sit down and think things through. In my mind, it heightens the likelihood that one of these days someone's going to realize, 'Oops! We've been doing this or that all wrong,' or 'Oops! We forgot about this or that. Time out while we shut down the whole works—life as we know it—to fix things.'"

"Y2K and the Halloween Virus are perfect examples of that," said John.

"Exactly," said his father. "And that's hardly the last time we'll have to deal with bugs like that. Just the other day, I heard this fellow on the radio talk about how vulnerable all this technology has made us. Sure, the computer has made us more efficient—you, not me—but now that everything is done over the computer, what happens if some hacker wants to get into a few of our systems and really screw things up? It's not hard to imagine how someone could stop everything cold, from the transfer of money to the distribution of food. Or worse, how a bunch of Russian terrorists could hack their way into the Pentagon and the Federal Reserve System and deliver an ultimatum to the effect of 'Deliver $100 billion in cash to bail out our central bank by Friday or we bring down your whole banking system and your defense systems to boot.' What I want to know is whether we're better off zooming around faster and more efficiently than ever before, acquiring more gadgets than we know what to do with and having access to all the information—notice, I said 'information,' not 'understanding'—if we expose ourselves to a catastrophic interruption and if we lose our humanity in the process."

"At some point, Dad," John said, "you have to look at what's behind it all, and I'd say it's the almighty dollar—which, if you're honest about it, I suppose, is what's been behind us since time immemorial."

"That's very true," John's father said. "And you've got to be facing that more in a public company than anywhere else."

John shifted his cushion so as to position himself in a patch of sunlight, closed his eyes and put his face into the warm rays. "You're right, Dad. Every year, we're asked to produce more and more, and our growth objectives in year two are not a percentage of our growth objectives in year one, but rather, a percentage of how we actually did in year one. In other words, if a manager's planned earnings this year are a million and he does a fantastic job and comes in with actual earnings of one and a half million, then he's measured next year not against the million but against the one and a half million. How can a guy keep dealing with that before he goes over the edge?"

John's father nodded in agreement as he poured himself another cup of coffee from the thermos. "I heard someone on the radio talking about that too," he said.

"You sure listen to the radio a lot," John said, kidding.

"Hey, talk radio keeps a guy on his toes during a slow day at the lumberyard, and on Saturdays I wouldn't miss Garrison Keillor and *A Prairie Home Companion* for all the venison steaks in my freezer. Anyway, on the radio a couple of weeks ago, I heard an interview of some former businessman who is teaching at a small college somewhere. He was telling how one day he realized he was part of the problem, and when he realized he was part of the problem, he had no honest choice but to drop out."

"What do you mean?" John asked.

"Well, what he was saying was this, and it's kind of scary, when you think about it. This businessman-turned-professor was saying that whenever he received his personal statements from his broker or mutual fund or whatever, he'd look at all kinds of performance factors - you know, annualized growth, appreciation year-to-date, five-year performance, that sort of thing, for every single stock and every single mutual fund he owned. For awhile there, he said, he wouldn't tolerate any return that was below twenty percent on an annual basis.

"But meanwhile, at work, he argued continuously with his boss about reasonable expectations for earnings growth for the division he managed. He complained exactly of what you were saying a moment ago—'If I say I'll do such and such this year and I actually do a lot better, then next year, the bar will be set even higher.'

"When he realized he wasn't going to sway his boss, he sat back to consider the sources of performance pressures in the organization. It was simple really, and it all came right back to himself."

"How was that?" asked John.

"Well, he asked, 'Who's putting pressure on me? Answer: My boss. Who's putting pressure on my boss? Answer: *His* boss, and so on, all up the line to the CEO.' Then he asked, 'Who's placing the pressure on the CEO? Answer: The board of directors. Who's pressuring the board of directors? The shareholders. Who are the shareholders, by-and-large? Large institutional investors, mostly funds—you know, one of the twelve thousand or more mutual funds that exist out there today. And who's demanding that the funds produce at least a twenty percent return year after year?' he finally asked. 'Oh my God!' he realized. 'It's guys like me.' He resigned, downsized his spending habits, got a teaching job and is now happy as a clam living on a lot less money and a lot less stress than before."

"I never thought it through that way, but Dad, the guy is absolutely right. We're all to blame for the growth addiction," said John. "It makes you realize that we've all bought into the greed system, whether we want to admit it or not. Sometimes I just want to throw in the towel, Dad, and come up here to make a living." It occurred to him, in a flash of fantasy, to leave a voice mail message with Heckler to the effect that he, John, would not be coming in to work anymore and that his last paycheck should be sent, severance package or no severance package, to John's home address.

John's father got up stiffly, took a few steps and arched his back to get the kinks out. "How 'bout we change the subject, then, and talk about huntin'?" he said.

"I'm all for that, Dad." Now it was John's turn to pat his dad on the back. It was his way of saying, 'I love you, Dad.'

They left the pack and their cushions at the big old oak tree and started up again, with John's father leading the way. As they walked along the sun-splashed ridge, they cradled their rifles. From a distance, they looked like hunters, but John, at least, still had his mind on other matters. After several minutes of hiking, John's father stopped suddenly. John followed suit and looked ahead. There, about thirty yards farther along the ridge, stood a large doe. It had come up one side, at right angles to the hunters' path, and since it was upwind, it had not detected their scent. Even though each of them had a hunter's choice license, which allowed killing a doe, neither John nor his father even bothered to try a shot. The deer would have disappeared long before either hunter could shoulder his rifle. As it was, the deer bounded into the woods and disappeared.

"That was our prize, John," said Marv. "Maybe we'll see it again tomorrow."

"Maybe," John said to acknowledge Marv. John was intrigued by his father's use of the word "prize." "I could really use a prize in my life right now," he said wistfully.

"Truth is, John" his father said, "every day of good health is a prize. You get to be my age and your prime concern is to make it through the day without some new ache, pain or a symptom of terminal disease. Beyond that, you just thank your lucky stars you've lived so long and that you have more days in the bank."

John laughed. "But not more days *at* the bank."

"Now that's a whole 'nother matter," his father agreed. "In fact, my radio experts tell me that banks as we know them, no matter how big they get, are nothing but dinosaurs. In fact, all the mergers and acquisitions simply mark the final stage of their existence just before extinction. In a few years, you'll see virtual corporations dominating the global economic scene—which, by the way, the experts say will usher in an unprecedented period of prosperity. I say, fine, as long as the technology doesn't crash. But whatever happens, John, you wait long enough and you'll earn your prize, I mean, a *real* prize. You might think you're in the doldrums right now, but sooner or later, you'll come across the Prize, as I call it. You might not even recognize it at first, but the Prize will change your life for the better. For some of us, the Prize comes slowly, gradually. For others, it comes all at once, in one great big heap dumped right at our feet. Either way, you'll get yours some day."

"Aside from your health," John said, "what's the Prize for you?"

John's father stopped abruptly. "Are you kidding? I've had so many prizes, I can't list them all. But I have to start with you, your sister and your mom," Marv said. "Okay, for you, maybe Sandy turned out to be a prize that faded away, but you have Jessica and Linnea, and who knows but that there's another woman out there for you, John. If you're talking a tangible prize, then my biggest *prize* is all of this," he said, as he raised his arms and gestured at the woods all around them. "And you know what, John? I wouldn't have found this prize if the bank hadn't laid me off the way they did."

John recalled the bitterness that had visited the family back in those days, months, even years, after his father had lost his job and while his parents tried to make ends meet. "But Dad, you went through a lot of pain and suffering after you got laid off," he said.

"Sure, but pain and suffering build character," his father said exuberantly. "It's where you wind up that counts, and for the kind of life your mother and I have up here, the pain and suffering was worth it."

John wondered where he himself would have wound up if the bank had not laid off his father and if John had been allowed to finish college at St. Olaf. "Maybe," he said, unconvinced.

"You'll see for yourself one day, John, trust me. In the meantime, hang in there. As long as you do the right thing, you'll come out just fine."

"That's a big 'if,'" said John. "If only I knew what was the right thing."

"I don't mean it that way," his father said. "I mean, as long as you do what's right by the people around you; as long as you do the right thing from a moral and ethical standpoint, you'll wind up in the right place with the right kind of prize."

$ $ $ $

The next day, Saturday, was just as warm and beautiful. The only difference, which neither father nor son needed to mention, was that there'd be no talk in the woods today. Only a whisper or two and lots of hand signals. Today they were after a prize of sorts, a nice-sized deer to shoot, for a year's supply of venison steaks.

They returned to Deer Ridge and walked stealthily along the top for about fifty yards, till they reached a fallen Norway pine, the victim of a lightning strike years before. There they stopped and slipped slowly down beside the log. With their rifles ready, they waited for their quarry. Not a word passed between John and his father, and they sat motionless. Around them, the air stirred now and again and rustled the crisp leaves that lay strewn around their boots. John caressed the stock of his Pre-64 Winchester Model 70 and contemplated how the Rifleman's Rifle had become a collector's item since his father had presented it to him exactly thirty seasons ago. It was a beauty, despite the scratches, or perhaps because of them, and John cherished it as a symbol of hunting tradition, reliability and experience. John closed his eyes and saw his father, another symbol of tradition, reliability and experience. What had happened to all the old-time bankers of Marv's generation—the bankers whose customer knowledge was stored in their heads, not in some mammoth database on a sprawling computer network; the bankers who were sharp with a pencil but warm in the heart; the bankers who treated customers as people, not markings toward calling quotas or commission earnings? Like a blazing gem, the sun ruled in the cloudless sky, and its gentle warmth lulled the men to sleep.

Z-Z-Z-z-z

In his dream, John went online to check the balance in his account. An edict had come down from Sycophant—why from Sycophant, John couldn't fathom—that if you hadn't balanced your checkbook recently, you would be summarily fired and without a severance package. John hadn't balanced his checkbook in ages.

Without warning, the computer keyboard magically became a piano keyboard. John panicked. He had never sat down at a piano in his life. How would he know which key to press for what command? Out of nowhere, a dark-haired beauty instructed him to press an ivory key, labeled, Enter. The computer cranked and churned for awhile, but at last, Current Balance appeared on the screen. The amount was $10 million. In the next scene, John found himself in a teller line at the bank. It took forever for the line to move. At the head of the line stood a man in a dark suit. His sunglasses were perched on tiny ears and a colossal nose. He insisted on depositing Monopoly money into his account. The teller wouldn't allow it, and the man demanded that he be granted an audience with Max Brinkman. Soon a couple of security guards appeared and whisked the man away. Next it was John's turn at the teller window. He tried to explain the error in his account, but the teller stolidly maintained that there was no mistake. The money was John's. John persisted, whereupon the teller turned into Heckler. Heckler threatened to call the FBI on the spot if John complained any further. Anxiety swept over John. The money wasn't his, and he feared he'd go to jail if the mistake wasn't corrected. But here was Heckler threatening to call the FBI if John insisted on a correction.

Z-Z-Z-Z-Z

John woke up with a start, but it could not have been as much of a jolt as it seemed. The enormous buck—easily 250 pounds—moved slowly in the creek bed below, oblivious to the hunters. John sized up the rack. It was a ten-pointer. A trophy, the likes of which he had never seen. The buck drank from the creek, while John began the succession of movements by which he would draw a bead on his prey.

First, John drew his right foot back slightly, then moved his left foot forward. Next, he realized that the visor to his cap, which, before his snooze, he had pulled down to shade his face from the sun, would interfere with his shot. He bowed his head ever so slowly until the visor rested on his right arm, which, in turn, rested on his raised right knee. He then dropped his head further to raise the visor. In careful rhythm with his breathing, John moved the rifle stock to his shoulder, and three breaths later, he raised the barrel. After drawing a bead on his target—just behind the buck's front shoulder and not too high—John flicked off the safety and slid his finger over the trigger. He drew one more breath and exhaled to steady his heartbeat and pinpoint his aim.

Then he realized. The buck wasn't his prize. It was his father's. John reversed the process he had just completed so painstakingly. In the meantime, the buck had moved no more than five yards farther up the creek bed, away from the hunters. With the rifle back across his lap, John pressed his right elbow slowly, gently against his father's side. Marv stirred slightly and grunted.

"Uh bk," John said for "a buck." He uttered it between his teeth in a barely audible voice. The rest would be up to his dad. John moved his head only as far as was required to observe peripherally his father's movements. Marv was a master, and he linked his patient motions into a seamless flow like a rivulet of rainwater that trickles down a rugged slope. The shot surprised John when it finally came. At the same instant, the buck dropped dead.

Marv turned to look at John. When their eyes met, John said softly, "That's a real prize, Dad, and I don't know anyone who deserves it more than you."

His father smiled in return. "Your prize will come, John," he said, "and no one will deserve it more than *you.*"

◆ CHAPTER THIRTEEN ◆

Lawsuit One

IF WILLIAM FRANKLIN'S MOTHER WAS PROUD OF HIM for having gone from dirt poor in rural Mississippi to rich and successful in that shining city in the North, she was equally proud of her oldest daughter, Magilda ("Maggie" to her friends and family), who graduated from Mississippi State with honors and went on to become a legal assistant in a civil rights firm in Jackson. As confident as she was smart, Magilda planned to go to law school and run for the state legislature someday. In the meantime, she put in long hours on the job and looked after her four brothers and sisters. When she heard of William's plight at HeartBank, she jumped all over the case.

"They didn't do right by you, Willy." She reached out to him over the phone, after he had explained how he was being squeezed out. "Now if you're any self-respecting brother of mine, you're going to get what's yours, you hear me, Willy?"

"Yeah, uh-huh." William had always looked up to his sister and admired her spunk.

"Don't 'Yeah, uh-huh' me. You're going to get what's yours, do you hear me?" She never settled for less.

"'Maggie, you going to be my lawyer?" William laughed. "Me and you, we can hold up this big bad bank."

"Willy, someday I'm going to be Chief Justice of the Yoo-nited States Supreme Court, mark my words, baby." Maggie laughed.

"That's for sure, Maggie."

"But in the meantime, baby brother, you going to have to get yourself a lawyer up in that frozen over hell of a place you wound up getting stiffed in. Just goes to show you, prejudice is alive and kicking in the cold north just as it is in the hot south. North, south, east, west—it doesn't matter, Willy. The color of your skin is going to be the same no matter where you go. That's why we got to stand up for ourselves, you hear me, Willy?"

"I hear you, Maggie."

"Here's what I'm going to do. I'm going to check with some lawyers here at the firm and get a recommendation, you know, a referral, for a lawyer up there in Minneapolis. Then, with your lawyer, Willy, you're going to get what's yours."

"Thanks, Maggie."

"No 'thanks,' Willy. That's what I do for a living—help people stand up for themselves."

And so it was that Justina Herz, Esq., social crusader, woman with a cause, civil rights lawyer, solo practitioner, came to represent William Franklin in his discrimination case against the bastion of white supremacy, HeartBank, National Association.

$ $ $ $

As a banker who had spent much of his career trying to collect on bad loans, John knew a good number of bankruptcy lawyers and other commercial lawyers in HeartBank's law department as well as in outside law firms. His duties had never required retention of an employment lawyer, however, and he was not acquainted with Joan Harstad, a ten-year veteran in the employment law division of HeartBank's law department, before she called John in early December.

"We got served with a summons and complaint yesterday, John. The plaintiff is a guy named William Franklin. I looked him up on the HR information system and saw that he reports to you. Is that right?" Joan sounded calm and collected, and her matter-of-fact reporting helped John maintain his composure.

"Yes, William, as we call him—I mean as he calls himself—is in my profit center. Actually, it's a cost center. I manage a cost center now."

"Whatever. I'll need to get some background from you on the claim. Is now a good time?" Joan sounded like the type who never strayed too far off the subject.

"Sure, Joan. First let me close my door."

"Good idea. While you're doing that, I'll e-mail the complaint to you so you'll have it in front of you. It'll just take a second. We scanned it into our system."

Two conflicting thoughts struck John as he put the phone down and rose from his chair. First, now that William had sued the bank, Heckler would be all over him, just as he was all over him about the Walden deal, and to the extent that Heckler had an ounce of sincerity in saying he'd reward John at bonus time if Franklin was gone by year's end, this lawsuit—damn it—would throw cold water all over his bonus. But second, and rather intriguing, was the fact that William had actually taken the initiative to sue HeartBank. It would serve them right, John thought, for enticing a naïve black kid up here and then dumping him in a corner of Heckler's world to fend for himself.

"Okay, Joan, I'm back."

"Good. Let's go through the complaint. I want your version of each allegation, and if you don't know things yourself, I'd like you to tell me who at the bank does know." For the next half hour, John and Joan discussed the purported facts on which William Franklin based his claim that HeartBank should pay him "damages of an undetermined amount but in excess of $75,000."

"How does he get to a figure in excess of seventy-five grand?" John asked.

"Oh, that doesn't mean anything in particular. It's standard practice for plaintiffs to state damages in that manner until they themselves establish what their damages actually are."

"And what do you know about his lawyer?" John asked.

"That's our problem. She's good. We've been up against her before and she's done better than just about anyone else in town could. She tends to sue first and ask questions later. Then she drives a hard bargain and often walks away with very attractive deals for her clients. I'm warning you, she won't let you take this case lightly."

"Great," John said. Forget the bonus, he told himself. "Is she with a big firm?"

"Nope. She's on her own, always has been." John had had enough experience with lawyers to know they made careers of cutting their opponents down every chance they could. It seemed as much sport as it was advocacy. He found it remarkable that Joan was saying nothing negative about the bank's opponent in the William Franklin case.

"Where do we go from here?" John asked.

"We'll need to retain outside counsel on this one, John. I'm recommending that we go with Lehigh Dickenson at Whiley & Cobb. He's a superb litigator who's recognized all over HeartBank as the kind of guy you want to settle difficult cases—and John, I'm telling you, based on what you've told me, this is a difficult case. I'll get in touch with Dickenson and let you know."

"Thanks, Joan."

"Sure, John, but your profit center or cost center or whatever it is will be paying for it." With that shot of realism, Joan signed off and left John to ponder the implications of William Franklin's lawsuit.

As soon as Heckler had learned of it, he stormed into John's office and slammed the door so hard that the photograph of John and his father in hunting gear fell flat, face down, on the credenza next to the door. "Goddamn it, Anchor, can't you do anything right? I told you to get rid of that guy by the end of the year, not to botch it so he brings a goddamn lawsuit against us. What the hell is with you, anyway?"

It was no use talking back. Heckler's temple veins stuck out, and his neck bulged against his tight collar. The arms were in fighting position too—hanging out and back a ways, which accentuated his growing paunch. He twisted his head and neck like a bull, pawing the ground, ready for attack.

"Didn't you offer him a severance package?" Heckler continued.

"I went through HR, Dennis, and they offered him the standard package for his job level and time with the bank." John said.

"Those dumb clucks, they don't know shit, Anchor. That was your mistake right there."

"Going through HR? I had to, Dennis."

"Not until you negotiated a severance package. You're the business manager, remember. HR has no business dictating to us." Heckler was so out of control now, John feared his boss might start tossing objects around the office. To defuse the situation, John decided to change tack.

"Sorry, Dennis. We'll get it settled right away. We've got Lehigh Dickenson at Whiley & Cobb working on it. He'll take care of it."

"Goddamn right he'll take care of it. And how much are we going to have to pay him besides paying Franklin?"

"I'll watch it carefully, Dennis."

"You got that right. Tell me when it's over, and it better be over soon and it better not break the bank or I'll bust your balls, you understand?" With that, Heckler repeated his door-slamming maneuver, except from the other direction. Perhaps the sound of the impact caused certain neurons to collide inside Heckler's brain, or maybe the thought would have occurred without the slam of the door, but in any event, Heckler turned right around and re-entered John's office and closed the door behind him, this time without knocking down pictures.

"Here's my deal," said Heckler, whose unexpected turn-around prompted a headline to flash into John's mind—"Unstable HeartBank Executive Guns Down Employee." "I'll take a special provision in December for thirty-five thousand dollars—we've got plenty of room for it. Now, come the end of January, if you've settled the case for that much, all in, including attorneys' fees, we'll call it even and I'll pretend I never heard of Franklin and that you never botched the assignment I gave you. For every dollar this goddamn suit costs us over thirty-five grand, all in, I take a buck off what you'd get for a bonus on March 15. For every dollar you *save* under thirty-five thousand, I'll *add* fifty cents to your bonus. Sound like a deal?" Heckler's strained grin revealed his crooked lower teeth. John had yet to recover from Heckler's sudden shift in tactics. Before John could respond, Heckler's grin gave way to grimness. "And if you can't settle this thing for fifty grand, all in, by the end of January, you don't get any bonus at all, is that clear?"

"Clear." John worked hard to utter the word.

♦ CHAPTER FOURTEEN ♦

The Diversity Club

THE DAY AFTER HECKLER'S GREAT HARANGUE over the William Franklin lawsuit, John donned the coat to his best banker-blue suit and headed over to the Metropolitan Club for the Diversity Council's meeting with the captains and Maximilian Brinkman. Like the vast majority of HeartBank's 60,000 employees, John viewed Brinkman as one in a league with famous athletes and Hollywood entertainers. His picture and quotations were ubiquitous, but the man himself was nowhere to be seen. Rumor had it that he spent lots of time on his sprawling ranch down in Texas. Of course, some people in the organization surely saw him plenty, and doubtless many employees had seen him on one occasion or another, but not the vast majority of employees. Not John. The Great Brinkman was almost like a legend, a myth, the great all-knowing Oz, who was one of the most powerful bankers in America. Now, thanks to Heckler's unwitting assistance by way of his appointment of John to the Diversity Council, John would be allowed into Maximilian Brinkman's inner circle, however briefly. John glowed with exhilaration.

The Metropolitan Club was an old, venerable, ivy-covered brick, richly paneled, elegantly furnished institution that used to be emblematic of exclusive wealth, power and privilege in Minneapolis, milling capital of the world. That was in its golden era, when the Club charter restricted membership to "outstanding and upright gentlemen of the monied class, refined in all matters of civil etiquette, demonstrably supportive of the refined arts and members of the white, Christian race." Social change during the twentieth century had demolished many barriers at the Club, but if your connections got you past the front gate and past the bald, chief butler-like ichthyosaur who guarded the grand foyer and seemed to know every passing member by name, you assumed a feeling of wealth, power and privilege, however fleeting.

When John reached the eight-foot-high, wrought-iron gates that separated the Club property from the sidewalk, he straightened his back and shoulders more than usual and imagined himself a power wielder on his way to broker a deal. This image vanished quickly, however, when the chief butler asked for identification. As the members of the Diversity Council had been instructed in an e-mail from Ms. Miller, John gave his name and said he was attending a meeting of HeartBank's Diversity Council. The guard pulled out a list of names furnished earlier by Ms. Miller's assistant, checked off John's name and handed him a round, plastic badge the size of the lid to a mayonnaise jar. When pinned to his lapel, it would label him as Guest in bold, black lettering. "It's up in the Mississippi Room. Go down the hallway and take the staircase on your left. You'll find Mississippi right across the hall at the top," said the guard. John decided the guard was a life-long employee of the Club, who had probably decried all the changes society had imposed on his lords' castle, but who, like everyone else, had adjusted to progress as far as he needed to for survival.

The guard then grasped the large, heavy iron ring on one of the double entry doors and opened John's way into the heart of the Club. Four inches thick, four feet wide and seven feet high, the dark, ornately-carved oak doors signified power far more convincingly—and, given the existence of a doorman, more conveniently—than did the metal imitations at the HeartBank Tower. John rehabilitated his image as power broker and proceeded down the corridor of wealth and privilege. He felt almost giddy, as he walked along the long oriental runner and past mahogany-paneled walls that bore numerous oil paintings of various Minnesota landscapes of the past, followed by a gauntlet of dead (judging from their old-fashioned poses and clothing) white guys in portraiture. A small brass lamp attached to the top of each ornate frame illuminated John's pathway. As he mounted the stairs, he gaped at the three large stained glass windows above the landing. One depicted a grain harvest, another, timbers floating down a river and the third, an ore-mining operation—wheat, wood and iron-ore being the resources that the Club's founding members had exploited to amass enormous fortunes.

John Anchor, power broker, returned to reality when he entered the Mississippi Room and saw his fellow Diversity Council members, each wearing a big, round Guest badge. He had not yet affixed his to his suitcoat, and reluctantly, almost ashamedly, he identified himself as a member of the non-elite. Three or four of the captains had already arrived too, and they conversed among themselves, in hopes their numbers would soon swell. None of them, John noticed, wore a Guest badge. One of their perks, John figured, was a fully paid membership at the Club. Their colleagues arrived late, and Brinkman himself, the Great Brinkman, was the last to appear, pursuant, John imagined, to carefully orchestrated logistical maneuvering. As in working out bad loans, John thought, timing is everything when it comes to projecting the right image for a CEO of Brinkman's stature.

In contrast to the dark hallway through which he had just passed, the Mississippi Room was light and airy, though the light green wallpaper patterned with gold *fleur-de-lis,* tall casement windows with white trim and lacy curtains, two oversized chandeliers, rich oriental carpets and elegant French Provincial furnishings reflected strict adherence to a decor code born of an era decades past. When all the VIPs who were expected (seven out of the ten captains who were Brinkman's direct reports) had assembled, Ms. Miller took her place on the speaker side of the lectern with Ann—the African American woman who served as the nominal co-chair of the Council—at her side and spoke into the microphone.

"I think we're ready to get started if everyone would like to have a seat," said Ms. Miller. What authority she must have felt, John mused to himself, to tell the most powerful men (for they were all men—and white ones, at that, although one, Bill Sadoff, happened to be Jewish) of HeartBank to sit down and shut up. Compliantly, the captains and their master and commander and nine of the ten members of the Diversity Council (John's compatriot from the middle-aged, white male ranks of the bank was out of town on business) sat down around three round tables covered with linen and set for a lunch—several steps of formality above what John was accustomed to at Betty's Place. "Thank you," Ms. Miller continued, with bright eyes and posture that seemed to lift her right out of her shoes. She was definitely on top of *her* game. "On behalf of the HeartBank Diversity Council, I want to thank Mr. Brinkman and all the captains for taking time out of their busy schedules and agreeing to meet with us here today. I think this kind of attendance shows how committed HeartBank still is to the diversity initiative." John felt his ears heating up. He didn't feel committed to diversity at HeartBank or anywhere else, for that matter, and yet he was on the Diversity Council. He counseled himself to keep his mouth shut, for fear he would be discovered as a reluctant conscript and not as a fervent volunteer. On the other hand, he wondered exactly how committed any of the captains or Mr. Brinkman was.

"Before we get to the agenda, I'd like to make sure everyone is acquainted with each other, so maybe we could go around the room and introduce ourselves." Now Miller had everyone by the ring in the nose. John wondered whether they would obey if she issued some whimsical directive like, "Now stand up, put your hands in the air so I can lift your wallets" or "Without standing up, reach down and grasp your ankles." One by one, people followed Ms. Miller's command. John noticed that in contrast to members of the Diversity Council, who introduced themselves by name only, the captains introduced themselves by title and domain.

"Good. We have a little presentation now that the Council would like to make to give you an update on what we've been up to. Ann, do you want to dim the lights and work the slides?" If Ann didn't have a speaking role, at least she got to do something productive. As Ms. Miller's co-chair-slash-assistant took her place at the table to the right of the lectern and projected the first slide onto a screen at the end of the room, Ms. Miller passed out a stack of the hard copies of the presentation. As far as John could tell, this was all Ms. Miller's show. If anyone had conveyed any comments to Ms. Miller or otherwise participated in producing the presentation materials, it was not he. Many of the bullet points on the screen, he noticed, were the same as those that appeared among Ms. Miller's comments on the diversity survey results that the Council had discussed the previous week.

Seated at the opposite end of the room, John could see all the other heads in the room without turning his. He observed, first and thoroughly, Brinkman over to the side of the middle table, arms folded across his chest. Dressed in a custom-tailored, gray cross-hatched suit with a red striped tie personally selected by Brinkman's clothier during a recent buying trip to London, no doubt, the CEO of HeartBank looked every inch a CEO. One of the tallest people in the gathering, Brinkman was in his late fifties and in very good shape. Streaks of gray along the temple areas of his abundant black hair imparted an image of maturity and experience to the dominating impression of vigor and agility. From every angle, John noticed, Brinkman's head cut a rugged, photogenic shape, much like a Hollywood figure—a large, square chin with a prominent dimple, a well-proportioned nose, brown eyes so dark and piercing that they looked black, ears drawn from a textbook and nicely landscaped by the hair around them, and a slight slope to the mouth—the combined impact of which reminded John of a general in command of his armies or a guy who couldn't be trusted, John couldn't decide.

Seated randomly among the three tables were the captains, or at least the seven who were neither clever nor lucky enough to be excused from attending. While Ms. Miller droned on, John watched the captains and wondered how each had risen to his particular position. Was it intelligence? Education? Pedigree? Personality? Timing? What allowed this particular crew, out of the tens of thousands of people at HeartBank, to rise to the top? John decided it was having the look and the lines. You had to appear as if you belonged at the top, and you had to read from a universally recognized script for inner circle executives. But take a guy like himself, for example. Smart? Okay, okay, at least he was no dummy. Educated? Well, he was no Ivy Leaguer, but wasn't the U of M better than a lot of other state schools, assuming you weren't a varsity athlete? Pedigree? Not exactly, but this wasn't Europe or the East Coast, for crying out loud. Personality? John had an adequate supply—for someone with a Scandinavian background. Maybe a bland personality (he never told lewd jokes) was his problem.

Out of the corner of his eye, John noticed Brinkman reach into his suitcoat for his cell phone. No one had heard it ring. The CEO flipped it open, leaned away from the table and spoke inaudibly into the phone. Only when he rose and walked slowly toward the doorway, with his right hand in his pocket and the other hand with the phone to his ear, did heads turn to watch him. Even Ms. Miller, who by now had died and gone to heaven, John thought, as she realized that of the total net worth in the room, hers was the only portion standing up, came back down to earth hard, when she saw the CEO walk out on her carefully rehearsed presentation. John assumed that Brinkman, the all-powerful, all-knowing Brinkman, had been summoned to lend his influence to one big deal or another. What

John didn't know was that the call was from one of Brinkman's Wall Street "sources," who had an urgent message: The second in command at Chase and heir apparent to the throne had lost a power struggle and was on the street. A nice severance package, mind you, and a very hot commodity. Chase's loss, any other bank's gain. Go short on Chase stock and you could make a bundle by the time the news goes out on the wire later this afternoon, Brinkman's source advised. Brinkman promptly closed out the call and placed another—to his broker. By lunchtime tomorrow, Brinkman would pocket a cool two million after taxes. The source wouldn't do too badly either, especially when his finder's fee from Brinkman was taken into account.

Soon after Brinkman rejoined his underlings and members of the Diversity Council, Ms. Miller finished her presentation. Her sidekick dutifully restored full light to the room, and Ms. Miller called on the HeartBank CEO to address the group. To mask his desire to be elsewhere, Brinkman rose with affected spontaneity and stepped energetically toward the podium, as he buttoned his suitcoat with an executive flourish. At the podium, Brinkman pulled a folded sheet of paper from his breast pocket, glanced at his notes and launched into his remarks.

"Thanks Susan. That was a very informative and impactful presentation, and I look forward to getting together on a periodic basis like this." Brinkman reached out to each side, the palms of his hands opened broadly toward his audience. His voice sounded the way he looked—confident and powerful. He then placed his hands on the sides of the podium as he always did on the many occasions when he addressed a crowd. "You know, you members of the Diversity Council, each and every one of you, are performing a very important role, and I just want to tell you on behalf of the entire corporation, how much HeartBank appreciates what you're doing. Diversity as a concept is long overdue and it's definitely here to stay at HeartBank. But we're going to need to keep up the momentum, and under Susan's leadership, I'm confident that you members of the Diversity Council can do it. Our most important resource is our *people,*" he emphasized the word with his voice and his hands, which rose sharply from the podium and floated back down again. "And diversity is the only way we're going to be able to enable *all* people to realize their full potential at HeartBank. Frankly, I'd like to see us quadruple our efforts on this front. The captains should be leading in this effort, and I'm going to be looking for specific diversity goals in their HBGBs♥ for next year."

John looked around surreptitiously at the captains and noticed two shift in their chairs and another two smirk at each other. The others hid their reactions. "Now, I'd like to hear from people in the room about how the captains and how I personally can help diversity along." John marveled at Brinkman's polish and ability to spin. Whether the CEO believed his own pitch, didn't matter. He'd said the right things to the right audience. As much as John's fellow members of the Diversity Council might criticize Brinkman for the lack of progress by women and minorities at HeartBank, they sat mesmerized by Brinkman's vacuous speech and overwhelming projection of image. This was the CEO talking about diversity. John wondered if Brinkman would actually read the letter that Ms. Miller had labored over so assiduously, the letter that would bear his signature and be disseminated to HeartBank's 60,000 employees.

The captains saw the bandwagon rolling slowly past them, and none wanted to be left behind. O'Gara initiated the climb aboard. "Max, it seems to me," the silver-haired dean of the captains said, "that the Diversity Council could achieve higher visibility if each of us could invite Susan or some other spokesman for the Council to attend our monthly group meetings. I know I'd like my people to get more exposure to what the Council is doing, and that would be an effective way to get the word out."

"That's precisely the kind of thing we should consider," Brinkman said. One by one, the other captains, including the ones who had smirked, joined in, each in an attempt to show greater diversity fervor than the guy before him. John wondered if anyone else on the Diversity Council saw that despite the lip service, none of the captains was wearing any clothes when it came to commitment. How many William Franklins are there at HeartBank because these guys don't know or care what really goes on? he asked himself. And by the way . . . holy smokes! He felt illumined, as if by divine revelation. How is it that every single one of the captains is a white guy in his fifties, maybe older? Ms. Miller coughed, and reflexively, John

♥Shorthand for "HeartBank Goals of Business", an HR term adopted throughout HeartBank. Each year, every manager in the corporation was required to drum up "HBGBs" (or "heebee geebees," as most middle managers called them) for discussion with and approval by the next level of management.

glanced in her direction. Yeah, his enlightened musings continued, and why is it that virtually every single HR person I've ever dealt with except for those in the so-called "advanced leadership" training seminars offered every year by HR, is a woman? Does HR discriminate against hiring men or is it not a male thing to go into HR? And now that I think of it, despite the Women Going for the Top campaign to place more women in top executive slots, most of the names in the top boxes of business line departments belong to men. Most operations departments, on the other hand, are headed by women, stuck in the bowels of nondescript buildings on the periphery of downtown Minneapolis. John had never asked himself such questions, and he felt private shame that he hadn't.

A set of waitresses appeared with large, oval trays loaded with light salads and plates of chicken breast with Minnesota wild rice and asparagus, as the diversity bandwagon labored to a crawl under the weight of redundant discussion. John noticed Brinkman check his watch at regular intervals. Taking her cue from the head waitress, Ms. Miller stood up, thanked everyone for attending the "great discussion" and suggested that they now eat lunch. Taking his cue from Ms. Miller, Brinkman stood up, and under the camouflage of commotion as the others re-positioned themselves for a chicken lunch, shook Ms. Miller's hand with both of his, said, "Thanks, Susan. Great job," and slipped out of the room for more important matters on his schedule.

As for John, he enjoyed the free lunch and participated minimally in the conversation at his table. After dessert, he rose and followed his fellow plebeians, who trailed the three captains who hadn't left early. John surrendered his Guest badge at the door and stepped back out into the brisk December air.

♦ CHAPTER FIFTEEN ♦

Lawsuit Two

LARGE BANKS, LIKE LARGE CORPORATIONS in any other industry, are not strangers to lawsuits. A multibillion dollar company, no matter how righteous and well-managed, cannot please all its constituents—customers, employees, shareholders and community groups—all the time. On any day of the year throughout the life of a Fortune 500 corporation, any number of lawsuits against the company rage, fester or smolder; take William Franklin's case, for example. However, it's not every day that even the largest corporation in America is sued for a billion bucks. At precisely 11:54:30 a.m. on December 7, a law student working part time as a process server for Opegaard Legal Services, stepped off the elevator onto the fifty-fourth floor of HeartBank Tower and rang the buzzer below the sign, next to a set of double doors, that read, For Service of Process, Ring Button Below. At 11:55, she served a summons and complaint on a legal assistant in the HeartBank Law Department designated to accept service on behalf of the corporation. The pleadings bore the caption, *Walden Financial Corporation, et al. vs. HeartBank, National Association.* That afternoon, Heckler received a call from Chuck Lindstrom, head of the litigation section.

"What the . . ." Heckler was so stunned that for once he couldn't bring himself even to belch a string of expletives. "I told Anchor . . . what's . . . what're they suing . . . over?" No doubt Heckler's career at HeartBank flashed in front of his eyes as sudation glistened on his crimson forehead.

"The complaint goes on and on about a deal we allegedly said we'd do and then backed off of, resulting in all kinds of damages to the plaintiffs," said Chuck. "Frankly, I can't see how they come up with even a tiny fraction of a billion dollars, but a tiny fraction of a huge number can sometimes work out to be a significant amount of money. How much do you know about this transaction, Dennis?"

Chuck's matter-of-factness did little to lower Heckler's mounting blood pressure. The fact that Walden had sued at all was enough to throw Heckler into a conniption, but a billion bucks? Wait till he got ahold of Anchor. Anchor! Where was he, anyway? "Just a minute, Chuck. Let me get John Anchor in here. It's his deal." Heckler's neck swelled within his collar, and reflexively, he twisted his head sharply to the right and back, as he linked John into the call. "Chuck? I have Anchor on the line now."

"Hi Chuck," said John. He wasn't closely acquainted with Chuck Lindstrom, but over the years, John had had periodic dealings with the senior attorney, particularly in the late eighties and early nineties. Back then, when John and Special Asses initiated lawsuits against borrowers in default, the borrower often counter-sued on the basis of "lender liability"—the allegation that the borrower had been harmed by over-reaching on the part of the bank, either in the process of granting the ill-fated credit, administering the loan or collecting on it. In several landmark cases across the country, defaulting debtors were allowed to dishonor their sizable debts *and* recover sizable, trumped up damages from their lenders. Over time, the pendulum had swung back toward the center, but it remained commonplace to have to deal with "lender liability" claims.

"Hi John, it's been awhile since I've talked to you. How've you been?" Heckler's head twitched again to one side, but this time Chuck's cool demeanor and not the heat under Heckler's collar caused the movement. The fact that John seemed acquainted with Chuck didn't sit well with Heckler either. Heckler hated lawyers. They only got in the way and charged you blind.

"Okay. What's up?"

"I was telling Dennis that we got served today with a suit by a Walden Financial Corporation and some related individuals. Dennis says you were involved with Walden in some way?"

"Oh, no!" John knew Heckler must be steamed enough to hire out as a wallpaper removal agent. "What's the claim?" If the Franklin complaint put Heckler into orbit, John wondered, what would this suit do?

"You mean the amount of damages they're seeking? A billion bucks." Chuck's voice revealed a crack in his cool exterior.

"A billion bucks?" None of the three men could see the other two wince when the figure was repeated.

"Yeah, a billion dollars. Before we hire outside counsel on this, I'm going to want to discuss the allegations with you. Can you come over first thing tomorrow morning?"

"Sure," said John. But he wasn't sure about anything anymore, least of all himself.

"That is, if he's still employed here tomorrow," Heckler in his barely confined fury vented impulsively. "I'll plan to be there in case he isn't."

"I'll expect you at 9:00 here at my office on fifty-four," Chuck didn't acknowledge Heckler's remark about John's possible absence at the scheduled meeting and closed out the conversation.

John didn't acknowledge the remark either, but it prompted a thought. Perhaps now Heckler would entertain the idea of a severance package. What with the Franklin complaint and now a billion frigging dollar lawsuit, John was a liability. An albatross. At this rate, in another month HeartBank would be in receivership with the Feds, thanks to the screwups of yours truly, the one and only John Anchor. "Yes. Here's my prize," John said aloud to himself as his face lit up. He sprang to his feet as he considered his father's advice during the hunting trip. Not only will Heckler love to dump me now, John thought, as he paced with his hands atop his head, but my price ought to be higher. Think of the money he'll save by canning me now, before I attract more litigation. He laughed. "Heckler," John said in his giddiness, "I want eighteen months' pay—a great deal for you, because you get rid of me now, today." Wait till Steve hears about this, he exulted.

The thought about his friend prompted John to pick up the phone and call Steve Torseth. They established another lunch rendezvous for the following day. Meanwhile, Chuck Lindstrom was back on the phone with Heckler. "Dennis, it's me, Chuck Lindstrom, again."

"Let me guess, I'm going to jail. That goddamned Anchor, sonofabitch. I told him not to trash the deal with Walden, and look what he did. He trashed the deal and got us sued. Just what I need. I'm gonna can his ass so fast he won't know he had one."

"Dennis, that's sort of what I wanted to talk to you about, in light of your comment when John was on the line. I mean, Dennis, you can't let John go as long as the litigation is pending."

"What?" Heckler's contempt lacquered the word, as he drew in a breath for the next verbal fusillade. "What do you mean I can't can his ass? Under the circumstances, doesn't it deserve to be canned?" Heckler stopped short of saying he thought the bank should can a few lawyers as well. Here was another one, trying to tell him, a business guy, who actually delivers something to the bottom line, what he can and cannot do.

"I'm saying, Dennis, it isn't advisable at this juncture to let a key witness go. In the first place, a judge or jury is apt to give the plaintiffs' allegations undue credit if John—the bad guy—is terminated by the bank. Assumptions about cause and effect, you know. Second, a terminated employee is not often a friendly witness. There can be retaliation, either outwardly hostile or passively uncooperative. I know you're upset, but I'm not sure that John necessarily did anything that merits his dismissal—at least insofar as the allegations are concerned—and like I said, even if he did commit some egregious acts here, it won't help our case if John is let go."

"Jesus rots!" Heckler fumed. "Okay, the asshole stays, but not a day after this lawsuit goes away." Heckler had no idea how accurate his threat would be. But he would never know and never care.

◆ CHAPTER SIXTEEN ◆

The Rejected Prospect

FOR ONCE, JOHN ARRIVED AT BETTY'S AHEAD OF STEVE, secured a booth and poured water from the plastic carafe when it arrived. He couldn't wait to tell Steve about developments at the bank and how they loomed large in his rekindled quest for a severance package. There were other things John didn't want to discuss, namely, his impending divorce, but surely Steve would have plenty to talk about. This would be strictly a business meeting. Soon John's eagerness turned to impatience. According to John's Timex, which was slow, it was a quarter to twelve—a full fifteen minutes past their appointed time—and still no sign of Steve. John was not a cell phone carrier, so he had no way to reach Steve.

Finally, Steve appeared at the front of the restaurant. The sudden change from the cold December air outside to the warmth of Betty's Place fogged up his glasses. He took them off and squinted as he wiped the lenses clear with the end of his scarf. John waved, but only when Steve had restored his own sight did he see John. Steve waved back and strode purposefully to the booth.

"You're a warm sight for cold eyes," Steve said.

"What took you so long?" John asked.

"Car trouble. My battery was dead when I went to start the car, and it took me a few minutes to find someone who could jump it." Steve rubbed his hands vigorously, then cupped them together over his mouth and blew.

"At your outplacement office?"

"No, at home. I decided not to go in today. With the holiday season going full tilt, I find it a bit depressing to hang out all day at the outplacement office. Nothing's going to happen this month anyway, and I figured, why not take the day off and stay close to home. Besides, it was so damn cold this morning, I didn't feel like freezing my butt off. It was much easier to look at the weather from our kitchen window."

"I'm glad you could make it, Steve."

"I am, too. We've been trying to stretch out the life of my car. It's an old Taurus with ninety thousand miles on it. It's starting to go. Over the past month it's been one thing after another. I don't know if it's going to survive the winter. You know, John," Steve opened his menu and scanned it hastily, "Something you have to think about regarding a severance package is making sure that before you say 'sayonara,' you've thought about refinancing, getting a car loan, that type of thing. The time to get an auto loan approved or refinance your mortgage is not when you're not working. Get all your loans before you bail out. I waited too long on the car. Now it's going to be hard to get a loan—when they get to the 'How many years at current employment?' part, what are you going to say? And you don't want to buy a car with a credit card—you still get tons of credit card applications in the mail, that's for sure. They all say, 'Because you're such a great credit risk, we're making available to you our Platinum-Plated Visa card with up to twenty grand of credit at our special, low, introductory annual rate of 3.9 percent.' I'll bet I'd get five card apps a week even if I were in bankruptcy. And then there are always the home equity loans for twice the amount of the *real* equity in your house, at a gazillion percent interest. You don't want to buy a car with one of those, either."

Louise finally appeared to take their orders. She wore a thick wool sweater with the sleeves pushed halfway up her forearms. "A little chilly out there today, isn't it fellas? I'm flattered you came all the way down here in the cold to see me." Her eyes glanced up furtively from her order pad as she cracked a smile in anticipation of a wisecrack retort.

"Sorry to disappoint, Louise, but you're wrong," Steve said. "We were hot out there for some chili in here."

"That's what I like to see," Louise gave her chewing gum an exaggerated chomp. "A little holiday season spunk. Chili for both the bankers today?"

"Yeah, extra hot, Louise. Right, Steve?"

"I'm paying," Steve said as he pointed to himself with both hands, "so I confirm that's right, Louise." He smiled at their waitress.

John was eager to tell Steve about his newfound shot at a severance package, but common courtesy dictated that he ask Steve first for an update on Steve's job search.

"AmBanCo offered me a job," Steve said.

"Congratulations!" John was genuinely glad to hear of Steve's breakthrough, though he was disappointed that lunches at Betty's would soon be a thing of the past.

"Yep, they offered me a job starting at $105,000 with a bonus of up to another thirty to forty percent, plus moving expenses."

"That's quite a Christmas present. You got the prize, Steve. Remember how worried you were about blowing the interview? Just goes to show you—just when you think you're down, you're not out." Given the good news and his own oddly improved crack at a severance package after weeks of abuse by Heckler, John was feeling uncharacteristically optimistic. He noticed, however, that his enthusiasm was not mirrored on Steve's face.

"There's a slight problem," Steve said.

"What's that? Your wife doesn't want to move to Charlotte?"

"How'd you guess? I turned down the offer, John." Steve's deadpan remark smothered the cheer that had risen over the table. John drew his hand over his chin in disbelief. A hundred and five thousand base salary was nothing to sneeze at, and a thirty to forty percent bonus was no joke either.

"You turned it down?"

"John, it just didn't seem right. You know the guy I was telling you about—the guy I interviewed with?"

"The guy with the—" John tried to suppress what he thought was inappropriate mirth, but Steve graciously let him off the hook.

"Yeah, the guy with the booger that backed in and out of the garage. Anyway, he couldn't explain to my satisfaction exactly where the job was going to take me, and the more I talked to him, the more I got the feeling that he didn't know where he himself or his department was going. I just thought, Geez, okay, so I accept the job, go through the commotion of moving my entire family out to Charlotte and everything that entails, work for a year and discover that I'm working for a dud. Where am I then, aside from being a million miles from my network back here, family, friends like you? The headhunter put all kinds of pressure on me—she was looking at a very nice commission—thirty percent of my anticipated first year income—but John, I just didn't feel right about it."

Despite his surprise, John tried to be reassuring, though he suspected that Steve had struggled mightily with the decision and still harbored second thoughts about it. "Sounds like you made the right decision. You know, Steve, sometimes you have to go with your gut. If you accept the first thing that comes along, you're just selling yourself short on other, better opportunities." His words lacked conviction, and the arrival of the chili distracted from whatever meaning they contained for Steve.

"Can I get anything else for you bankers in the fast lane?" Louise asked.

"No, we're set, Louise," Steve answered for both of them. He opened his package of oyster crackers and dumped them into his chili. John wondered if his remark of reassurance had even registered with Steve. "Something you worry about at this stage is how to manage your savings."

"What do you mean?" John said.

"Well, here's the situation. Nothing's going to happen between now and the first of the year. People are too focused on year-end stuff, too busy, too distracted by a hundred other things, not to mention the holidays, to be interested in interviewing people. So realistically, the earliest anything will happen is January. I mean interviews. Then it'll be another month before any offers develop. That's the best case scenario. What if nothing pans out? What if it takes another couple of months to generate an offer? What if it takes even longer? What if the economy tanks in the meantime? Christ, I'm already five months into my severance package. Another four and it runs out." John swallowed hard. Steve was not doing well, and what made John think he could do any better with a severance package? What if the economy *did* tank? What if Heckler gave him only six months instead of nine or a year? If his search turned out to be anything like Steve's, with a six-month package, John would have only one month left. On the other hand, given all that John had been through over the past several months—the lateral move to a dead end job, the lawsuits, his divorce—surely things were bound to turn around, and surely a nice severance package would bring the equivalent of a clean slate to his life, a chance to reorganize his priorities. Besides, how much more abuse could anyone handle from a guy like Heckler? Moreover, how much choice would John have, anyway? By all indications, the Walden suit put a limit on his days at HeartBank, no matter what.

"Here's the dilemma. I've got a little saved up that I can access—you know, funds outside my IRAs and 401(k). Problem is," Steve said, as he and John synchronized the movement of their chili-laden spoons, "it's all in stocks—or nearly all of it. The market has had quite a run, but sooner or later, we're going to see a big correction, like the one we saw earlier this year. Who knows when it's coming, but what if it happens right when my severance runs out and I need to liquidate stocks to pay the bills? I don't want to be selling when the market is way off."

"I hadn't thought of that," said John.

"Okay. I've whined enough. Any more and this chili will turn on me. Tell me how you're doing." John felt inept at responding to Steve's woes. He wanted to talk about his own situation, and he hoped Steve would be of greater comfort than he had been to Steve.

"Where should I start?" he said. John took another spoonful of chili and pushed his bowl aside. He enumerated his burdens, from his impending divorce to the William Franklin case and the Walden litigation that swirled around him at the bank. John's own lamentations, combined with Steve's predicament, diminished John's enthusiasm for a severance package of his own. Nevertheless, he mentioned his plan to Steve.

"Holy Jesus!" Steve said, as he pushed his glasses back to the bridge of his nose. The volume of his outburst startled John. "I've got to keep closer tabs on you before you walk into the next buzz saw. Geez, John, I'm sorry."

"Thanks, Steve, but I'll be all right. So, what do you think are my odds for a decent severance package?"

"Hard to say, honestly. But wait a second. What kind of severance package are you going to have to pay your wife?" Steve's tone conveyed a sincere concern for John and respect for John's stoic posture and steady voice.

"I'm paying plenty on account of the kids. What else am I going to do?"

"Man, I'm sorry."

"It's okay, really, it's okay, I'll be just fine. So what do you think are the chances of Heckler's giving me a good severance package?"

"If Heckler thinks he has a good reason for giving you the ax, your chances might not be great for a home run. At a minimum, though, given your level and everything, I'd think he'd give you four to six months. Jesus, how do I know?" This time around, Steve didn't offer to be John's agent.

"But if I approach him before year end," said John, as he tried to convince himself of his leverage against Heckler, "when he's flush in year-end earnings and can afford the expense, maybe he'll be more generous than he would be early in the coming year."

"Maybe." Steve didn't offer ringing concurrence. Louise brought the bill, and when John moved his hand toward it, Steve snatched it away. "My turn," he said. "I'm tired of people treating me like a welfare case. I'm not on welfare. I can handle it, okay?" The hardness in Steve's tone startled John. He backed off and uttered a muffled thanks.

"It's too cold out there to say goodbye on the street," said John. "You're going to have to assure me before we leave that you're okay." Steve expressed his acknowledgment of John's request by scratching his head with both hands, then using his forearm to sweep the cracker crumbs in front of him from the table. He prepared to deliver.

"There's this woman in Minneapolis, who turns on the radio one morning and hears on the news on 'CCO that someone is driving the wrong way on the eastbound side of I-94 between Minneapolis and St. Paul. Concerned about her husband, a banker who's on his way to a meeting in St. Paul, she calls him on his cell phone. 'Hello,' he answers. 'Honey!' she shouts. 'There's a crazy driver going the wrong way on the freeway you're on. You should get off at the nearest exit.' 'One crazy driver?' he says. 'Hah! There are *hundreds* of them, and they're *all* going the wrong way. But what do you expect out of people from St. Paul?'"

"This is the time of year for a few extra laughs," John said, relieved that Steve still harbored a reservoir of humor. He and Steve donned their overcoats and gloves, braced themselves for the wind chill outside and headed out the door. On the sidewalk, they pulled their collars up and shook hands without removing their gloves.

"Merry Christmas, Steve," said John.

"Thanks, John. You too. Damn but we sound like a couple of old farts, don't we?"

"What do you mean?" asked John.

"In this age of the Kwanzaa card and political correctness, when's the last time you heard someone say 'Merry Christmas' in public?"

"I guess I'm a creature of habit. I still call the Fourth of July the 'Fourth of July,' and when it's Christmas, I say 'Merry Christmas.' So long, Steve."

"See ya."

As they turned their backs to each other and walked in opposite directions, each thought himself luckier than the other. More than the seasons had changed over the past four months.

♦ CHAPTER SEVENTEEN ♦

Forg(er)ing Ahead

WHEN JOHN RETURNED TO HIS OFFICE, he found a Collateral Exception Approval Request form on his chair. Attached was a handwritten note from a salesman in Sycophant's division.

> John—
> Here's a CEA for a transaction with Equitar Properties I need to get closed right away. Please sign the form and get it back to me A.S.A.P.
> Bob Swenson

Swenson, a former Gopher football player and a sharp dresser, with every one of his light brown hairs in place at all times, could sell wind chill to Minnesotans in January, but he was a pain in the neck to John's Collateral Control Division. Collateral Control ensured that all the collateral documentation required by the bank in connection with a real estate loan was actually obtained at closing. Any exceptions required approvals from the head of the applicable lending division—Skip (Sycophant) Schuneman, in this case—and John, as head of Collateral Control. A deviation from this policy would result in a write-up by the internal auditors and a slap on the wrist, a warning or, in extreme cases, job termination, depending on the severity of the violation.

Swenson often pushed the limits of permissible exceptions, and the request now before John called for waivers of several crucial items—"Survey," "Phase I Environmental Report" and "Flood Plain Insurance." John walked through a maze of cubicles to Swenson's office, where the veteran backslapper was blowing hot air at someone over the phone. With his big hand, which several heavy rings made even bigger, Swenson motioned John to sit down. When he had finished his long-winded, run-on sentence, Swenson covered the lower half of the phone and addressed John.

"You got my note?" Swenson smiled. He was an affable guy, especially when he was trying to put one over on somebody, which was most of the time. John wondered what he was like when he wasn't trying to con someone. The animated salesman suddenly shifted the phone back to his mouth and uttered an "ah hah!" with a false tone of sincerity to acknowledge the person on the other end of the line.

"Yes, I got your note, Bob. And I've got some problems with it," said John.

Swenson feigned bewilderment as he covered, then uncovered the phone. "I see," he said into the phone, before slapping his hand back on it.

"Do you want me to come back?"

"Really?" Swenson issued another phony acknowledgment into the phone. Then to John he said, "No, no, don't go away. Let me close the call, it'll just take a second." He turned his full attention back to the phone, and after sounding like Mr. Sincerity while simultaneously rolling his eyes and entering some information on his notebook computer, Swenson got rid of the call. "Okay, Johnny, what can I do for you?"

No one called John "Johnny," but Swenson added a *y* to any name that could accommodate one. Swenson was one guy with whom John had no desire to be on familiar terms.

"Look, Bob. You just can't close this loan without a survey, a Phase I and either flood plain insurance or evidence that the collateral doesn't exist in a flood plain. I mean, these are major exceptions."

"Let me ask you a question, Johnny," Bob said. John went on alert. The classic "Let me ask you a question" line signaled a sleight of speech in the offing, and John was not about to be cornered by a smooth-talking sales guy.

"What's that, Bob?"

Swenson cleared his throat and carefully arranged his words, much as a magician manipulates the deck before directing his audience to pick a card.

"What kinds of things can I get you . . . ," Swenson cleared his throat. He then lowered his voice and said, "short of these things . . . ," He cleared his throat again and continued in his normal volume, "that will make you comfortable with this transaction?"

It's amazing, John thought, how the word "comfortable" can actually make you *feel* comfortable, especially when you're sitting next to a guy who has assumed a very relaxed position. Swenson leaned back in his chair, stuck one hand in his pocket and leaned his head against the fingers of his other hand while he rested his elbow on the desk. John noticed he himself was slouching. He sat up to retain a hold on his senses. "Frankly, Bob, nothing can make me comfortable except a certified survey, a Phase I report and flood plain insurance or a flood plain letter."

Swenson nodded slowly. "Johnny, we'll get whatever we can to satisfy you, right after closing."

"But after closing, Bob, the horses are out of the barn. You need those items up front or you'll never get them."

"I hear you, Johnny, I hear you. But I've got to be honest with you. The building we're taking the mortgage on is smack dab on the middle of the parcel. In all honesty, there's no problem with the building sitting on a boundary or anything like that."

"I have no idea about that, Bob, and besides, there can be other survey issues with respect to the property."

"Johnny, I hear you, but this is a clean property, believe me. We're taking out TransCapital Insurance on this one, and I don't have to tell you, Johnny, that TransCapital doesn't do a deal without strapping up the borrower eight ways to Sunday, so you know this property is clean. Besides, the loan is guaranteed by some heavy hitters. The last thing we'd have to do here is foreclose on the property. I mean, it just isn't going to happen, Johnny."

"Bob, look. I'd like to help you out, but in good conscience, I really can't sign off on your request."

"Johnny, I hear what you're saying, but Skip signed off on this. In the remote chance that the loan goes south and in the even remoter chance that we give up on the guaranties and decide to foreclose on the property, there's only the most infinitesimal chance that survey problems, environmental problems, that kind of thing, are going to limit the value of our collateral. Besides, we're way over-collateralized the way it is. So if remote on top of remote on top of infinitesimal on top of no way will this go bad, Skip takes the risk. We won't hold you accountable."

Swenson was full of it. "Bob, maybe you and Skip won't hold me accountable, but the auditors sure will."

"I hear you, I hear you." John was proving to be a hard sell, and Swenson was no dummy. Time to switch gears and tackle the real issue—Swenson's commission. Swenson was on the threshold of the twenty percent commission bracket. The deal at hand would put him over the top and move him from fifteen percent. The additional five percent on origination fees and estimated first year revenues amounted to an extra ten grand in Swenson's pocket. The salesman dropped his pretense of being relaxed, leaned forward and assumed a deadly serious countenance. "Let me level with you, Anchor. You prevent this deal from closing in December and Schuneman will make sure your ass stays in Collateral Control for the rest of your life. When he takes over from Heckler—and rumor has it that's going to happen one of these days, once Heckler gets his promotion—Schuneman can be either your friend or your enemy. You don't want to be his enemy, you understand? Now sign the goddamn form before I have to tell Schuneman you're not playing ball."

"I've got an idea," John said. He himself was not about to compromise sound lending practices, but there was certainly someone else around who would and could.

"I'm all ears," said Swenson.

"Why don't you get Heckler to sign it?"

Swenson leaned back in his chair. "No offense, Johnny, but we already thought of that. Problem is he's out of town and we can't get ahold of him in time for the closing—it's this afternoon."

John disdained just about everyone in Sycophant's group. They cut corners wherever they could—anything necessary to make a fast buck. The same went for Heckler. Swenson's threat against John carried next to no weight. In the first place, it was presumptive of Sycophant to think he was Heckler's successor. The more likely scenario was that Heckler would blow himself up sooner rather than later, and Sycophant, who was so closely tied to Heckler, would go down with Heckler's ship. Blowhard was the far more likely candidate to succeed Heckler. In any event, wouldn't the Franklin complaint and the Walden lawsuit extinguish John's misery once and for all? John almost laughed at himself for taking Swenson's overreaching request so seriously. Who the hell cared? Now it seemed more like a game. Should he stiff Swenson and Schuneman just for old times' sake, or should he just give the juvenile delinquents free reign in the candy store and make one last contribution to the ultimate demise of Heckler? In the end, John came down on the side of integrity. When in doubt, do the right thing, he thought.

"I guess then you're out of luck," said John. He rose out of his chair and returned to his office.

Swenson went to Sycophant, and Sycophant knew better than to coerce John. After three more failed attempts to reach Heckler, Sycophant calculated the deal's first year fees again, looked at his division's year-to-date income statement and forged Heckler's signature on the form. He handed it back to Swenson and said, "Our lucky day."

♦ CHAPTER EIGHTEEN ♦

Negotiations

JUST TWO WEEKS BEFORE CHRISTMAS, it turned so warm that the artificial snow in the display windows of Dayton's Department Store threatened to melt. Normally by this time, Minnesotans were hunkered down for a long spell of Alberta Clipper cold fronts and dangerous wind chills. Maybe it was the warm weather or perhaps the holiday season or possibly neither. Maybe it was that the Equitar deal had put the entire department over the top, enabling Heckler to maximize his bonus for the year. In any event, John found his boss nothing less than ebullient the next morning.

John's hope soared. Finally, everything was in alignment. As his father had promised, eventually everything works out. The failed plan several months ago, the unpleasant job of terminating William Franklin, the lawsuit it prompted, the Walden scam, the lawsuit *it* brought, all the Blowhards, the Sycophants, the Swensons, the Hecklers, for crying out loud, the entire bank were just about to become minor distractions of the past. John was on the threshold of his grand escape. Soon he could start his life afresh. He'd be free of a spouse who didn't love him, he'd be free of a job he could never love, he'd be financially free to rediscover alternatives, he'd simply be free.

"Got a minute?" John asked, as he leaned into Heckler's office.

"Sure, sure, come on in, Anchor," Heckler said out of one side of his mouth, while a giant, unlit cigar wobbled on the other side. The Minnesota Clean Air Act prohibited smoking inside public buildings, but since when did rules stop Heckler? As long as he lets me go with a decent severance package, John thought, he can blow all the smoke he wants. John took a step into Heckler's lair and closed the door softly behind him. "Anchor, you take life way too seriously," Heckler said, as he moved to his chair and plopped himself down. "You're going to get old long before your time. What you need is a good cigar," he continued, as he pulled his stogie out of his mouth, ran it under his nose and stuck the end back into the inside corner of his cheek. Wearing a bow tie that was in the shape of holly leaves, with two big red berries in the middle, and suspenders bearing little Santa faces instead of the usual dollar signs, Heckler looked like a retail banker trying to be jolly. "What is it now? Let me guess," he jeered. "We're getting sued again." Heckler reached down, opened a drawer and pulled out an air purifier, plugged it in on the credenza behind him and turned it on. Next, he pulled out a lighter and flicked it. He moved the flame toward the end of his cigar but didn't light it.

"No, Dennis, we didn't get sued again," John sighed.

Heckler laughed. "We didn't? Well now, there's something to celebrate. Happy Holidays, Anchor!" He continued laughing until John shifted in his chair, as he faced Heckler. Then without warning, Heckler changed moods, yanked his cigar from his mouth and spit a piece of errant tobacco off to the side. He then riveted his eyes on Anchor and bared his crooked lower teeth. "Then tell me why the hell you're in here with the door closed."

In one sense, John found relief in Heckler's sudden change of direction. There would be no need to dance around the business at hand. At the same time, John wondered if Vesuvius wasn't about to erupt. Better to shoot fast, John told himself, and be done with it.

"Dennis, I figure now would be a good time for me to leave the bank, and I'm here to talk about a severance package." There, he'd done it. It was so easy when you just compressed your words together and blurted it out. That would be his advice to whoever might seek it. Don't agonize for months. Don't ponder, wonder, worry. Don't hesitate. Just go in and ask for it. If only he'd been that direct back in September. With a guy like Heckler, you had to be direct. You had to look him straight in the eye and say exactly what John had said exactly the way he'd said it. *Time for me to leave, I'm here to talk about a severance package.*

Heckler moved the cigar to the center of his mouth and focused his eyes on the tip, as a three-inch flame leapt from his lighter. His cheeks collapsed as he drew in, and regained shape as smoke billowed into the air. John could see that Heckler was ready to negotiate. Once he gets the cigar lit, John assured himself, he'll be ready to golf, and when Heckler approaches the office putting green, the horse trading will begin.

"I can't." The words were laden with cigar smoke.

"What?" John said in disbelief.

Heckler pulled the cigar from his mouth. "I said, I can't." Smoke drifted over the desk, and like enemy soldiers, John and Heckler peered at each other through the haze of no-man's land. The room grew silent except for the steady, muffled blowing of the ventilation system. This was no holiday season, John thought, Heckler's attire to the contrary.

"What do you mean you can't?" John finally broke the silence.

"Lindstrom says you can't let someone go when they're in the middle of a lawsuit. Says it looks bad if you can the asshole who caused the problem for the bank. *And* my friend, Lindstrom doesn't even know about your other lawsuit." Heckler poked the cigar deep into the back of his cheek, stood up, pulled loose the bind in his underwear and moved toward the windows. John's hands felt cold as his fingers tightened on the arms of his chair. He stared straight ahead at Heckler's empty chair. "Anchor," Heckler continued, "there's nothing I'd rather do than watch the door hit you in the ass as you walk out of here. You and me just don't see eye to eye. Never did, never will. You've caused me so much grief, my patience is up, but my hands are tied."

"It's a bogus suit," John mumbled.

"What's that?" Heckler spun around and walked back behind his desk, as cigar smoke trailed behind him.

John cleared his throat. "It's bogus," he said, this time with conviction.

"Well, let's hope it is, Anchor, because the sooner it's gone, the sooner *you're* gone. The day after that lawsuit is over, you've got yourself a package. Deal?"

"What kind of severance package are we talking?" Half a loaf—a severance package in the future—was better than no loaf, John thought. Heckler slowly moved out of his chair again and approached the putting green. He rolled a golf ball over the edge of the window ledge and onto the floor and gripped the putter that stood in the corner.

"Six months," said Heckler, as he lined up his putt.

At least he's negotiating, John reassured himself. "A bonus of twenty-five thousand for the year, plus fifteen months' severance pay and out-placement."

Heckler stood up and shouldered his putter. "Let me tell you something, Anchor. Pigs get fat, but hogs get slaughtered, and you're in danger of being a hog." The cigar distorted his words, but John heard them. At least I didn't start too low, John told himself. "My bonus deal still stands—you know, the deal I gave you over Franklin's case. I'll guarantee you fifteen if you settle the case like I told you—end of January for thirty-five grand, all in. For every dollar over thirty-five grand, you lose a buck. For every dollar under, I'll give you half a buck on top of the fifteen. For severance, I'll give you nine months. Outplacement? Okay, that's standard. Nine months' worth. That's my deal, take it or leave it." Heckler lined up his putt again and sank it.

"Twelve months," John said. He stood up slowly and crossed his arms across his chest. He uncrossed them when Heckler bellowed back.

"I said, a deal's a deal, take it or leave it!"

"I heard you." By now Heckler was champing on his cigar and the putter was back in the corner. Negotiations were over. John's career at HeartBank was over . . . except for two minor details: resolution of a couple of lawsuits.

♦ CHAPTER NINETEEN ♦

Under Watch

In the meantime, Heckler basked in the extraordinary revenues that fell to his domain in December, thanks in large part to the Equitar loan. The deal closed in December, because no one who saw Heckler's signature on the Collateral Exception Request form knew it had been forged. As it turned out, no one would ever be the wiser, though over the life of the loan, more than one employee in the Collateral Control Division would question why in the world Heckler would have signed off on such exceptions as the form contained. As a result of the December closing, Heckler's department booked the $100,000 origination fee—one percent of the principal amount of the loan—in the current year, and yet, Heckler could count the deal toward his next year's plan of $100 million in new loans. Both effects put Heckler in a party mood. But Heckler made two mistakes. He invited O'Gara, his boss since Dunn's demise, to the party, and he forgot about the cleaning crew.

Heckler had been one of Brinkman's direct reports for only two days, certainly to the disappointment of Sycophant, a direct report of Heckler. Forty-eight hours in a position just two layers down from the CEO was hardly enough to satisfy the Sycophant's appetite for power and prestige. The management bulletin that announced, "Dunn will pursue other opportunities outside HeartBank," also stated, "Effective immediately, National Real Estate Services, headed by Dennis Heckler, will report to Mike O'Gara." The next day, Heckler put himself on his best behavior and took the elevator to the sixty-ninth floor to meet his new boss.

O'Gara was a "hands off" manager who thrived on glad-handing a crowd but who preferred to give people under him "the maximum latitude to make money for the bank." Everyone knew O'Gara's signature phrase to mean, "maximum latitude for me to avoid true management duties." Pushing sixty-two, O'Gara had the senatorial look, except that his head was way undersized for his bulk. Nonetheless, his craggy face, wavy gray hair and a trademark handshake, which included a pat on the shoulder with his left hand, would have made him a winner on the hustings. However, O'Gara preferred to golf (in Minnesota during the summer, elsewhere when the state's climate was less felicitous or downright inhospitable), watch his personal investments and attend social functions. Although his favorite gatherings were large business association luncheons and benefit dinners for local charities, his forte was "working the crowd," not addressing it. He had a knack for knowing exactly when he should make the rounds from table to table, shaking hands and impressing people with his ability to remember their names and personal trivia. He also loved to hand out HeartBank lapel pins in tiny plastic bags as if he were handing out campaign buttons. People at HeartBank thought he'd run for governor or the U.S. Senate someday. He never would. Golf in Florida was too much fun. Besides, as impressive as O'Gara was inside a crowd or seated up on stage at annual meetings, he was scared to death of having to say anything in front of a sizable audience.

Behind the scenes, O'Gara was less affable. He hounded the bank's personal investment officers, with whom he maintained his trading accounts. On days of market volatility, he was known to call those poor folks half a dozen times. Having worked his way up the ranks, O'Gara now focused on retirement. Accordingly, he was no agent for change. He simply wanted a smooth landing. No shake-ups, no daring moves, no blow-ups, just maintain the status quo until he could cash out, golf and glad-hand full time. He had not greeted kindly the news that Heckler would now report to him. Heckler's reputation alarmed O'Gara, and other captains speculated that Brinkman's decision to move Heckler to O'Gara's world after the break-up of Dunn's organization was to keep O'Gara on his toes, take him off easy street for a while and remind him that there is no such thing as a free lunch. In fact, during the captains' meeting that Brinkman held to announce Dunn's departure, Brinkman said to O'Gara, "Now it's your turn to babysit Heckler, and if necessary, to sit on the baby."

Now with Heckler in his office, O'Gara wondered how he was going to sit on Heckler. That was why O'Gara called on his right-hand lieutenant, Fred Vohlmann, to sit in on the meeting with Heckler. Vohlmann was every bit the sycophant that Sycophant was, but Vohlmann was simply more intelligent. The two of them—O'Gara and Vohlmann—went way back. Actually, Vohlmann's father, a crusty old banker who had owned Sibley National Bank in St. Paul, had hired O'Gara right out of University of St.Thomas to return a favor by O'Gara's uncle benefitting Vohlmann's brother-in-law. Years later, when HeartBank (the old Heartland National Bank) had bought Sibley National, old man Vohlmann took the booty received for his Sibley National stock and left the Land of 10,000 Lakes for the links of Florida. Although it took the acquisition of Sibley to get O'Gara out of downtown St. Paul, he had applied his Irish charm very effectively across the river and schmoozed his way into the top echelons of the new Minneapolis-based HeartBank. In deference to his old mentor, O'Gara had taken the young Vohlmann under his wing.

Under his father's abusive shadow, the younger Vohlmann, now thirty-eight, suffered an inferiority complex. However, instead of becoming a gay artist, like Brinkman's son, or a trust baby like the scions of so many other wealthy executives, Vohlmann became a workaholic to prove himself. O'Gara took full advantage of Vohlmann's capacity for work and put him in charge of "special projects." Among his peers, Vohlmann became known as the "*Ja wohl!* Man." In fact, Vohlmann could be counted on to roll up his sleeves and put out just about any fire without getting burned, and more important, without O'Gara's getting singed. It was thanks largely to Vohlmann's efforts that O'Gara had survived for as long as he had.

Vohlmann stood about as tall as Heckler—right around six feet—but carried less weight and none of the sleaze that oozed from Heckler. Also, whereas Heckler was *going* bald, Vohlmann was already so bald that his pate was a fire hazard in a room with bright lights. Terribly nearsighted, he wore out-of-date, thick-rimmed glasses with lenses so impenetrable, you couldn't tell what he had for eyes. He wore any suit, as long as it was dark blue—so dark, you wondered if it wasn't polyester. He seemed to own only white shirts and ties in shades of blue and gray, and no one ever saw him in any shoes besides black shells with rubber soles. Eager to please his boss, Vohlmann joined the meeting with Heckler like an intern full of first day enthusiasm and took copious notes, right from the start.

"Thanks for coming up here, Dennis," O'Gara started off the meeting. "Would you like a cup of coffee?" Vohlmann closed his notebook in anticipation of an affirmative answer.

"Yeah, thanks, I would." Vohlmann sprang to his feet.

"You want some too, Mike?" he asked.

"Yes, please, Fred," said O'Gara. Fred needed only two hands for the coffee run. From his arrival at the office—often before five-thirty in the morning, till he left, usually after seven o'clock at the other end of the day—Fred kept his own mug full of coffee. While steam rose from his fifth refill of the morning, Fred rushed off to the coffee room to fetch cups of caffeine for O'Gara and Heckler. By the time he returned, O'Gara had lost control of the meeting. Heckler blathered on about what a "great" year National Real Estate was having, how "great" his systems area was, what "great synergies" were being pursued and why it would be "great" to accommodate projected growth by moving up to the twenty-fifth floor, which Heckler had heard was slated to be vacated soon. Heckler made no mention of the Franklin suit or the Walden case. It made no sense to tarnish unreality with reality.

"That's great, that's great, Dennis, I'm glad to hear it." O'Gara himself was such a bull-shitter, he could hide well his distrust of Heckler. "It sounds like you've got just a great business down there. Keep it up, keep it up."

Heckler felt smug, knowing O'Gara would be easy to fool and assuming an air of contempt for O'Gara's little servant, whom Heckler believed he could snow as well. But the little servant broke Heckler's run with the ball. "Did you bring any numbers with you?" Vohlmann asked, as he brought his HeartBank mug to his lips and drew a sip of hot coffee.

"Yeah, we'd like to see some numbers," O'Gara chimed in. For a banker, O'Gara was terrible with numbers. Decades ago, he had divulged his secret—numerical dyslexia—to his wife, but he had managed to hide it from everyone else. Ironically, among the rich and influential members of the community—business executives, corporate and non-profit board members—O'Gara had fostered a reputation for being "a numbers guy," merely by lowering his right bushy eyebrow so it heavily shadowed his eye and raising the left bushy eyebrow about two inches in the opposite direction. He then curled his upper lip and turned down the corners of his congenial mouth so far he looked almost petulant and said, "Can we see some numbers?" or "It'd be helpful to know the numbers." The local business press loved O'Gara, and only recently a feature article in *Minnesota Business* asserted generously, "Don't let that broad smile and hearty handshake fool you though. Mike O'Gara knows his numbers, and whether it's a St. Thomas Booster Club meeting or a loan review session, he'll be asking about 'the numbers.'" He could ask all he wanted, but he would never understand the numbers.

Heckler handed O'Gara an income statement for the year-to-date as of November 30 and the next year's budget for National Real Estate. Vohlmann pulled his chair closer to O'Gara so as to look on and asked, "Do you want me to make copies?" Not even he knew O'Gara's secret.

"No, Fred that's okay." It was one of O'Gara's numerous tricks of his dyslexic trade. With just one copy in four hands, it was easy to yield possession to Vohlmann. Ever the eager beaver, Vohlmann was bound to start asking questions. O'Gara could then ad lib, throw in an echo question or affirming comment and slip out of the hot seat. Yet, all the while, even with a guy like Heckler, O'Gara could leave the impression he was the one calling the shots.

O'Gara was right. Vohlmann studied the statement and asked Heckler what sort of December he was having.

"Tremendous. Just tremendous. My people—they're finding deals all over the place. We just closed a *really* big deal with Equitar Properties—a $10 million deal—that is so rich for us, you got to wonder, How long can the bank afford not to find me more bonus money for my guys?" Dennis opened and closed his jaw as if he had a wad of gum in his mouth and smiled his crooked smile as his eyes darted back and forth between O'Gara and Vohlmann. He was testing the prospect of a bigger bonus—not for "his guys" but for himself. O'Gara gave him no clues. Vohlmann looked down at the statement. "Next week, as a matter of fact," Heckler continued, "we're throwing a big party to celebrate the tremendous year we've had, the great month we're having, thanks to Equitar, and the great year we're going to have. Did I tell you? We've got plenty of deals in the pipeline to start first quarter with a bang."

"That's great, just great," O'Gara lied. He didn't care. He disliked Heckler's cockiness and used-car salesman appearance, and he'd heard stories about Heckler's being out of control.

"We'd really like to have you come down for it. You know, meet the troops in the trenches," said Heckler.

"We'll try to make it," O'Gara answered, without conviction. He didn't bother to ask for the time or date.

Heckler possessed two motives for having extended the invitation. First, he wanted to highlight the financial success of National Real Estate, heighten his chances for an exceptionally big bonus and advance his visibility over his new set of peers who reported to O'Gara. Second, he wanted to send a message to O'Gara to the effect, *This is my empire. You are welcome to visit, but don't mess with it.* Heckler still seethed over Brinkman's decision to break apart Dunn's old world and merge the pieces into the empires of the remaining captains. Heckler had never had much respect for Sycophant, but Sycophant had managed to convince Heckler of one thing: he, Heckler, was the most qualified person to succeed Dunn. Much to Heckler's surprise, no one else shared that assessment.

At the conclusion of the meeting, O'Gara extended his hand to Heckler and patted the side of his arm. From a vantage point four inches higher than Heckler, O'Gara noticed the grease in Heckler's hair. Nonetheless, he remained in glad-hand mode. "Great to see you, Dennis. Thanks again for coming up."

"Sure thing." Heckler resented the pat on the arm. It put him in the same league as the masses whom the glad-hander greeted as a matter of course. Heckler was not one of the hoi polloi. He was HeartBank CEO material—a guy who, in Sycophant's words, was "the smartest person I know." O'Gara would just have to be managed, and glad-handers were easy to manage.

No sooner had Heckler disappeared from earshot, than O'Gara dispensed with his affected affability and sat down to serious business with Vohlmann. "I don't like that slime ball," O'Gara set the tenor of the discussion. "He's a twerp. . ." O'Gara caught himself. He had never looked up the word, but if anyone looked like a twerp it was his protégé. At the same time, O'Gara was smart enough to recognize this twerp's value. "Sorry," O'Gara said. Just as he could arrange his eyebrows to feign interest in the numbers, O'Gara was blessed with additional facial muscles that could pull down his lower eyelids without any change in the rest of his face. It conveyed an appearance of contrition, reserved only for special occasions.

"It's okay." Vohlmann didn't get it. He assumed it was the dollar signs on Heckler's suspenders, not the upside-down V-shaped furrows on his own forehead that had prompted the word "twerp."

"Look, Fred. We'll find out when Heckler plans to hold his little bash—and with a guy like him, you can be assured it's going to be a *bash*." O'Gara's tone imparted none of the affability he projected in public. "I'm not attending, but you will be."

"Sure," Vohlmann said. The upside-down Vs on his forehead disappeared, and smaller ripples appeared above his high-riding eyebrows.

"I want you to gather intelligence on Heckler. I don't trust him, and I sure don't want him blowing up my three-year plan before three years are up." O'Gara confided in Vohlmann that at sixty-five, O'Gara would ride into the sunset. In the meantime, O'Gara would do his best to position Vohlmann.

◆ CHAPTER TWENTY ◆

The Party's Over

DESPITE HIS VOLATILITY, TEMPER AND ABUSIVE EGO, Heckler knew how to have fun, often in ways that were more becoming of his high-flying, real estate developer tycoon borrowers than of his banking brethren. Not that the latter didn't know how to have fun, just not out in full public view.

Heckler assigned party duties to his loyal assistant, Carol Wahl. Carol wore heavy make-up, bleached her hair badly, chewed gum that snapped and crackled, and walked around in her stocking-feet by two in the afternoon, earlier on Fridays. She was nothing to look at, and her smoker's voice was nothing to listen to, but she had a knack for covering up for Heckler—his affairs, his questionable expenses and a host of lesser infractions. He rewarded her handsomely with perks disguised as legitimate business expenses.

The party budget was whatever Carol wanted to spend. She reserved the ground floor of Barry's Bar and Billiards, a place in the renovated warehouse district on the north side of downtown, where, in Carol's words, "people could get wild and crazy." It didn't occur to Heckler that it might not be the most prudent thing in the world to invite O'Gara to a party at such a place, but then again, Heckler's ego sometimes got in the way of prudence. An open bar, combined with loud music in a place where the floor got hosed down every night after closing time, was not bound to impress a guy like O'Gara, whose prime concern was his image. Fortunately for O'Gara, he stayed away. Unfortunately for Heckler, Vohlmann didn't.

Lots of Heckler's minions got wild that night. John Anchor was not among them and wouldn't have been wild even if he had attended. Others would have been had they attended. The difference was that John didn't want to attend. Even back in college, he had avoided loud, drunken frat parties, and he never felt comfortable at large gatherings of any kind. His fellow absentee peers didn't attend because they had prior party commitments. Prior commitments, not discretion, would keep them out of trouble.

With Carol's help, Heckler could have taken care of the damage bill discreetly—they'd had plenty of experience at that sort of thing—but ultimately, such a measure would prove pointless. There was nothing discreet about the damage itself—two pool tables destroyed, three shattered windows, a smashed up juke-box; and the mangled grill of a pickup truck that was passing by the entrance to Barry's Bar and Billiards just as an empty beer keg got hurled out the door by a couple of over-exuberant party-goers.

When Heckler regained his senses the next morning, he felt relief in knowing that Vohlmann had left before the ruckus—and before Heckler's fist fight with Blowhard, who himself had been no picture of sobriety. Heckler himself had seen Vohlmann to the door and bade him a contemptuous farewell. What Heckler didn't know was that soon after the party was underway, Erica, John's assistant, had casually divulged to Vohlmann the existence and magnitude of the Walden case. Heckler's fate was sealed in more ways than one.

On the following Monday morning, O'Gara's secretary placed a call to Wahl with instructions to have Heckler appear in O'Gara's office at 10:00 sharp.

$ $ $ $

"I don't like surprises," O'Gara said, with his hands on his hips and both eyebrows casting angry darkness over his glare, "but I come in here this morning, and I get surprised by the biggest goddamn, fucking lawsuit this bank has seen since Brinkman took over." Sweat beaded on Heckler's forehead, but O'Gara's outrage felt like a cool fresh breeze. Heckler could blame the suit on Anchor. He could blame only himself for the party, and so far, it seemed, O'Gara didn't know about the party.

O'Gara turned slowly around, as Heckler repositioned himself in his chair. "Just a week ago, you come in here and give me a report and you don't say one goddamned word about this little lawsuit of yours."

"Let me explain," Heckler said, eager to slam Anchor.

"First you let *me* explain." Without Vohlmann around, O'Gara could get worked up when he had to. "You're one lucky son of a bitch that I found out about this lawsuit the way I did—through Vohlmann. Good man, that guy. It seems he was talking to one of your folks at your little celebration Friday night, and he finds out about it. Now if I'd heard about this from someone else—let's try Brinkman, for example—you'd be in boiling oil, not just the scalding water you're in. I know your reputation, Heckler, and from now on, you're going to tell me about every little problem that arises in your crappy little department, you understand?"

Heckler's blood pressure soared. "Crappy little department"? Who did this idiot think he was? Heckler had never held much respect for the gladhander. Now he despised the old man.

"You don't know what you're talking about." Heckler cast off all sensibilities. This was no way to manage O'Gara, but Heckler was so far out of touch he couldn't see that the fuse to his self-destruction was short and lit.

$ $ $ $

It didn't take long for tales from Barry's Bar and Billiards to reach O'Gara. However, he reacted with relish, not anger. Now he had just cause for ousting the repugnant Heckler. Not that on any day of the week there wasn't just cause for firing him, but the same held true for lots of people in an organization the size of HeartBank. Granted, Heckler was an extreme case, but everyone was vulnerable to a point, and in times when massive layoffs weren't necessary, firing someone at Heckler's level for anything besides outright fraud, embezzlement or egregious behavior, subjected the firing manager to increased scrutiny. The bash at Barry's Bar and Billiards couldn't have occurred at a better time, as far as O'Gara was concerned. He directed Vohlmann to get in touch with HR and have them do the dirty work—the investigation, preparation of the severance package and the rest of the bureaucratic nonsense that had to be completed before Heckler could be told to "seek other opportunities."

At half past two in the afternoon of an overcast day in early January, two guards from Central Security stepped off the elevator on the fifth floor and found their way to Heckler's office. O'Gara didn't want any trouble, and HR had recommended what they described as an "escorted departure."

"We're here to secure your pass, sir, and walk you to your car," the stockier of the two guards said to Heckler. Like a wounded lion cornered in the back of his den, Heckler stood with lower lip protruding, shiny and red. His eyes bulged and his paunch heaved in and out between the dollar sign suspenders as he breathed. There was no sunshine to reflect off his cufflinks. In fact, Heckler wasn't wearing any. He'd rolled his sleeves up his forearms to help Carol pack up his mementos. His hands rested on his hips. Carol, who stood amidst packing boxes next to the credenza behind Heckler's desk, sobbed. Her makeup smeared under a stream of tears.

After a long stare, Heckler finally spoke. "Okay, let's go." He rolled down his sleeves as he moved toward the doorway and pulled his suitcoat off the hanger on the back of the door. It was impossible to humiliate Heckler, just as it was impossible to intimidate him. The show was over. Time to move on, and move on he would, successfully at that. In one final directive, he turned to Carol and said, "After you've packed up the boxes, take the rest of the day off."

$ $ $ $

O'Gara was scheduled to meet with Heckler's direct reports at 4:00 that afternoon. By now, word was all but official, and speculation ran rampant. Who would succeed Heckler? What would happen to the department? Sycophant was in somewhat of a panic, now that the horse to his wagon had been cut loose. While Blowhard walked the floor and openly distanced himself from the past regime by maligning Heckler, Sycophant slipped out of the office shortly before four o'clock and rode the elevator to the ground floor. He then walked across the cold hard granite to the elevator bank for the sixtieth through the seventieth floors and waited for O'Gara to appear.

Every time the doors to an elevator opened, Sycophant cleared his throat and checked his posture. After a dozen false starts, Sycophant had his man.

"Mike," Sycophant extended his hand.

Instinctively, O'Gara shook hands and patted Sycophant on the left shoulder.

"Skip. Good to see you." Sycophant basked in O'Gara's acknowledgment. Surprised but immensely pleased that O'Gara remembered his name after only a couple of brief encounters at various manager functions over the past several years, Sycophant stood confident he had trumped at least Blowhard for Heckler's job.

"Are you headed for five?"

"Yes, as a matter of fact."

"Good, good. We're looking forward to it."

"Well, the circumstances aren't great, but we need to reassure people that we'll get control of the situation," said O'Gara.

"In that regard, Mike, I'm ready to do whatever would be helpful. I mean, Heckler was totally out of control. I tried to tell him, but it was no use. To be honest, Mike, we're all really relieved." It was a lie. Some were relieved, but some weren't. Sycophant was among the latter—unless, of course, it opened up a whole new opportunity for himself.

"Skip," Mike said, turning his face toward Sycophant, as they strode down the lobby, "I really appreciate that." O'Gara's lower eyelids dropped, and Sycophant felt assured the promotion would be his.

"Any time, Mike. You, know, I've got a lot of questions, which, between you and me, are pretty significant as far as the department goes. Depending on what your schedule is over the next couple of days, maybe you'd like to talk."

"That'd be great. We'll be in touch on that, definitely," said O'Gara. Sycophant managed to lash himself closely to O'Gara as they alighted from the elevator on the fifth floor and walked into the conference room where the rest of Heckler's direct reports were gathered. With consummate skill, Sycophant wound up sitting on O'Gara's immediate right. This was not lost on the others, particularly Blowhard.

"Well, folks, you've probably heard by now," O'Gara began, "that Dennis Heckler will be seeking opportunities outside HeartBank. I think this is best for Dennis and best for HeartBank. Now, I know you're all good people and that this is a good department, and I'm confident that we'll all get through this just fine. What I'd like to do is meet again next week, when you can give me an idea of what are some of the pressing issues concerning the department and how we can move forward in the best way for the shareholders. Let me suggest next Wednesday at 7:00 in the morning. How does that work for everyone?" It was a terrible time, but no one protested. Everyone nodded in complete assent. "Good. Now, in the meantime, are there any questions?"

One of the direct reports asked, "Do you have any idea yet about Heckler's replacement?" John guessed that Blowhard and Sycophant thought they knew. Each looked at O'Gara, ostensibly for a confirming response.

"No, I don't. We'll be conducting a search in the very near term. I can't tell you just when we'll have a decision, but it will be a strong choice, whoever it is." O'Gara fielded a few more questions and adjourned the meeting.

During the next week, productivity plunged, as people in the department speculated about who would succeed Heckler. The doors to offices that had doors were closed most of the time, while people behind them conspired, speculated and jockeyed for position. Only one person out of Heckler's empire of six hundred employees said anything remotely positive about him, and that was Carol Wahl, who guarded his old lair as if he still owned it. Among the pretenders, namely Blowhard and Sycophant, an unofficial contest raged as to who could most thoroughly malign Heckler.

With Heckler's abrupt departure, John Anchor saw the promise of a severance package evaporate. Sure, Heckler had made the deal in his capacity as John's manager, but what was the likelihood that Sycophant or Blowhard or anyone else, for that matter, would honor the arrangement struck with Heckler? John's relationship with his two most ambitious peers was strained at best. Undoubtedly, Sycophant viewed him as uncooperative, independent and unreliable. John's refusal to sign the Collateral Exception form in the Equitar deal was ample evidence that John wasn't a team player. He became wholly suspect, however, when he failed to attend a meeting arranged by Sycophant to prepare an agenda for the next meeting with O'Gara. Blowhard had probably written John off long ago, when the latter's pattern of leaving the office before six o'clock was well-established. How could a non-contender influence Blowhard's prospects one way or another? It was unlikely anyone important would ask John's opinion. Thus, ironically, Heckler's demise left John in the lurch. Gone with Heckler was the hope of parole.

At his next meeting with "Heckler's orphans," as O'Gara called John and his peers, O'Gara shocked Blowhard and Sycophant and surprised everyone else by announcing that effective immediately, Fred Vohlmann would be the new head of National Real Estate Financial Services. O'Gara had reached the decision without deliberation, for he needed to know only that Heckler's department was totally out of control and that there was one man with proven ability to get things under control—the workaholic, all-obedient Fred Vohlmann.

"Clean the place up, get it back on track and deliver a year to eighteen months of solid performance and you'll be ready for something really big, Fred," O'Gara told his protégé.

"I'm up to the job, Mike."

"Then it's yours, along with a nice pay hike, a company car—you've got to drive something other than that ridiculous Saturn, for crying out loud, something befitting your position—and a title. By the way, how does 'senior vice president' sound?"

"Anything to please the shareholder." O'Gara wondered sometimes about Vohlmann. He managed to turn everything to "shareholder advantage," even when it wasn't.

"Well great. You can take over immediately. I'll grant you whatever it takes to get that crazy place under control. I don't need to know anything except that it's under control, understand?"

"Understood, Mike." That evening, Vohlmann and his wife visited the Audi dealer on Highway 61 near their home in White Bear Lake.

◆ CHAPTER TWENTY-ONE ◆

Severed Hopes

In Minnesota, forecasts of sub-zero temperatures are invariably more accurate than are forecasts calling for snow. Snowfall varies significantly among areas in close proximity with one another. However, the Siberian Expresses that sweep over the North Pole and down across Canada, and the Alberta Clippers that stream into Minnesota from the frozen reaches of western Canada, carry air so cold and dense in such a broad band that the whole state plunges into a deep freeze. Fashion goes out the window, as Minnesotans, rich and poor, stylish and not, urban and rural, go for warmth.

The day of John's first lunch of the year with Steve brought a bona fide Siberian Express. Temperatures had plunged to minus thirty-four overnight, and by noon, the mercury struggled to break minus thirty. Black ice—frozen exhaust on road surfaces—produced treacherous driving conditions and made Steve late for lunch. The plate glass windows in the front of Betty's Place were so thickly glazed with frost that the place looked closed. Inside, John stamped his feet on the floor to recover some feeling. Just the six-block walk from HeartBank Tower had felt like an arctic expedition. A wind chill of minus seventy had frost-nipped John's nose, and it would smart for a few minutes once it began to thaw. Fewer patrons than usual occupied the tables and booths, and they looked set to stay until spring.

John took a booth way in the back and waited another fifteen minutes before Steve appeared. Like others who entered Betty's Place that day, Steve wore a heavy overcoat, leather chopper mittens, a wool scarf and headgear that would make any Siberian feel right at home. Steve's glasses fogged up instantly as they met the warm air of the restaurant, and he had to warm the lenses for several minutes before they'd stay clear.

"Son of a gun, it's cold out there," were Steve's first words, as he joined John in the booth. "Makes me wonder why I didn't take that job in North Carolina. Happy New Year, John!"

"Same to you, Steve." The two friends shook cold hands warmly. "This weather is crazy, isn't it? Can you imagine snowmobiling in this?"

"No, and it's something I have no interest in trying to imagine." Steve said, as he rubbed his hands together furiously. As close as they were, Steve shared none of John's love of Minnesota outdoors life.

Louise arrived wearing a Vikings jacket. "Geez, Louise!" said John. "Can I borrow that?"

"Not until I don't need it," Louise said. She chomped on her gum unusually hard, as if it would keep her warm.

"Then tell Betty to crank up the heat in this place. Food's going to get cold, not to mention us." John fired back. Steve kept rubbing his hands, and John noticed that his friend had yet to remove his fur-lined bomber hat. "See how cold Steve is here? If he has to eat in that thing, he's going to embarrass me." Louise looked around. A number of diners wore scarves and heavy sweaters, but none wore a hat.

"We've got the heat turned up as far as we dare without the boiler blowing up," said Louise. "I'd recommend you guys order our 'soup sand' special today. It's chicken noodle, real hot, and since you braved the Siberian Express to come down here today, I'm going to arrange for you to get bowls with the special, instead of cups."

"Sounds good to me," said John. "Make the sandwich a ham and cheese."

"Got it. How 'bout banker number two?"

"Louise," Steve said with a strained face, "I'm not a banker anymore."

Louise dropped her hands to her sides. "So what are you now?" She no longer chomped on her gum.

"Unemployed. Have been for months."

"You mean out of work?" Louise said in disbelief. She didn't notice the man in the next booth, who turned at her words.

"Sh-sh-sh!" Steve held his finger to his lips. "Someone might hear and want to hire me."

"I'm sorry to hear that."

"What, that someone might want to hire me?" Steve said.

Louise blushed. "No, no, that's not what I meant, I mean, I'm sorry to hear you're out of work. I mean, I was out of work once, and it wasn't easy."

"Don't worry about it, Louise. You see, what I'm worried about is that if someone gives me a job, John here will quit buying me lunch."

John knew Steve well enough to discern the stress in his face and the strain in his voice. He admired Steve's attempt at humor under the circumstances. Louise marked down a 2X beside John's order and tore the green slip off her order pad as she walked back to the kitchen.

"So what's with the head gear," John asked. "You leaving that on for lunch?"

"Maybe," Steve said, and "Maybe not." Steve placed his right hand atop his oversized hat and slid it down off his head to reveal hair so short it looked like pencil shading on a shaved pate.

"What the hell happened to you?" John made no attempt to hide his astonishment.

"It's part of my new approach to financial planning. Shorter hair means less frequent haircuts, which means lower cost to the household. In my case, you don't know when I'm going to be working again."

"For crying out loud, Steve. Are things really that bleak?"

"Let me tell you exactly how bleak, my friend." Steve leaned his arms on the table and lowered his voice. "I'm afraid, John, that it's going to be forever before I find a job. I'm a loser. A total loser. Either that or I'm being punished for a heinous crime I didn't commit. I've decided God has it in for me."

"What's this? You're talking nonsense, Steve." John sat back, disturbed by his friend's bitterness.

"Am I? I don't think so. I have to confess, John, I started praying real hard, ever since Christmas. I mean, I know it sounds ridiculous, but I didn't know what else to do. You hear about people who are down and out who turn religious and everything turns around for them. Well, I tried that—I wouldn't admit it to anyone else, so you've got to keep it confidential—but I've actually had days where I thought I was losing it. I got down on my knees and clasped my hands like this." Steve squeezed his hands so hard, white bands appeared under his fingernails. He looked outside the booth to see if anyone was listening or watching. "But it's all a hoax, John. Or the Almighty Creator just doesn't care, I don't know which. I mean, who with my background can't get a job in this economy, huh?" John didn't know what to say, and even though he wasn't thirsty, he poured water from the table carafe.

Steve continued. "Take the other day, for example. I actually had a job interview. Can you believe it? Loser here had a job interview. Ten o'clock Monday morning last week. I'm thinking, Great! A perfect way to start the new year. So I do all my homework for it, show up right on time, sit around until about nine-thirty and finally get introduced to the big cheese who's going to interview me for a sales management position. About five minutes into the thing, I have to sneeze. *Atchoo!*" With his dramatic flair, Steve demonstrated a sneeze, just as Louise appeared with the soup and sands.

"Chicken noodle's just the thing for a cold," she said.

"Thanks, Louise." Steve looked at her and turned back to John. "You know how the mucous always runs after you sneeze? Well, that's what happened to me. Of course, I didn't have a Kleenex or handkerchief or anything like that, so I'm just trying to keep the nose from running out of control–you know, taking deep breaths through my nose, one, to control the running and two, to dry it up so I wouldn't need a Kleenex. Well, it kept on running. The old sump pump behind my nose worked in reverse, no matter how hard I inhaled. Finally, not hearing a thing the big cheese was telling me, I figured it was time to go for it and sniff real hard and loud. I did, but still, my nose ran like crazy–worse. Now I could feel it run right out the garage and down the driveway toward my lip. So, what do you do when you're in an interview and your nose runs away from you and you don't have Kleenex. What do you do?"

"Geez, Steve, I suppose, well, I'd ask for a Kleenex or something."

"Aeaeh!" Steve made the sound of a game show buzzer, as he took a spoonful of soup. "You use your sleeve. Only guess what?"

"What?" John suspended his spoonful of noodles half way from his bowl to his lips just long enough for one noodle to slip out. The splash back into the bowl left a tiny spot on John's tie.

"It wasn't a runny nose."

"Huh?"

"It was a *bloody* nose. And a gusher too. Right there in front of this guy. He doesn't know what to do. He doesn't say, 'Sorry, can I get you a Kleenex,' or 'Geez, maybe we could take a break.' No, the asshole just continues yapping. By this time I'm slouched in my chair, with my head flung back like this." Steve pushed his glasses up his nose and leaned his head back. John couldn't restrain a laugh. He didn't see Steve as a loser at all, but as a guy who would always be blessed by humorous circumstances—or maybe *cursed* was the better word. "So there I am in this position, with a blood-stained shirt cuff—my right cuff, mind you—and in barges one of the cheese's direct reports to hand him something. The door was open and the guy hadn't seen me. 'Sorry,' he says. I roll my head to the side to see him and then stand up, keeping my head horizontal, mind you. I stick my hand out to shake but he sees the bloody cuff and blood all over my hand and backs away. Meanwhile, his boss—and my boss perhaps, if I hadn't gotten a goddamn nosebleed right in the middle of the damn interview—just keeps yappin' and says I applied for the sales manager job. Doesn't say I'm a candidate. Just says I *applied* for it. Well, needless to say, I didn't get an offer. What a humiliating experience!

"Then, just this past Monday," Steve took a bite from his sandwich and resumed talking after a couple of munches, "I had an eight o'clock interview with a financial advisory firm over in St. Paul. Wouldn't you know it, but the night before, I toss and turn all night, worrying about the interview. Then, with about an hour to go before the alarm goes off, I fall into a deep sleep. I sleep right through the damn alarm. I wake up at seven, look at the clock and go directly into panic mode. I drive like crazy, but the traffic is terrible. I'm going all over the place—and on the shoulders—and blast through the control lights on the entrance ramp to the freeway. I pull up to the parking lot of the building, just across the river from St. Paul—and re-enact the Olympic hundred-meter sprint to the door. I take the elevator up to the fourth floor, inhale deeply and with exactly a minute to spare before my nine o'clock appointment, I enter the office suite of the company." John chewed slowly in anticipation of Steve's next misadventure. "I announce myself to the receptionist and she says, 'Oh, didn't he call you? He had to go out of town today.' So there I am, all dressed up, in adrenaline up to my eyeballs and the damn guy is 'out of town.' Worse, he hasn't returned my phone calls."

John leaned back against the hard straight wall of the booth. He felt distressed by his friend's misfortunes. Across from him sat an eminently employable man; a well-educated, intelligent, witty, honest man with an impressive résumé as an effective, successful middle manager of a large bank, who thought he had to shave his head to make ends meet; a rational guy who admitted praying to God. John struggled with his current circumstances, certainly, but his struggle for vocational meaning seemed whimsical when juxtaposed with Steve's despair. Maybe a severance package isn't something to be wished for, he thought.

On the other hand, John questioned the cause of Steve's predicament. Was it not a fluke? If the economy was no longer roaring, if the Dow Jones wasn't exactly rocketing toward new highs, business still flourished. Good jobs existed. John strove to reassure himself that Steve's woes arose from a combination of bad luck and rotten timing.

"So how about you? How are *you* doing?" Steve's genuine interest in his friend's affairs chased the despair from Steve's eyes.

"I'm fine." To have said anything less sanguine would have mocked Steve's tribulations. "On the other hand, there's turmoil all around me."

"Like what?"

"Well, for starters, Heckler got fired. So, under less than honorable circumstances, he got the severance package he wouldn't give me."

"You're kidding!"

"I kid not. The man threw a big Christmas party to celebrate his numbers for the year. People went nuts—I mean *really* nuts—and Heckler got the ax."

"So are people in your department celebrating the exile of Napoleon?"

"They aren't celebrating so much as maneuvering. You have your corporate climbers who scheme against each other to succeed the exiled emperor. Then you have your 'not ready for prime time' players who aim to succeed the corporate climbers. They compete against each other as well, but they also try to curry favor with the corporate climbers so that when the music stops, they'll land in favorable chairs—or at least in some kind of chairs. Then you have some who say to their friends, 'This place is nuts. I think it's time to look for a job somewhere else.' They come to work later, leave earlier, talk on the phone in low voices and copy files they think will be valuable elsewhere. Finally, you have the people who are oblivious to it all. The people who don't care; who just keep coming to work, doing their jobs, day in, day out, year after year until their wrinkles deepen, their hair whitens and they fade into the background."

"And where do you fit in?" Steve asked.

"I'm the guy who got stuck on the roller coaster that won't stop. It's like everyone else at the amusement park is in the house of mirrors or eating cotton candy, playing the rigged arcade games, gawking at the bearded lady or riding the merry-go-round, while I'm riding this wildly out-of-control roller coaster. I just don't know how to get off."

"A few months ago, I would have said, 'Jump!' but now I'm not so sure, John. When you're like me, with my head stuck in the cutout atop one of those caricatures that's set up for photographs – in my case, a clown bum with a bag on a stick over his shoulder – you wish you were just plain moving."

"But even if I wanted to jump, I'm not sure I can."

"Why not?"

"Remember, I told you the bank got sued over a couple of things I did?"

"Like firing that black guy. And wasn't there some huge lawsuit?"

"A billion dollar case. I thought it was my ticket to a severance package. Trouble was, according to Heckler, the bank couldn't let me go until the litigation was resolved some way. It would look bad for the bank if the guy who 'caused' the claim was canned. But Heckler made a deal that I'd get nine months' severance once the case went away. Now that he's gone, I don't know what I have."

"You have whatever the emperor promised, as long as he was emperor when he promised it."

"Yeah, I suppose, but who's going to believe a thing that's attributed to Heckler? At the rate I'm going, I'd have to sue the bank for it. I have no idea how the new guy would react to it."

"Who is the new guy?"

"His name is Fred Vohlmann. No one knows a thing about him, except that he's a gunner, a corporate climber. We get to make our first impression on him at a direct reports meeting tomorrow morning before sunrise." John said.

"Before sunrise?"

"Reveille is at 6:30 on the dot."

"Reveille? At that hour? Sounds like you're going to boot camp."

"Yeah, I'm afraid it might be one of those 'frying pan to the fire' deals. What would you rather have—whacko insane man Heckler or Mr. Marine Sergeant?"

"Just hope you don't have a whacko insane marine sergeant. There's more than one in the suit of a boss."

"Frankly," said John, scanning his side of the table for spilled soup and leaning his elbows on the edge. "I don't care at this point, as long as I wind up with a severance package sooner rather than later." In having described his circumstances to Steve, John decided that the chance to be free of corporate nonsense outweighed the risks of the unknown—despite Steve's misfortunes. John's father was right—you have to do the right thing.

"Be careful," Steve said. "You might get what you wish for."

John offered to pay for lunch, and Steve offered no protest. It was now more important to guard his savings than to avoid humiliation.

"So where did you say this guy Vohlmann is from?" Steve asked, as they waited for Louise to bring back change for the twenty.

"He's been at HeartBank for quite awhile—a stint here and there, each one a rung higher on the corporate ladder. His old man ran the old Sibley National Bank over in St. Paul."

"That reminds me," Steve said with a smile lifting the corners of his mouth. "Did you hear about the Norwegian who moved from Minneapolis to St. Paul?"

"No," John said. "You mean someone actually moved *to* St. Paul?"

"He was a little confused, I have to admit," said Steve, "but he improved the IQ of both cities."

The two men warmed themselves with the chuckles that followed. Then they wrapped themselves for the plunge back into the cold outside, hesitated at the door and finally faced reality.

$ $ $ $

As the two friends leaned into the Siberian-American air and bade each other farewell, the phone rang in Max Brinkman's office. He stepped back from the window, through which he had been gazing out over the forest of exhaust plumes that rose from the buildings downtown, and punched the speaker button on his phone.

"Yes,"

"It's T.C.," said Kathy, Brinkman's secretary.

"Ah-ha! Send him through." It was T.C. Buckmaster, Brinkman's longtime friend and rival, a classmate in the commercial bank training program at the old Manufacturer's Hanover Bank, a tough competitor on the golf course and on the ski slopes, a veritable high stakes gambler and CEO of TexAm, Inc., the world's largest supplier of oil drilling equipment.

"T.C." Brinkman greeted him. Just a phone call from someone in a southern clime like Texas was a welcome break from the absurdly cold Minnesota weather. "Happy New Year!"

"Same to you, Cowboy." The native Texan had assigned the nickname to Brinkman back in their days at Mannie Hannie Bank in New York. Born and raised in Rutherford, New Jersey, just a stone's throw from Manhattan, and educated at Princeton, Brinkman was no Texas-style cowboy. However, during one of their breaks in the training program at Mannie Hannie, T.C., who looked every inch the Texas cowboy—hence the initials—hosted his Yankee friend down in Texas. Although Brinkman had done many a wild thing by that stage of his life, he had never before ridden a horse on the open range. Outfitted in full-fledged Texas-style riding clothes, courtesy of Buckmaster Stables on the Buckmaster Ranch, Brinkman impressed his host and guides as a born cowboy. The nickname stuck, at least as far as T.C. was concerned.

"News has it you boys up there in Mini-*soda* are freezin' your gonads off."

"News has it that you boys down there think Minnesotans are as dumb as they are tough, for choosing to live in a place where the wind chill hits a hundred below."

"Your words, not mine, Cowboy," T.C. laughed so forcefully that the speaker phone rattled. "When you planning to show you're smarter 'an all those dumb Swedes and Norwegians up there?"

"You got something in mind?" Brinkman asked.

"How 'bout a couple rounds at Desert Mountain?" T.C. divulged the purpose for his call.

"Sounds like a perfect reason to clear out of here. When are you thinking?"

"Day after tomorrow. We can fire up the Gulfstreams tomorrow night for a tee time first thing in the morning, what do you say?"

"I say my bird will get there ahead of yours."

"Dinner after golf says it doesn't, and just to make it fair, I'll fly to Jackson, Miss and start from there."

"You're on."

"Good. Tell your skipper to arrange with the tower for clearance at seven bells, on the nose, and I'll do the same. Then I'll phone you and give the count down, so our birds will start their rolls at exactly the same time.

♦ CHAPTER TWENTY-TWO ♦

The Power Bettors

BRINKMAN'S PLANE, A GULFSTREAM VI, won the race, primarily because Buckmaster's pilot refused to fly through storms that hung over central Louisiana. To rub it in, Brinkman arranged for a car and driver to meet Buckmaster's plane. As the tall, lanky, silver-haired Texan emerged from the aircraft, the driver alighted from his car, jogged to the vanquished and handed him a note.

> T.C.–
> I'm already here. Tired of waiting, I arranged a car and driver for you.
> See you at the club.
> Cowboy

Buckmaster looked around and noticed the HeartBank jet was parked only a short distance away. Its pilot was still in the lighted cockpit. Just as Buckmaster suspected, Brinkman himself had arrived only minutes before. "Cowboy'll pay for this," Buckmaster pushed his index finger into the driver's chest. "Come on! Let's saddle up and *ride!*"

As the car sped along the tarmac to the road leading away from the airport, Buckmaster pulled a hundred-dollar bill from his clip and held it up for the driver to see in the rear-view mirror. "Here's a C-Note that says you can get me to the Master's Hotel before the smart alec who ordered you up. Show me you got some spurs, boy." The driver checked his mirrors, scanned the road ahead and pressed his foot down hard on the accelerator. While the car raced past other vehicles–including Brinkman's–in the darkness, Buckmaster phoned ahead and arranged for half a gin and tonic and a full whiskey on the rocks to be waiting at a table for him and Brinkman.

Upon arriving at the hotel, Buckmaster hurried to the bar, found his table, assumed a relaxed position and waited for Brinkman to appear. Minutes later, Buckmaster waved. "Over here, Cowboy!"

"Sonofabitch," Brinkman said under his breath. As he approached the corner that the Texan had staked out under autographed pictures of famous golf pros, Brinkman noticed that Buckmaster was well into his drink.

"Time you got a new bird," Buckmaster laughed. "How the hell are you?" The two rivals shook hands and bantered. Nothing had changed since their training days back in New York City, when after the close of business on the last working day of the month, they'd find their way down to a bar on Hanover Square near Wall Street, have a few drinks and then race—each in a cab—to the apartment they shared up on the East Side.

Though they had shared many experiences back then—as well as an insatiable lust for one prize after another—Brinkman and Buckmaster had reached the training program at Manufacturers Hanover from quite different approaches.

Brinkman came from an upper middle class family that had migrated down from New England in the late 1880s. His mother was a quiet woman who preferred drives in the country, books and the arts over the noise of her three children and the rise of industry around Rutherford. Brinkman's father posed a marked contrast to his wife. A big, strapping, fearless man, Clayton Brinkman was an engineer by education and training, whose shrewd ways had led to advances far up the chain of command at Consolidated Edison. He believed in the ultimate power of machine over man, but he also believed that he was the man to drive the machine. At ConEd, he ruled by decisive command, and if he was responsible for the prodigious growth of the company's capacity, he was also responsible for the wake of sacrifice and destruction in the lives of his employees. He had little time for his wife's diversions, and though he tolerated them in her, he insisted that his children—two daughters and Max—follow his example, not hers. He was every bit as hard on them as he was on his minions at work.

When it came to college and a major, Clayton chose Princeton for his son. It was the place for math, physics and other subjects that would lead to a career in engineering and business. Also, it was a place where he could keep a closer eye on Max than if he went to a New England Ivy League school or M.I.T., Rensselaer Polytech or, God forbid, any other school. A moderately successful student, Max developed an interest in business and finance. He acquired a taste for power, women and fast living. As did his competitors, he viewed money as the currency of power.

After graduation, Max eschewed the world of engineering, machines and technology, and signed up for the year-long bank training program at Manufacturers Hanover. Clayton Brinkman was not amused. His daughters could choose whatever they liked, as long it was in law or medicine. Max had to be an engineer. Clayton saw money men as parasites, leeches and Jews. Raw materials and the industry that reshaped them were the true source of America's wealth, and the future belonged to men who could develop and harness new industrial technologies. Clayton's heroes were people like Thomas Alva Edison and Henry Ford, not the J.P. Morgans or the E.F. Huttons. Max viewed the world as a giant boardgame, in which he was destined to be a major player. People like his father could build factories to their hearts' content, but people like Max would own and control them—buying, selling, financing and trading.

As a consequence, father and son experienced a falling-out. They would have little to say to each other before Clayton died of a stroke at the age of sixty-nine. Often challenged and prodded by Buckmaster, Max reached high, hard and far and made an exceptionally positive impression on people who counted at Mannie Hannie. Fresh out of the training program, Max was offered a commercial lending position normally reserved for people with far more experience than he possessed. He outworked all his competitors and developed a sixth sense for political maneuvering. By the age of thirty-four, Max had climbed to the head of mid-Atlantic, middle market commercial lending at Mannie Hannie. Chemical Bank then enticed him away with an expanded role and the promise of bigger rewards within a few short years.

After five years, however, Max suffered one of the few setbacks of his career. Several of his older rivals resented his meteoric rise and conspired to teach him a lesson. They launched a campaign to force him from contention and did one better: they ousted him from the bank altogether, but not without a generous severance package. By this time, divorced and estranged from his son and daughter, Max seemed to have hit the wall. It was only a breather. His next stop was at Chase, where again, he pushed out his elbows and climbed aboard the fast track.

At fifty, Maximilian Brinkman left New York to lead HeartBank, as chairman and CEO. In six years, his bank vaulted in size to $115 billion in assets and $1.2 billion in earnings. Buoyed by a big bull market, HeartBank stock had appreciated over four hundred percent since Brinkman had taken over. He was on top of his game.

T.C. Buckmaster was on top of his game, too. Born and raised in Texas, Buckmaster came from a family of frontiersmen, ranchers, wildcatters and opportunists. During the Great Depression, T.C.'s father, William Buckmaster, took the oil money that his family had steadfastly refused to invest in the stock market and bought up all the land and oil drilling equipment he could lay his hands on. In time, William became a legend of wealth.

Like Clayton Brinkman, William Buckmaster distrusted money men, particularly if they "talked New York." For that very reason, however, he insisted that his son "go live with the enemy for awhile to learn his ways." The plan then called for T.C. to return to Texas to take over the family empire. T.C. followed through, but his pet project was TexAm, which he shepherded from a mere holding pen for the oil-related assets his father had accumulated over the years, to an acquisitive oil conglomerate listed on the New York Stock Exchange. With $135 billion in assets and close to $2 billion in earnings, TexAm stock had increased more than tenfold since the company's founding in 1970.

In the bull market of the 1990s, the stampede mentality prevailed in most markets. When the stampede reached ground occupied by the boulders of Asian financial crises, meltdowns in Russia and troubles in Latin America, the bulls simply raced around the obstacles. Here and there a bull stumbled, but the stampede continued. If the herd was headed for a precipice, people like Brinkman and Buckmaster, for the most part, were safe. They were the cowboys driving the herd. From their elevated saddles, they could see what was coming in time to save their own hides.

Buckmaster ordered another gin and tonic, pulled out two Nicaraguan cigars that he'd acquired for the occasion and handed one to Brinkman. "So," the Texan started, as he lit a match and held it out for Brinkman's cigar, "what I want to know is with all these goddamn bank mergers and acquisitions goin' on, how soon will there be one big bank in this country?"

"About the same time there's one big goddamn oil company in the world," Brinkman said in a mocking tone, as Buckmaster sucked a match flame into the end of his cigar.

"I ain't in the oil business proper, if that's what you're gettin' at." Buckmaster said around both sides of his cigar, clamped by his incisors. "Let the Exxon-Mobils and the Saudis worry about the oil business. I'm in the acquisition business first and the oil business second. What I see coming is a huge opportunity to buy up everything in sight–rigs, rights and royalties–and control oil from west Texas to Kazahkstan." He inhaled and let out a cloud of smoke. "How 'bout you, Cowboy? What business you in? I suppose you're gonna tell me you're in the banking business. You're sure not in the *acquisition* business."

Brinkman inhaled and blew back Buckmaster's smoke with a cloud of his own. "Banking as we once knew it is dead," he said. "If all you do is take deposits and make loans, you're already dead. The capital markets today are so much more sophisticated, so much more efficient, conventional bank loans will in time become a thing of the past. To stay in the financial services game today, T.C., you've got to have lots of fee-based businesses and you've got to find ways to gather assets–other people's assets. Heap technology on top of the equation, and you've got a very different looking financial world in a few short years."

The men lifted their elbows from the table in order to accommodate the drink waiter, who put down Brinkman's second drink and Buckmaster's first full one. "Well, Cowboy, given the way things have gone with banks over the last couple of years, isn't it about time you joined the big leagues? You've been awfully quiet, and in the winter, especially, I worry that you're stuck in a blizzard somewhere or all boozed up in one of those gol' dang ice houses."

Buckmaster's latter reference recalled the time a couple of years before when his friend had invited him up to Minnesota in the dead of winter. It had been on a bet–as so much of their activities together were. The two men had gazed out on ice-covered Lake Minnetonka from the great room of Brinkman's mansion, and Buckmaster had inquired about all the "shit houses" parked in clusters all about the frozen lake. "Don't tell me there are that many people without plumbing in these parts," he'd said, only half-joking. Brinkman himself considered ice fishing to be a little weird, just as he did a lot of things in Minnesota, but after several Minnesota winters, he had learned enough to be able to explain that the shacks weren't outhouses but warming huts well-stocked with booze and fishing gear for people who actually wanted to venture out when it was thirty below, auger a hole in the ice and drop a few fishing lines into the icy black waters while they got good and happy with alcohol. No stranger to fishing—he was a regular deep sea fisherman down off the Texas coast—Buckmaster had wanted to try "ice fishing" and laid down a bet that he could catch something bigger than what Brinkman could. They spent the better half of a Sunday out on the ice in the well-appointed ice-house of the CEO of Kar-Co, Eliot Samuelson, a member of HeartBank's board. Neither the Texan nor the transplant from the East caught anything, "not even ice," jested their pixilated host.

"No doubt about it," Brinkman said. "Banks are involved in an end game right now—eat or be eaten. Just look at all the big names that have disappeared over the past few years—our own Mannie Hannie, of course, Chemical, Citibank, NBCD, NBD, First Chicago, PNC, Texas Commerce, Barnett, First Interstate, First Bank, NationsBank, Norwest, BT . . . and it's not over." Brinkman took a swig of his drink, then drew on his cigar till the tip glowed menacingly, and blew the smoke out of the corner of his mouth. "So, you've got everyone in a frenzy—go out and merge for the sake of merging, because it's the game of the day. Hell, most mergers are thought out about as well as a stampede is coursed out by a bunch of dumb steers on your ranch. There are exceptions of course, but by and large, megamergers haven't delivered the goods."

"Well, you in the game or ain't you?" Buckmaster squinted from the lingering cigar smoke as he took a sip of his drink.

"In the end, the real competition isn't from other banks. It's going to be from the Merrill-Lynches, the American Expresses, the Microsofts, the non-banks. When banks merge, theoretically they can squeeze out all kinds of cost savings—systems consolidation and job duplication—and increase market share. That helps in the short run, but eventually, you've got to increase the combined market shares and revenues, and unless you can provide all the customer service, all the financial products that a broad-based outfit like Merrill-Lynch provides and with the efficiency that high tech brings to the picture, you'll be dead in the water."

"You know what I think? I think you're chicken shit," Buckmaster said smugly. He picked up his drink and swished it around before taking a gulp. "I've been watching your heartbreak bank, Cowboy. After all, I own stock in the lousy thing."

"And you can thank me for the fact that it's outperformed the market over the past five years." Brinkman saw a major challenge shaping up.

"Bullshit," Buckmaster only half-believed anything he himself said, but his belligerent tone often obscured his own bullshit. It wasn't who was right or wrong, it was who could win that counted. "All bank stocks have gone to the moon over the past five years. Hell, a monkey could have been runnin' a bank and made money over the past half decade."

Neither man was drunk, but each talked and reacted as though he were. Brinkman's eyes widened. "And some of the monkeys got eaten for lunch."

"Oh, so are we admitting you bankers are a bunch of monkeys after all—some having been eaten, some not?" Buckmaster let out an obnoxious laugh muted by his cigar.

"And who's running the oil business but a bunch of grease monkeys?" Brinkman shot back.

"Call 'em chimps." Buckmaster lowered his voice and narrowed his eyes. "But T.C. Buckmaster ain't no chimp, Cowboy. He's a gorilla, and I'm takin' the chimps to the cleaners." He sucked on his cigar and twisted it as he slid it in and out between his lips. "Now, what I want to know is whether the man runnin' HeartBank is a chimp or a gorilla."

"I'm not playing zoo," said Brinkman. "I'm picking the cherries that the monkeys, the chimps—and the gorillas—are leaving behind. We've been acquiring the little community banks all over the map, all for a song. We strip them of inefficiencies, put them on a common operations platform, give them product to sell and in no time flat, they're improving our margin and growing the bottom line."

"Cowboy, I've been watching you. And I say you're chicken shit. Hell, you'd have to go out and buy a thousand of those itty-bitty banks before you equal one serious acquisition that the big boys do." Buckmaster insisted on pushing Brinkman around, as if they were rivals on the playground. "When you gonna be a big boy?"

"You wait and see, T.C.," Brinkman pushed back. "I've got a dual strategy that will make me the biggest of the big boys by the time the end game is over."

"Oh yeah? Ha!" Buckmaster bellowed. "What's the secret plan?"

"HeartBank is going to continue the cherry-picking at the same time that it invests in technology. You just wait, T.C. HeartBank stock will be Heart*Break* stock for all who don't own it. In a few short years, we'll be offering our customers across the country—hell, across the world—all conceivable financial services through an automatically managed account that can be programmed according to a customer's needs and objectives. It will be in a constant state of flux, as it seeks the cheapest loan rates, and the best yields for your specified risk tolerance. Let's say you own stock in ABC Company through the account. Your total annual return in dividends and appreciation is fifteen percent, and the risk according to a computerized formula, taking into account all sorts of financial ratios and other factors, is eleven on a scale of one to twenty, twenty being high. Now, let's say there's a business in Hide-Your-Bad, India that's willing to give you eighteen percent for the same risk. Your 'smart' account, which is constantly searching the world for the best opportunities, will make the switch automatically. Same on the debt side. If your account finds a cheaper mortgage, it will trigger the refinancing automatically. You'll even be able to make purchases of goods and services the same way. For example, input a request for a car with certain specs, and presto, the account will locate the best deal and make the purchase for you. Capital markets—hell, all markets—will become efficient beyond our current comprehension, and the world economy will soar into an era of unprecedented wealth—only by that time, I'll have so much of it personally, you'll be heartbroken." Brinkman inhaled deeply and flicked the ash off his cigar.

"What've you been smokin' there, Cowboy? Sounds like a bunch of techie dope to me. A chicken shit smokin' dope, now there's somethin' to see!" Buckmaster was having fun. He downed the last of his drink and rattled the ice around in his glass.

"Before you know it, T.C., CEOs of other banks, large and small, will be begging me to buy them before I put them out of business, as they realize their banks can no longer compete with my high-tech machine. You wait and see. Then it'll be a buyer's market, and I'll be the only buyer."

"Well, however you want to slice it, Cowboy, dinner at The Opulate in Vegas, with the chef's personal special and two bottles of *Chateau Petrus* and a good-looking broad to go says you're chicken shit."

"What do you mean?" Brinkman asked.

"I mean you're too chicken shit to close on a $25 billion merger by the end of the third quarter. I don't care how you structure the damn thing, so long as the deal is worth a minimum of $25 billion and as long as you come out on top. None of this merger of equals stuff that leaves you in the number two number one position."

"Now wait a minute, T.C." Brinkman put his drink down more forcefully than he had intended, and some of it sloshed over the rim of the glass. "Why would I take on a bet like that for a transaction that is pretty much contrary to my whole strategy?"

"To show you've got the maracas, which I don't think you have."

Brinkman narrowed his eyes and ground his teeth. His face, already flush with drink, turned darker. Buckmaster was picking a fight, and the Texan's challenge gave Brinkman an idea. Loan Star Bank, a super-regional bank holding company, was headquartered right in Buckmaster's backyard. Based on the numbers that Brinkman had last seen reported by Loan Star, the Texas bank was probably worth close to $25 billion. In a stock swap with a slight premium, Brinkman figured, he could easily put a merger deal over the bar set by Buckmaster. Loan Star stock had had quite a run over the past several years but had stalled out over the past twelve months. Its chairman, Clinton Blusser, was running scared. He'd be easy to snag. So would Brinkman's board of directors. It was time to shut the Buckmaster up.

Buckmaster assumed from Brinkman's silence that the bet was on. He pulled a pen out of his shirt pocket and scribbled the terms of the deal on the back of a napkin. "I'm takin' this to dinner at The Opulate," Buckmaster said, "for redemption." Brinkman blew one last cloud of smoke in Buckmaster's direction and extinguished the remains of his cigar.

"Have you got a tee time?" Brinkman changed the subject.

"Eight o'clock."

"I'm looking forward to cleaning your clock."

"How 'bout my shoes?" With that, Buckmaster crushed the end of his cigar on the butt Brinkman had just placed in the ash tray. "Waiter," he called out gruffly. The waiter hurried over to their table.

"What can I get you, Mr. Buckmaster?" he asked.

"Put the drinks on my room tab." Buckmaster then rose from the table and extended his hand to Brinkman. "I can't wait to see them maracas of yours, Cowboy," he said wryly. "In the meantime, get a good night's sleep. Don't forget—I've been practicing, and if tradition serves us well, there'll be lots of bettin' on the course. Good night Cowboy."

"Goodnight, T.C."

♦ CHAPTER TWENTY-THREE ♦

The New Guy

NEVER BEFORE HAD JOHN AND ALL OF HIS PEERS shown up on time for a direct reports meeting, but all knew it would be advisable to be punctual for their first meeting with Vohlmann. Only no one yet called him "Vohlmann" or "Fred." He was simply "the new guy," and it had been tough to obtain any intelligence on him.

The cold snap continued. Overnight, the mercury had plunged again to a near-record low, and the usual phenomena associated with extreme cold—black ice on the roads, thundering ice on the lakes, stubborn car batteries, frost nip on the walk from the bus stop or parking lot—prompted ample chatter before the new guy entered the conference room. Nearly everyone sat with a large serving of coffee purchased from the Moose Mocha at the end of the skyway leading into HeartBank Tower. For most, it was the day's second large dose of caffeine.

Finally, at precisely 6:30, before there was a hint of morning light outside, the new guy entered the room. "Good morning!" The words shot out of his mouth as if they'd been spring-loaded. Everyone around the table, already at attention, replied in kind. "I'm Fred Vohlmann, and I'm glad to be here." The compression of words and voice left no doubt that he was the new *boss.* From the dispenser that sat in front of him on the table, he poured himself a cup of diluted sludge and took a big gulp. For him, it was well beyond the day's second large dose of caffeine.

"Let's go around the room and get acquainted, starting with you." Vohlmann turned to Jason Wysgaard, seated at his immediate right. John noted to himself that it wasn't Sycophant.

"Jason Wysgaard, head of Information Services." Vohlmann made a check mark next to the bespectacled techie's name on a sheet before him, took another gulp of coffee and eyed his next subordinate. All eyes remained fixed on Vohlmann.

"Jenny Jacobson, head of Loan Processing." Jenny, a short, plump woman with a sense of humor and a life outside of work, was one in the bunch John liked, and he hoped she would command respect and resources under the new guy.

"Pete Cunningham, Mortgage-Backed Securitization." John noticed that Blowhard's sleeves were rolled down and wondered whether this was on account of the cold weather or in an attempt to put his "best arm" forward for the new guy. John also wondered how long it would take the new guy to call Cunningham "Blowhard" or the equivalent.

"Debra Tarwinski, Risk Management," the Police Woman identified herself. She looked nervous and turned to her right as the words left her mouth, as if to avoid scrutiny by her new boss.

"Skip Schuneman, Fred, National Sales—CRE—Commercial Real Estate." Sycophant cleared his throat and tried to look like the executive he wasn't.

Vohlmann gulped so hard this time, he slurped. "Good, Skip," Vohlmann offered. Sycophant took him literally, but no one else did.

"Joe Laverne, Strategic Planning." A dapper dresser with nowhere to go, Joe was one of Heckler's foster children, the people whose names appeared in boxes off to the side of the departmental hierarchy on Heckler's disorganization chart.

"John Anchor, Collateral Control." Vohlmann lifted his coffee cup to his mouth and poured his sight into the cup just as John spoke. When the drained cup swung back down to the table, Vohlmann's eyes were trained on the next person. Later in the day, John would encounter Vohlmann in the corridor just outside the new guy's office, offer a "Hi, Fred," but receive only a "Hi, there," in return. Not until John's first "one-on-one" meeting several days later would Vohlmann link John's name and face.

"Cyndi Callahan, Administration." She was another foster child, and no one around the table knew exactly what Cyndi did all day, except her nails. Once in a while, though, she changed filters in the coffee machines no one used.

"Judy Bauer, Tax-Exempt Financing." She brushed her tinted blonde hair nervously behind her shoulders.

"Wow! There sure are a lot of you," Vohlmann said. "We should have had name tags for this meeting." Nervous chuckles echoed around the table. Not even all the foster children were present; the less confident ones thought it was safer to lie low. John surveyed the faces gathered with him and saw in each the instinctive question, "Will I be demoted or fired?" As for himself, John thought about the severance package that had eluded him. Maybe the new guy's my hope, he thought.

Vohlmann poured himself another cup of unctuous caffeine and surveyed his assorted crew of subordinates. "Maybe I should give a little background on myself. I'm new to real estate *per se,* but I've been in banking all my life and I've enjoyed every minute of it. Grew up in White Bear Lake, went to University of Wisconsin-Eau Claire, where I majored in accounting and got my MBA at St. Thomas."

Vohlmann poured himself another cup of coffee and took a sip. "I think this is a great bank, and I know this department has been impacted by some issues, but if we're proactive and work as a team, we can make it a great department, because I know there are lots of great people here. Finally, I just want to say that if I've learned anything through my business career, it's this: Value-added comes from the empowerment of people."

A plus for enthusiasm, John thought, but C minus for the jargon.

"Now, I know Mike O'Gara real well—for fifteen years, I've worked for Mike—and I can tell you, if you haven't heard, he's a numbers guy. So I'm a numbers guy. When you talk about your business to me, make sure you know the numbers, because I know Mike will be asking me. On the other hand," Vohlmann took a gulp of his grey-brown beverage and slurped again, "although the bottom line is important, it's not everything, and I want people to understand that. If we can't have fun doing what we're doing, then we should pack up and find something else to do." Although the compression in Vohlmann's voice suggested that his brand of fun differed from John's, the words sounded good.

"So you know my work style," Vohlmann continued. "I come very early—six or so—and I tend to leave at about seven o'clock in the evening. I don't expect others to keep those kinds of hours, but I tend to notice who sneaks in late and who sneaks out early." In other words, John said to himself, he does expect us to keep ungodly hours.

"I'm highly organized, and when I ask for something from you, I'll assign a deadline and log it into my computer. My tickler system has a great memory, and if I don't receive what I'm expecting a day ahead of the deadline, I'll e-mail you a reminder. If you're late—well, let's put it this way—don't be." We're in the army now, John told himself, or is it the Marines? Somehow, though, Vohlmann didn't look like the military type, certainly not of the brass variety.

"I communicate primarily by e-mail, which I find to be a great means of communicating, especially late at night, weekends or when traveling. If my door is closed, which will be a lot of the time, it means I don't want to be disturbed." John wasn't the only one to swallow hard.

"I'm also big on diversity. This is a great initiative, and I'll be giving you each some major diversity goals for the year. We can talk about these during one-on-ones, which we'll be scheduling with each of you over the next couple of weeks." John relaxed over Vohlmann's statement. Despite the dubious merits of the diversity program, John figured it could only help that he was actually on the Diversity Council. "In conjunction with this great initiative, I will be stressing diversity training and employee recognition and development programs, and as managers, you should make sure these are included in your HBGBs."

"Which reminds me," Vohlmann drew more morning fuel from his cup. "When we meet in our one-on-ones, I want to discuss your HBGBs. We'll make appropriate adjustments, and then I'll want to adopt modified HBGBs by the end of February, at the latest. Also, I'll distribute an informational form, which I'd like each of you to fill out in advance of our one-on-ones. These are numbers-oriented but also call for market information, if you manage a line group, or operational information if you're in a support function. They're pretty detailed and they'll help focus our discussions." John got the distinct impression that he wouldn't be talking fishing or deer hunting during his one-on-one with the new guy.

Vohlmann drank the rest of his coffee and let his cup down carefully onto the table. He looked around at his attentive subjects and with his eyebrows pushing deep furrows into his forehead, he concluded his agenda. "Any questions?" he asked. There were, but none was asked. "Great! We'll meet every Thursday at 6:30, right here. Can everyone make that?" It would be nearly impossible for some and a major inconvenience for the rest of the group, but no one protested.

As people shuffled out of the room, Sycophant fought his way against the tide to ask Vohlmann a question. "Back to his old ways," John said out of the corner of his mouth to Jenny Jacobson.

"Somehow I don't think Vohlmann is the kind of guy who warms up to apple-polishers," Jenny said, with twinkling eyes. "Sycophant could be in for some rough sledding."

Vohlmann immediately turned to the task of scheduling one-on-ones with each of his newly inherited direct reports and e-mailing to each of them the promised form to be completed. One question that did not appear on the form but that he asked everyone in person was, "So, tell me about each of the other direct reports. Who's a keeper and who isn't?" Jason Wysgaard and Cyndi Callahan wouldn't commit. Debra Tarwinski thought everyone should go—except herself, of course. Joe Laverne, who noticed the numerous books by Stephen Covey and other self-appointed management gurus on the shelves behind Vohlmann's desk, offered that "while *we* direct reports had our differences, they weren't something that a few management seminars couldn't correct." Joe's explicit inclusion of himself among the direct reports worked its psychological magic on Vohlmann, who thereafter treated him as a full-fledged "team member." Vohlmann thought Joe displayed common sense, too. Blowhard blathered on interminably about "what you ought to do about this and that," and without naming names, he complained about people who were "all butter and no bread." Vohlmann wasn't sure what that meant, but ironically, he interpreted it as a reference to the likes of Blowhard himself, not to individuals like Sycophant, whom Blowhard actually had in mind. Sycophant, meanwhile, hanged Heckler in figurative effigy. He then cleared his throat and expressed with a confident tone that Vohlmann and he should be able to get along with everyone, but if anyone gave Vohlmann difficulties, he, Sycophant, "would be more than willing to coach the wayward individual." Vohlmann sincerely appreciated the offer. Jenny was perfectly candid and told who should stay, who should go and who was a maybe. She won credibility when she identified Blowhard as one who should go but lost it when she recommended dismissal of Sycophant and questioned the worth of Wysgaard. Unwittingly, she worked against John when she volunteered that he was definitely a keeper.

"John, in fact," she said, "is someone you definitely don't want to lose. He didn't exactly thrive under Heckler, and I think he got kind of discouraged until you came on board. John has been in real estate ever since he arrived at the bank. I don't know exactly how long that's been, but it's got to be longer than nearly anyone else here. He's a good guy, too."

Not knowing the first thing about real estate and worse, not knowing anything about the people in the department, except what he had gleaned from the one-on-ones, Vohlmann was keenly interested in knowing whom he could count on. He turned over a page in his notebook, wrote down John's name and underlined it. "What does this guy look like?"

"Thick red mustache and reddish, sandy hair."

Vohlmann twitched, then tapped his lips with his pen. "Oh yeah," he said and poised his pen to write. "Exactly what does he manage?" Jenny explained, and Vohlmann dutifully recorded everything. He looked forward to his meeting with this man Anchor. Vohlmann would have his chance beginning at 9:00 the following morning.

$ $ $ $

On the eve of his meeting with Vohlmann, John sank his hands into his pockets and paced the floor of his one-bedroom apartment. To save money, now that he was on his own, he'd found an old but adequate place on the west end of Grand Avenue over in St. Paul for just $450 a month. He followed a general route between the corner of his bedroom in the back to the living room in front. Each time, he altered the route slightly to avoid the same squeaky floor boards on consecutive rounds. Immersed in his thoughts about work, John allowed over a half hour to pass unnoticed. When the heat came on and the ancient pipes running to the radiators banged around like loose hardware on a steam locomotive, John lost his concentration. He donned his winter workout clothes and running shoes and stepped out into the night.

The clear air was dense with the cold, and traffic sounds traveled well, which gave John a heightened sense of awareness. He began running immediately and assumed a pace fast enough to stay warm but slow enough to allow concentration on the matter at hand. The change in command at work had not altered John's mind about leaving the bank. Among managers in the department, the consensus was that Vohlmann was a turnaround guy, sent on a mission to impose martial law, clean house and put the department back on track. After considerable deliberation, John determined that he did not care to work under such conditions, and that he ought to take up with his new boss, at the earliest opportunity, the matter of a severance package. However, what if Vohlmann rejected John's claim for a severance package? Nevertheless, a deal was a deal, and Heckler had

had every authority to make the deal with John—come the end of the Franklin and Walden cases—and John would have his nine months' severance package. The question then, was how to raise the issue with the new guy and obtain his affirmation of the accord John had reached with Heckler.

After a mile or so, John resolved that in the meeting he would not belabor the department's sordid history but simply seek affirmation of his deal with Heckler. Over the next mile, at a slowing pace, John played, modified and replayed an imaginary tape of his anticipated conversation with Vohlmann. "Heckler promised me a deal." No, "Heckler *gave* me a deal, and I was wondering whether you'd approve . . ." No, "The *bank* gave me a deal, and I'd like to tell you what it is." Yeah, that was it.

By the third mile, John was imagining Vohlmann's possible reactions. "Heckler didn't have authority," or "Let me think about it," or "I'll have to get approval from Mike," or "Absolutely not," or "What? You can leave *now,* as far as I'm concerned—but without a severance package." What then? What would he himself say? "Okay, just kidding," or "Look, this bank gave me a deal and I'm holding people to it," or "You can tell my lawyer that"? What lawyer? Every lawyer that John knew, worked for the bank. Besides, he couldn't see himself as a plaintiff in a lawsuit. Only whiners and fools went around suing people.

As John approached Memorial Park at the end of Summit Avenue, overlooking the bend in the Mississippi, he saw the Minneapolis skyline all aglow, like a sparkling crown. Wells-Fargo Center, with its setbacks and elegant lighting, looked like the crown jewel. Next to it rose the classic IDS tower, the tallest building in Minneapolis until the HeartBank Tower, several blocks away, soared above it by fifteen floors. Comfortably warm by now, John stopped running and walked to an outcropping just beyond the park monument. There he obtained a commanding view of the city, which, despite the hour—about eight o'clock—seemed to pulsate with the work of business people, lawyers and accountants, who burned the late-night oil. It reminded him of a giant casino, where stakes were high and fortunes were won and lost; a constellation of crap shoots, roulette wheels, black jack tables, wine, women and song, where you had to be present to be a player. John felt more distant from it than he ever had before, but he didn't know if he longed to be a player or was relieved that he wasn't. A stir of the frigid air brought a chill, and John realized that most of the lights he saw illuminated the work of office cleaning crews, not office workers. Perhaps someday, John mused, the cleaning crews—mostly recent immigrants—would capitalize on their access to all kinds of sensitive information across thousands of desks and take over the casino. He retreated from the outcropping and jogged home.

$ $ $ $

When John's turn came the next morning, Vohlmann started off the conversation cheerfully. "I understand you're a keeper," he said.

"Well, yeah, you might say that," replied John. "I mean, my group maintains all the collateral documents associated with loans the department books and ensures that what we receive is what is required pursuant to departmental standards."

"No, what I meant is that you individually are a manager I should try to keep on board."

"Really?" John felt at once flattered and disheartened. It was the first compliment in years that he'd heard from a superior, but on the other hand, it threatened prospects for a severance package. "Gee, thanks, uh, that's great, I, uh, appreciate that." He stumbled and struggled to restore the viability of his plan. "But actually, you see, I was planning to leave—"

"Leave?" With his eyebrows, Vohlmann signaled surprise and consternation. "Have you got an offer somewhere?"

"No, it's just that I was promised a severance package once certain litigation affecting the department is concluded."

"A severance package? Litigation? You don't mean that billion-dollar lawsuit. Are you the one involved with that?" Vohlmann took a swig of his addictive beverage, though the revelation that it might be John who was involved with the Walden suit seemed to have twice the impact of a shot of caffeine. "What does a severance package have to do with . . ." Vohlmann continued, as confusion appeared in his eyes. "Oh, I get it. Heckler fired . . . wait a minute. *You* aren't suing the bank, are you?" The puzzlement in Vohlmann's face yielded to a scowl.

"No, no, no, nothing like that," John said, in a quick attempt to dodge the image of complainer, whiner. "You see, he and I had our differences, you might say. There were a couple of lawsuits—a discrimination case and a lender liability suit, I guess you'd call it—over incidents he thought should be resolved one way and I thought should be addressed in another.

Well, see, I wanted to leave the bank and he agreed, but I guess the law department said I'd have to stay on until the litigation was resolved—it would look bad for the bank if I left before that—and then Heckler negotiated a severance package with me." John felt as though he'd finished a minor workout. He'd broken a sweat, but now the issue of a severance package was distinctly on the table.

"Well, I don't want to talk about Heckler, though I've certainly heard lots of stories about him. In any event, now that he's gone, I assume, I mean, I'd sure like you to stay." Vohlmann sounded earnest enough, but exactly what kind of boss would he be? So far under the new regime, John felt like a Marine, and he'd never held a very positive view of the military. The bank was the bank, and John remained convinced that his career had stalled out over more than Heckler's abuse. John just wasn't cut out for large corporate life, and as long as the bank—any bank, for that matter—was run by people who allowed a guy like Heckler to rule for years and by people whose careers actually thrived on the presence of a guy like Heckler, John knew he himself would never fit in. Okay, fine, the tyrant was gone, but not the tyranny of a place where advancement depended on mediocrity, greed, lust for power and disingenuousness, not more admirable traits. Yet, John knew the world was an imperfect place, and, as Steve Torseth was discovering, the world could be a frighteningly insecure place. Still, as John's father had advised, you have to be true to yourself. In the compressed time allotted by the pause in the conversation, John failed to reconcile his experiences with Vohlmann's words of encouragement, even flattery. Before John could add another word to the conversation, Vohlmann revealed his own decisiveness. "Look," Vohlmann said. "I don't want to talk about your situation any further right now. As far as the big lawsuit goes, O'Gara explained to me that we've got the legal eagles up in the law department and Bakke & Fulsom all over this one. I've got a meeting scheduled with the lawyers this afternoon to get up to speed. The other lawsuit is news to me, so maybe you can fill me in, but I'd like some background on the big lawsuit too. In any event, when the lawsuits gets resolved, maybe then we'll see how you're doing."

John relaxed with the realization that he now had it both ways. Vohlmann hadn't slammed the door on the severance package, hadn't denied Heckler's authority to make such a deal; at the same time, John could adopt a wait-and-see approach to his continued employment at the bank.

In fact, John felt downright positive about his position. He could use the next few months, or whatever it took to resolve the litigation, to contemplate the next step in his career. If things in fact worked out under Vohlmann, well, then, great. If they didn't, presumably there'd be a severance package at the end of the road.

Vohlmann proceeded to question John about the Franklin and Walden suits, and in contrast with the vitriol and tension that had characterized discussions with Heckler, the conversation with John's new boss was direct and objective. Vohlmann took careful notes, but he expressed no lesser opinion of John, either verbally or visibly, as the result of John's association with the cases. In fact, there existed no reason for Vohlmann to blame John for anything quite yet. If the bank achieved favorable results, Vohlmann could claim credit for himself, and if the bank lost, Vohlmann could point the finger at Heckler or Heckler and John, if that became necessary. Furthermore, Vohlmann could pin responsibility on John with the advantage of hindsight. For now, however, Vohlmann could give John the benefit of the doubt and allow the lawyers to do their thing. If it came out in the litigation that John was to blame, well, fine. Vohlmann could join in the chorus, and against the backdrop of the law department's advisory regarding HeartBank's retention of John pending resolution of the litigation, Vohlmann could elude criticism for not having fired "a bad apple" early on in his regime. For Vohlmann, keeping John aboard was a "no lose" proposition.

♦ CHAPTER TWENTY-FOUR ♦

The Deposition

"HAVE YOU EVER BEEN DEPOSED?" asked Wickley, John's lawyer, or rather, the bank's lawyer, in the Franklin case.

"No," said John.

"Okay, let me explain a few things," the lawyer said. Zane Wickley was a young, hard-working, aggressive lawyer at Whiley & Cobb, and he was convinced that he was partner material. Among the existing partners, however, the jury was out. He was a little like a bulldog at a collie show. He could do all the required routines, but he'd always be a bulldog, ugly and tough. To succeed at a firm like Whiley & Cobb, that is, to make equity partner, you had to be hard-working, aggressive *and* ready for show. Zane simply wasn't ready for show, and until he learned to comb his hair, tuck in his shirt, lose a little weight, which he had carried around since his hapless childhood, and talk about something other than his latest discovery motion, he wouldn't be ready for show.

The Franklin case had come into the firm by way of Lehigh Dickenson, who was *all* show and the honorary chairman of the "schmooze committee" at the firm. Dickenson hadn't taken a deposition in years, but he managed to attract a steady stream of HeartBank work, which he passed on to office grinds like Wickley, all of whom competed for favor with the partners who could make or break a senior associate's own bid for partnership. As in the Franklin case, Dickenson often turned over matters lock, stock and barrel to one of the grinds, like meat to a pack of hungry wolves. In more high profile cases, Dickenson sometimes handled a dispositive motion hearing, if the client wanted to attend and Dickenson was assured of winning.

Wickley's office, located on the north side of the IDS Tower, was about half the size of an average partner's office and ten times as messy. With papers, briefs, books and CD-ROMs stacked on every level surface, Wickley's cubbyhole was no place to receive a client. In fact, there was no room for a client, especially with Wickley in the room. Thus, the lawyer's secretary had reserved one of the floor's conference rooms for the session between Wickley and John.

As a real estate banker, John couldn't help but view the enormous conference room and its elegant wood paneling, oil paintings, high-backed leather chairs, silver samovar and mahogany table from a strictly financial perspective. Depending on the term of their lease and the depreciation schedule for all the buildouts and furnishings, John thought, this is expensive space we're in, particularly when you consider that the room is about twenty-five feet by fifteen and we're the only occupants. No wonder the firm's hourly rates are so high.

"A deposition is a chance for the other side to grill you into barbecued chicken," Wickley explained from his chair at the foot of the conference room table. Seated in the first chair around the corner from his lawyer, John wasn't the kind of client who would wilt in the face of brusqueness, but he wondered if this gruff lawyer, who looked angry and rumpled before his time, approached all clients this way. Better to be ruffled up by your own lawyer first, John told himself, than to be grilled by opposing counsel without a taste of abuse beforehand.

"So what can I expect?"

"First of all, the deposing lawyer will ask you all kinds of personal, background-type questions. You know—where do you live, where'd you go to school, where've you worked, that kind of thing. Then, after they've dug everything out of your deep dark past—and everyone has one—they'll interrogate you about all sorts of irrelevant details relating to your current job. They'll circle around like a fox around the chicken yard, with its eyes on the prey, and if you're stupid or scared or both, they'll swoop in for the kill." Wickley shoved his hand to his throat and released a guttural "Ya-a-a-c-c-h-h!" so suddenly, John jumped. "My job is to object to questions when appropriate. Your job is not to be stupid or scared."

"Generally, I'm not stupid," said John, "and I don't scare easily."

"I'm glad to hear it," Wickley said, "but there's something else you need to be."

"What's that?"

"You need to be laconic."

"Laconic?" John didn't know if he was or wasn't, but he suspected that had he attended law school, he would know.

"You know, a man of few words," Wickley rolled his eyes. "When you're asked a question, don't blab, just answer the question as narrowly as you can. If the question doesn't quite get to the point, don't volunteer anything. Otherwise, you're bound to say something that can be used against you somehow or that will trigger some ideas, some other avenues of inquiry that will hurt our case. Make the other lawyer work at it, figure things out."

"Which raises the question—who *is* the lawyer representing Franklin?"

"Some woman named Justina Herz," Wickley said, with a tone of contempt.

"Justina Herz? What firm is she with?"

"Firm?" Wickley laughed. "You haven't been through one of these types of cases before, have you?"

"What do you mean?" John didn't see the humor, and he was fast developing a dislike for this slovenly cynic who was representing HeartBank in the case at hand.

"Let me explain something to you, Mr. Anchor. Legitimate lawyers like those of us here at Whiley & Cobb—with a few exceptions that we'd all like to ignore, I admit—take on *cases.* Other make-believe lawyers out there take on *causes.* They'll take on anyone who has a beef against the establishment, and they're generally pains in the ass. Generally, they can't make any money doing what they do, so it's no wonder they rarely wind up in legitimate firms. However, once in a while they hit pay dirt—you know, they'll get some big settlement or verdict over some dumb ass issue. Then, all of a sudden, they buy fancy cars and big houses like partners at a megafirm like ours, but generally they're Democrats for life."

"So this Justina Herz is one of those types? Have you dealt with her before?"

"Not directly, but her name's been around. She was in the papers awhile back in connection with the Indians' attempt to hold up highway construction over a bunch of stupid bones and broken pottery they claimed was sacred or some idiotic thing like that. Beyond that, all I know is she's a solo practitioner with an office in a low rent building and she's Jewish."

"Jewish?" John surprised himself. Rarely in his life had he uttered the word "Jewish," for he simply had never had the occasion to do so. Besides, it sounded as if you were prejudiced or something if you mentioned "Jews" or "Jewish" in this neck of the woods, unless, of course, you were talking about World War II and all the horrible things Hitler had done to those people. Wickley's intemperate remarks, especially in this initial encounter, made John uncomfortable. "Dare I ask what significance that has?"

"Given all the things she is—a woman, a civil rights practitioner with low overhead, and Jewish to boot—she's probably liberal off the charts and a lesbian besides."

"Lesbian?" John wasn't sure he knew any lesbians, although, in retrospect, he suspected that the single woman who lived on the corner in his old neighborhood—the one who owned the industrial-sized snow-blower—was maybe lesbian, but so what?

"*And,* my friend, she's probably grilled lots of chicken in her career." Tiny beads of perspiration appeared on Wickley's nose and forehead. "So, we'd better get ready."

$ $ $ $

The following day, John opened his closet door and ran his hand across the half dozen suits that hung there, ready for action. He eyed them the way a football coach views his roster. There was the MVP quarterback—the expensive suit that he had bought at Dayton's with the gift certificate John's folks had given him on his fortieth birthday. Then there were the solid performers, maybe not franchise players but reliable veterans—the three suits he'd bought on clearance at respectable stores in a mall. Next to these were the second-stringers—suits he'd purchased at discount stores as backup when the "starters" were at the cleaners. He selected his MVP suit, dark blue with widely spaced pin-stripes, a heavily starched white shirt and his best tie, a red-and-silver-patterned Armani that his sister had brought back from her trip to San Fransisco last year.

He dressed, looked himself in the mirror and told himself he was no grilled chicken. No unattractive, radical lesbian with a short haircut, a large snow-blower and a law degree was going to get the better of him. As much as he disliked Wickley, he would follow the lawyer's instructions and be tough and "laconic." If nothing else, at least the whole sordid experience had expanded his vocabulary.

For Wickley, it was just another day of battle. He wore the same suit,

John noticed, and the same shirt—he could tell by the light stain in front—and tie he had worn yesterday. John hoped Wickley wasn't wearing the same socks and underwear. They met in the lobby on Wickley's floor of the IDS Tower and trekked together through the labyrinthine skyway system from the central business district of downtown Minneapolis to the last building served by the second story walkways. Their destination—Justina's office—was two blocks beyond the outer limits of the skyway system. John felt like a hunting dog on a tight leash. Under normal circumstances, John's gait carried him abreast of most other pedestrians, but with Wickley in tow, he had to shorten his strides and slow his pace.

Outside the skyway system, Wickley stepped up the pace but only marginally. "Christ but it's cold out," Wickley muttered.

John wanted to say "So move faster and you won't be out in it so long and you'll feel warmer besides," but he just pressed on with his lawyer. They were definitely in the lower rent district, where old, red or dirty-yellow brick was the predominant building material. Occasionally, a date from the late nineteenth century was etched in a large chunk of limestone at the top of a façade. John figured that the higher energy bills faced by the owners of these tired old buildings were offset by lower taxes. He also noticed that the cars parked in the lot where a building had been razed were predominately cheaper Hondas, Toyotas and rusted Fords and Chevies, not the more expensive vehicles that occupied downtown parking ramps.

"Here it is," Wickley's voice wobbled as he looked up at the numerals carved in the lintel over the entrance of the tired building where Justina Herz practiced law. John followed Wickley up the five stone steps that led to a set of double doors with brass handles in need of a shine and large plates of thick, beveled glass. The clank of the latch, as John opened the door, reminded him of the old library at the University. Inside, the men stepped onto a black-and-white tile floor, dulled by time and the dried grit of winter deposited from the footwear of visitors. Directly ahead of them was a bank of four elevators, and off to the side hung a directory bearing the names of current building occupants. Some of the white plastic letters were missing, as was the case with the *z* in "Herz"; it lay at the bottom of the directory casement.

After Wickley pressed the brass button marked UP next to the nearest elevator, the motor switched on and groaned inside the shaft. John looked around for a stairwell and had plenty of time to consider how long it would take Wickley to huff and puff up four flights. Finally, the elevator car clanked to a stop on the ground floor, and the heavy brass doors, which hadn't shone for decades, slowly drew apart. Good thing to have your lawyer close on this elevator, John chuckled to himself. Trouble is, thought John, Wickley wouldn't be the one I'd want to represent me if the cable broke. The doors closed and the car vibrated as the motor churned. The two men traveled to the fourth floor in the time it would take a HeartBank elevator to soar twenty stories. They stepped off into a vestibule the size of a large closet and lit by a dim light overhead. They eyed their choices among three, dark wooden doors. Two bore no lettering. On the third appeared, Justina Herz - Attorney at Law.

Wickley turned the knob and cautiously pushed the door into a small waiting area nearly the size of the elevator vestibule, separated, by a wooden counter, from a slightly larger office. John's image of Justina changed to a gray-haired war-horse, perhaps in the style of Miss Jasper, his seventh-grade English teacher, who spit when she uttered "parse," her favorite word; poured red ink over every assignment you turned in and handed out D minuses as if she enjoyed it. A stingy, faded rug lay in the center of the waiting room, and three straight-backed chairs sat inhospitably against the off-white plaster walls. The only sign of hope, John thought, was a framed Blaylock photo of a wooden canoe pulled halfway onto shore in the wilderness. Under the photo was the title, *Boundary Waters.* John replaced Miss Jasper with his great aunt Bertha, an earthy, frugal Danish immigrant, who loved to fish on the small lake hidden on her farm near Tracy, Minnesota.

On the other side of the counter was a jumble of old wooden office furniture: a desk—similar to Miss Jasper's, actually—several file cabinets, two tables and an odd chair here and there. John noticed that despite the volume of papers, files and books that occupied just about every level surface, these items were arranged very neatly, much as Aunt Bertha ordered her busy kitchen. Straight ahead were three large, double-hung windows, which, judging by the distortions in the glass, John figured were probably originals. On one of the walls hung a pendulum clock, an antique, to be sure, whose steady "tick-tock" ruled over a quiet domain. The only signs of modernity were a PC and a phone on the desk, and even these were at least several generations behind what was state-of-the-art.

While John stood wondering what kind of law was practiced in such a low-tech, out of the way office, Wickley read the sign next to the classic bell on top of the counter. Please Ring Bell to Announce Your Arrival, it directed. With a heavy hand on the ringer, Wickley challenged the preeminence of the stately wall clock. He waited a couple of seconds and rang again. From a room on one side of the office, there emerged a heavy-set woman in her early sixties, dressed in a timeless navy blue skirt, matching jacket and white blouse. She took short steps and leaned from side to side—a regular waddle. Arthritis in the knees, like Aunt Bertha, John told himself. Moreover, she wore a kindly face like that of his great aunt, and a smile. John beamed. He was about to be deposed by an Aunt Bertha. Maybe his luck would extend to some milk and cookies after the deposition, just as Aunt Bertha used to serve after John and his dad helped with chores during their visits out to her farm.

"Here, I can let you in," the woman spoke. She opened the door that made up a section of the counter and allowed the men to join her in the office. She uttered something to Wickley, which John heard to be "Justina," and led the men into a small, windowless conference room just off to the side of the office.

"I was just about to get some coffee. Can I get some for you gentlemen?" she asked.

Wickley turned down the corners of his mouth and shook his head. "No thanks," said John. Okay, he told himself, so it's coffee instead of milk, but surely Aunt Bertha would have offered me coffee if she had ever seen me grownup. With that, the woman left the room, and Wickley and John found their places at the conference table. John eyed the furniture, clearly hand-me-down pieces from an era long past. Perhaps the table and chairs had belonged to one of the original tenants back in the 1890s.

"She doesn't look like the type who grills chicken," John said, smugly. It was about time that a hard cynic like Wickley meet one of the Aunt Berthas of the world and see first hand that not all disputes need be reduced to a "barbecue" of litigation before they could be resolved.

Wickley twisted his mouth into a half-smile, half-smirk. "The old lady is the court reporter, *stupid.*" Except he didn't say "stupid." He didn't have to. John felt stupid and naïve. He also felt instant perspiration flow from every pore in his body. He'd forgotten about the role of the court reporter, and about what Wickley had said regarding his (or in this case, her) administering an oath and taking down every word, every "uh" and "um" and every "duh" as well, so that he'd look like a complete illiterate (Wickley's word) when anyone read a transcript of his deposition. And if this kindly woman wasn't Justina Herz, then what kind of woman could he expect for a Justina? He suspected she was no Aunt Bertha, but a Miss Jasper, who would doubtless have some favorite "grill words" of her own; a woman from the old school, who parsed for a pastime and probably spit venom when she talked; an oddity among lawyers of her generation, who were nearly all males; a woman who could make your ears sweat. Surreptitiously, John wiped the clammy palm of his right hand on the side of his suitcoat. When Justina Herz entered the room, which she was bound to do at any second, and shook his hand—assuming she observed any of the conventions of the business world—he didn't want to reveal any more vulnerability than that which was probably written all over his face.

"Miss Jasper's revenge," John mumbled.

"Huh?"

"Nothing," said John. Now all he could do was submit, get it over with and escape the clutches of Miss Jasper reincarnate. A moment later, a set of determined footsteps echoed across the floor of the office—from another room, John realized, on the side opposite the conference room. No waddler *this* walker, John thought, as his breathing quickened.

"Hello. I'm Justina Herz." If John made it to his feet, he didn't know how he'd remain standing. He couldn't feel his knees, and his head threatened to float away altogether. Appearing through the doorway was a much younger woman—probably early thirties—of instantly recognizable beauty. Not the kind whose features you had to ponder before you determined she was attractive or good looking or, at least, not bad looking, but a woman whose dark, intelligent eyes, radiant skin, rich brunette, loosely wrapped hair, red lips, straight white teeth and figure that even under a conservative business suit boosted John's pulse rate, formed what John could see only as the perfect woman. This woman can grill chicken all she wants, he thought.

"Zane Wickley." John's lawyer showed no emotion, and after perfunctorily shaking hands, he stepped back to allow John to do the same. But for John, it was no perfunctory handshake. He clasped Justina's firm but feminine hand and felt its warmth, energy and character, much as he would try on an expensive leather glove in the *L'Homme Unique* section of Dayton's—a section John had visited but never patronized. Light-headed,

John managed to look into the eyes of this remarkable woman, and they struck back with a penetrating look into his thoughts.

Justina took a seat at the side of the table opposite Wickley and John, and the court reporter waddled in with a cup of coffee to see her through the deposition. All eyes followed the older woman, as she situated herself next to her stenotype and made the necessary adjustments to the tape recorder, the computer and an overhead projector, which fed projections onto the wall behind her.

"Could I see the caption, please?" the court reporter asked. Justina pulled some papers from the stack she had placed on the table and gracefully extended the pages to Aunt Bertha, who punched some keys on the stenotype. To John's surprise, the name of the lawsuit jumped onto the screen.

Hennepin County District Court

State of Minnesota

William Franklin

vs.

HeartBank, National Association

Now he'd be able to see instantaneously how illiterate he sounded. The court reporter eyed John and Wickley, turned her view to Justina and nodded. "Ready?" she said.

"Go ahead and administer the oath." Justina said, in a voice that reminded John more of a conversation over wine at a nice restaurant than a grilling by a litigator.

"Raise your right hand." The court reporter faced John, with her own hand in the position she expected from John. "Do you swear to tell the truth, the whole truth and nothing but the truth, so help you God?"

"Yes." The question jolted him back to reality. The lawsuit. William Franklin, Heckler, HeartBank, Wickley. With the solemnity of the oath, John felt as if he were about to experience his fifteen minutes of fame, or, as Wickley had warned, more like an hour or two of it. The court reporter regained her chair and looked at Justina, who sat back, straight, confident and beautiful.

"Could you please state and spell your name and give your address for the record?" Justina's eyes sparkled, and John tried to slow his pulse by taking a deep breath.

"John Anchor, first name J-O-H-N, second spelled A-N-C-H-O-R."

"What kind of name is that?" John wondered what that question had to do with the lawsuit, but he detected a friendly curiosity in her tone and it helped him relax.

"Actually, it's Danish—sort of." John returned curiosity with curiosity, which, he noticed in his peripheral sight, caused Wickley's face to snap to the left and remind John to be laconic.

"I see. I have a Danish connection of my own," she said, almost under her breath, before she returned to the prescribed routine of a deposition. "And your address?"

"Seventeen fifty Grand Avenue, St. Paul, Minnesota." Justina turned her head slightly, though her eyes remained on John. He thought he detected surprise in her face.

"Lived there long?"

"Only a few months."

"Are you married, Mr. Anchor?" Justina asked, her head now turned slightly in the other direction and a faint furrow in her forehead.

"Divorced." Justina's face relaxed. The question prompted him to want to drop his sight to the ring finger of Justina's left hand, but he dared not do so until she herself shifted her gaze from him.

"Where did you attend high school and what year did you graduate?"

"Armstrong High in Robbinsdale, Class of '76."

"Did you attend college?"

"Yes. I went to St. Olaf for a semester, then transferred to the 'U,' where I graduated in 1981."

"What was your major?" Justina looked at John expectantly.

"Business Administration." He thought he saw a flicker of disappointment in her face.

"Starting with your first job after college and continuing through your present position, would you please give me a summary of your employment, by name of employer, your position, title and responsibilities. Take your time." As he gave his background, Justina leaned forward and poured herself a glass of water from the pitcher on the table. Without thinking, John lowered his sight to Justina's left fingers, wrapped elegantly around the side of the glass. He saw no ring and fixed his gaze just a moment longer to confirm there was none. He watched as Justina took a sip of water, and moistened, her lips looked delicious. He wondered what it would be like to kiss them, and for an instant, John fantasized about phoning Justina—after the lawsuit was over, of course—and asking her out, as unlikely as her assent might be.

When he had finished reciting his employment history, John poured himself a glass of water and sat back, even more confident that Wickley had over-prepared him for the deposition.

"What do you do in your spare time?" The question and a hint of a smile on Justina's face piqued his curiosity about this process that was supposed to have been an ordeal. Before John could respond, a rough blast erupted next to him.

"I have to object, counsel," Wickley bellowed. His volume was disproportionate to the size of the room. "I don't know where you're going with that question."

Without moving her eyes from John, and in a steady tone, Justina said, "You know as well as I that under the rules, I can ask damn near anything I want to ask, counsel. Please answer the question, Mr. Anchor." John expected a retort from Wickley, but none came forth. Was Justina correct? Could she ask "damn near anything she wanted to"? Or was Justina's even-keeled self-assuredness simply a tactic for which the bully Wickley had no response? An uneasy silence filled the room, and John realized that as between himself and Wickley, the decision to answer the question was now entirely John's.

"Well," he said, hesitantly. "I guess if I could, I'd spend my spare time at my folks' lake place up in northern Wisconsin. I don't mind being in the city and all, but I guess I prefer to be out in nature." He stopped there. He was about to say "huntin'" or, more appropriately, in the presence of a woman as strikingly beautiful and undoubtedly as intelligent as Justina Herz, "hunting," but it occurred to him that a radical civil rights lawyer wouldn't take too kindly to a white male who designated "hunting" as his favorite pastime. Moreover, he remembered the excoriating ridicule that his ex-wife Sandy had hurled at him regarding the barbarity and cruelty of shooting deer. No doubt Justina was an animal rights activist as well, and if John had any hope, however fantastic, of making a positive impression on her, it was probably wise not to mention "hunting."

"When you're not up at the lake, what do you like to do in your spare time?" Justina asked.

"I wish I had more spare time," said John. "If I had it, I suppose I'd find a million things to do with it. Right now . . ." John's voice trailed off. Enticed into an almost conversational mode, John wanted to explain that he was struggling mightily with his life, his career, his objectives; that he spent most of his free time studying up on various ways to change his circumstances—going into business for himself, moving to new surroundings and starting work and life afresh, even going back to school, but to become what? In the end, however, he couldn't bare his soul to her or she'd get the wrong idea as to who he was. He was John Anchor, Vice President at HeartBank, National Real Estate Services, dressed in his MVP suit, in the throes of a lawsuit, a nothing lawsuit compared with the billion-dollar lawsuit that stood between him and his severance package. He was what Steve Torseth had labeled him. He was a schmo—today, tomorrow, forever.

"You were going to say, right now . . .?" Justina prompted him.

"Right now, I'm just trying to get by," John closed down, as much as he closed out the thought.

"Well, let me ask you this, Mr. Anchor. Do you do much reading?" Despite the earlier exchange between Justina and Wickley, John wondered where the question was heading and just how far astray the lawyer could go. He looked at Wickley for some clues and saw the face of a debarked bulldog confined to a kennel while an intruder walked by.

"Well, yes, I guess, you know, the usual, papers, periodicals, that sort of thing."

"What about books, Mr. Anchor. Do you ever read books? I mean novels, fiction and the like?" John could almost feel the heat coming out of Wickley's ears, but he heard no objection. The dog was still in the kennel. Novels? Fiction? In truth, John thought, he liked novels. His mother had seen to that. For every hour he had spent in sports or fishing or hunting with his dad, she insisted that he read fifteen or twenty pages, and not just anything, but excerpts from a list of books she had compiled during her years as an English teacher. He would never have admitted it to his football buddies or baseball friends, but he actually enjoyed those books. Not since high school, though, had he found time to escape to a quiet reading corner like the one his mother had established in his boyhood home.

"Yes, as a matter of fact. I mean, I like to read novels, but I never seem to have the time for it." Justina's face brightened, only then to frown ever so slightly, like the sun going in and out and back behind a thin layer of cloud.

"What kind of novels?" Furrows appeared in Justina's forehead, like small animal trails across fresh snow. John realized there could be a wrong answer to the question, like "Tom Clancy" or "Stephen King" or "John Grisham," but he didn't care for those writers and had never cracked one of their books. Still, against what would she gauge his answer? Gloria Steinem? He searched his memory for some of his boyhood novels and blurted out a few titles.

"Last of the Mohicans, The Scarlet Letter, Uncle Tom's Cabin." Uncle Tom's Cabin? John blushed. There it was on the screen behind the court reporter, suspended in time, frozen in print, *Uncle Tom's Cabin.* This, he figured, had to be the lawyer's ploy. To lull him down some path in the woods, which seemed so pleasant, innocent and irrelevant, until he found himself in the oven of the wicked witch, to be cooked and devoured—like grilled chicken. But wait. *Uncle Tom's Cabin* was sympathetic toward blacks. It was the most popular abolitionist novel of its time, one of the most popular novels of all time; John recalled his mother's instruction. Surely, it was a favorable thing to have mentioned it.

"Then you're familiar with the plight of African Americans in this country, going way back." John wasn't sure if Justina had asked a question or not. Before John could decide, however, Wickley slammed his pen down on his tablet and threw his full slovenly weight at the statement or question or whatever it was.

"This is preposterous!" Wickley exploded. The dog was out. "I'm not going to allow my client to sit here through some sort of goldarn"—the way he said "goldarn" signaled that Wickley had narrowly avoided "goddamn"—"political interrogation. If you want to run this deposition like some kind of radical, left-wing political campaign, you're going to have to get a court order, which you're not going to be able to do." Whether or not he was right, Wickley's outburst struck John as an inappropriate reaction to someone as beautiful as Justina and in the presence of someone like an Aunt Bertha. Besides, maybe under their "rules" this was a perfectly legitimate line of inquiry. John suspected that Wickley was simply nervous because he was not in control, and to compensate for his relative weakness against the one who was in control, Wickley was staging a conniption. John had seen the tactic used often by desperate debtors in his days as a workout specialist.

"Call it what you want, counsel, but with or without a court order, I'm entitled to inquire into the witness' thoughts and opinions regarding people of color." John was impressed by Justina's coolness under the blast from Wickley.

"Bullshit!" Wickley dropped his thin veil of restraint and bared his fangs. The word echoed from the wall behind the court reporter. "You're harassing the witness and you're making a mockery of this deposition. You continue like this and we'll be packing it in, Ms. Herz." John worried that Wickley was serious, and that his audience with the beautiful Justina would come to an abrupt and sour end. He hoped she would back down but didn't expect it. She was more than a match for Wickley.

"Let me try this," she said calmly. Wickley's red cheeks flapped as he huffed. Justina's tactics clearly had him off balance. "If you had a choice between attending a Twins game and a symphony concert, which would you choose?"

Without warning, John's lungs released a hearty laugh. He noticed Wickley himself guffaw in disbelief, right into the back of the chair. If Justina no longer led John down a pleasant woodland path, she still had him very much in the woods—an *Alice in Wonderland* woods perhaps. If Justina had said "Vikings" instead of "Twins," she would have encountered puzzlement undisguised by levity, and John would have answered, "Vikings game" reflexively. However, the Twins were a joke, and in whatever kind of *Wonderland* he now found himself, the Twins remained a joke. Justina's serious countenance struck John as incongruous.

"A symphony concert, definitely," John answered, almost mockingly, and thought he detected approval, even delight in Justina's face. He began to wonder if she wasn't an extreme eccentric, maybe even insane, though she certainly didn't appear so, aside from her bizarre questions. Crazy people looked crazy, not beautiful.

"Who are your favorite compos . . . Strike that." Composers? John thought. Was she about to ask me who my favorite composers are? She is completely off her rocker. And in any event, I don't have any favorite composers; I don't even know of any composers, except, I guess, Bach and Beethoven, guys like that.

"Let me ask you this. What sort of training does HeartBank require of its managers?" Justina asked, right out of left field, or maybe it was center field. Up to now, she'd been in left field.

"Well, uh, geez, it depends, I guess." Management training? John fumbled for a plausible answer. Most of the training calendars that found their way onto his desk got discarded—after they surfaced among all the other papers, which usually occurred several weeks after the calendars were obsolete.

"It's an ongoing process. Management training. It's a continuous cycle of courses and training." John felt moisture form under his collar.

"Does any of the training cover matters relating to discrimination in the workplace?" Tough question. John didn't know specifically if any of the courses on those calendars did or didn't relate to discrimination. He assumed there must be something—just about every conceivable harebrained subject appeared at one time or another, like his favorites, "Treating the Deaf with Deference" and "Visualizing Blindness: Understanding the Full Meaning of Diversity."

"Yeah, I think so—I'm sure." John felt Wickley's shoe and remembered the instruction, "Don't say if you don't know." Too late.

"You think?" Oh no! You live and learn. Surely there were courses on discrimination. Wouldn't that be covered under the umpteen courses on diversity?

"No, I'm sure there are." Justina looked unconvinced.

"Describe the ones you have taken." Back onto the barbecue grill with *Uncle Tom's Cabin.* But wait. If John had never actually taken one of those management courses, pertaining to discrimination or otherwise, surely his membership on the Diversity Council should count for something.

"Well, actually, you see, I'm on the HeartBank Diversity Council." Wickley's shoe kicked again, but this time, John thought Justina had been caught off balance.

"You are?" She allowed genuine surprise to surface. "Tell me more about this. How long have you been on the Diversity Council and how were you appointed?" John explained, and while Wickley fidgeted helplessly, John and Justina engaged in a dialogue about the Council. Alert now to the dangers of Justina's questioning, John trimmed his answers of any personal editorials, which he knew could only set him back. Undaunted, Justina continued circling around for what John feared was the ultimate kill. He decided that her disarming beauty, coolness under fire and off-balance questions made her exceptionally good. Good and dangerous.

"On the day that you first met with William Franklin—I believe you testified this was last September 26, is that correct?"

"Correct."

"On that date, you talked with William about his recruitment by the bank, isn't that right?"

"Yes." Time to be careful. Time to be laconic.

"And he told you all about it didn't he?" John nodded in reply. He could see the gloves coming off. He visualized her soft, elegant hands as fists, hard against his jaw. "Could you express your answer verbally for the record, please?" The directive reminded John of Miss Jasper's frequent command to enunciate.

"Yes, uh-huh."

"What did he tell you about his recruitment experience?"

John contemplated his response. The questioning had veered away from simple "yes"-"no" to short essay. Perspiration threatened to break out again under his constrictive collar. "He said the bank had told him about the job they were offering him." He stopped, confident he hadn't tripped a land mine yet.

"Did he mention who it was at the bank who had talked to him?"

"No, he didn't."

"Do you have any idea who it would have been?" Wickley's kick in the leg suggested how John should answer.

"No."

"Who at the bank participates in recruiting?"

"Objection, lack of foundation. Mr. Anchor is a manager in the real estate department, not a member of the HR staff."

Justina looked unfazed, but she re-phrased the question, nonetheless. "Are you familiar with the recruiting process at HeartBank?"

"You mean recruiting in general or recruiting minorities?"

"Either. Both."

"Sort of."

"Describe your familiarity." Now he was in a jam. The fact was, except for his brief encounter with William Franklin on that fateful day back in

September, John had had next to no exposure to the bank's recruiting, whether of minorities or anyone else. So, now, did "sort of" constitute a lie? After all, he was under oath. President Clinton had been impeached for lying under oath. A normal citizen could be sent to jail. Better back track to avoid the slammer.

"Well, actually, I'm not very familiar with the recruiting process." John felt the heat return to his ears. He was near the barbecue pit now. Not necessarily on the grill, but close enough.

"Fine, but William Franklin was placed in your department, National Real Estate Services, is that correct?" Justina tightened the ring.

"Yes."

"Do you know how his assignment to your department came about?"

"Uh, no, not exactly."

"Was it Mr. Heckler?"

"I don't know."

"Mr. Heckler is your boss, is that correct?"

"Was. He was fired a few weeks ago."

"Oh he was, was he? Let's talk about that for a moment." No hiding it now. John was in a veritable sweat, and no wonder. Justina was on a roll—and completely by rote. How many litigators at Whiley & Cobb—including the slob sitting next to him—could grill chicken like this lawyer?

Despite numerous objections by an agitated Wickley, Justina managed to extract from John the generally shared perception of his former boss. She then zeroed in on the bull's eye. "So you were told to fire William Franklin, is that correct?" The most delicious lips of John's interrogator were now flame-throwing lips, and Justina the beautiful now became Justice Hurts. Like a deer in a hunter's gunsight, John started one way—to qualify "fire"—only to remember "laconic," then to feel stupid for taking so long to respond and finally, just plain cornered.

"Uh-huh" is all that came out, and John flinched when the court reporter, who hadn't spoken since the beginning of the deposition, interjected.

"Was that a 'uh-huh' or a uh-uh'—a 'yes' or a 'no'?" she asked.

"It was a yes."

"And that was on September 26 of last year, correct?"

"Correct."

"And when you told him he was going to be fired, isn't it true that you expressed to him your opinion about how HeartBank had treated William?"

"Uh-huh. I mean, yes."

"William has told me what you said—"

"Are you giving evidence or taking evidence, counsel?" John saw a sneer across Wickley's face but Justina's icy glare wiped it off.

She turned her piercing eyes back to John. "May I remind you, Mr. Anchor, that you're under oath. Do you understand what that means?"

"Yes."

"What does it mean?"

"For crying out loud, Herz, you're harassing the witness again and you're out of line!" Wickley's tie clasp struck the table hard enough to nick the wood, he stood up so fast, but Justina beat him standing.

"No, *you're* out of order, and while I'm at it, bully tactics don't work on me. Now sit down and behave yourself." She left Wickley speechless and standing, while she resumed her seat and said directly to John, "Tell me what the oath means." Justina, twenty-three - Wickley, zero. John said to himself.

"It means I swear to God I'll tell the truth."

"You have the basic concept down. Now, given the fact that you swore to God to tell the truth and given the fact that William Franklin remembers exactly what you told him, I want you to tell me what you told him about how you thought the bank had treated him."

Make that Justina, twenty-three - Wickley, zero - and John, the loser. John gulped. He'd go to jail if he lied under oath, but on the other hand, his chance for a bonus would vanish if he told the truth. Before he could formulate his answer . . . but there was nothing to formulate. He remembered very clearly what he had told Franklin. John had only wanted to be honest with the poor guy, and look what had happened. Franklin had gone straight to a goddamned lawyer—and a goddamned good one, at that—with John's words, ready for suit, no tailoring necessary. Why was it that every word in business was fodder for litigation? During his entire career in banking, John had been warned time and again, by veterans, colleagues, bank lawyers, not to say this or that "or you could get sued." Well now, after all these years of *not* getting sued over a careless or innocent word or conversation, John had gotten whacked twice—first by William

Franklin and soon thereafter, by the scam artist, Prachna. Good enough reason to be laconic at all times.

"I told him I thought he'd gotten a raw deal and was the victim of racism." The words, spoken spontaneously months ago, like a child blowing seeds off a dandelion stem, reappeared on the court reporter's screen as if they were chiseled in granite. *I told him I thought he'd gotten a raw deal and was the victim of racism.*

Wickley groaned deeply and slammed his pen down on the table. "I want a recess," he blurted, as he struggled to his feet.

"You'll get a long one shortly," Justina said. "I'm almost through with the witness." Wickley dropped back into his chair as if someone had kicked him behind the knees. John raised his hand to his tie knot and shifted it back and forth in an attempt to relieve the tightness around his neck. Grilled chicken.

"Describe for me what you meant by racism." This chicken would be well done, and with it, his bonus would be charred to a crisp. John felt as if he were bending over a bed of hot coals.

"Well, uh, what I was referring to was his treatment by the bank. I mean, he was sort of a pawn, if you know what I mean. I mean, it looked to me like the bank had gone out to recruit him just so they could show they had minorities working for them . . ." Wickley kicked an audible "huh" right out of John, and *laconic* popped up on his mental screen as if it were emblazoned behind the court reporter.

Justina went on to sear the chicken, and by the time she said, "I have no further questions," John felt as if he'd been through a workout at the gym. His MVP suit was headed for the cleaners—assuming, that is, that his lawyer didn't kill him first. The fantasy of asking Justina out now seemed preposterous. While John extinguished even the deepest subconscious notions of romance with Justina, Wickley jammed his papers into his briefcase and without observing even a modicum of civility toward opposing counsel or the court reporter, stormed straight out of the conference room. Like a dog caught between a stranger who had just jabbed him with a sharp stick and his owner with a raised club, John went with his owner, for he knew the club wouldn't hurt any more than the sharp stick. Wickley's fury blew papers right off the neat stacks on the tables and chairs as he blasted his way contemptuously between the conference room and the door to Justina's low-rent office suite. John attempted to pick the papers off the floor, until he realized Wickley was moving so fast that John was likely to lose him. When they reached the elevator vestibule, Wickley groaned in disgust and turned directly to the door to the stairwell. When he's mad, he moves, thought John.

The perspiration on his skin and in his clothes froze instantly as John stepped out into the frigid air. Wickley showed no reaction to the seventy-degree change in temperature from the inside of yesteryear's building to the outdoors of current-day Minneapolis. He fixed his mad gaze straight down the sidewalk and pounded his heels into the pavement in utter contempt of the patches of ice and snow that would have threatened the balance of the most agile athlete. John worked hard to stay abreast without slipping.

"Why the hell didn't you tell me you were going to do that?" Wickley's voice cracked.

"Do what?" John asked.

"Blow my fucking case! Hell, I didn't have a fucking case to begin with, but why in God's world didn't you tell me that shit before I went in there and made a complete fool of myself?"

"I did tell you."

"You told me you told him he'd gotten a 'raw deal.' 'Raw deal' I could have dealt with. 'Victim of racism' I can't, pal, and thanks for the embarrassing surprise. You bankers are all the same. What's the deal anyhow—you got to have an MBA in stupidity to work there or what?"

"Sorry."

Wickley didn't hear, or if he heard, he didn't care. "Getting my ass kicked by a lousy, two-bit solo practitioner who bills out at probably a third of my billing rate—if the lesbo, radical, left-wing bitch even bills—is not my idea of professional gratification, you goddamned idiot. What the hell am I going to tell Dickenson?" Wickley was no longer talking to John, if he'd been talking to him in the first place.

"Who's Dickenson?"

"Don't ask." Wickley slammed on the brakes and with eyes ablaze, singed John's retinas. "And if you ever find yourself in need of a lawyer again, you stupid idiot, don't call me." Wickley started up again so fast, John nearly lost his balance. Upon entering the skyway system, John slowed his pace and let Wickley disappear into the crowd.

If Wickley had flipped out and made a mockery of client relations,

John had to admit to himself that it was he, John Anchor, who had blown the case. No, it was he who had created the case and delivered it on a silver platter to William Franklin and again to his lawyer. It would never settle within the range that Heckler had set and Vohlmann had affirmed regarding John's bonus. Franklin's suit was now worth a lot more than fifty thousand dollars, and for each settlement dollar over that amount, John's bonus would be reduced by a buck. John deserved to be called "stupid idiot." Stupid idiot. That's exactly what he was, all the way around. His job sucked, his whole career sucked, no, let's be honest about it, his whole life sucked, not because of tyrants like Heckler, not because of cheating by Sandy, but because John himself was just plain stupid. That's what the Franklin case was all about. That's what it had exposed. What he needed now more than ever was that severance package, so he could just quit this place, go a million miles away and start all over again and not be so stupid. In the meantime, John needed to pull himself together and scramble to pick up his daughters in time for dinner and the Lynx game afterward. How could he begin to tell them how he felt? How could they begin to understand? More than ever, he wanted a talk with Steve.

♦ CHAPTER TWENTY-FIVE ♦

Crazy Man

THE MERCURY HAD BEGUN ITS CLIMB late the night before, as a warm front, with the portent of snow, had moved in from the west. By the time John exited the tower on his way to Betty's Place, the temperature had to be pushing thirty-two. John's shoes crunched on the wet grit underfoot, and he hugged the inside of the sidewalks to avoid the road spray kicked up by passing traffic. A few minutes later, Betty's came into view, and standing there already was Steve, wearing an open coat with gloveless hands on his hips. He sported his bomber hat, flaps up, at a jaunty angle.

"Tropical heat wave to remind us of heaven," Steve said, with a smile extending from ear to ear. Given Steve's sunny face and confident stance, John figured his friend had finally found work. For the moment, John forgot his own woes and greeted Steve warmly.

"I don't know about heaven," John said, "but maybe March."

"At least the deep freeze is behind us. Days are getting noticeably longer, now, you know."

"I wouldn't have noticed. Whether in the daylight or the dark, we still have a solid month of winter left."

With that exchange, the two friends entered Betty's Place and found a booth. To John's astonishment, when Steve removed his bomber hat, he revealed a shaved pate, as shiny as the head of a professional wrestler in the spotlight, not just a butch cut like the last time. "What the hell?" The words spilled out of John's mouth.

"What, the Jesse Ventura look?" Steve passed his hand proudly over the top of his smooth head. "I decided that if I'm going to save money on haircuts, I ought to go all the way and really save money on haircuts. Now I shave it every morning, along with my face. What do you think?"

I think, you don't have a job or even a good prospect, or you wouldn't be talking like that—or looking like that, John said to himself. "I think you must be in the Navy Seals," John said, in reference to Governor Ventura's frequent invocation of his Navy Seal experience. "Who knows, you too might be governor some day."

"I told Beth I'm going to keep it shaved until I land a job." Steve said, as he poured the water.

"Uh, no offense, Steve, but how are you going to get a job, looking like that?"

"Jesse Ventura got a job looking like this." He had a point. Just then, Louise pulled up to the booth, and with a big *'pop'* of her gum expressed her reaction to the flesh-colored bowling ball on top of Steve's shoulders.

"You got cancer—if you don't mind my asking—or is this a delayed fad in reaction to Gov The Mind?" Louise pulled out her order pad and pen. She wasn't expecting an explanation any more than she needed one.

"By popular demand, Louise. All the beautiful women out there wanted to see Steve the Body, so I decided to humor them." The men placed their orders.

"Back to your question, John, about 'the look.'" Steve passed both hands over the top of his head, as if to brighten the polish. "I'm a new man. Born again, and the head shave is like a daily reminder that I'm a follower of Christ Jesus. Every day, I can pour water over my head in remembrance of my baptism by the Holy Spirit."

John lowered his glass from his lips without taking a sip. Born again? Christ Jesus? Holy Spirit? John had had an acquaintance once in college, back at the "U," Chip Gulliver, who had fallen into one of the many cults that seemed to recruit on campus—the Moonies or some similar group. After a few months with the cult, Gulliver began to talk utter nonsense, gave away all his belongings and then disappeared altogether. For the first time in years, John thought about those cults, thought about Gulliver.

"Whoa, Steve! Back up a second." John wasn't sure how far he needed Steve to back up, but worry about his friend's job prospects had turned into a very different sort of concern. He had to save Steve before it was too late. "Is everything okay?" John asked.

"Is everything okay?" Steve let out a hearty laugh. "My friend, not only is everything okay, it's truly great." He pushed his glasses back to the bridge of his nose—at least that little piece of Steve hadn't changed—

placed his arms on the table and leaned toward John. "I've found Jesus, or more accurately, he's found me, and John, it's made all the difference in the world. Maybe I don't have a job, maybe I don't even have a good prospect for a job now, but in the end, Jesus will take care of me and my family. For the first time in my life—the first time, for crying out loud—things are beginning to make sense. You know, we humans are so arrogant, so sinful. We think we know exactly how to go about things, how things ought to be; we think we have 'the plan.'" Steve raised his hands off the table and with his first two fingers on each hand made little quotation marks in the air. "All God can do is shake his head and laugh. But mostly just shake his head. 'The plan'"—Steve marked another set of quotation marks in the air—"is God's plan, and whatever dreams we ourselves might harbor, his plan rules." Steve took a sip of water, and by the power of suggestion, John too lifted his water glass.

However, John carried it only halfway to his mouth before he set it back down. There entered his thoughts the terrible possibility that Steve had simply snapped under the pressure of unemployment, of his self-perceived failure as an educated, experienced, middle-aged middle manager, husband and family man. There in front of John sat the funny, intelligent, not altogether goofy looking—when he had hair, at least—all-around good person, his long-time friend and confidant, at least in a work setting, who had flipped his lid, gone gaga, whacko.

As if prompted by something in the water, Steve surged ahead. "Now my plan is to follow God's plan, and what better plan could there be?"

"And what's that plan?" John could not bring himself to say, "'God's plan." It might signal the wrong message. It might be misinterpreted by Steve and be viewed as active encouragement of Steve's insanity, if in fact one could encourage such a thing. Besides, it occurred to John that diners at neighboring tables might be able to overhear the conversation.

"That's the interesting part, John. I don't know yet what the plan is."

"Sorry Steve, but how can you follow a plan if you don't know what it is?" John realized he was trying to reason with a crazy person.

"I'll find out."

"How and when, Steve?"

"In due course. Through daily prayer, I ask my Lord Jesus to show me the way. Show me what he would have me do with my life."

The food arrived just in time, like a temporary cure, John thought, for

Steve's insanity. Louise slid down John's side of the table the ham and cheese with fries and left Steve with the bowl of vegetable beef soup. Where could John possibly take the conversation now? The weather? The Timberwolves? His own woes of late? But where would he begin with his own trials and tribulations? Whatever he said, it was all too likely to fan the flames around God and Jesus talk. Better stick to small talk, he advised himself. However, before he could steer clear of anything provocative, Steve pre-empted him.

"So how's everything under the new guy?"

"Fine, just fine."

"No it isn't. Let me ask again. How's everything under the new guy?"

Steve was definitely insane, John concluded. "Well, okay, it's kind of wait and see." John hoped the mild qualification would satisfy Steve.

"Wait and see about a severance package?"

"Yeah, wait and see."

"Have you brought it up with the new guy?"

"Yeah, as a matter of fact."

"And . . . ?"

"He's going to take another look at it once the lawsuits I'm involved in are resolved." So far, so good. Maybe this insanity thing was like a zigzag run down the edge of a football field. Now you were inbounds, now you were out.

"And how are the lawsuits coming?" The question felt like a jab with an ice pick.

"Not so hot, I mean one of them. The other one, the big one, hasn't really taken off yet, but I have to meet with the bank's lawyer tomorrow about it."

"What do you mean by one's not going so hot?"

"Hell . . . I mean, heck,"—John corrected himself without thinking, then almost chuckled aloud for having altered his diction because of the "God effect"—"I really shouldn't be upset about it. It's close to being settled, just not on terms that are very favorable to the bank and certainly not very favorable to my bonus prospects. I guess I'm still feeling burned by my deposition experience." John remembered why he had set up lunch with Steve in the first place.

"What happened?"

"I got deposed—yesterday."

"That happened to me, once, years ago." By God? John worried. "It was a lender liability suit against Fake Bank—a non-starter claim, as it turned out. A guarantor claimed the bank had told him they'd never go against the guaranty, and well, I guess it came as a big surprise when they did go after him. I got all nervous about the deposition, but it turned out to be slow, boring and mostly irrelevant, as far as I could tell. The case just faded out after that."

"Well I got grilled, just like chicken on the barbecue."

"Sounds like fun."

"Well, it was a very strange experience. The lawyer on the other side—this was the discrimination suit I told you about, remember?" Steve nodded acknowledgment. "—was gorgeous, and she started out almost as if we were having a get-acquainted conversation, about books and whether I liked the Twins, what I majored in in college. She's not with any firm you'd recognize. In fact, she's not even with a firm. Just on her own, some kind of social do-gooder type who goes after the bad guys of the corporate and Republican world. I was actually falling for it, you know, feeling very relaxed and even very charmed by this woman, and it even crossed my mind to ask her out after the case is over, but then she grilled me like chicken. My lawyer, this . . ." John started to say "asshole" but caught himself ". . . slob from Whiley & Cobb went ballistic afterward. Truth is, Steve, I really did screw up."

"How do you mean?"

"Well, I told this guy William Franklin, the black guy who's suing the bank, that he was the victim of racism, and I guess that pretty much cinched his case against HeartBank."

"I still don't see how you screwed up."

How could Steve respond this way if he was in possession of his senses? Wickley was beginning to look normal. Normal? Hardly, but still, how could Steve question the stupidity of John's statement to Franklin if Steve was sane?

"Steve," John said, with an ironic smile. "I basically handed the guy a loaded pistol and said, 'Here, aim this at the bank and pull the trigger and you win yourself a hefty severance package in the form of a winning discrimination lawsuit.'"

"Was it true?"

"Was what true, that he has a winning case?"

"That he was the victim of racism."

John hesitated and scrutinized Steve's face. Despite the shaved head and the Jesus talk, Steve seemed perfectly lucid. John looked around to assess the risk of eavesdropping by neighboring diners. In a lowered voice John said, "No one at HeartBank would ever dream of admitting it and most would deny it occurred, but I'm telling you, Steve, as sure as I'm sitting here, that William Franklin was nothing but a pawn in the corporate diversity game. It wasn't just Heckler, it was the whole organization. I can't prove it, I mean, I can't point to anything specific and say 'Look, here it is, outright discrimination, a bunch of whites dressed up in hoods and sheets yelling 'Nigger,' but there's racism at work, nonetheless. And it gets terribly complicated, because the William Franklins get hired and dumped somewhere, and then one of two things happens. Either the guy is left to fend for himself—good luck, if you're black as coal and from a place like Atlanta, and you're here in subzero winter, surrounded by Minnesota nice—or, if you dress and talk white enough, you're promoted right smack dab over the better-qualified whites, who, right or wrong, develop resentment and fall into a reactionary, racist mode—never out in the open, of course, but it's there. Then, of course, there *are* plenty of people, you discover, who have got to be racist, the way they talk in private. Anyway, based on what I'd observed about how blacks and certain other minorities are sprinkled around a place like HeartBank, and given what William himself had described about his own experience, I gave him my comment—that he was the victim of racism—and he ran with it."

"So what's so bad about your telling him, if you honestly believed it?"

"Steve, for Christ's sake." The word "Christ" was out before John could stop it, but Steve seemed unfazed. "It's so fucking unprofessional." John could feel himself blush.

"That's something I've learned not to do since I met Jesus," said Steve, gracefully. "It simply pollutes our speech. After all these years of swearing, it's tough not to, but I pray every day that I'll be able to control my tongue, all in his honor."

"Sorry." Sorry? Why was it necessary to apologize to a crazy person?

"It's okay. I'll pray for you too." Pray for me? John had never been particularly superstitious, but he worried that Steve might cross the line with his Jesus stuff, wake up in the middle of the night and lay some sort of curse on John, just like that, just because of a dysfunctional synapse.

Prayers were fine, but not if they led to curses, and John's visceral reaction was that a narrow line separated prayers from curses. "I know what you're getting at, and I'm telling you, John, it's time that good people like you inside the amoral corporation stood up and said 'This is wrong. I don't care if the bank is going to get sued, I don't care if I'm going to get fired—with or without a severance package—but this behavior on the part of an individual or by the organization as a whole is just plain wrong.' The world is screwed up, my friend, if you think you screwed up because you spoke the truth. In the end, you have to do the right thing, especially when conventional behavior is the wrong thing."

Do the right thing. His father's advice, exactly, and John couldn't think of a saner person than his father. But his father had all his hair and a job—albeit at a lumberyard—and didn't go around preaching about God and Jesus. When the check came, Steve snatched it right out of Louise's hand. Unemployed, no prospects on the horizon and he grabs the check like it's his prize, thought John. On balance, Steve's definitely off balance. But what to do? As the two men donned their overcoats, John watched his friend carefully and pitied him.

Outside, Steve stuck a toothpick in his mouth and, just as in old times, John anticipated, prepared to tell a funny story. After the shock of seeing Steve in a condition of mental imbalance, John needed a funny story more than ever.

"John, I'd like to invite you to prayer group." John shivered and buttoned his coat. So it was a cult after all. "We meet every Thursday morning at the Lafayette Club, where one of the group is a member. People generally arrive at around seven o'clock for breakfast, followed by scriptures and a prayer session. You're certainly more than welcome."

What further evidence did John need? No cult would meet at the Lafayette Club, and surely, no prayer group would meet at the old, uppercrust club on the shores of Lake Minnetonka. I've got to call Beth, he told himself, and find out what's really going on. Maybe I can help her help Steve. If ever there was a chance to do the right thing, now was the right time. "No, uh, thanks, Steve, but I don't think so," as he instinctively took a step back from what he considered to be a sick man.

"Well, if you ever change your mind; if you meet Jesus on the street someday—today, tomorrow or next year—or if you don't meet him on the street and you'd like to meet him at the Lafayette Club, you'll be more than welcome."

"Thanks, Steve. I appreciate it." And whatever it is that has snapped inside that shaved head of yours, I really, truly feel sorry for you, your wife and your family.

John strode back toward HeartBank Tower until it occurred to him that it was imperative to reach Beth before Steve returned home. He broke into a trot, but by the time he reached his office, he realized he had done so probably before Steve had even reached the parking lot. John punched in the Torseths' home phone number and waited for Beth to answer. Although John and Steve had been friends for years, their friendship revolved almost exclusively around work. John had met Steve's wife only a half dozen times, if that, and under the circumstances, he felt awkward even before she picked up the phone.

"Hello?" It was a woman's voice.

"Beth?"

"Yes, who's this?"

"John Anchor, remember me?" John figured it must have been a year or better since he'd last seen Beth—at a Christmas party put on by a group of "Fakers" (current employees or alumni of Fake Bank).

"Oh, yes, sure. How are you?" Her voice betrayed no sign of distress.

"Fine, fine. I was just calling about Steve, you know, to see how he's doing." A pregnant silence followed, a sure sign, John thought, that something was awry. He began to worry that Beth would break down, that he'd get sucked into a conversation from which he couldn't easily extricate himself, and Steve would enter the house and wonder what was going on and go completely berserk, and who knows, shoot his wife, then himself.

"I thought you were having lunch with Steve today?"

"I did. I mean we did. That's why I'm calling." John figured Beth would appreciate that he called so soon after having witnessed Steve's mental disturbance first-hand.

"Is something wrong?" The surprise in Beth's voice threatened to complicate the conversation. Didn't she realize Steve was off key? Maybe she's too close to him, John thought. On the other hand, there's the shaved head. She ought to see the strangeness in that.

"Well, no," John didn't know how to broach the subject. "I mean, what's with the shaved head?" It was all John could get out. Except in a swearing context, "God" and "Jesus" were simply too awkward to mention. Someone else would have to bring these words up before John would feel comfortable mentioning them, and he hoped that Beth would say them and give him an opening.

"Oh." She laughed. "People who know Steve are kind of taken aback by it, especially now in the dead of winter. I'm getting pretty used to it, and it seems to help his mood, so I'm all for it. By the way John, I just want to thank you for calling. Outside of people in the prayer group, no one will have anything to do with Steve. None of his old friends or acquaintances at Fake Bank ever calls to see how he's doing, let alone to offer any help." There was that pair of words again—"prayer group"—uttered by Beth, as if it were perfectly normal to do so. John now realized the situation was worse than he'd imagined—in desperation, Steve's wife had fallen prey to the cult as well. Or was she nuttier than a fruitcake too?

"That's too bad," he said. "I'll make a point to stay in close touch with Steve." John meant it. He didn't know what else to do but keep close tabs on his mentally unstable friend and apparently, his unstable friend's unstable wife. The psychology business or psychiatry business—he wasn't sure of the difference beyond intensity levels in need and treatment—was totally alien to John. He was wholly out of his league and worse, he didn't know a soul who was in the psychology or psychiatry league, except, of course, all the psychology majors that wound up working in the HR department at the bank.

"Please do," Beth encouraged him. "By the way, how are you doing? Steve mentioned that you yourself were trying to get a severance package."

"Yeah, sort of. Still working on it." The concept scared John. If the severance part of severance package pushed you over the edge as it had Steve, it no longer seemed to be something a rational person would wish for.

"Good luck." Beth's voice was too cheerful. John knew better, but he wondered for an instant whether insanity was contagious.

"Thanks, Beth." With that, John ended the conversation, perplexed and disappointed in himself. He had tried to do the right thing but had failed in the execution.

◆ CHAPTER TWENTY-SIX ◆

The Meeting

BEFORE VOHLMANN CALLED THE MONDAY MORNING staff meeting to order, the room was abuzz with the news that had bludgeoned everyone on the way to work: Lake Bank, HeartBank's rival down the street, was to be acquired by Citigroup. Headlines reminiscent of JFK SHOT IN DALLAS screamed from the newsstands on the street corners of downtown Minneapolis, and all the local morning radio shows covered the story, just as they carried school closings and road conditions the morning after a paralyzing blizzard.

"Three thousand jobs, mostly middle management, kaput," Blowhard said, as he rolled up his sleeves to start the day for his hairy forearms. He was right for once, at least according to the news reports. "And they're offering big packages to all managers who get the ax." That part had not been reported. "A buddy of mine says they're handing out twelve months, in some cases, fifteen months."

John thought about Steve, who had less than three months left out of only a nine month severance package, and now, to boot, Steve would be competing with all those former colleagues of his at Fake Bank. On the other hand, John figured, Citigroup's acquisition of Fake Bank would compound the pressure on HeartBank—the only major bank still headquartered in the Twin Cities—to join in the M&A game. This pressure, John figured, heightened the chances that his litigation contingency would be overwhelmed by mass layoffs and that his nine-month severance package would expand to twelve months or better. Furthermore, as he had decided long ago, once he left HeartBank, he was leaving banking altogether, so the prospect of thousands of bankers on the street didn't particularly worry John. No, on balance—the plight of his friend notwithstanding—today's news wasn't all bad.

Vohlmann entered the room about ten minutes late. "Sorry, folks, for the delay. I was on the phone with Mike talking about the big news. Really, I think this is actually great news for us. It'll create such chaos in the local marketplace, we'll be able to clean up. I can tell you, our friends at Lake will lose market share from day one. They'll be so preoccupied with the acquisition, conversion issues, layoffs, turf wars—I hear a number of their national lending groups are now going to be based in New York—it'll look like a disaster zone over there in no time and for a very long time. Mike says this is a tremendous opportunity for us, and you know, I think Mike is absolutely right."

"I heard rumors that HeartBank is now a target of Chase," Sycophant said. John couldn't tell whether Sycophant's tone reflected concern or one-upsmanship.

"I haven't heard anything to that effect," said Vohlmann. "In fact, if you read the story in the *StarTribune,* Brinkman was asked that very question—I mean, whether Citigroup's move would force HeartBank to take action. He was quoted as saying that HeartBank had no current plans to merge with anyone else; to acquire or be acquired 'just for the sake of doing a deal,' he said, so I think we can all be confident that HeartBank won't be thrown into chaos the way just about every other major bank has been over the past few years. Mike reassured me too and said that Brinkman is too independent to want to be a copycat."

John wasn't buying, and he wondered how many others around the table weren't convinced that HeartBank wouldn't fall next. After all, its stock had been in the doldrums for a number of weeks, and its P/E—price to earnings—ratio had fallen behind the bank stocks that were considered long-term survivors. If Vohlmann was hanging his hat on "No current plans," then Vohlmann was either fooling himself or trying to fool others with the corporate line. In reality, "current" meant, "as of the very moment I say 'current.'" A message waiting back at the CEO's office or a phone call that afternoon could very well put "current" in the past. But so what? The sooner Brinkman plunged HeartBank into the mergers and acquisition game, the greater the likelihood that John would have his severance package, and twelve months or more, at that.

Little seemed to knock Vohlmann off task, and after no more than five or ten minutes of discussion about the demise of Fake Bank and its implications for HeartBank, Vohlmann turned to his agenda.

"As you can see from the agenda I'm passing around," Vohlmann said, as he licked his thumb to separate copies in his hand for distribution, "there are several initiatives we need to work on. First is the Fall Festival Virus Contingency Plan." Originally named the Halloween Virus because it was set to go off around the world next October 31, the potentially catastrophic virus had been renamed by HeartBank pursuant to pressure from the Diversity Council. "Some people"—just who, John couldn't imagine—"might be offended by the word 'Halloween,'" Vohlmann had explained once, with a straight face. Irrespective of what it was called, the virus threatened to erase files and applications from the vast majority of computers around the world. Or so the world was told. According to conventional knowledge, a disgruntled employee at World Online—now the biggest online service in the world—had created the virus about a year before and ensured that virtually every member of WOL picked it up and spread it. The crime was uncovered six months later, and since then, untold billions of dollars had been spent in an all-out effort to eradicate the errant virus before what the popular media were calling "Doomsday."

Vohlmann looked down the table at his systems person. "Jason, maybe you could tell us what's up with the contingency plan."

In front of Jason Wysgaard, whom everyone called the Wizard or just the Wiz, was a stack of handouts, with the stapled corners one precisely on top of another, curled higher than the other corners. "Yeah, what I'm going to pass out is a Fall Festival Contingency Plan matrix, with instructions and format guidelines." The Wiz shipped half the stack down the table to his right and half to his left. While John watched the papers flow like white pincers around to his place at the table, he wondered why the head techie in the department hadn't sent the materials to everyone by e-mail.

"What you'll see on the matrix are a number of contingencies we tried to imagine, situations that could arise if the virus shows up in some or all of our computers. If you turn to the second page, for example, you'll see some of these." Like a flock of pigeons taking flight, pages turned around the table. "The first one assumes we have a system-wide failure—all our systems go down. Now go over to the next column and you'll see the proposed solution—lease extra computers. In the next column, you'll see timing constraints. In the next, certification that the leased computers are Fall Festival-safe and finally, if you flip to page seven"—although the pages weren't numbered—"you'll find a second matrix covering the backup contingency plan, in this case, the contingency being that the leased computers aren't Fall Festival-safe." Again, a great fluttering fanned across the conference room, as John's peers, like a classroom of children following the directions of a visiting prestidigitator, obediently followed the command of the Wizard and flipped through the handout to the backup matrix. They turned at different speeds, and the inevitable, "What page?" accompanied the search. John worked hard to suppress a laugh. The Wiz was serious, but there was nothing particularly unusual about that. The Wiz was a wiz at being a wiz; at pulling the techie wool—or more accurately, the cloak of techie geekspeak—right over everyone's eyes. What struck John as funny was how everyone else at the table appeared to be taking the Wiz so seriously—all except Jenny, he hoped, but she was sitting next to him and it was hard to see her facial reaction. He leaned toward her to find out.

"Sounds like the techies found their sequel to Y2K," John whispered in a test of his colleague's reliability.

Jenny turned her chubby face toward John but showed no humor. Tiny weights of disappointment lowered the corners of John's mouth. However, as he turned his face back toward the Wiz, Jenny leaned over to give her reply. "No, it's better than that. The techies found their sequel to the actual virus scrubbing."

John whispered back, "If they were so damned good at scrubbing—as they told us they were—why do we need the contingency plan? And how many goddamned contingency plans do we need?"

"As many as it takes until the techies take over and HeartBank becomes TechBank."

"John, did you want to say something?" Vohlmann interrupted. John straightened up like the target of a reprimand in grade school, although he wasn't sure whether Vohlmann had issued a reprimand.

"Uh, well, actually, I had some questions about this." All gazes turned to John.

"Shoot," said Vohlmann.

"I was just a little curious as to why we need to spend so much time and money building contingency plans." John felt a jaw open under each set of eyes that was trained on him. To question the Wiz in public bordered on sacrilege. "First of all, for months now, we've been told how many resources were needed for the scrubbing project." John couldn't bring himself to say "Fall Festival," and "Halloween" at this point would have drawn gasps, so he avoided both terms. "Time and again, we coughed up the resources. Then, in the monthly updates, we were told how far ahead of schedule we were, how—thanks to the efforts of our IT staff—we were in fine shape." John was on a roll, but he knew he was in dangerous waters—and all because he had been caught whispering to Jenny. Oh, if only he'd kept his trap closed altogether, he wouldn't be slitting his throat in public. Without looking at him, John could see the Wiz scowl. "Yet, despite all that, now we're told that the scrubbing might not have worked and we need to do up contingency plans." John felt emboldened to proceed, and before he noticed from the cold stares around the table that no one—except for Jenny, though her support, if it was there, was totally silent—agreed with him. "It makes me question the cost of all the scrubbing or maybe the competence of the people doing the scrubbing." He had done it. He had grabbed the knife or maybe it was his Cross pen, with the point exposed, and jabbed it smack through his Adam's apple.

"If that's the way you feel," Vohlmann said, eyebrows higher than ever, "then maybe you need to dialogue with Jason off-line. Jason, why don't you continue taking us through the matrix."

John blushed. Dialogue with the Wiz off-line? That was a shallow encryption for "You're out of line, so drop it." The person next to him shifted his chair to open the distance from John. The Wiz, meanwhile, droned on about his convoluted matrix, while one set of eyelids after another around the table drooped, despite the number of empty coffee mugs in the room. John was too upset to be drowsy or to listen, but he noticed that Vohlmann himself suppressed a succession of yawns. When the Wiz had finished, John watched in amazement as Sycophant snapped to full consciousness, raised his hands off the table and clapped. Once, twice and three times—but on the third clap, John heard someone else clap from the other end of the table and another and another, until everyone, even Jenny, John realized, was clapping. John couldn't clap, and he did a poor job of feigning a coughing fit.

"Excellent job, Jason," said Vohlmann, and he sounded as if he meant it. He poured himself another cup of coffee and turned to the next item on the agenda. "Moving on," he said, "some of you have probably heard about the HeartSmart initiative. Corporate Marketing is rolling it out in a number of departments this week, and I'd like us to be leaders in the fantastic effort. I've asked Craig Fiskbeck to help us understand what it's all about. Craig, you've got the floor."

John cringed. Vohlmann had just yielded the floor to the Minister of Propaganda, also known as the Minister of Bamboozlement. "Thanks, Fred," the Minister said. "I have a little presentation about HeartSmart, which the bank, from Mr. Brinkman all the way down to Mike, is pushing really hard. I attended a roll-out meeting last week and got a sneak preview of the program. Its going to make a huge difference at HeartBank–a difference we're all going to notice, whether we're employees, shareholders or customers." John caught himself with mouth shifted to one side like a skeptic and shifted it back and forth to stifle a snicker. The Minister of Propaganda was worse than Sycophant. No one took Sycophant seriously, except, of course, Sycophant, but John noticed that Vohlmann treated the Minister like a holy man.

"Could someone get the lights, please?" said Vohlmann. Sycophant leapt to the call while others took turns at the two large coffee urns for refills.

"I think you're going to like this videotape," the Minister said, as he pointed the remote control device in the direction of the equipment at one end of the conference room. Suddenly, music boomed like a row of cannons, woke up the two decaf drinkers in the room and yanked Blowhard's finger right out of his nostril. The others grimaced, instinctively smacked their hands over their ears and watched the Minister fumble desperately with the remote to tame the volume. To the accompaniment of a drum roll with trumpets in the background, the HeartBank logo appeared–a red heart superimposed on the North Central area of a green map of North America, with thin lines branching out to smaller red hearts on the West Coast, the South and the East Coast–tiny at first, then larger, larger, like some kind of alien blob until it threatened to charge right off the screen and swallow up everyone and everything in the room. Then, with a cymbal crash at the end of the drum roll, the logo disintegrated, and in its place sat Max Brinkman at a carefully choreographed angle on the edge of his massive desk. He appeared without his suitcoat, but his handlers' lame attempt to project a casual image was undercut by Brinkman's starched, white custom-tailored shirt and his Galento tie. As the trumpets faded, the CEO spoke to the masses.

"Hi. I'm Max Brinkman, CEO of HeartBank." John noticed Brinkman's eyes move from left to right in a telltale sign they were following a teleprompter. "I'd like to talk to you about an exciting new program here at HeartBank. It's called 'HeartSmart.' Over the coming months, HeartSmart will gain tremendous momentum and will propel this great organization of ours to even higher levels for the benefit of our customers, our employees and our shareholders. What is HeartSmart? Let me explain. HeartSmart is a program designed to encourage the development and implementation of good ideas—across the company—that will improve the way we do business, enhance our revenues and reduce our expenses." With these dazzling remarks, Brinkman moved away from his desk, slowly and stiffly, so as not to miss a word on the teleprompter. If you pay a guy enough dough, John thought, he gets to work from a script. "Our greatest resource besides our technology is our people . . . and their ideas. Let's take a look around the company at some examples of HeartSmart ideas."

John gave his head a quick shake in astonishment over the words, "besides our technology." Had he really heard that correctly? He looked around the room for confirmation, for a sign of surprise or outrage, but he detected none. Surely, he thought, the PR folks who wrote the script would not have Brinkman say something so preposterous. But just then, Jenny rolled her chair closer to John's and whispered in his ear. "It's nice to know we're moving up in the world," she said, sarcastically. "I thought it was technology first, capital second and people third."

John turned toward her so she could see the disbelief in his face. How in the world could the scriptwriters have Brinkman say such a thing, or had the CEO insisted that it be written that way? And why wasn't the room abuzz if it wasn't asleep? John whispered back, "I have my first HeartSmart idea: can the video." Jenny coughed to stifle a laugh.

By this time, the action in the video had moved from Brinkman's office to the scene of a HeartSmart idea in process. The setting was a modest conference room, and around a table sat an African American woman, an African American man, an Hispanic- or Indian-appearing woman, a man in a wheelchair, an Asian woman and a white man, who watched a white woman next to him signing for the deaf. Jenny leaned forward discreetly toward

John and said in a barely audible voice, "Are we working at HeartBank in Minneapolis or Bank of New York in Manhattan?"

John whispered back, "The only place you'd see a group like that around here is at a meeting of the Diversity Council."

"I think your idea about distributing the reconciliation report is a good one, Steve," said the African American woman.

The camera shifted to the white man, who faced the signing woman. He signed in return and the woman said, "Thank you."

"By changing the routing so it comes directly to us from output services," continued the African American woman, "we'd get it a whole day earlier and the mail room wouldn't have to handle it twice."

"That's right Sharon," the man in the wheelchair said. "And besides, the business development people who got it before us didn't need to see it. This idea will save them time too.

"This sounds like a HeartSmart idea to me," said the next woman, with what John thought was an Hispanic accent.

"What's a HeartSmart idea?" asked Sharon.

"It's an idea that will somehow improve the way we do business, increase our revenues or decrease our expenses," said the woman who John thought was Hispanic. "It's real easy to submit a HeartSmart idea. You fill out this form," she said, as the camera zoomed in on a pre-printed form with the HeartBank logo on top. She was definitely Hispanic, John decided, probably Mexican—"I always carry several with me, in case I have a HeartSmart idea I want to submit. I just fill out the form—it's real easy—and send it to the HeartSmart Committee. The Committee meets every two weeks and reviews all the HeartSmart ideas that have been submitted. All ideas are recognized with a HeartSmart certificate of appreciation. The ones that are accepted are assigned to an implementation team. Anyone whose HeartSmart idea gets accepted receives a fifteen-dollar credit toward a share of HeartBank stock."

Jenny leaned toward John's ear and said quietly, "And how much of a credit do I get for watching this asinine video?"

John smirked and whispered back, "Not nearly as much as Brinkman gets for reading the script."

The deaf man in the video signed and his signing partner said, "I'd sure like to add to the HeartBank shares I already own."

Music swelled and the setting now became a long row of cubicles somewhere in the Tower. John recognized them as S-cubes, the smallest of the four standard sizes at HeartBank. The camera moved down the row and settled on one occupied by a young blond man, barely out of college, John thought—a "baby banker." The baby banker sat alone at a desk the size of a high-chair tray, with nothing on it except a phone and a small pad of paper. He was on the phone. "Sure, Mr. Johnson," he said, into the phone, "I'd be glad to provide you with the name and number of a personal banker. Let me find out and I'll get back to you . . . Goodbye." The baby banker hung up the phone, opened a drawer to his mini-desk and pulled out a sheet of paper—what's this? A HeartSmart form. In neat, block letters, he wrote "provide every banker with a list of names and numbers of personal bankers, by location."

The canned music swelled while the voice of Max Brinkman, like the great Wizard of Oz, spoke to the audience. "There is no idea too small to be HeartSmart. This banker did the right thing by following up right away on a chance to better cross-sell our products. He's well on his way to earning more shares of HeartBank stock. . . Let's have one more look at a Heart Smart idea."

The setting changed once again, now to a private office, smaller than Vohlmann's but larger than John's, and certainly neater, with furniture more attractive than were the fully depreciated items in John's office. Several large potted plants—the kind you'd be allowed to lease from Backstrom Florist, John thought, if your office were a video set—occupied the background. A woman with Scandinavian-wanna-be blonde hair coloring, dressed in a dark blue power suit and a white blouse but with a silk scarf of pastels tied stylishly around her neck—by the video handlers, no doubt—gazed out the window while she tapped a big red HeartBank pen against her lips. A female voice—presumably hers—echoed in the background. "I wonder how my processing division can be more pro-active in interfacing better with the product development group." The woman's blue eyes narrowed with thought, then widened with revelation, as she punched the air with her pen. "That's it. I could have them form an interface task force to identify ways the product development team can communicate better, so that the processing team will know what new products are being developed, and the processing team can give their input in advance." The woman threw her head back, beamed a big smile at the acoustical tiling above and to distant triumphal music, flung her pen into the air and watched the red implement rotate in slow motion across the room. The rotation accelerated until the pen changed into huge block letters, which then landed horizontally across the screen. That's Heart$mart! the inscription told the viewers.

The trumpets crescendoed until cymbals cut them off. In the final scene, viewers returned to the cavernous office of Max Brinkman, who had resumed his half seat on the edge of his desk. "So you see, HeartSmart ideas can come in all sizes, at all times, in all places, from all people at HeartBank." His head moved from side to side like a TV anchorman's—or like that of a slick salesman in an infomercial. "Before you get back to work . . ."

John turned his head slightly in Jenny's direction, then moved his mouth a little farther and chided, through his clenched teeth, "Yuh, gt bk t wrk, Jnny."

". . . I just want to say this. You've helped make HeartBank the great company it is today. By focusing on HeartSmart ideas in the weeks and months ahead, you'll make HeartBank an even greater company—for our customers, your fellow employees and our shareholders."

"And Chase's shareholders after they take us over," Jenny said back to John.

Music blared while credits rolled against a background filled by the HeartBank logo—"Pizzazz Productions, Makeup by Calypso, Plants provided by Lingon Florist"—he was right about the potted plants being leased—and a host of gaffers, tweakers, boomers and what-nots. John estimated the ratio of video production people to video stars at about ten to one and said to Jenny, "I've got another great HeartSmart idea regarding promotional videos like this one."

"What's that?"

"Sell them to Blockbuster Video for rental in the comedy section."

"In other words," Jenny said in return, "the video is what you'd call a 'HeartSmiles' idea." The two laughed, and for a split second, John lost control of the flatulence he had been feeling since his breakfast of oatmeal. Besides John himself, no one but Jenny heard the little *'thblit.'* Jenny shook as she struggled mightily to stifle a laugh. Not since the same thing had happened to him during a final exam in college, had John found himself in such embarrassing straits. But unlike then, when all he could do was remain hunched over his exam blue book and pretend that someone else had farted, John could dilute his embarrassment by making light of this butt burp.

With his own shoulders shaking in laughter, John leaned toward Jenny and said, "Hey, do you think I can get credit for an idea that rhymes with 'HeartSmart'?" With a noise like air escaping from a balloon, Jenny blew laughter straight out of her mouth, but few people noticed as they adjusted their chairs, opened the blinds, flipped on the lights and poured more coffee.

"Thank you, Craig," said Vohlmann. "That was a fantastic video. Is there any more you'd like to say about HeartSmart?"

"No, except each manager will be getting a copy of the video today or tomorrow, together with an information packet, blank Heart Smart idea forms and a quick guide card like this." The Minister held up a laminated, eight-by-five card with the HeartBank logo on one side and print on the other. "The quick guide card is an easy-to-look-at card with information about how to submit a HeartSmart idea. Any questions?" With puckered lips, the Minister surveyed the room for questions but none came forth. John wondered how long he himself would take to lose the quick guide card amidst the mounds of papers atop his desk.

"I can't over-emphasize how important this new initiative is going to be," said Vohlmann, in support of the Minister of Bamboozlement. "At a meeting of Mike's directs yesterday, we learned that Brinkman has told the stock analysts he expects us to realize over half a billion dollars of value—that's about a buck a share—over the next five years."

The extraordinary claim triggered John's skepticism. He also seized on Vohlmann's statement as a chance to redeem himself from his exchange of humor with Jenny—Vohlmann must have observed it disapprovingly. To veil his doubt and ulterior motive, John assumed a serious tone and countenance and interrupted. "That's an enormous bottom-line figure, Fred. How does he come up with that?"

Vohlmann showed no sign of questioning John's motive. "I think how he gets there, John, is by the two HeartSmart ideas per person per year with a revenue enhancement or cost savings per idea of one thousand dollars. Spread across—what do we have, 60,000 employees, something like that?—you get to over $100 million per year. Over five years, you do actually come up with over half a billion dollars of shareholder value." *Shareholder value.* Everyone used the term as a way to justify anything from stupidity to deception to falsehood. "Now," Vohlmann continued, with the interior ends of his eyebrows rising into his forehead, "I don't know if they're present valuing—and taking into account a growing employment base and increase in the number of HeartSmart ideas and the value per idea over that five-year period or not. I have to think that if you take all those things into account, you're probably going to see a much bigger number than half a billion. That's why this initiative has so much potential."

John raised one eyebrow and nodded slowly back at Vohlmann, as if Vohlmann himself had devised the brilliant plan to boost the price of HeartBank stock. When Vohlmann asked, "Any other questions?" and looked around the room for them, John jotted down some words and turned his notepad inconspicuously so Jenny could read them. *I'd call it potential fraud!* Jenny narrowed her eyes and nodded ever so slightly to signal her agreement.

"Good," Vohlmann said. The emphasis implied that he was relieved by the absence of any questions. "Now I'd like to turn to OFAC—the next item on the agenda." The dreaded OFAC. It sounded obscene. It was obscene. In fact it was an acronym created by none other than the U.S. Government. John had recently read about it in a corporate-wide memo. The memo was a doozy.

> To: All Managers
> From: OFACCAU
> Re: OFAC Training and Compliance Monitoring
>
> The OFAC Compliance and Audit Unit ("OFACCAU") is responsible for OFAC training, compliance and audit functions throughout HeartBank relating to regulations of the Office of Foreign Assets Control ("OFAC") under the Office of the Comptroller of the Currency. OFAC requires that all national banks develop policies and compliance monitoring programs to ensure regulatory compliance. Each division of HeartBank is required to have appropriate policies and procedures in place and to report all compliance activities to OFACCAU. Compliance activities include, but are not limited to CBT courses, quarterly reports showing that every employee who is subject to OFAC has taken and passed the required courses, and monthly reports to the regional office of the OCC listing all financial transactions and certifying that the bank

has not entered into any prohibited transactions. This is in addition to any ongoing reporting required in connection with suspected Specially Designated Persons ("SDP"s) or involving Specially Designated Nations ("SDN"s).

All Compliance activities must be documented with OFACCAU within the applicable time periods. Any exceptions must be approved by Legal and Audit and must be signed by at least four levels of management. Any questions should be directed to OFACCAU.

cc: Blake Huntington, General Counsel
Will Flaske, Chief Officer of Audit

John could not remember having heard of OFAC before the memo, but he assumed it had been prompted by the Chechen money-laundering scandal that had gotten Puritan Bank into so much trouble a year before. As far as he was concerned, OFAC applied to international transactions, and HeartBank's real estate business was strictly domestic. Very few HeartBank divisions, in fact, had any international connections. It was a bit curious, of course, that the memo had been so widely distributed, but it wasn't the first time that untold thousands of HeartBank employees had received a memo relevant to fewer than a hundred. John suppressed a jaw-straining yawn.

"I asked Stephanie Krimpsky from Audit for some clarification," said Vohlmann. Krimpsky? John wondered if Vohlmann realized Krimpsky was the wrong person to ask for clarification. Years ago, John had consulted Krimpsky about environmental audits of real estate collateral. In response, the beady-eyed anorexic woman had embarked on a half-hour harangue about the bank's potential legal liability for infractions of CERCLA, the backbone of federal environmental cleanup legislation. In her opinion, HeartBank should have entirely avoided real estate collateral—and accordingly, real estate lending. Krimpsky wasn't called the Crimp for nothing. You could see in her thin, straight lips and humorless eyes a need to chase the fun out of work. She was put on the planet to stop risk—any risk associated with business—dead in its tracks. If you were generating revenue for the bank, you were probably assuming far too much risk, is how John interpreted the Crimp's view of the banking world.

"Non-compliance with OFAC could impact us in ways we don't want to be impacted," said Vohlmann. There was that word "impacted" again, abused just as Jenny always said it was. "Wisdom teeth, not people are impacted," she was fond of saying. John stole a glance at her, and she placed her hand gingerly against her cheek and strained her face to mime a toothache. "Stephanie"—the *Crimp,* Fred, the *Crimp*! John laughed to himself—"sent me some proposed policies and procedures for us to review." Vohlmann licked his thumb, preparing to circulate another round of waste paper. "She said responses were supposed to have been in by last Friday, but they're giving us an extension—till noon today—to get ours in."

John fumed inside. It was the same old story. Some anonymous person or committee within the bank would issue an idiotic, overreaching, irrelevant, proposed edict for comment by the business lines. However, the chance to comment was unreasonably brief—a day or two, sometimes a week, if you were lucky. If you managed to find time to comment on or, God forbid, question the proposed edict, your chances of affecting it were slim to none. So why did they solicit comments in the first place? It was a chance to stick your neck out and vote without having a chance for your vote to count.

"Can I ask a question?" Jenny asked, as the handouts made their way around the table. John wanted to cheer her on. Jenny was good at questioning things, and anything relating to OFAC deserved to be questioned.

"Sure," said Vohlmann. John wondered whether Vohlmann would use the same word if Jenny asked, "Can I have an answer?"

"Who drafted the proposed policies and procedures?"

"Uh, good question. I suppose . . . I think someone in Audit. Audit or Legal. Why do you ask?" Curiosity spread across Vohlmann's face.

"It would be helpful to know who actually drafts this stuff so we know what was intended and the extent to which they understand our business. This is the first time I've seen the proposed . . . I'm not sure if anyone else . . . Has anyone seen this before?" Jenny held up the handout as if it were a small, undesirable fish and surveyed the faces around the table. A few audible denials accompanied shaking heads. "Just look at this," Jenny said with a directness she reserved for occasions like this when she wanted to jolt people to their senses. "It says, we're all supposed to take an OFAC-rated CBT—everyone with any customer contact. But what does that mean? What on earth is an OFAC-related CBT?"

"It's a CBT—computer based training—course about OFAC, which you can access on the LAN."

"No you can't." Blowhard weighed in with a volume that caused more than a pair of eyelids around the table to snap open. "I tried last Friday but couldn't find it. I called Audit and they said it wasn't available. Didn't know when it would be." Every once in a while, Blowhard piped up when you wanted him to.

"I'm sure it will be soon," said Vohlmann, optimistically.

"That's the first question," Jenny said. "How soon? And once it is, what's our deadline for completing it?"

"End of the month, is what Audit says," Blowhard said.

"End of the month?" Jenny said, with disdain in her voice. "Who in Audit says end of the month?"

"The Crimp," said Blowhard with a straight face. John couldn't believe it. No one had ever said "the Crimp" in a meeting like this before. Maybe Blowhard wasn't such a bad character after all. John glanced at Vohlmann for a sign of disapproval but detected none. Maybe Vohlmann hadn't heard "the Crimp."

"Wait a second," Jenny said. She was gathering steam now, and John wondered how long it would be before Vohlmann took the conversation "off-line." "What authority does the Crimp have to set the deadline and on what basis? And how the hell can we meet such an arbitrary deadline when we can't even get access to the CBT course? Fred, this is really something we ought to contest. I mean, if the course isn't available—and I don't even know who's responsible for getting it on the LAN—by the deadline, how are we supposed to take the course in time? And that all begs the question of how everyone in the department is going to find the time to take it. So, when we get audited this year, are we going to be written up because we failed to take this OFAC-CBT in time?"

"Maybe we need a little push back," Vohlmann said, using "push back" in the way HR used the words. "I'll try to dialogue with Audit about it, but I think you all need to be prepared to get your people taking the CBT course as soon as it's available. Stephanie . . . What are you calling her . . . the 'Crimp'? Why do you call her that?" A burst of laughter filled the room, but it stopped abruptly when people realized Vohlmann wasn't joining in. "Come on, people. Stephanie said the CBT course shouldn't take more than an hour-and-a-half. I'm sure people can fit this in without a big problem—you know, over the lunch hour, before work, after work or over a weekend." No one saw any humor in what Vohlmann suggested.

Like a man in the water clinging to the side of a capsized boat, John felt a strong urge to let go and swim ashore. His thoughts drifted from the conference room, away from techie talk, HeartSmart ideas and OFAC-CBT to the hope of a severance package. He remembered—later in the morning, he was scheduled to meet with the lawyers about the Walden case. Then he would be able to gauge, perhaps, just how far he would have to swim, how long it would take to resolve the case and approach Vohlmann about a severance package. Meanwhile, Vohlmann's meeting continued, and though John remained seated at the table, his attention never returned to the room. Not until he heard, "That's it. Thanks for coming, everyone," did John snap out of his daydream. He followed the others out of the conference room and watched them head for the lavatories, urged by their consumption of diuretic beverages.

◆ CHAPTER TWENTY-SEVEN ◆

Summary Judgment

IF ZANE WICKLEY WAS A LAWYER John avoided and despised, Tom Kinder was a lawyer John enjoyed and respected. A senior partner at Bakke & Fulsom, Tom Kinder enjoyed a sterling reputation among all who knew him. According to Chuck Lindstrom, the in-house HeartBank lawyer responsible for retaining outside counsel, Tom was known throughout the Twin Cities legal community as a tough but fair-minded litigator, and it had not taken John long to agree with Chuck's assessment. John recalled cheerfully his first encounter with Tom. An imposing figure with weathered skin, thinning, light brown hair and unhurried motions, Tom Kinder exuded confidence and experience. When he shook hands with John and Chuck on the occasion of that first meeting in the Walden case, Tom projected, with hazel eyes and a pleasant smile, a look of warmth, sincerity and trustworthiness. As Tom led his clients from the reception area to his corner office, he greeted everyone, from secretaries to partners, with equal affability and respect.

While Tom went after beverages for his guests, John surveyed the office for more insights into the lawyer on whom he would pin his hopes for an early resolution of the Walden case—and a severance package. He liked what he saw. On one wall was a hunting scene—two men with shotguns aimed at a flock of ducks flying over a marsh, their bird dog at their side, at the ready. On another wall hung a gigantic physical map of Alaska. Crowded onto a credenza were numerous family photos, a stack of plaques that Tom had apparently never gotten around to hanging and various novelties, including an antique toy tractor and wagon. Tom's partner-sized desktop reminded John of his own chronically cluttered workspace, but among the pleadings, folders and notepads was a skiing magazine and the latest issue of *The Economist.* John derived hope from the good omens around the room. In contrast with Wickley, here was a lawyer with whom John would get along, and he figured that his rapport with his lawyer had to bode well for a swift, favorable outcome of the case.

That was back in November, back when Tom had reassured John and Chuck, "This isn't a case that three middle-aged white guys can't handle." They had laughed confidently. But now it was March, and the case had not gone away as easily as the three middle-aged white guys had thought it would. Tom's opening round—a motion to dismiss the lawsuit—had failed, as had settlement negotiations, if that's what you called Walden's offer to settle for $35 million, HeartBank's counteroffer of thirty-five thousand and the response by Walden's attorney too profane for the mild-mannered Tom Kinder to repeat to his clients. After five day-long depositions, boxloads of documents, ten grand worth of legal research and a thirty-page brief, Tom was ready, he said, "for a motion for summary judgment."

"It's a motion that says, 'Look judge,'" Tom had explained, "'there is no dispute over the material facts of this case, and as a matter of law, you should rule in our favor.'" When John had read Tom's brief, he was convinced the judge would rule in favor of the bank. How could it be otherwise? A week later, when John received a copy of the opposing brief filed by Walden's attorney, John jumped straight out of his chair and punched his fist into the air in celebration of the victory that was sure to be his. You did not need a law degree, you did not need to wear a black robe to see not only that Tom Kinder was the better lawyer but that their side held all the cards.

It was now approaching "show time," as Tom referred to court appearances. John and Chuck had been invited to meet with Tom up in his office before the three of them headed for the winning show on the grand stage of a courtroom in the federal courthouse down on Fourth Street. "So, what odds are you placing on our chances?" John said confidently. He knew that no lawyer worth his salt ever guaranteed the outcome of anything in litigation, but under the circumstances, John figured the odds of winning ought to be north of ninety percent.

"Our chances?" Tom sounded surprised by the question. "Oh, I'd say about sixty/forty, to be honest about it." John looked for a glint of humor in Tom's face, or at least his eyes, but he found none. Tom was dead serious.

John's mouth suddenly went dry, and he swallowed hard. "Only sixty percent?" He felt the flash of searing heat that you experience the instant you realize you forgot to attend an important meeting. Going into Tom's office, John had placed his odds of an early severance package at ninety percent. If Tom, the great Tom Kinder, assigned only a sixty percent chance of winning summary judgment, then the chances of a severance package in the foreseeable future had also dropped to sixty percent.

"Summary judgment is tough to win, especially in a case like this, where you have all kinds of facts, statements, conversations, interpretations of documents, that sort of thing." Tom said. "Now, I think we're entitled to summary judgment, and we certainly have the law on our side and enough in the depositions, our affidavits and the documents to show the judge that when it comes right down to it, none of the material facts as we see them is controverted by the plaintiffs, but it's going to be tough." Tom's phone buzzed, and it irritated John until he realized Tom was ignoring it. "However, there's another reason to bring the motion and that's to educate the judge about the case and to show the plaintiffs that we aren't about to back down." Tom looked at his watch. "Well, I suppose we'd better get on our way if you want to get good seats for the hearing."

While Tom packed his briefcase, John cleared his throat. "Tom," he said. He wanted to ask what the next step would be if the judge denied the motion for summary judgment, but just as he was about to speak, he decided posing the question in that way might jinx the outcome.

"Yes?"

"Uh, in how many of your cases do you move for summary judgment?" John composed the question to avoid the jinx.

"Depends. If I think I have a decent shot at winning or, in a case like this, where we ought to win and I want to educate the judge, then I'll bring the motion."

"Ought to win." John repeated the phrase to himself. All the way to the courthouse, he said, "We ought to win," like a mantra, just as he had silently recited the words, "I'm going to get a BB gun for Christmas," for an entire day in early December when he was ten. It had worked then. It ought to work now. He ought to win. He ought to get his severance package. As the trio approached the towering glass-and-Kasota stone courthouse, John dropped behind Tom and Chuck and slipped into his mouth a full stick of cherry DentDream. No doubt they would wind up sitting close together, talking back and forth about the case, and John figured he might want to participate in the conversations.

John could not remember the last time he had been inside a church, but this courtroom reminded him of one. The benches looked like pews, and with just five minutes to go before "'show time," they were filled with men and women in dark suits and solemn faces, who spoke only in low voices. Tom led his clients to an opening in a pew up front on the left. John looked around with curiosity. He had been in courtrooms before, but only in state court, and never in one like this. It was the size of a cathedral, for crying out loud, with wood everywhere. The sixteen-foot-high walls—they had to be at least that high—the ceiling, the floor, the choir box, the judge's throne area, or seat or whatever it was called, the pews, the floor, the tennis court-sized tables where the lawyers sat, were covered with wood the color of the waffles in the photo on the box of Franklin's Frozen Golden Waffles, which were the kind John ate every other morning for breakfast. The Great Seal of the United States filled the wall behind the judge's leather throne, and down below stood an American flag and a blue Minnesota flag, each on a pole ten feet high with an eagle the size of a downtown pigeon on top. The place was high-tech, too. Ubiquitous PCs, computer notebook hookups and the latest in audio-visual technology reminded John of a TV church he sometimes saw when he flipped channels on a Sunday morning. Windowless, the place was well-illuminated by wall sconces and two large lights, suspended from the mile-high ceiling like a couple of UFOs. A short wall separated the congregation from the area reserved for the choir, the high priests and God—Judge Kanker—who John imagined would be larger than life.

It was here that a judge could play God and determine the fate of crooks and criminals, decide the outcome of disputes involving mere mortals. It was here where the judge could advance John's quest for a severance package, and the beauty of the matter lay in the fact that all the judge needed to do was say, "You win" to one side and "You lose" to the other—it did not matter who won or lost, as long as the case was decided. Win or lose, John could then march into Vohlmann's office and say, "Okay, the case is over, now let me go." But as hope swelled in his chest, John remembered what Tom had explained about summary judgment. "Losing a summary judgment motion doesn't mean the other side wins the case, unless there's a cross motion—or counter motion—for summary judgment, and in this case, the other side hasn't brought one."

Tom, meanwhile, looked around for his opponent, Jeffrey Rangle, the high-voiced, greaseball of a lawyer who represented Walden *et alia,* the plaintiffs, or Walden "and Al," as Tom referred to the Latin phrase for "and others." He spotted Rangle in a pew on the other side of the aisle. "There's Rangle," Tom said to John and Chuck in a voice just above a whisper. The two HeartBankers turned their heads to see the man Tom was up against. John thought Rangle looked like a shoe salesman. The relatively young lawyer—thirty or thirty-five, maybe—sported shiny, dark, tightly wavy hair and eyes that fleeced everyone he looked at. Unlike everyone else in the room, the Shoe Man was not wearing a dark suit. Dressed in anticipation of greater success than he had yet seen in his practice, he wore a well-tailored gray plaid suit and a wide red tie that screamed with geometric designs in yellow, black and white. John remembered Rangle from the deposition, which had been a piece of cake after John's experience in the Franklin case. Rangle had tried for more than half a day to elicit something worthwhile out of John; concerted preparations and John's firm grasp of the matter had kept the bad guy at bay. According to Tom after the deposition, "Rangle didn't even score a flinch out of you, John."

Suddenly, all heads turned to the front of the courtroom as a door appeared in the wall and a woman with an official gait marched forth. She stopped in front of one of the tables and addressed the congregation. "The first two cases scheduled for hearings have been settled, so the first matter on for hearing will be Walden, *et al*"—Walden and Al—"versus HeartBank, National Association. Counsel, please take your places." So saying, she turned on her heel and disappeared through the door that then blended back into the wall.

Tom grabbed the handle of his briefcase, sidestepped his way to the end of the pew and entered the sanctuary with the Shoe Man directly behind him. Tom claimed the table on the left, and his opponent walked to the one on the right. Everyone watched as Tom pulled out a yellow legal pad and the Shoe Man hooked up a laptop. In nervous anticipation, John chomped on his gum. Soon the judge would appear and the lawyers would argue. Though the odds of winning the motion for a severance package were only sixty percent, they were still better than even.

"All rise!" Again from nowhere, the woman announcer reappeared and barked the command. The congregation obeyed barely in time as a little man in an oversized black robe ascended the throne. "The United States District Court for the District of Minnesota, Fourth Division, is now in session, Judge Ernest Kanker presiding." Perspiration formed on John's palms. If Judge Kanker did not have the stature one would expect of an exalted member of the judiciary, he certainly bore the face of a "hanging judge." His narrow eyes ran parallel to the horizontal lines in his forehead, his long, humorless mouth and the straight crease in his chin. His thick wavy white hair rested in heavy tufts atop his oversized ears and contrasted with his ruddy face. John tried to imagine what the man must have looked like as a kid, but could not. Maybe he was the kid everyone picked on, John thought, so he became a judge to get back at the bullies.

The judge sat down on his high-backed leather throne, which had been preadjusted to enhance his height. He picked up a gavel and gave it a quick rap. "Sit down," he said in a raspy, contemptuous voice. Like a crowd of school children, the congregation in their dark suits—and the Shoe Man—obeyed. "Gentlemen . . . and ladies," the judge feigned self-correction, "it looks like we have a few ladies in the crowd today . . . we have settlements in the first two cases, so the first matter I'm going to hear is Walden versus HeartBank. Is that who's ready to go here?" The judge peered at Tom, then at the Shoe Man. The two lawyers stood up and affirmed the judge. "Okay then, can I have appearances."

"Tom Kinder with Bakke & Fulsom representing HeartBank, the movant, your honor."

"Jeffrey Rangle, Rangle and Associates, for the Walden parties, the plaintiffs," said the Shoe Man.

"Summary judgment, is that what you're here for, Mr. Kinder?" John's heart pounded. Why was there any question about it?

"That's correct your Honor."

"You already moved for dismissal, didn't you?" The judge said in a tone that suggested he needed a refresher on the case.

"That's right, Your Honor."

"And I denied that motion, didn't I?" John chewed his gum more aggressively. He did not like the tone of "didn't I?"

"Yes, Your Honor," said Tom, with continuing deference.

"And now you want me to give you summary judgment?" John thought he saw a smirk forming on the judge's face. He also noticed the Shoe Man straighten his shoulders with a certain smugness.

"That's right, Your Honor. We believe summary judgment for Heart-Bank is appropriate."

"Well, now," the judge said. His smirk was official, now. "What in the world makes you think it's appropriate?" John's heart raced. The hearing hadn't even started—or had it?—and the judge had already made up his mind.

Tom stood still and tall, but his back was facing John. What color was Tom's face? Was it red? Was he nervous? Was he perspiring? John chewed his gum so hard he forgot to keep his mouth closed. He looked at the judge and for the fraction of a moment, thought he had eye contact with the judge. Tom said, "If Your Honor would like to hear arguments—"

The judge cut him off. "Counsel, I've read your brief and I've read Mr. Rangle's brief, and I have to tell you, you're bringing a tough motion. Now, if you have something more to add, I'm certainly willing to hear it, but I'm just telling you, you're bringing a tough motion." John watched the Shoe Man shift his weight confidently and assume a look on his face that seemed to say, "Gotcha, big-firm lawyer. Didn't think I had a case, didja? But now the judge is trashin' your motion before it's even heard."

"We'd like to proceed, Your Honor."

"Very well then," the judge said with a sigh.

Tom was holding up well under pressure, but John felt as if he were inside a huge inflated balloon with the opening pinched between the judge's thumb and forefinger, and now the judge was releasing pressure and allowing the air to rush out, taking with it all hope of an early resolution to the Walden suit and all hope of a severance package in the foreseeable future. Only if Tom Kinder could persuade the judge to pinch the opening of the balloon, only if Tom could dodge the defensive rush, avoid being sacked, launch a Hail Mary pass and . . . well, there just wasn't much air left in the balloon. Tom picked up his yellow pad from the table and strode to the lectern that faced the judge and stood between the two tables. With remarkable coolness, Tom slipped his left hand into his pocket and rested his right hand on the edge of the lectern. "Your Honor." John stopped chewing his gum. It was utterly tasteless now, and he wanted to be rid of it. "What you have here is an attempted bank robbery. No guns, no masks, no note to a teller, no escape vehicle involved, but an attempted bank robbery, nonetheless, and based on the uncontroverted evidence in this case and as a matter of law, summary judgment is not only appropriate in this case. It is imperative. It is imperative for the preservation of integrity, for the protection of the rules of commercial engagement among members of society.

For if this case is not put to rest here and now, if HeartBank is not granted summary judgment, Your Honor, the plaintiffs will have succeeded in breaching the code of legal and ethical conduct that ensures order in our society. The plaintiffs will have succeeded in robbing a bank."

Tom is taking the high road, John thought. He's tackling the judge's skepticism straight on, and it's beginning to work. The smirk is gone from Kanker's face and he's resting his head against his hand, forefinger on the temple, middle finger on the mouth in the position that means a person is giving serious consideration to what is being said, according to what I learned back in my "Body English for Business" class at the University. Was not Tom the best litigator in town? Couldn't he win this—wasn't he winning this—after all?

"Your Honor, Mr. Rangle has developed a number of very creative theories of liability here, but at the end of the day—in fact, at the very beginning of the day—they amount to nothing more than this: If you run a business, whether it's a large bank or a little corner grocery store, and I come in off the street—no, I don't even do that, I just call you over the phone—and I propose a transaction that you think from the get-go is not something you want to enter into, for whatever reason—it's too good to be true, you don't know how you're going to be compensated, you can't understand it, it doesn't make sense to you, or worse, as is the case here, you're afraid it might actually violate the rules and regulations of the Office of the Comptroller of the Currency—OFAC, specifically, or Office of Foreign Assets Control—you are obligated to enter into that transaction, simply because I've proposed it. Your Honor, if that's the law of this land, then suddenly this becomes a land without the freedom to contract or not to contract. It becomes a land without commerce as we know it."

Go Tom! Hope, deader than a doornail just moments ago, was showing signs of life. And to boot, Tom was bringing OFAC, those dreaded regulations that had been on Vohlmann's agenda just this morning, into the picture, however indirectly. How ironic that they should be good for something. With hope renewed, John revived his gum and chewed with fresh enthusiasm.

"Furthermore, Your Honor, despite attempts to shower this case with depositions, interrogatories, boxes upon boxes of documents and other discovery, the salient facts here are real simple, straight-forward and under the plain light of day, not open to question."

"Stop right there, counsel." The judge seemed to be looking out at the congregation on John's side. "You," he pointed. John turned around to see who was the target of the impromptu order. "No, you in front." John glanced back at the judge, than at the others in the front pew. "You in the middle!" The judge yelled. John looked at him and pointed to himself. "Me?" he mouthed the word. "Yes, I mean *you.* Stand up." John did as he was told. "What's your name?"

"John Anchor."

"What case are you with?"

"I'm with HeartBank, Your Honor."

"You're the banker? Come up here." What in the world did the judge want? John looked at Tom for clues, but he found only puzzlement. John turned and nearly tripped on Chuck's feet as he moved toward the aisle. He couldn't feel the floor under his feet, and his lower legs, his knees, then his entire body went numb as he approached His Honor. The courtroom turned perfectly silent, as every pair of eyes followed John. Without warning, the judge ripped a sheet of paper from his legal pad. "I want you to take this," the judge said. "Here, take it!" He yelled and shook the paper so hard it crackled like fire. John obeyed. "Then I want you to take that gum out of your mouth and stick it on the paper." John wondered if he had ever turned so red in his life. He had certainly never been so humiliated. The bizarre scene had sucked all the saliva right out of John's mouth. He removed the gum, and with hands shaking, he tried to put it on the paper. He fumbled it, and to his horror, it rolled off onto the floor and bounced. John stepped back to see where it had landed, and as he did, he felt his right shoe cushioned by something. The gum. He had stepped right onto the gum. Now the gum stuck fast to the floor and to his shoe, with a hundred rubbery strands in between when he lifted his foot.

"Great! Now you've got it on the floor of my courtroom." The judge's voice boomed so loudly it bounced around John's head like hammer blows. "Stop!" the judge shrieked. "Don't move." Cold with shock and hot with embarrassment, John wondered if the moment of death could be any worse. "Take your shoe off." Chuckles rose from the direction of the pews. John dared not look at Tom or anyone else. He removed his shoe and remembered at the very instant he saw his toe, that in the rush to get dressed that morning, he had not changed the sock with a hole so big that his entire big toe was exposed. Worse yet, he had deferred clipping the nail, a reduction of which was long overdue. He quickly leaned down to pull the sock forward, but it was bound tightly around the base of the toe. It would take some effort to free it. "Look at me." John aborted his effort and looked at the judge. He watched in fear as the man's eyes bulged. "I'm ready to hold you in contempt of court, you hear me?" The judge screamed.

"Yes," John said, but without saliva to lubricate it, the word stopped short of his lips.

"I said, I'm ready to hold you in contempt, did you hear me?"

John tried to clear his throat but there was nothing to clear. He strained to speak. "Yes," the word came out hoarsely. By this time the tittering in the pews had swelled to out-in-the-open laughter. From his elevated platform, the judge looked menacingly at the pews, slammed his gavel down and roared. "Order in this courtroom!" Like canned laughter in a sitcom, the ruckus stopped instantly. John stood where he was, waiting for the next blow, the next freeze-frame in this film of personal horror and humiliation. He stole a glance at Tom, who remained at the lectern. One-half of Tom's mouth seemed upturned with a trace of mirth. The other half was definitely down-turned, pulled by shock, dismay, panic, John did not exactly know. Silence now weighed down so heavily it threatened to squeeze the air right out of the courtroom.

The judge remained standing, with one hand leaning on his gavel and the other pressing down hard on top of the wall in front of his throne. He looked more than angry, John thought. He looked evil. "Mr. Kinder," the judge addressed poor Tom in a low, grave voice. "You have a lot of nerve coming into this courtroom accusing the plaintiffs in your case of bank robbery. It seems to me that there's a lot more to this case than meets the eye, or at least, your eye, and I urge you to try to settle it on reasonable terms before you ever show up here again, is that clear?"

"Yes, sir." Tom looked like a big golden retriever stoically taking the harsh rap for something the cat did.

"And as for you," the judge turned to John, who stood motionless, his big right toe exposed and his shoe in his hand, connected to the floor by long rubbery strands of cherry DentDream. He might as well have been standing there buck naked. "I never ever want to see you or anyone who is related to you or acquainted with you *ever* chewing gum, in my courtroom or anywhere else in the world, *is that clear*?" The judge gave the last three words such propulsion, they flew forth in a spray of spit. "I'm going to call a twenty-minute recess while I get the custodian to clean this mess up and restore order and dignity to this courtroom." With that, he slammed down his gavel, stormed down the steps from his throne and exited the courtroom with his robe flowing rapidly to catch up.

♦ CHAPTER TWENTY-EIGHT ♦

Merger!

WHEN THE CLOCK RADIO SUMMONED JOHN into consciousness the next morning, his first thoughts were not pleasant. Like a bad case of the flu, the memory of yesterday's horror scene in the courtroom swept over him. He now faced the prospect of an interminable sentence at HeartBank. After yesterday's disaster, the Walden case would never settle, and according to Tom Kinder, a trial of the matter was unlikely that year. Then there were all the appeals and procedures that Tom had said could tie up for years a case of this magnitude. It would be forever before a severance package became a reality. In the meantime, John would just have to endure, scarred by yesterday's humiliation and stuck fast in the mire of OFAC directives, technological contingency planning, computer helpdesk run-arounds, HeartSmart ideas, employee recognition programs, Diversity Council meetings and whatever other make-work distractions and obstructions corporate bureaucracy threw into the mix.

John rolled over and faced the clock. It was 5:56. Why on earth should he get up? Why should he go into work today? What was stopping him from calling in sick? He could just leave a message for his assistant, Erica, and be done with it. He would spend the day running errands, go for a jog, maybe even take in a movie. He could go down to the Dunn Brothers coffee shop near Macalaster College, drink mocha and catch up on some reading. He could just walk up Grand Avenue and contemplate his future, contemplate alternatives to his utter lack of desirable prospects at HeartBank. Maybe he could even call Steve. Steve? John remembered. Steve, the poor man, was in terrible shape. Maybe there was a reason for everything. Maybe John was supposed to be humiliated in the courtroom so he would not feel like going into work today so he would think to call Steve so the two could have lunch so John could reassess the situation so John could help Steve. Maybe that was what this was all about. The time was now 5:59. A few more flashes of the colon between the fives, and the numbers would flip to 6:00 even. The news at the top of the hour, John thought. I'll catch the news and then get on with the day, my day, not HeartBank's day.

"Good morning," said an announcer's voice, after the serious-sounding musical salutation marking the top of the hour faded away. "This is Andrea Munson with the news. Yesterday's announcement of Citigroup's intended acquisition of Lake Bank has put increased pressure on other banks to join in the latest wave of consolidation affecting the banking industry or be left behind. We spoke yesterday with Bill Brehmer, a bank stock analyst with Jamison & Reed." John threw back the covers, spun his feet down onto the floor and sat attentively on the edge of his bed.

"I think we're going to start seeing another push toward consolidation," the all-knowing stock analyst said. "With the acquisition of Lake Bank, Citigroup can project itself into a major new market, and I think the pressure will really be on other banks here and in Chicago to punch back. With the retail and business products that a Citigroup can offer the Upper Midwest market, it will be hard to compete unless you can provide the same product offerings with the same efficiency that an organization the size of Citigroup can and will give this market. I've got to believe that HeartBank has something in the works, or if it doesn't, it should, if it wants to survive in this era of bank consolidation."

"That was Bill Brehmer with Jamison & Reed." The announcer took over. "In other news . . ."

John stood up and walked to the bathroom. He thought about what Blowhard had said at yesterday's meeting, something about Fake Bank's offering whopping severance packages to middle managers, and he remembered Sycophant's remark about Chase's taking over HeartBank. Suddenly, John's face lit up. "Yes!" he shouted at the walls of his apartment. If the stock analyst was right and the pressure was on, maybe HeartBank would merge or acquire or be acquired after all, despite the public statements—albeit qualified—by Brinkman to the contrary. Then, maybe, no, no, then probably, no, let's make it *definitely,* they'll offer severance packages by the boatload, and I'll just jump on the boat before they realize I'm handcuffed to the Walden case, thought John. It would only be a matter of time, surely, before HeartBank was swept off its lonely perch by the wave of consolidations.

John took that day off and recharged his morale in all the ways he had considered, except that he never got around to calling Steve. The truth was, John did not know what to say to a friend in the throes of a nervous breakdown.

More days passed, and gradually, the humiliation suffered in the courtroom was eclipsed by growing rumors fueled by Citigroup's acquisition of Fake Bank. From a salesman in Jenny's division, John heard that one of the captains had been seen perusing Chase's annual report while waiting at LaGuardia for a plane back to Minnesota. From someone in Small Business Lending came the report that a group of strangers were sighted in a conference room supposedly doing due diligence—the process of account and systems review that preceded an acquisition. John's friend in Corporate Accounting, the quiet and reliable Paul Dahl, was never in and did not return any of the three voice mail messages John had left over as many days. Blowhard said a "highly reliable" contact of his at Fake Bank had said HeartBank was "next in line for a big announcement." And whether it meant anything or not, John noticed that Sycophant was right. Vohlmann's door *was* closed more often than usual. It was hard to know what to believe and what to question, what was fact and what was baseless rumor, four unreliable, anonymous levels removed from fact. Wholesale gossip and speculation consumed so much time at the office that Vohlmann saw fit to send a broadcast e-mail and reveal to everyone in the department that he had yet to master the keyboard or English or both.

> Lately there has been lots of rumors circulating about a possible take over of HeartBank. None of these are true. I talked to Mike O'Gara and he assured me that HeartBank is not on the block at that time. you can be sure HeartBank wont initiate any M&A activity just because other banks are do it and will not do so unless it is in the clear interest of the shareholders to do so. Therefore I ask that you not engage in the idle speculation and get back to the kind of work that I know you all do so well, which is what makes HeartBank so successful. Remember, lets be Heart Smart for the share holder!

The e-mail did little to squelch the rumors, and there were as many people who saw it as a cover-up, as there were who concluded that

Vohlmann was in a dangerous state of denial, had been ordered to keep quiet about any impending merger or was simply out of the loop.

$ $ $ $

John would remember the day, the third Monday in April. When he stepped outside his apartment, he was just about blinded by the snow that remained from the previous Saturday's surprise storm. Although his watch showed only 7:15 in the morning, the mercury must have already climbed above forty. Water trickled off the roof of his building, and rivulets of melting snow washed down the sidewalk and street out in front. From the front steps, John pretended he was looking at the Mississippi River from an airplane. At this rate, grass would be showing all over the place by sundown. John took a deep breath and smiled. It was a new day, a new week and a new season, all rolled into one. Time for a fresh beginning, he told himself. Time to get off the dime at work, quit the idle speculation, even if that was what the boss had ordered, clean up his office, clear out his e-mail and just wait for an acquisition or merger announcement. It was bound to occur sooner or later.

On the bus to work, John pulled a small notepad from his briefcase and dug around for a pen. The items for his To Do list formed faster than he could jot them down. In no time, he had two pages' worth, sufficient enough to keep him busy for a week. When the bus pulled up to his stop at Fifth and Marquette, he stood tall and hopeful. A renewed sense of direction overtook him—get things in order, wait for the big announcement, get the package and start a new life. John waited for the others to disembark before he himself alighted from the rear half of the articulated bus. The exit positioned him directly in line with a newsstand, and as he moved around it onto the sidewalk, his eyes snapped onto the headline like a magnet onto metal. HEARTBANK JOINS MERGER MOVEMENT in letters meant for a billboard.

John nervously fished around in his pocket for some change, slipped it into the coin slot and grabbed a newspaper, the last one in the stand. So HeartBank merges, but with whom? There it was, under the main headline: "HeartBank announces $27b merger with Loan Star Bank of Dallas." What? Loan Star? What in the world? John stepped across the sidewalk, found a dry spot for his briefcase and began to read the front page. Then, just as abruptly, he decided to march straight down to his office and read it there. As he strode down the sidewalk toward HeartBank Tower, he mused how in an instant, in a flash of time, his To Do list had been altogether scrubbed in favor of:

1. Buy newspaper
2. Read article about merger.

John made it all the way to his floor without encountering a single acquaintance, and he seemed to be the first one there as well. Not even Vohlmann was in. John strode into his office, dropped his briefcase next to the door and dropped into his chair to devour the news.

(Minneapolis) Max Brinkman, CEO of HeartBank Holding Company, announced today in New York that the $115 billion bank holding company he has led for the past six years has signed a definitive agreement to merge with the $80 billion Loan Star Corporation of Dallas, Texas. The value of the merger has been placed at about $27 billion, in a deal that will result in Loan Star shareholders' receiving seven shares of HeartBank stock for every share of Loan Star outstanding. The new company will be called Heart-Star Bank and will be headquartered in Dallas. Clinton Blusser, currently CEO of Loan Star, will be chairman of the new organization, and Maximilian Brinkman will be named CEO. "This transaction will benefit HeartBank and Loan Star shareholders alike," said Brinkman, " by opening new markets, providing more cross-sell opportunities and achieving greater efficiencies. What we have here is an entity that can compete with the biggest of the biggest." The merger is contingent on regulatory approval, but is expected to close later this year.

John read the entire first page before he turned to the supporting articles inside. Nearly the entire first section of the paper was consumed by the story.

Hope surged when he came across a paragraph about the anticipated effect on jobs.

The effect the merger will have on jobs is not clear. "We anticipate there will be some dual functionality throughout the organization," said Blusser, "and over time there are likely to be some redeployments, as we strive to make the most efficient use of our most valuable assets—the employees that have made HeartBank and Loan Star the successful companies they are today."

Between the lines, John thought confidently, are a rash of severance packages too numerous to publicize. Just look at the choice of words, the code embedded in terms like *dual functionality,* meaning *redundant,* meaning *layoffs*; *redeployments,* meaning *seeking other opportunities,* meaning *layoffs*; *efficient use of our most valuable assets,* meaning *fewer people,* meaning *layoffs*; *layoffs* meaning *severance packages.*

When he finished with the paper, John noticed his voice-mail light was on and checked his messages. The first was a broadcast message from Max Brinkman himself.

> Good morning. This is Max Brinkman, CEO of HeartBank. Well, by now you've probably heard the news. Last night, the HeartBank Board of Directors approved a $26.7 billion merger between HeartBank and Loan Star Bank, a terrifically successful bank holding company serving the southwest region of this great country of ours. I know this comes as a surprise to most of you, but I'm convinced that this makes the best sense for our shareholders, our customers, our employees and our communities. The new entity will be much stronger, more productive, more efficient, more competitive than either HeartBank or Loan Star could be on their own. I personally am very excited about what we can achieve in working together to make the new company, called HeartStar, become a giant of 21st century banking.
>
> One of the toughest decisions we had to make about the new company was the location of the headquarters. As you know, I'm a big fan of the Twin Cities, and Minnesota truly offers some of the greatest advantages for the headquarters of a company like the new HeartStar. However, it's important that we locate our headquarters where our greatest growth will occur—the American Southwest.
>
> In the days and weeks ahead, you will hear more about plans for the new organization. In the meantime, congratulations to you all for your fine efforts in making HeartBank the great company it is and for contributing to the success of the new HeartStar. Together, we can build one of the strongest banking organizations in the world.
>
> Thank you, and have a great day.

There was nothing about jobs and no word about when the merger would close.

Pressed by a need to trade exclamations and speculations about what lay ahead, John stepped out of his office to find someone. Erica, his assistant, had just arrived at her cubicle and was busily arranging things on her desk while her computer booted up, much as a pilot checks miscellaneous lights and switches on the dashboard while the engines warm up.

"Hear the news?" John asked her.

"What news?" Erica's gum popped.

"The merger."

"Twins and the Vikings?" Erica said with a straight face. Actually, with all the debate over the past several years about building a new sports stadium, possibly two, to replace the Hubert Humphrey Metrodome, the prospect of the anemic baseball team's merging with the robust Vikings made a good joke. Erica could be funny sometimes without even trying—or knowing.

"No, Erica, HeartBank."

"HeartBank?" A look of surprise and puzzlement, but mostly puzzlement, snapped Erica's eyelids wide open. "Does this mean we'll lose our jobs?"

"I hope so, I mean, they say probably not," John caught himself.

"When will we find out?" Concern replaced the puzzlement in Erica's face.

"Don't know, Erica, but it'll get very interesting around here."

By now, the troops were streaming into the cubicles, like cattle back to their stalls, only it was the reverse of a farm routine. On a farm, John thought, the livestock returned to the barn at dusk. Here the animals returned at dawn. At the start of any typical Monday, one could walk the floor and find a number of pairs of co-workers, the earlier bird sitting, the later bird standing, with hands around coffee mugs, chattering about their weekend activities. Today, John noticed, everyone was standing, and not in pairs, but in groups of three or more. Palpable excitement, mingled with anxiety, filled the floor, as ventilation fans blew at full force to clear out the dead weekend air.

John walked to Jenny's office and found her standing in the doorway, talking with a couple of subordinates. When John approached, Jenny's underlings dropped back.

"Happy Merger Monday," Jenny's voice rang out.

"Who's merging now?" John filled his voice with a sense of urgency for the answer.

To John's surprise, his tone worked on one of the subordinates, a new hire whose main mission in life was to make sure people knew he was an MBA from Columbia. In this effort, he had been largely successful. Everyone in the department called him "Heights," after Columbia Heights, a working-class suburb of Minneapolis. John's affected surprise gave Heights an opportunity to impress his boss' peer. "You haven't heard?" Heights said earnestly. "HeartBank and Loan Star."

"You've got to be kidding." John teased further.

Heights beamed with pride for being in the know. "Nope. I just got a voice mail message from Brinkman making the announcement."

"Really?" The teasing ended when Jenny giggled. "Has anyone seen or talked to Vohlmann yet?" John directed his question to Jenny.

"You must not've checked your e-mail yet. He sent one first thing this morning—we're having a direct reports meeting at 9:30."

To ditch Heights, John entered Jenny's office as he addressed her. He gave Heights a little credit for catching on and moving on. "Jenny," said John, "I wonder how long Vohlmann has known about this. He's been touting the party line—you know, Brinkman's line—right up to our last direct reports meeting. Remember the bit about how HeartBank doesn't currently have any plans to play 'monkey see, monkey do' with all this merger stuff? But don't you think he's known for awhile?"

"I don't know, but you've got to think people at O'Gara's level have."

$ $ $ $

Nobody in the department, and for that matter, no one anywhere at HeartBank, accomplished anything over the next two hours. When Vohlmann's directs assembled in the large conference room, as caffeinated by the merger announcement as by espresso, John wondered what sort of spin Vohlmann would put on the decision to do what Brinkman had consistently said HeartBank would not do.

"Okay, people, you've all heard the news—we're merging with Loan Star. Personally, I think this is just terrific news. First thing this morning, I attended a meeting of O'Gara's direct reports, and I have to tell you, everyone is really excited about the merger. We pick up six new states, and with the added cross-sell opportunities, I think we'll be able to expand our revenue base way beyond what we could have done on our own."

John wondered what kind of dope Vohlmann and his "really excited" colleagues had been smoking. Less than a week ago, the party line, as parroted by Vohlmann, the corporate climber, had been quite the opposite. HeartBankers, so went the word, were in the catbird seat in this "age of merger chaos." While the competition worried about merging computer systems, corporate culture clashes, plunges in productivity, customer confusion and a host of other merger-related difficulties, HeartBankers could remain outward-focused and, in the official language of the corporation, "win marketshare." In fact, merger mania had spawned a full-fledged propaganda campaign at HeartBank called "Steal a Heart," by which some marketing genius was referring to a customer's heart. After distribution of a million posters, brochures and trinkets promoting "Steal a Heart," the campaign was abruptly halted when several community groups supposedly complained about the message this sent to troubled youth. Now John wondered if the campaign had not been stopped for another reason.

Vohlmann continued with unabated but unsubstantiated enthusiasm, and then entertained questions.

"If this is such a great thing for the shareholder," Blowhard said, "why was our stock down five-and-a-half bucks at just before ten o'clock this morning?" People gasped at Blowhard's question, which filled the room like a cloud of nerve gas. Leave it to Mr. Hairy Forearms to have an up-to-the-minute stock report. However, while others groaned, John found himself giving silent credit to Blowhard for having asked the most pointed question right off the bat. It caught Vohlmann off guard.

"Is it really?" Vohlmann made no attempt to hide his surprise, as he poured himself a cup of coffee, probably his tenth of the day already. John could see the wheels in Vohlmann's head grinding away like an overworked hard-drive cranking up in a PC. "I think what you're seeing is the market's surprise, not its disapproval." Vohlmann said limply. "Once Brinkman gets the full story out about what great potential this has for us, I think you'll see a big resurgence in the stock price." John could see the skepticism in peoples' faces, but no one pressed Vohlmann. The boss had just pulled a mangy, stuffed rabbit out of a prop hat, and everyone, including Vohlmann, knew there were no more rabbits, mangy and stuffed or otherwise. No sense in embarrassing a bad magician further. However, a long pause exposed palpable fear around the room about how Wall Street was receiving the news, and the implication for jobs, stock options and HeartBank shares in 401(k) plans.

John, on the other hand, saw hope in what others feared. Sure, a five-and-a-half point drop in HeartBank stock, which had been trading at around fifty the day before, put a major dent in his personal portfolio, but that was all long-term money. In twenty years, when he expected to retire, if there was still such a thing as HeartBank stock or HeartStar stock or whatever the hell stock it was going to be, or even a stock market or even a world, for that matter, a five-and-a-half-point blip today, followed by a couple more blips of a buck or two over the next twelve to twenty-four months, would not even be a memory, in the overall scheme of things. No, of far greater significance was the effect a badly received merger would have on job cuts and . . . severance packages. Who knew what was planned in the way of employment reductions, but a bad reaction on Wall Street was bound to pressure management to show more expense takeouts from the merger. And what would give Wall Street a bigger, faster takeout than across-the-board job cuts?

Suddenly, the Sycophant cleared his throat with a big *'hurrumph'* and asked, "Fred, any word on severance policies that we're supposed to report to our staffs?" The question yanked the wax right out of John's inner ears. He envied the Sycophant for his chutzpah, if not for his arrogance. Sycophant always referred to the people in his group as "staff," as if he were some big-shot executive and they were his servants.

As if the question had been planted and the whole scene carefully choreographed, Patsy Dillon, the HR person assigned to Vohlmann's department, entered the conference room just as Sycophant floated his question. What was she doing there, John asked himself, unless it was to deliver the black news about layoffs . . . and to spell out the severance package policy that would allow John to forget all about the resolution of the Walden case?

"What timing," said Vohlmann. "I invited Patsy to talk about that very subject."

"Thanks, Fred," the petite HR woman spoke. Behind her back, she was called *the* Patsy. She had "let's all feel good about ourselves" written all over her small white teeth and fine, soft features, but John noticed deepening creases of concern in the faces around the table. "A meeting of all the HR group leaders was held this morning, and we got some direction on a number of fronts. However, there will be lots up in the air for quite awhile, and we'll just have to wait and see on a lot of things, as to what will be impacted. There are a couple of things we know at this stage. First of all, it's important to take a big deep breath and tell ourselves that everything is going to be just fine," the Patsy said. "Many of us feel threatened by change, but we shouldn't. We often assume, just assume, that change will negatively impact us, when in fact, sometimes, we need to seek out the wonderful and exciting opportunities it can create. We just have to give ourselves permission to relax about it."

Discernable anxiety filled the room at the same time that John felt rising delight. For all who heard, the Patsy's talk about "change" and "seeking wonderful and exciting opportunities" formed a transparent veil over the much-feared phrase, "seeking other opportunities"—the unmistakable, universal corporate euphemism for "fired" and "layoffs." The Sycophant looked shell-shocked, his dreams of becoming CEO someday nothing but a small puff of gray smoke rising above his head. A disturbance appeared in the enlarged eyes of the Police Woman, and the concern on her face made her look homelier than usual. For John, on the other hand, the words pointed in the right direction.

"Second, they're telling us that effective immediately, a hiring freeze applies to all departments across the company," the Patsy said. John noticed that Blowhard's mouth hung open wider than usual, as it did not when he was about to nod off but when he was caught off guard. The Patsy continued. "If you need to fill an open position, you need to hire strictly from within the company." Yes. A hiring freeze was a sure sign of layoffs, massive layoffs, thousands of layoffs, layoffs that would sweep John away—with a severance package—and the plaintiff's lawyer in Walden would hardly notice. At long last, it was here. The elusive, the unattainable, the mirage, the severance package. Thank you, Mr. Brinkman. John felt giddy to the point of embarrassment. How could he take such pleasure from an event that would wreak havoc on the lives around him, the people who were deathly afraid of the flood waters that would carry them out the door of HeartBank and into the cold cruel world of unemployment and direct competition with one another for fewer and fewer jobs in the banking world? For John, the bell was ringing. For the others, the bell was tolling.

"Finally, and this is very important . . ." The Patsy's thin voice cut through the anxiety-laden air. No one stirred. Coffee mugs froze midway between the table and faces in shock. People stopped cold, part-way through a shift in posture. The air grew as quiet as the vacuum of space, as everyone hung on the Patsy's voice. ". . . they're telling us that except for a few headquarters jobs, there is no intent to incent early retirement or other resignations. There will be no mass departures or severance packages." *There will be no severance packages. There will be no severance packages.* The words reverberated inside John's head. "They've been looking very closely at the Lake Bank merger, which is not going very well, and seeing that if we incent people to leave, we're likely to lose people we don't want to lose."

The Patsy's statement felt like the blow of a two-by-four across his chest, while the others around the table sighed like a group of aerophobes whose plane had landed safely on the runway. No layoffs? No severance packages? But how could that be? The newspaper had reported that Brinkman expected to achieve expense takeouts of close to a billion dollars a year beginning only twelve to eighteen months into the merger. How could he possibly achieve that without significant reductions in the work force, since employment expenses were by far and away the single largest expense of the bank? What were they telling the employees of Lone Star Bank? The same thing? No layoffs?

The Patsy talked more about what she did not know, what no one knew yet, about all the effects of the merger. It did not much matter. Disruptions, changes and restructurings would make life difficult over coming months, but at least the managers around the table would have their jobs. Relief brought color back to everyone but John. Over him a gloom descended, a foreboding gloom like that which visits Minnesota in early November, when all color has faded from the earth, and naked trees, stark against snow clouds, shake in the icy wind, a portent of the long winter ahead.

He recalled the last few hours and relived the pain of the rise and fall of his hopes. No one, but *no one* had foreseen the merger, at least not in the short run or intermediate term, even. Then, with explosive power, the merger news had broken over downtown Minneapolis, over the whole state, across the nation. Stymied by Walden and knocked in the jaw by Judge Kanker, John had found hope in the merger news, which would crush the bar to a severance package. Now it was hope that lay crushed.

The meeting ended and people dispersed. Stunned and depressed,

John retreated to his office and closed the door behind him with more force than he had intended. It was almost a slam, and it reminded him of a scene in a movie where, cuffed and shackled, a prisoner is returned to his cell after his petition has been rejected by the parole board. The door is shut with extra, mocking force, and the prisoner returns to his occupation of marking time. John sank into his chair and stared at the papers strewn across his desk.

It occurred to him to quit, right then and there. March into Vohlmann's office, toss his security pass onto Vohlmann's desk, say "I quit" and leave without further ado. Maybe "I'm outta here" was better or "See you, Fred. Time for me to get a life." But he knew he could not do that. He needed the money. Support payments, bills, car lease payments, rent, it all added up all too fast to all too much. No, he needed the money. It was more realistic, he thought, to find another job and then toss his security pass onto Vohlmann's desk. With everyone distracted by the merger, no one would notice he was actively looking for another job. Another job. Where would he find another job? What kind of job did he want? What kind of life did he want? The questions only mounted until the whole idea collapsed like a jumble of Janga pieces. What he needed was time off, weeks of it, months of it. Time off to contemplate his life, its direction, his likes and dislikes, the range of possibilities.

He needed to talk to Steve. Steve? If only Steve were able to talk sensibly and not be nuts or part of a cult or both. It felt like eons since John had thought about his wayward friend. Remember that time at Betty's Place, John mused to himself, when Steve offered to serve as my agent for negotiating a severance package? Couldn't I use him now! John realized how strained his face had become. It was all in the eyebrows, tensed up and pulling toward the center of his head, just above the bridge of his nose. He placed his fingers on the place and felt the deep, short, vertical furrows that formed there, then relaxed and felt the furrows disappear. Why not give Steve a call? John thought. If he truly is nuts or immersed in a cult, he couldn't be any nuttier or more cultish than some of the corporate loyalists at HeartBank. Just then, John heard his computer beep, once, then twice. Who was sending e-mail on a day like today?

John swung around in his chair to check his in-box and found a message from Vohlmann and another from Corporate Marketing. He clicked on Vohlmann's, and italicized red text—Vohlmann's attempt at originality—leapt to the screen. It was addressed to G=NRES, which meant everyone in the department. John prepared himself for fractured sentences, misspellings and typos.

> Good Morning Every One!
>
> By now you've heard the great news about HeartBank merging with Lone Star Bank in Dalles. This is truly great opportunity for us. Instead of going with just any bank, Mr. Brinkman and his team has chosen a very synergistic combination. I think were foing to see tremendous shareholder value come out of this strategic merger. I know many of you are concerned about what the merger means in the way of jobs but you don't need to worry about that or how you'l be impacted. Except for a few headquarters jobs there is no intent to cut large numbers of people. I think this is truly great news. So now we can continue our work and benefit from the new synergies that the merger will provide. Their will be many announcements over coming weeks and I and the direct reports will keep you informed. Thanks and congratulations on being part of this exciting team!
>
> Fred

Bullshit, John thought. What did Vohlmann know about "synergies" and "strategy"? For that matter, who in the whole corporation knew a darned thing about the so-called synergies, and who were the geniuses that had figured out the strategy behind the merger? He wondered how many senior managers like Vohlmann around the bank were sending off drivel like this to calm the troops. John closed Vohlmann's e-mail message and opened the one from Corporate Marketing.

This ought to be good, John told himself. Since the first of the year, Corporate Marketing had launched one propaganda blitz after another. Each one focused on HeartBank's independence, hometown flavor, Upper Midwest roots. One of the latest media campaigns, in fact, had preyed upon the disaster at Fake Bank—middle management leaving in droves and service failing miserably in all corners of the merging bank. We Know our Customers by Heart, claimed the latest HeartBank ads. On television, the ad showed HeartBank employees greeting a grandfatherly customer by name as he strolled across the lobby of a HeartBank branch. The ad then showed the man making a deposit at a teller window. He has forgotten his account card and apologizes, but the teller will have none of it. "That's no problem at all, Mr. Anderson," she says, "I can find your account right away. Would you like to transfer some of it to your savings account today?" John wondered what sort of spin Corporate Marketing would assign to the day's startling news.

The e-mail was addressed to all managers, and, given the number of unnecessary layers of management at HeartBank, John wondered why the message had not simply been sent to all employees. In a show of defiance, he clicked on the "forward" icon, entered G=NRES Anchor and typed at the top of the text screen, "In the spirit of open communication, I'm forwarding the message below, which Corporate Marketing inadvertently neglected to send to you directly." John then clicked on the "send" button before he pulled up the original message again to read it.

> Congratulations on being a part of today's exciting news! The merger between HeartBank and Loan Star will create the eighth-largest bank holding company in the United States, with the new entity, HeartStar, holding over $195 billion in assets. "We will now be able to compete on a much broader footing," said Max Brinkman, CEO-designate of the combined company, "and I'm very excited about the opportunities it will create for all our stakeholders—customers, employees, communities and shareholders."

John scoffed at the screen when he saw Brinkman's quotation. Every release that ever came out of Corporate Marketing contained at least one quotation from somebody, and John wondered how many people really believed that the quoted individual had actually sat down with a copy writer and given out statements for publication. John continued reading.

> Now it's time to make it all happen. Over the weeks and months to come, many decisions will have to be made regarding the integration of HeartBank with Loan Star. To ensure that announcements of all major decisions are communicated broadly and on a timely basis, Corporate Marketing will e-mail announcements to all managers. . . .
>
> This afternoon, a press conference will be held in the auditorium

> on the third floor of HeartBank Tower. All managers are welcome to attend. We look forward to seeing you there!

Below the text appeared an attachment icon. John clicked on it, and up popped a document entitled, "Text of Remarks by HeartBank Captains/ Press Conference–HeartBank Tower." He scrolled down, read a few lines of text and burst out laughing. Corporate Marketing, the Ministry of Propaganda, had outdone itself with a script so contrived, it included "uhs" and "he-he-he-hes" and even directives to "clear throat here." John read Mike O'Gara's opening lines.

> *M. O'GARA*: That's right, Max. [*clear throat here*] I think the merger is going to uh catapult us onto center stage as far as a world class financial services company. [*spread arms far apart*] But more than that. The merger has community written all over it, [*bring hands together like the hands in the old Allstate Insurance ad*] and the fact that we're moving the headquarters won't affect our commitment to our Twin Cities and Minnesota communities one bit. You all know how committed I personally am to Minnesota, growing up here and all, but [*laugh a little here*] I'm looking forward to salt-free driving in the winter down there in Dallas. [*join laughter here if there is any*]. [*assume serious look before resuming*] In all seriousness, I think you look at what's best for the community when you make decisions, and moving the headquarters to Dallas is the right decision, all the way around. However, just to show our continuing commitment to the local community, HeartBank will redouble its efforts in the area of charitable giving in the Twin Cities and throughout the states of the uh Upper Midwest [*wait for applause*]. . .

John noticed that his lower jaw hung down twice as far as he had ever seen Blowhard's. What filled the screen before him was the most amazing thing ever to have come out of Corporate Marketing. Imagine, he thought, having not only a script, but one that directs every pause, every gesture, and receiving the compensation package of an O'Gara on top of it. Something was wildly out of whack. Were the captains just a bunch of puppets? Was Brinkman a greater control freak than anyone had imagined? Or was it Corporate Marketing, the veritable corporate Ministry of Propaganda, that was completely full of itself and out of control? And whose idea had it been to send the script to just about everyone in the world?

John's PC beeped to signal the arrival of another e-mail message. He closed the press conference script and returned to his inbox screen. In bold type at the top of the 575 messages that still occupied his inbox was another one from Corporate Marketing. He clicked on it, and with each word of the message, John's smile expanded till he let out a hearty laugh. The dispatch read:

> The attachment (press conference script) to the previous e-mail was sent inadvertently. Please disregard it and send it back. Do NOT forward it to others and do NOT save it. Thank you for your cooperation.

This one belonged in the *Guinness Book of World Record Stupidity.* The sender was identified simply as Corporate Marketing, which is how it always came. No one in the Ministry of Propaganda wanted to be held accountable. On the other hand, this message, not to mention the inadvertent transmittal of the script itself, revealed stupidity so extreme, thought John, that someone's head was bound to roll right out a window of HeartBank Tower.

By the time John reached the auditorium on the third floor of the Tower, the place was so jam-packed that the security guards were turning people away. He suspected that like him, most bankers had shown up to see how well the captains did with their scripts. However, like countless colleagues, John was left to hear about it second-hand.

The merger dominated the next day's newspaper, and the press conference received ample coverage. On the front page, in fact, was a photograph of O'Gara himself, the caption underneath reading, "Mike O'Gara doubles HeartBank charitable giving." John pondered the photograph and the caption. As usual, the press had gotten it wrong. John remembered specifically O'Gara's script. The exact phrase had been "*re*double its efforts", not "*double* its efforts." The script version, John thought, purposely gave the bank some wriggle room. The reported version was black and white. *Double* meant double. John wondered if O'Gara had mistakenly strayed from the script or the reporter had purposely put the bank in a bind.

Whatever HeartBank intended to do, double or *re*double, John questioned the bank's motive. Was it old-fashioned, Minnesota-style generosity at work or was it an attempt to thwart the community activist groups (which seemed to abound in the Twin Cities) that would otherwise extort the bank by lobbying the regulators to withhold approval of the merger until substantial handouts were made to the activists?

Just as John turned the page, Jenny appeared in the doorway of his office. "Did you go to the press conference yesterday?" she asked.

John put the newspaper down and folded it deliberately once, then twice. "I couldn't get in," he said. "Did you?" Jenny always had her ear to the ground, and undoubtedly, she would be a far better source than the newspaper for up-to-date news, not to mention the latest scuttlebutt. He hoped she would interpret the folded newspaper as an invitation to step into his office to talk at length about the merger.

"Are you kidding?" she laughed. "After that little e-mail boo-boo from Corporate Marketing yesterday, I just had to see those jokers live. I knew it would be crowded so I went over early. I stopped by your office but you weren't around." John was pleased to see Jenny advance into his office and drop into one of the chairs in front of his desk.

"Thanks just the same, Jenny," John said. "How did they do?"

"None of them is headed for prime time, except Brinkman," Jenny said. "Now there is one cool, smooth CEO." In her royal blue dress, Jenny did not look unattractive. Slightly overweight, John thought, but not in a way that detracted from her looks. Her eyes projected intelligence, and John wondered how many Jennys there were at HeartBank, who were not about to be fooled by corporatespeak, whether it originated from the top or from Corporate Marketing.

"Did they really follow the script?" John asked with a hint of doubt in his voice.

"Pretty much," said Jenny. "Can you believe it? I sat next to a group toward the back of the auditorium, and someone had the script so they could follow along. They got to laughing so hard they had to leave."

"I'm surprised the press didn't get ahold of it and turn it into a comic strip," John said.

"It already is," Jenny said. Though there was no need to do so, she covered her mouth to catch a laugh.

"What do you mean?" John said.

"It's another scene from Dilbert. Think about it, John. Every day around here there are a thousand Dilbert scenes. They're what give Scott Adams' creation such appeal, but the press is far too full of itself to consider any of the scenes 'news' in the conventional sense."

"I suppose," John sighed. "Did they take many questions at the press conference?"

"Yeah, mostly about the headquarters' moving and what effect that is going to have on jobs in the Twin Cities. No hard-ball questions though. I kinda think they were all planted, but I don't know for sure."

"So Jenny," John said with a shift in tone suggesting that a serious question was in the offing, "what do you really think is behind the mer—"

"Oh-oh!" Jenny surprised John with her outburst as she snapped her posture out of a slump and exclaimed, "You won't believe this. On the way back, my friend in Investments said she'd overheard O'Gara say after a few drinks at some sort of function last night that the whole merger was the stupidest decision he'd seen in all his years as a banker. Then, apparently, he made some comment about how it would've been nice to have heard about it before the morning news."

"You mean he didn't know about it until the world knew about it?" Incredulity spread across John's face.

"John, I don't think anyone except Brinkman knew about this before it was announced to the public."

"But Jenny," John's common sense was trying to override his astonishment. "How could one person make any kind of determination that a merger of this size would work? The captains, or at least some of them, had to have known what was happening. I mean think about it. When HeartBank goes out and acquires some puny community bank somewhere, just think how it's done. I mean, we send out a big SWAT team—all in secret of course—but a SWAT team nonetheless, including M and A guys, lawyers, auditors, bankers, numbers people. They scour the target like it was a full-blown audit. Then they gather for exhaustive debriefings, and then they decide whether it's a bank we should buy and at what sort of a premium. An assimilation plan is put together as part of the same process, and presto, you have an acquisition," John's voice trailed off, "that makes sense and adds real value to the stock." In recounting the normal process, John realized maybe Jenny was right, and if she was, the merger with Loan Star was preposterous. How could the analysis, the decision, begin and end with one person, with the solitary person at the top? He and Jenny looked at one another, and each saw the other's thoughts. The Loan Star merger was a decision looking for a rationale.

Jenny was the first to speak after the revelation struck them silently, simultaneously. "Are you thinking the same thing I'm thinking, John?"

"I'm afraid to answer that, Jenny, but if what you're thinking is that not more than three or four people at HeartBank had any input on the merger decision, the answer is 'yes.'" John spoke as if he were a police detective one step away from naming his suspect.

"And I say Brinkman hatched this from the confines of his cranium, such as it is." Jenny named the suspect for John.

"Brinkman is no dummy," John said, "but honestly, how does it work that one person in an organization of over 60,000 employees has such a corner on knowledge and strategic brilliance that all by himself, he can set off a nuclear device in the middle of so many lives . . . and portfolios, if you take the shareholders into account?"

Jenny formed a silent "oh" with her mouth and placed her hands on her cheeks. John realized that simultaneously, he and Jenny had come to the same revelation. He left it to Jenny to talk first. "My God, John," she said and rose from her chair. "Do you realize all these mega-mergers we read about probably work the same? One or two people at the top, in their infinite wisdom, decide that a bunch of 'synergies' and 'expense takeouts'"—Jenny applied a sarcastic tone to the terms—"exist between their business empire and someone else's. The top one or two in each of the companies to be merged get together in secret to decide who's going to run the new company, where the headquarters will be and, most important, how big their personal takes will be. Then they pay a couple of investment bankers to say 'it's a good thing for shareholders,' hire a couple of gigantic Wall Street law firms to slam the deal together and boom!" Jenny clapped her hands together. "They drop the bomb. Now," she said, as she placed her hands on her hips and leaned slightly forward, as if to issue a reprimand, "what I want to know is where else in society is power so concentrated?"

John admired Jenny for her feistiness and her intelligence. He wondered why she had not become a lawyer or head of her own business. "You're absolutely right," he said. For some reason, a chess analogy sprang into his mind. When he was a kid, he had played it occasionally with his dad, but he had not sat down at a chessboard in years. "Do you play chess, Jenny?"

"Sort of, why?"

"In a lot of ways this whole merger mania reminds me of a surreal chess tournament at some posh hotel in New York. The CEOs of the merging companies are up in the penthouse suite, seated at an expensive chess board—you know, one of those super-expensive commemorative sets you see advertised in an avant-garde catalogue that carries nothing you need and nothing you can afford. They're wearing smoking jackets, puffing on expensive cigars and sipping brandy served by a couple of Sycophant types. They're playing a high stakes game, but not to worry for the loser. He'll walk away from the game with untold millions—he'll just have to rehabilitate his ego a little bit." Jenny nodded slowly, deliberately. She grasped the analogy.

"Meanwhile, down in the ballroom of the main floor, the lesser masters are engaged in a major tournament. All who are allowed to enter are contenders, but not all who leave are. The winners get tidy cash prizes. The losers get consolation prizes—not to be sneezed at—and leave the hotel to find another game, another tournament. Every once in a while, a tournament official exits the ballroom and jots down the score on a giant scoreboard, so people in the lobby can see who's winning, who's losing."

"I like this." Jenny smiled.

"We're the people out in the lobby, milling about, awaiting the outcome. For us poor slobs they've set out big metal bins of pop cans in ice. Me? I'm one of the guys on the floor, scrounging around for the empty pop can that says, You Won $100! on the bottom."

"The only part you left out, John, were the whores in the penthouse." Jenny laughed, and John joined in. But then she turned serious. "John, you're right. We're just pawns. And worse, we're captive pawns. They've rigged it so people will leave because they're not happy with the merger, not because they've been laid off. They'll make it so lots of people leave voluntarily—that way the bank won't have to come up with a boatload of severance packages."

When John heard "severance packages," he felt a twinge of pain in the back of his head. For an instant he wanted to tell Jenny all about his tribulations around his quest for a severance package—he had told no one at the bank about it—but he quickly extinguished the temptation.

"I've got to think this is all very carefully orchestrated," Jenny said, her eyes alight with indignation. "Think about it, John, they've even structured it so our stock options won't vest. Normally, they'd vest upon a change of control of the company, but because this is a so-called merger of equals, there's not a change of control."

Just then the phone rang. Instinctively, John answered it, without regard for Jenny's presence in the room. "John Anchor," he said. It was Steve Torseth. "Steve!" Observing the surprise and distraction in John's face, Jenny winked, waved and moved to leave John's office before he could stop her.

"To be continued," she said on her way out.

"I called to see how the heck you're doing, my friend." Steve said. He sounded perfectly normal, and before John could think about it, he pictured his friend as Steve used to be—thick, curly, dark hair and glasses slipping down his nose, witty, good-natured and interesting. It took John a moment to remember Steve had gone off the deep end.

"I meant to call you yesterday, but I have so much going on I just didn't get around to it."

"Yeah, a lot's going on," John said cautiously. "What's up with you?"

"Life," Steve said. John cringed. Steve still needed help, he thought. "That's the other half of the reason I called you—to tell you what I'm up to. John, I can't wait to tell you. How about lunch a week from Friday? I've got an appointment downtown then, early afternoon. I thought we could grab a bite beforehand. What do you say?"

Something was going on with Steve, certainly, but there was a tone of confidence and genuine hope in his voice. For a moment, it occurred to John that insanity was not all bad if it worked to lighten one's burden. If in fact it was insanity and not the influence of some cult. No good could come out of any cult. Whatever it was, it piqued John's curiosity. "Sure, sounds great. I'll see you at Betty's at noon."

"'Can't wait. God bless."

God bless. Why did he have to say that? It was as if he had said, "I am nuts," or "Yes, I am in a cult." But then again, maybe it was a cry for help, and if John was any kind of friend, he would listen and try to help.

♦ CHAPTER TWENTY-NINE ♦

God Blessed

JOHN LEANED INTO THE HEAVY DOOR and pushed his way onto the sun-washed sidewalk outside the HeartBank Tower. It was the sort of day that said, "You weren't meant to work in an office." Like any Minnesotan, he knew the year was good for about five days—total—like this, when the temperature was around seventy degrees Fahrenheit, the sun ruled in a cloudless sky and not a single insect buzzed in your ears. Yet, at the moment, it seemed that they all could be like this and that he should adjust his lifestyle accordingly. Ideally, he'd even find a job that allowed him to work outdoors full-time. He slung his suitcoat over his shoulder, and with a spring in his gait, he hiked down Nicollet Mall to Betty's Place.

At Eighth Street, John heard his name from behind. He turned around and saw Steve running toward him. To John's relief and curiosity, Steve had hair. Not a lot of it, but enough to be noticeable from a distance. But what was he doing at the very center of downtown, when usually he parked in the low-rate district on the other side of Betty's Place? A job, thought John. He's landed a job.

"Steve!" John called out. "I'm surprised to see you *here,* he said, hoping for confirmation that Steve's life had turned around, that a job had replaced despair, that work had chased away insanity and rescued Steve from the cult. The two friends shook hands and stood on the corner.

"I was in a hurry, and figured I'd park where I knew I'd find a place right away."

"But—"

"I know what you're thinking. It's expensive. But you know what? I don't have to worry anymore." Steve smiled broadly as he pushed his glasses back onto the bridge of his nose. "Hey, let's walk."

John followed Steve's lead toward Betty's Place. This was a new Steve. "Written all over you is a job, Steve, am I right?"

"Oh?" Steve slapped John on the back and left it there, as if to push John along down the sidewalk. "I've got a job and a whole lot more, but you'll have to wait until there's a turkey sand with mayo on rye in front of you and a grilled cheese with fries in front of me."

John stepped away from Steve and pretended to throw a punch. "No fair, Steve."

"Yes, fair, and I'm buyin', which is fair also, considering how you stood by me when I was down and out."

"Nah," John protested. He felt embarrassed that he had not done more for Steve. A lunch here and there, but what had he really contributed to Steve's cause beyond that?

"Yep. And in the meantime, I get to hear all about your merger with Loan Star."

The friends made their way to Betty's Place and found a booth in back. They had hardly slid onto their benches when Louise came by.

"Well look who's back from wherever the hell you've been. Where *have* you been?" Louise said, like a mother hen to her wayward chicks after an unexplained absence.

"To hell and back," John said. Before the H word was even out of his mouth, John wished he had thought of something else for Steve's benefit. But then again, Steve was smiling, so maybe it was okay.

"Well, with all those bank mergers going on, your lives must be pretty hectic," said Louise. What made Louise so endearing, thought John, was that she could be droll and ironic without realizing it.

"Just a little," Steve played along.

"Say, I've been meaning to ask you guys." Louise turned her face into a composite of question marks. "Now that HeartBank—that's my bank—has merged with this Loan Bank, or whatever it's called, can I still use my HeartBank checks?"

"Actually, Louise," John said with as straight a face as he could muster, "the merger won't take place for a few months yet, and yes, your checks will be just fine."

Louise sighed with relief. "That's a load off my mind. You know, I've never been behind on my bills, ever, and I was scared to death that I'd have to order new checks and they wouldn't arrive in time and I'd be late on my bills. Can't have that, you know."

"Take it from me, Louise, you have nothing to worry about."

"Thank you, thank you. You're a real sweetie, you know that?"

"He's a good man, all the way around, Louise," said Steve.

"What'll it be, then, for my banker friends?"

Before John could respond, Steve spoke up. "A turkey sand with mayo on rye for the good man, and grilled cheese with fries for me."

"And in the beverage department?"

"A diet of Coke for me and a Pepsi large for him," Steve said. John nodded in agreement.

"Comin' up," said Louise with a flourish of her pen on the order pad.

Steve poured some water, pushed the glass toward John, poured his own glass of water and rested his elbows on the table. "So tell me everything about the merger. It sure took the world by surprise."

"It certainly took everyone at the bank by surprise."

"What do you mean, everyone? There must have been plenty of people at the muckety-muck level who knew about it." Steve said.

"I don't think so." John shook his head.

"They'd have to," said Steve. "I mean, how could anyone know whether it's going to work unless they consult a few people who are in a position to know?"

Steve sounded so eminently reasonable and showed no signs of insanity or cult membership. There was the "God bless" yesterday, which was decidedly unlike the old Steve, but John decided that was a little like your congestion breaking up at the tail end of a cold. Officially, the cold was over. Drainage didn't count. "I can't argue with that," said John. He proceeded to describe what he had observed so far and his suspicions that the merger was a one-man decision—two-man, if you looked at both sides of the merger and counted Blusser, the CEO of Loan Star.

Steve looked too surprised to worry about the slippage of his glasses down his nose. "How on God's green earth can that happen?" Uh-oh, thought John. There was the G word again, but not necessarily inappropriately. "What you're saying is this? That the CEO goes to a name-brand Wall Street investment banking advisory firm and says, 'Hey, I want to merge my behemoth company with another behemoth company—can you give me a fairness opinion?' The Wall Street firm says, 'Of course it'll work for the shareholders,' crunches numbers to support the conclusion and issues the fairness opinion without having consulted with the people who are capable—or not capable—of making the numbers work. Is that what you're saying?"

John nodded.

"That's preposterous," Steve said.

Steve was definitely sane, at least for the moment. "For a price, people will say and do just about anything," said John.

"Amazing, isn't it?" Steve said. "Amazingly corrupt."

"Yes, it is, actually." John had not thought of it exactly that way, but Steve was right. "Unconscionable, too, the way a decision like that can throw so many lives into chaos. Who knows when and where and how it'll all shake out? And who knows in the end whether it was all for the better? We'll never know."

"John, I'd bet your merger is no different from any other mega-merger. They're the ill-conceived offspring of nefarious affairs—affairs of the ego. For the guys at the top, it's no longer about money as money is understood by you and me. It's about power as measured by money. All this hype about the trend toward consolidation, about squeezing out expenses, enhancing efficiency, is just that—hype. There's certainly no proof that it's true in the long run. If it is true, why don't the fees that banks charge ever go down after a merger?" Steve was visibly steamed, much to John's relief. It was a sure sign that he was thinking straight.

"In contrast to how the bank approaches a small acquisition, the mega-merger is nothing but a roll of the dice. It's nothing but a big blind bet, for crying out loud, made by the CEO on his car phone, for all we know. What amazes me, Steve," said John, without breaking stride when Louise arrived with their food plates and beverages, "is how so many people join blindly in the bet. The investment advisors, who, of course are paid to bless the bet, the lawyers, who, we all know, are nothing but hired guns to begin with, the board of directors, who—typically, what the hell do they know?—and then the muckety-mucks one or two levels down from the top, who, in this case, at least, weren't given the courtesy of a 'heads up' but clamber aboard just as fast as they can for fear of being left behind."

"You're right," said Steve, as he poured a generous serving of ketchup across his French fries. "It's a grand, open conspiracy of corruption, and few people with anything to lose stand up to say, 'The emperor is wearing no clothes,' and no one with nothing to lose who does stand up to say 'The emperor is wearing no clothes,' has a voice that is heard." Steve took a big bite out of his grilled cheese, chewed it down to size and resumed talking. "You know, John, all of this is the whole reason I ain't working at a *big* corporation, and the reason you shouldn't be."

All the clues Steve had brought to lunch—parking in the high rate district, growing his hair back, sounding rational again—suggested that he had found work at last, and the emphasis on "big" in his last statement all but told John so. "So you've—" John started, but Steve cut him off.

"How can you stand working there at a time like this? I mean, John, you're in the den of iniquity, don't you realize that?"

"It's not exactly kindergarten, where all the boys and girls are told to be nice to each other, if that's what you mean," said John. "But for starters, I'm not in line for a severance package any time soon, and frankly, Steve, I need the dough before I quit. I can't just toss in my resignation like I'd toss a Frisbee across the lawn. In the meantime, I'm kind of absorbed by it, by the chance to say from within, 'The emperor is wearing no clothes,' as you put it."

"Don't kid yourself, John," Steve said bitterly. "Not to denigrate your position in the hierarchy, but you say that from within and you're going to sound like a mouse squeaking. The only way someone like you can be heard is through one of those lawsuits—what do they call 'em?" Steve searched the ceiling to John's left. "A shareholder suit." He thought he'd found it. "That's it. A shareholder suit, or something like that, a shareholder something kind of suit. I read about one in connection with Citigroup's merger with Fake Bank. Some group of Fake Bank shareholders sued, claiming it wasn't in the best interest of the shareholders. In effect, they were saying, 'The emperor is wearing no clothes.'"

John swallowed the half-chewed piece of sandwich in his mouth and took a swig of water to wash it all the way down. He then had room to ask, "What's happening with the lawsuit?"

"Oh, like all lawsuits, it's languishing in the courts somewhere. The Fake Bank merger will be ancient history, probably, by the time anything happens to the suit, but at least a few people will have a chance to be heard."

Steve had given John an idea, but he wondered what to do with it. "I wouldn't know where to start with something like that," said John, in the hope Steve would encourage him. "I mean, all the lawyers I know already represent HeartBank in one way or another."

"What about . . ." Steve stopped and used his napkin to wipe some errant ketchup from his upper lip. "What about that attorney who was suing you on that discrimination claim?"

"Justina." John felt himself blush. He had said "Justina" as if he were on familiar terms with her. "Justina Herz. Yeah, exactly." After the disastrous deposition in the Franklin case, and the $100,000 settlement, John had long put the lovely Justina Herz out of his mind. But the searing memory of that experience had been overtaken by subsequent events. He now had a perfect reason to see her again. "Steve, you're a genius." John felt a certain giddiness rise in his chest. "She makes a living going around suing big corporations, fighting for the little guy. She'd be perfect."

"Why don't you give her a call, then?"

"I will. Definitely. Thanks, Steve, for the idea." Unwittingly, unexpectedly, Steve had unleashed nostalgia, hope, romance and excitement inside John's lonely, middle-aged heart, to run free until John could come to his senses. John replenished the water glasses and took three sips of water to cool down the burn in his ears. They felt as red as the ketchup.

"We've talked enough about the merger." John seized on a ready diversion. "What's up with Steve Torseth?"

Steve drained his Diet Coke and made a loud gurgle with his straw. When he looked at John, Steve lit up the booth with his smile. "I not only have a job, John. I have an entire enterprise." Steve extended his hand across the table and said, "Shake hands with Steve Torseth, Executive Director of Christian Community Enterprises."

John played along, but Steve's sudden lapse into insanity—or was it humor?—chilled John's ears. What on earth was he talking about? John groped for words. "You're what?" he asked, inadequately.

"John, it's the greatest thing that's ever happened to me. Now I suspect you thought I'd gone off the deep end the last time we met," said Steve, "but I experienced a real turnaround in my life—isn't that another name for the restructuring of a troubled company, a 'turnaround'? I didn't know where I was headed, frankly, but I could feel it was somewhere new and exciting and fulfilling. I tell you, John, it was real. It's still real. I'm talking about my faith, John, and if that makes you uncomfortable, then, well, it proves its power, doesn't it?" Steve's remarkable outburst pinned John hard against the back of his booth. "But whatever you think, whatever anyone thinks, this faith experience of mine—John, it's a direct result of the hardship, the pain, the questioning I went through during my search for meaningful work, the direct result of my severance package—has made me a new person, given me new life, given me purpose."

John was so flabbergasted that it did not occur to him to look away from Steve to see who might overhear the extraordinary speech. With his eyes trained on Steve, John failed to notice the spot of dried ketchup at the corner of Steve's mouth until Steve himself discovered it with his tongue and cleared it with his napkin. "Now, let me tell you what I'm up to. After lots of prayer, I realized that I was going about my job search all wrong. I was struggling in vain for what I thought would please me instead of what would please God. When I changed the question to 'Show me the way to what will please you O Lord,' the answer came. The answer was: an enterprise to help people in the inner city find a way out of their poverty, out of their hopelessness—not by giving them a handout but by giving them a hand. Giving them decent housing, job training, jobs and—here's the exciting part, John—firsthand experience at owning and operating a business.

"Here's how it works." Steve was on a roll. John had never seen such fire in his friend's eyes, such light in his face. "We go out into the rough-and-tumble neighborhoods and recruit people for the program. We take all sorts, as long as they understand and sign a pledge to abide by the rules—no drugs, no trouble with the law, respect for others and others' property and to be the best that they can be. We then sign them up for training, which includes some classroom instruction, in some cases, private tutoring, and lots of on-the-job training in one of what we call our Inner Enterprises. Our Inner Enterprises are various shops and stores that serve the very neighborhoods in which these people live. For example, we have several mini-marts where local residents can buy many of the things that they would find at a Target or a Wal-Mart. The store inventory consists of seconds or returns, but perfectly good merchandise, donated by the Targets and the Wal-Marts that we've enlisted in the program. Our trainees, then, under the supervision of volunteers and a few paid staff, run the store as if they owned it. You'd be amazed at how hard and how smart they work and how it changes their lives, John."

"What . . . uh . . . what do you do for funding?" John fumbled for the words.

"That's the miraculous part of this, John." Steve clasped his hands together and leaned into the table. "Weeks ago I got involved in this prayer group. We met every week out at the Lafayette Club, and it was an amazing time to share experiences and so on. I got to know some remarkable people, and a number of these remarkable people were remarkably wealthy. When I floated my idea for Christian Community Enterprises and laid out a business plan, they were eager and rather hefty contributors. Not only that, they also called up their networks of wealth and before I knew it the money came rolling in. I couldn't believe it." Steve hesitated. "Actually, John, it didn't take me long before I realized it was all in answer to my prayers, and now I believe anything's possible through prayer. You ought to try it yourself, John."

Intrigued and bewildered by all that had tumbled forth, John also marveled at his friend's new-found purpose in life. He wondered whether he himself would ever find anything as meaningful. His thoughts drifted to this woman Justina, whom he hardly knew. Heck, whom he did not know at all. He imagined himself telling her all about Steve's venture and winning accolades from her merely for being a friend of the founder and leader of a non-profit organization as innovative as this Christian Enterprises outfit, and as successful as it would surely be.

Steve continued with irrepressible enthusiasm. "We've barely been open a month, and already we're seeing results that would give you goose bumps, John. You ought to volunteer. At least come down and see how we operate. Who knows, John, next year, when we open programs in Milwaukee and Chicago, you could be working full-time with us. Wouldn't that be terrific?"

There was no denying that Steve had finally arrived. "You ought to be real pleased with yourself, Steve," said John. He meant it.

"The credit goes to God, John. He simply works his wonders through his people." John shrugged, not so much from disbelief as to head off a shudder that might be misperceived as a nervous tic. Whatever had gotten into Steve had made him formidable. John wondered if there was anyone at HeartBank right now—besides Brinkman, he supposed—who possessed half the drive of a Steve Torseth.

Steve took care of the bill and left a five-dollar tip. "Aren't you being a little generous, Steve?" said John. "Next time when I'm paying, she'll expect the same and be disappointed when I leave a lot less."

"So? Leave five bucks and she won't be," was Steve's rejoinder, as the two men stepped out onto the sidewalk. John waited for Steve to crack a smile, but none appeared. The Executive Director of Christian Community Enterprises was dead serious. The men walked a few strides in silence before John recovered from his brush with embarrassment.

"Steve," John said, as he offered him some cherry DentDream and unwrapped a piece for himself, "I'm really happy for you, but I'd be even happier, I mean laugh happier if you could bless me with a funny story." John thought it would please Steve to hear the way John used "bless."

"Like old times?"

"Like old times."

Steve threw his head back with a laugh. "Okay, there are these two Swedish bankers, Sven and Ole, who are volunteers for Habitat for Humanity. They're working the roof job together, and it's agreed that Ole will haul tools and materials up to Sven, and Sven will nail the shingles down. Well, Sven climbs up and gets ready to nail the shingles, but next thing Ole knows, Sven is chucking down one nail after another. 'Yaysus Kreestoos!' says Ole. 'Vhat de hell ya doin' dere, chuckin' dem nails dahn like dat?' 'Vel,' says Sven. 'Da heads are all on da wrong end of ta nails!' 'Ah!' yells Ole. 'Ya dum Svede! Dem nails are fur da udder side of da house!'"

The story carried the men laughing to the corner of the IDS Center. "Here's where I have my meeting." Steve motioned with his head and reached with his eyes. John stopped and offered his hand. "Thanks for putting the merger into perspective," he said.

"Thanks for being you." Steve shook John's hand vigorously. He then reached into his suitcoat pocket for his wallet and pulled out a business card. "Here. Give me a call sometime and I'll give you a tour of our facilities. I think you'll find it interesting. So long, and God bless." With that, the amazing Steve disappeared into the crowd of lunchtime sun-seekers returning to their work stations.

♦ CHAPTER THIRTY ♦

Justina

"ERICA," JOHN CALLED AHEAD TO HIS ASSISTANT'S CUBE, but she had not yet returned from lunch or wherever she had gone. Lately, he had noticed, Erica had been stretching her lunch hour to a lunch hour-and-a-half. It vexed him like a mild rash under the band of his wristwatch. If he were a manager with any sort of backbone, John told himself, he would say something about it, like "Look, I've noticed you're not here when I need you. We need to abide by the rules around here, you know," but no, no, no, that was much too rigid, unnatural. Besides, if word ever got around, the HR folks would frown on that sort of thing. He would have to take a softer approach, like, "Erica, I'm certainly willing to accommodate you if you need a little extra time here and there, but we're depending on you back here and . . ." What was he thinking? He had stretched his own lunch time lately, from ninety minutes to two hours, and then there were the untold hours he squandered on unproductive activity and idle chat, especially of late, although it was not so much idle chat as it was active speculation. For crying out loud, how could he even think of reprimanding Erica when he himself was out of line half the time? He would well deserve the name Hypocrite if he chose to criticize her. On the other hand, what kind of spineless manager was he, anyhow? But he wasn't any kind of manager. He was John Anchor, wandering in a never-ending search for himself, for his niche in life, all of which required . . . *a severance package.*

He rummaged around the drawers in Erica's cube—at least in the ones that weren't locked—for a Minneapolis phone directory. John wondered what she could possibly be hiding in all those locked drawers, but it probably served him right that he couldn't gain access to them. He knew he shouldn't rifle through her office. It felt a little like searching a woman's purse for a package of gum. You just didn't invade someone's privacy like that. However, John was desperate to find Justina's phone number. Not so much desperate, he realized, as he stood up and put his forefinger to his lips, as simply overtaken by the thought of striking up a relationship with that very unusual, attractive woman. But what was he thinking? What would she possibly see in him? He was a fool to think she would have the slightest interest . . . no, no, he wasn't giving himself credit. That was half his problem generally, wasn't it? If he gave himself half the credit that Blowhard and Sycophant gave themselves, he would be way ahead of the game.

John wandered back into his office, and weighed down by his thoughts, he dropped into his chair. Why was he going to call Justina? Would it sound phony to use the merger as an excuse? Would she laugh at him for asking about a shareholder suit or whatever it was called? What was that kind of suit, anyway? Would she have the foggiest notion of what he was talking about? And if she summarily dismissed the idea, as in "I don't do that kind of law," then what? "Okay, then what are you doing for dinner tomorrow night"? But she must do that kind of law. Didn't she like suing big corporations? Wasn't that the kind of law she practiced—suing big corporations, whatever the claim might be? John leaned his elbows on his desk and sank his forehead into his hands. He realized he had not bothered to remove his suitcoat, but more important, he had not closed the door. When he had taken care of his coat and the door, it dawned on him: He didn't need to know where Erica hid the telephone directory. He could simply call directory assistance.

John wrote Justina's number down on the backside of a piece of junk mail that competed for exposure atop his desk. It occurred to him to jot it down neatly on one of his own business cards and put it into his wallet, but he figured that sort of permanence would jinx the call. Besides, he reasoned, either the call would go so badly that he would never want or need the number again, or they would fall madly in love with each other on the first call, and as a natural consequence, he would automatically memorize the number without ever having to see it again. Yet, having the number was a long step away from calling it. With pensive furrows in his forehead, John rose slowly from his chair and paced the floor in front of his desk. He needed to think this through. What would he say if he got Justina's voice mail? "Justina, this is John Anchor from HeartBank," he said aloud. He repeated himself, but with better enunciation. No, he coached himself, better to be natural. "Justina, this is John Anchor from HeartBank, and I have a matter I'd like to discuss with you when you have some time. Could you please call me at . . ." That was better. But what would he say if she answered and with a serious, business-like tone? John then scolded himself. Just call, for Pete's sake.

He punched the numbers and listened for the connection. The phone rang once, twice. John wasn't sure whether he was relieved or disappointed that no one was answering. Suddenly, the ringing stopped. "Justina Herz," she said. John's heart jumped.

"Hello, Justina," his voice cracked on the *lo* of "hello," and he blushed. He was forty-two, not fourteen, for Christ's sake. "This is John Anchor over at HeartBank." His voice echoed in the void on the other end of the line. Had he disconnected the line?

"Oh, John. I wondered when . . . I mean, I'm glad . . . How are you?" she said with a tone that sustained his blushing. He pinched the bridge of his nose and closed his eyes to picture Justina at her desk, in her office.

"It's pretty interesting here with the merger and all."

"I suppose. I've been reading about it. Is it going to affect your area much?" Her response was not what John expected. It was not the response of a radical left-wing lawyer, who pursued not so much a living as a cause, the cause being frontal attacks against corporate America.

"It's hard to say quite yet. I'm sure there will be changes, but they have yet to be announced," said John. He worried that the pretext for his call—an inquiry about a shareholder suit—would evaporate and leave him in an awkward position. "Actually, that's why I'm calling—the merger, I mean."

"What about it?" Justina asked. Her voice didn't suggest the sort of curiosity John had hoped it would elicit.

"Well, it's hard to talk about it here at the office, and I was hoping maybe you'd have a little time when I could talk to you about some concerns I have about the merger."

"I'm free after four this afternoon. Does that work for you?"

Maybe there was a God after all, John kidded himself. "That should work." He finished the conversation with amazing calm, having avoided choking on his own excitement.

Justina was in with a client when John arrived, just before four. He knew by the sign next to the bell on the counter.

> I'm with a Client. If you have a delivery and need me to sign, ring twice.
>
> If you're here for an appointment, ring 3 times.
> If you're here for any other reason, ring 4 times.
>
> Thank you,
> *Justina L. Herz, Esq.*

Definitely low-tech, he thought, and a refreshing departure from attempts at advanced automation at the bank. He consulted his watch and decided to wait another five minutes before he disturbed the peace.

Behind the closed door of Justina's office flowed the muffled strains of music. Piano music. Serious, classical music. The kind that John rarely heard and had never understood but never necessarily disliked, either. Like most people he knew, John thought classical music was the exclusive domain of the very wealthy and the very sophisticated, or at least the very sophisticated. He doubted that people like Max Brinkman or that guy Blusser, CEO of Loan Star, listened to classical music. It was more likely to be lawyers at one of the big firms John had dealt with that actually went to symphony concerts. Though, come to think of it, over the years, John had received numerous invitations from lawyers for Twins games—okay, okay, more recently it had been Vikings and Timberwolves games. Who watched the Twins anymore? And once, five or six years ago, before they were divorced, John and Sandy had been invited out to dinner at a fancy restaurant and then to a musical—*Phantom of the Opera*—by a lawyer seeking work from the bank. But never once had John received an invitation to a symphony concert. Maybe that was because he was a schmo, and no one wanted to embarrass him by dragging him to a place where he would stick out like a sore and ignorant thumb. One thing was certain, however. Over his twenty-year banking career, John had been in the office of many a lawyer, and never had he heard classical music playing in any of those offices.

His musings reminded John of his deposition with Justina and her question, "Given a choice, would you rather attend a Twins game or a symphony concert?" and he remembered with relief his response—"a symphony concert"—though it had been prompted by his dislike of the Twins. But now what? How would he deal with Justina's interest in classical music? She would see straight through any attempt on his part to show any interest, and yet she would just as likely be disappointed in him if he declared right up front his complete ignorance when it came to serious music.

Just then, the door to Justina's office opened, and like a client processional, the piano music crescendoed to accompany an elderly couple, who shuffled forth. Behind them emerged Justina. She was still every bit as beautiful as he had remembered all these months. Her dark, penetrating eyes and luxuriant hair gave her an exotic appearance, John thought, and her supple figure, enhanced by an accentuating red dress, moved in lithe contrast to her clients' stiffness. John realized that Justina's exchange of farewells with two slow-moving old folks was all that stood between him and shameless desire. With a pleasant smile to hide his impatience, John waited for the processional to end.

"Hello, John," Justina said, her eyes smiling deep into his thoughts. Now it was purely an ingrained sense of propriety that bridled John's desire. He shook hands and greeted the woman who, social crusader though she might be, could melt hearts at a glance.

"I like the music," said John spontaneously. It was true. He didn't have the slightest notion of what it was, but he liked its soothing quality, which conveyed a sense of something higher, greater than what customarily filled John's existence.

"You like Mozart?" Justina asked, expectantly.

For an instant, John hesitated. He stood perilously close to bluffing—or was it having his bluff called? Either way, it would not lead to a happy outcome. Better to do the right thing and come clean, admit his ignorance, sooner rather than later. "Yes, I do, very much, actually," he said. "But—"

"I have a weakness for his piano concerti," she interrupted. "Maybe it's because in my heart of hearts I always dreamed of being a concert pianist. Whatever it is, I just can't get through a day without listening to a Mozart piano concerto. I got into the habit of having music on most of the day and discovered that clients like to hear it as well."

"You play the piano?" asked John.

"Well, I try to keep it up, but it's been years since I studied," Justina said, as she stepped toward her office and motioned for John to follow. He marveled at the gentle curves between her hips and her waist. "How about you?" she asked. "Do you play an instrument?" She motioned for him to assume a chair in front of her orderly desk while she held the sides of her dress in a subconscious gesture of modesty and gracefully lowered herself into another chair.

"Well, actually—" John started. Time to come clean.

"Or are you an armchair critic and connoisseur?" Justina smiled and revealed impeccably straight, remarkably white teeth.

"No, I've never studied a musical instrument," John was pleased that he had picked up on Justina's use of the word "studied," which he figured was a sophisticated form of "took lessons." "And I really don't know much about, uh, classical music." He blushed when he realized how close he'd come to saying "serious" before he thought of the word "classical" and how stupid "serious" probably would have sounded to the trained ear of someone like Justina.

"That's what I like in a man . . ." she tossed her head back with a gentle laugh, "Modesty." John noticed her tender neck and the pleasing line of her chin, but as she brought her head down, her interrogating eyes prompted an unpleasant memory. With a sharp, quick pain in his temples, he remembered his deposition in the William Franklin case, his dashed hopes for a severance package, the merger, his latest lunch with Steve Torseth, the pretext for his meeting with this . . . this extraordinary woman, this beautiful, warm, friendly, sensitive, sophisticated woman. In the next instant, Justina too lost her smile, perhaps in reaction to John's sudden return to reality, but maybe because after all, she was a hard-nosed, cunning, calculating lawyer, who went around suing the pants off big corporations and making mincemeat of the Zane Wickleys of the world. The piano music was nothing but the blossom on a Venus flytrap, if in fact blossoms even occurred on the killer plant.

"But you're not here to talk about music, are you?" Justina said solemnly. John fought off the shudders.

"No, I'm not," he said, shifting in his seat. A moment ago, his heart had skipped a beat when Justina had sat down on his side of the desk. Now he wished she were not sitting so close. As if she could read his mind, she rose and stepped around to her chair on the command side of her desk, but John noticed none of her attractive features, just that her dress was very red.

"So what brings you here?" Justina asked. She drew a tablet from the desk drawer and lifted a pen from a small wooden tray atop the desk.

John cleared his throat. "It's the merger. From what I see of it, Justina, it was an idea hatched in a vacuum without any real foundation when it comes to shareholder value. I mean, they say it's for shareholder value, but I'm telling you, it's not. It can't be. If it works out for the shareholder, it'll be one big happy accident. I'm seeing all kinds of signs that no one, not even the highest ranking executives below the CEO, knew about this before any of the rest of us did. And without anyone's input—other than the CEO and the investment bankers who we all know are simply paid fantastically huge fees just to bless the deal, not to analyze it in any meaningful sense of the word—how could the board of directors approve such a transaction? Now we poor slobs, the employees, are being ordered to figure out how to make the transaction work. It's as if the CEO comes along, rips the front wheel off my bicycle, rips the back wheel off your bicycle and then tells you and me to figure out how to put our two bicycles together so they'll go faster and more efficiently. He gets a ton of money whether the idea works or not. But what do the shareholders get, and what do the customers get? I might ask too, what do the employees get, but when it comes to us, who really cares?" John's impassioned speech drew him to the edge of his chair while it moved Justina to the back of hers. Only when he finished did he realize she had not taken any notes.

"I see," she said, skeptically. John searched her face in vain for a sign of indignation. "John, excuse me for asking, and this is just so ironic, but as I recall from your deposition, didn't you say you're forty-two?"

"Yeah, why?" John asked, perplexed. What did his age have to do with anything?

"Well, I'm just wondering how employees over forty will be treated in the merger. It's the point where we start seeing age discrimination. You're in a protected class now, you know," said Justina. It had never occurred to him that he was in a "protected class," and yes, it was very ironic that William Franklin's lawyer would suggest that John himself was a victim of some sort of discrimination.

"Well, uh, geez . . ." John felt his face blushing to match the color of

Justina's dress. So this is how the lovely lawyer viewed him—as a senior citizen, for crying out loud? An old fart in the same boat as the really old fart who had shuffled from her office a few minutes ago? Is that what she thought of him? "I never thought of myself as in need of that kind of protection. I mean, really, I can't imagine that sort of thing will happen." John's humiliation was turning itself around. Time to take the offensive. "I mean, after all, Justina, look at Brinkman, the CEO, Blusser, the CEO of Loan Star, all the senior management at HeartBank and for all I know, the senior execs at Loan Star—they're all over forty, every last one of them, and a lot, I know, are over fifty." There. He'd re-established his youth, his virility, his power. Forty-two wasn't old at all, when he compared himself with the powermongers at the top of the bank.

"How about your boss? How old his he?"

"Uh, thirty-eight, I think," said John. He swallowed just in time to avoid choking on some saliva.

"That's the one to look out for," Justina said, with her arms folded across her chest.

It was all a bad idea, thought John. I come in here with a headliner case, a good excuse to get to know the woman of my dreams, and she waves it off and treats me like a guy who's over the hill. He felt embarrassed, even angry, and he had half a mind to ask the beautiful Justina how old she was. Maybe not forty, but past thirty-five, he bet, and what's the difference, really, between thirty-five and forty?

"Well, time will tell. Just something to keep in mind," she said. Time as in years will tell, he thought. "But back to the basis for the merger, I'm intrigued but really not surprised, I guess." Justina leaned forward and picked up her pen but with both hands and not as if she were prepared to use it. "As you can tell, I'm usually suing corporations, not representing them, and over the years, I've seen all kinds of corporate actions that are less than praiseworthy. Many, of course, are downright actionable, and if you know how to uncover things, you can find glaring evidence of egregious wrongdoing." John liked the words, but they lacked the indignation, the passionate condemnation he had expected from a left-of-center lawyer who made her living suing big corporations. "However, quite honestly, John, you do have to know how to choose your battles." He hated that phrase, "choose your battles." Over the years, all too many people had advised him to "choose your battles." In fact, he had often told others to "choose your battles," the universal code phrase for "fold camp on this one—you're not going to win it."

"What battles do you choose?" John asked in frustration.

"The battles I think I can win," Justina said, sharply.

"But maybe if I explained things in a little more detail you'd decide this was a battle you could win."

"What you contemplate here, John, is what's called a shareholders' derivative suit. I remember that much from law school. I know a few lawyers who handle those kinds of suits, but it's tough pursuing them against big corporations. They can be enormously expensive to prosecute, and unless you join up with other firms, someone with a practice like mine can't afford to handle one. And besides, in the HeartBank merger, do you realize how hard it would be to prove your allegations? I mean, no offense John, but unless you have access to highly classified or rarefied financial information and you're prepared to spend lots of money on financial experts, accountants and economists, the odds of getting anywhere with a derivative suit are very low."

"I see." John's voice trailed off.

"None of which is to say I don't sympathize with you—I have no doubt you're right." Justina leaned her elbows on her desk and rested her chin on the back side of her hands. Her dark eyes softened, and she looked straight into John's. He thought he detected a longing in her face, perhaps a hint of sadness, and he found solace in the hope that she really did sympathize and really had no doubt he was right. She showed no sign of wanting to end the interview, despite her decision to avoid a battle with HeartBank.

A radical impulse swept over John. Maybe a shareholders' derivative suit was out of the question, but a most beautiful and intriguing woman was sitting directly in front of him and looking right into his inner feelings. The voice of chance, the voice of courage swelled within him. Now was the moment to seize control of his life, to take a risk, to pursue what fate had placed before him, within sight, within grasp. Now was the time to ask Justina the daring question flat out, even if it meant rejection. He inhaled deeply and pictured himself on the deck of his parents' pontoon boat, ready to dive into the icy waters of Petty Lake. Ready, get set, jump! he told himself. "What are you doing for dinner?" he asked.

"I'm having it with you at the Northern Pines," said Justina. "What did you have in mind?"

John's chest went arrhythmic. How in the world did she know about Northern Pines, his favorite Sunday morning haunt and a place within walking distance of his apartment on Grand Avenue? This was fate, and fate, for once in his life, was smiling on him. "That, that . . . sounds great," he said, with a subconscious nod.

"Then let's go. Justina rose like a royal figure, stopped the music and walked toward the doorway. John stood frozen in a state of pleasant surprise, and when she saw that he had yet to move, Justina stopped in the doorway, placed her lithe hands on the doorframe, looked at John with smiling eyes and bent her head in what seemed to be a yearning manner. For all he knew, a meteor had crashed into the building, killed them both and dispatched them to heaven. Not a bad way to go.

Enroute to the Northern Pines, John learned to his amazement that Justina lived in an apartment building just up the street from him. He had tried once to find out where she lived, but she had eluded him and actually many other men, with an unlisted number and use of her parents' address in the St. Anthony Park section of St. Paul. Justina, however, explained that she had seen him in the Northern Pines on a number of occasions. She herself liked the place because of its northwoods décor, including half-log siding and carved pine furnishings, a stone fireplace and reading nook in back and all varieties of collectibles, from antique skis to old fishing gear adorning the walls. It reminded her of the Boundary Waters Canoe Area, a scenic wilderness area she had never visited but longed to see.

After they found a table, Justina confessed to what she was really after during her deposition of John in the William Franklin case. "I don't know what came over me," she said. "I mean, it was so unprofessional of me, but I have to admit, there was something about you that I found—still find—very intriguing and attractive, and I saw it as a unique opportunity to confirm my initial impressions."

"I know I caved in the case, but did I pass the test?" John smiled.

Justina gracefully placed her elbows on the very edge of the table, rested her lovely chin on the backs of her hands, ignored the waiter who had just appeared, and silently but affirmatively answered John with eyes and a smile that told him she was in love with him. Her skin looked so perfect and pure and her makeup, ever so slight—it didn't need to be otherwise—was expertly applied. John wondered if he was looking any younger, given the pleasantness that swelled within his chest.

"I'll come back," the waiter said, as if to himself, and slipped away without having disturbed the lovers' trance. John's eyes, meanwhile, surveyed what he realized might well be the Prize, this remarkable person who returned his gaze. All matters of work and the world, the merger, the Walden case, the severance package fell deep into an amnesic gorge. To sleep with her, to make love till he was one heart, one soul with her . . . John had never felt so wonderfully, insanely smitten by whatever had now taken hold of his senses.

The waiter must have been regarding them perceptively. He didn't return until John and Justina had gently ended their ardent gazes into one another's face. They ordered as if surprised that they were in a restaurant. Sensitive to their main purpose, the waiter recorded their selections quickly, smiled courteously and slipped away. Justina herself then slid gracefully from the booth to repair to the restroom, but John remained spellbound by his remarkable fortune. As his mind glided like a featherweight, however, he realized how precious little he knew about this woman, Justina Herz. Where had she grown up? Where had she gone to school? Had she been married before? Did she have any children? He guessed not. What did she do on Friday evenings, on Saturday afternoons? What sort of people did she hang out with? He knew she liked nature, but she didn't look like the rugged type. What on earth would she think if he divulged his interest in deer hunting at his parents' cabin? There were a million questions, and what of the questions she would have of him? How would the answers play on the lovemaking that he, as any man in sync with his instincts, was drawn, pushed and urged to imagine?

Only much later would Justina bring John to understand that however unfamiliar his background and interests were to her, it was his genuine interest in hers that had sustained her infatuation through its transformation into interminable love. But wouldn't Justina's past and upbringing interest any man who had half his wits about him?

Born and raised in the village of St. Anthony Park, an enclave of academics and bookish professionals in the northwest corner of St. Paul, she graduated with a poli sci major from what John knew was the most liberal of liberal arts schools, Macalaster College, which straddled Grand Avenue, just west of Snelling Avenue in St. Paul. For law school, she went on to the University of Minnesota, which, Justina explained proudly, certainly attracted a superb faculty and a bright student body, even if it wasn't Harvard. There she met Doug Stenkrud, the son of a doctor from Rochester, Minnesota, whom she married a month after graduation, against her parents' better, albeit unspoken, judgment. While Doug pursued a big firm practice, Justina stuck with her politically liberal principles and went to work for Southern Minnesota Regional Legal Services or "SMeRLS" as it was called by its passionate staff of activist lawyers, who represented the indigent and downtrodden members of society in the southern half of the state. After her divorce, Justina quit SMeRLS and moved back in with her parents, professors at the "U," before she summoned the gumption to open her own practice in Minneapolis.

If Justina's *curriculum vitae* was solidly Minnesotan, her family roots were not, and her parents, whom she loved and admired, still felt like outsiders, despite having lived and worked in the Twin Cities for thirty-five years. Justina's parents were born in Germany just before the War, and after *Kristalnacht* in 1938, her two grandfathers—friends and fellow faculty members at Heidelberg—led their families to the relative safety of Denmark. "My grandparents always spoke affectionately of the Danes," said Justina. "The Danes risked their own lives to save Jewish lives, and my grandparents often said that goodness was part of the Danish national character.

"William Buchwalter, my maternal grandfather, landed a teaching position in the Physics Department at Princeton, and my father's father, Paul, took a job at NYU. Despite their separation in the New World, my grandparents remained close friends, and my parents knew each other from childhood. Like their parents, they pursued academic careers and obtained their degrees, from undergraduate to PhDs, at Columbia. In 1962, my parents joined the School of Education at the University of Minnesota. Except for trips to conferences and visits to their stomping grounds on the East Coast and occasional sojourns to Europe over the years, they never ventured far from the ivory tower of their academic posts on the east bank of the Mississippi River. Vikings football, ice-fishing and lake cabins, central to the life of any self-respecting Minnesotan with Nordic roots, I suppose, remain curiously primitive and alien concepts to my family.

"They shared with me their academic and artistic pursuits and their passion for political justice, both at home and abroad. They participated actively in the civil rights movement in the early sixties, and during the Vietnam War, they joined hands with student protesters. Nicaragua, the anti-nuclear protests, and any number of local causes, from the farmers' fight against foreclosure in the mid-eighties to desecration of Indian burial grounds to the campaigns of Paul Wellstone, were rallying cries for my parents. More than once they spent the night in jail for civil disobedience. They could never understand why the passion of the sixties had cooled and why so many Minnesotans now seem more interested in primitive pursuits of pleasure than in the issues of the day."

To John, all this was wildly exotic. He himself, of course, had never experienced directly any left-wing politics, and to the best of his knowledge, he had never even met anyone who had participated first-hand in that sort of thing. He didn't oppose left-wing views necessarily. He simply had never formed political views one way or another. It was akin to his likes and dislikes for music—he had none of either until, he realized, he had heard that classical piano music wafting from Justina's office a few hours before, which by now, seemed like a wonderful lifetime ago.

"Your parents must really take pride in the sort of law practice you have," said John. Justina laughed, and he thought he discerned a slight bitterness in it.

"Sure they're proud. It's the only kind of lawyer you can be and still have their respect," she said. "In their eyes, I'm fighting all the good fights—you know, on behalf of abused women, victims of racial and sex discrimination, Native Americans fighting development of ancient burial grounds, tenants facing unlawful detainer actions, targets of consumer fraud and senior citizens robbed of their due, whether it be adequate housing or Medicare payments. And more than once I've sued most of the banks in town on behalf of a widow or single mother whose account had been overcharged for overdraft fees."

"But you've never represented a middle-aged white guy in a shareholders' derivative suit against a big bank," John said. Who cared about HeartBank one way or the other, now that they were love birds in flight?

"Sorry to disappoint," said Justina with a smile over the top of her water glass, which she held between her hands. "Do we have to break up if I don't take your case?"

"I'll give you time to reconsider," he teased.

"Good," said Justina. As she sipped her water, John saw the lemon slice graze her lips. "Truth be known, John, I really struggle with my practice sometimes, and that's the part I don't think my parents understand. I mean, so much of my time and effort go unpaid. Over the past four years, John, I probably haven't averaged more than about forty thousand dollars a year, after rent and office expenses. That's only slightly more than the annual salary of a typical SMeRLS staff attorney with my level of experience."

John knew she wasn't making a fortune, but forty thousand dollars? He hired people—kids, really—out of the bank's training program for more than that.

"So, what would your parents think of your going out with a banker? I mean, maybe they'd go for my Danish background, but it sounds like everything else about me is probably totally alien to them, being professors and all and not being from Minnesota."

"If they see true love in you, they'll love you, John, whether you're Danish, Jewish or something else."

John wasn't sure what she meant, and one question led to another till he heard the story of Justina's divorce from Stenkrud. It reminded him, of course, of Sandy and Stu, except that Justina's recovery seemed to have been much more painful and protracted than his. She had gotten divorced four years into her marriage, when she discovered that her husband, who had never billed less than two thousand hours a year at the prestigious Twin Cities firm of Briggs & Stanton, had logged substantial non-billable time with a firm secretary. Stenkrud's indiscretions shattered Justina's love for him and so offended her sense of trust and loyalty, Justina explained, that she went into seclusion and plunged into depression. After crawling back into the light, she couldn't bear to date anyone. Eventually, at her parents' urging and with their arranging, she dated casually, always Jewish men. Her mother, especially, wasn't about to see her only child hurt again. Despite the obvious fact that Justina would have been quite a catch, few of her dates had led to a second or third.

"Uh-oh," said John, only half in jest. "Does that mean I get dumped after the next date or the one after that?"

A genuine look of concern crossed Justina's face, like an isolated rain cloud over a surprised group of picnickers on an otherwise sunny summer day. "I didn't mean for that to sound as it did, I mean . . ." She blushed ever so slightly and drew her hand to her mouth. "You're different."

John realized by her reaction that he had approached the line of taking advantage of Justina's insecurity, just to test, then strengthen his attraction to her, but he knew that would be unfair. The way she was treating him showed him he was different. To suggest he felt otherwise would have been dishonest and manipulative. At thirty-four, she had more or less surrendered to the probability that she would remain single the rest of her life. She bore a heavy heart, and the great love that resided there had languished, John guessed, as on a bed of steel in solitary confinement, sentenced to life imprisonment without parole. Whatever she saw in him, she saw it clearly, and it was up to him to carry her away from prison, not to torture her with the prospect that he would abandon her there.

Though the newfound lovers forgot what they had ordered by the time the food came and forgot what they had eaten by the time the bill was paid, they would remember forever those moments at the Northern Pines, each like a petal in an everlasting bouquet. By the time the softly-lit ambiance of the restaurant yielded to full lighting and the cleanup crew's impatient noise, which signaled it was closing time, the sun had slipped well behind the horizon. However, comfortable warmth lingered in the springtime evening. They strolled one block over to Summit Avenue and down the sidewalk past stately mansions, past the pleasing architecture of the St. Thomas campus, all the way to the park atop the bluff that overlooks the Mississippi, all the while, voice in ear, all the while, hand in hand.

John and Justina could have sold tickets to their moonlit embrace. Against the backdrop of two bright stars over the skyline of Minneapolis, the lovers' affectionate kiss produced an image of everlasting love—at last, for each of them. His desire to transform their vertical embrace into a carnal recline was given every encouragement by her lips, her tongue, her hands, her barely audible words of infatuation and the way her pelvis pressed against his. With miraculous alacrity, John had not only healed her heart; he, John Anchor, a middle-aged, middle management, middle-of-the-road kind of guy had sparked a flame that now burned hot in that heart.

He surprised himself when he pushed away, stepped toward the edge of the bluff and peered out into the night.

"What's wrong?" she asked with alarm in her voice.

What was wrong was that everything seemed so right. If John had learned anything in life, it was that if by chance, just by chance, things should go right, it was only a signal they'd go wrong again soon. If Justina was the Prize, there were only two possibilities: All too soon, she would see that he was, after all, a schmo who knew nothing about classical music and a whole lot of other things, or, like everything else in his life, his relationship with her would fail of its own accord. John stared at the sparkling skyline up the river, while his desires wrestled with despair. How could he continue to deny who he really was—the deer-hunting, ignorant schmo? Yet, how could he be himself and not disappoint her? He wasn't about to give up deer hunting, but he honestly liked the classical music, and maybe if he learned something about it on his own, he could go to a symphony concert without embarrassing her. There had to be one of those *Dummies* books he could pick up tomorrow, and yes, depending on what it prescribed for him, the dummy, he'd buy a couple of CDs—but he didn't even own a CD player, so he'd have to buy one of those too.

"John?" Justina said cautiously. "Are you okay?" She stepped toward him and yielded her slender hands, which he took into his. He drew her into a tight embrace, with his cheek against hers. "I'm afraid of losing you," she whispered.

John released her so he could smile into her face, which glowed in the moonlight. "And I'm afraid of losing you, Justina." He drew her close again, and their lips merged. John's carnal urgings, fueled by Justina's sensuous movements under his touch, nearly overwhelmed his reason. A younger man would have succumbed, but John sensed that to plunge into love-making that evening would only jinx all hopes for a lasting relationship. He took Justina's hand, and the two began their stroll back to Grand Avenue.

By the time they reached her car outside a darkened Northern Pines, it was agreed they would go out to Lake Harriet two days later, Friday evening, to hear the Saint Paul Chamber Orchestra in one of their summer concerts. "Chamber Orchestra"? Was that related to the Chamber of Commerce? John wondered why the St. Paul Chamber of Commerce was putting on a concert over in Minneapolis, but he dared not ask.

◆ CHAPTER THIRTY-ONE ◆

Behind the Scenes

LIKE A TORNADO BLASTING HAVOC across a Minnesota barnyard, Jenny rushed into John's office and slammed the door behind her. The disruption whipped a couple of papers right off his desk and prompted John to straighten his posture.

"John, you won't believe what Paul Dahl told me at lunch." Jenny's eyelids retracted to reveal her irises in full. The fact that she had called the finance man by his real name told John big news was about to break. Normally, Jenny referred to Dahl as "Fill-in-the-Blank Finance," in recognition that he was the man for reliable, inside scoops pertaining to HeartBank. "I just got back from lunch with Fill-in-the-Blank." Jenny tried to recover some composure as she plunked herself down in the chair facing John's desk. "He spilled some very amazing beans."

"You have my attention." John let out a laugh.

"We were right, John. The merger was hatched by Brinkman in a vacuum and fed to five guys only—that's five, John." Jenny held up her right hand and made her stubby fingers as long and straight as she possibly could. "Fill-in-the-Blank was tapped to help out just four days before the announcement, so he got to see everything, John."

"Fill-in-the-Blank was in on the merger decision?" John asked.

"Here's how it came down, according to Paul," Jenny said. She pulled up her chair and leaned her forearms on John's desk. Intrigued, he himself leaned forward until he realized their faces didn't need to be that close. "As of the Friday a week before the merger announcement, the only person at HeartBank who knew a damn thing about it was Brinkman himself. On that day, he brought General Counsel, Blake Huntington, into the know, along with Flaske, head of Audit, and Frank Johnson, Fill-in-the-Blank's boss. Now, on the Thursday before the merger was announced—so we're down to four days before—Johnson tells Brinkman that he, Johnson, just can't get everything done that he needs to get done before the target date for the announcement." Jenny talked so excitedly that a fleck of spit hit John in the face. He wasn't sure if Jenny even noticed, so rather than draw attention to it, he let it be. "So Brinkman tells him he can bring someone in, on the condition that the person be sworn to absolute secrecy. Fill-in-the-Blank gets the nod and is told he has to maintain two calendars—a real one and a fake one. He's told to keep the whole thing hush-hush, even from his wife. They tell him he has to fly to New York right away to work with the investment bankers, but he has to book his flight through Chicago. They come up with some story for his assistant, wife, co-workers, that he's working on some project down there. His assistant books a round-trip to O'Hare, but Paul then has to book his own flight from O'Hare to LaGuardia and back to O'Hare. That's it, John. Only four days out and only five guys out of 60,000 employees—or however the hell many we have—know about the merger. No one else finds out—not O'Gara, not a single one of the captains—until we all find out." Jenny's excitement revealed the veins in her neck. "Now, think about it John. You know that Huntington, Flaske, Johnson and our friend Fill-in-the-Blank aren't complicitous."

"Aren't what?" John hated to interrupt, but he figured if he didn't, he'd be missing out on an important word.

"Okay, it's not really a word, I admit, but it should be. I mean, those four guys aren't part of any complicity. They aren't dealing with strategy, you know, the question of whether the merger is a dumb idea, a plausible idea or a brilliant idea. They're dealing strictly with the regulatory issues, OCC, SEC issues, that sort of thing. They didn't have any choice in the matter, just to follow orders, just to help the outside lawyers, the investment bankers, just to feed them information so it could all happen according to Brinkman's timetable. Bottom line, John, it was Brinkman's decision—alone.

"According to Fill-in-the-Blank, Brinkman signed the definitive agreement with Loan Star on the Saturday morning before the merger was announced. The HeartBank board of directors met by phone Saturday evening to approve, and a full day later—Sunday evening, Brinkman informed the captains." Jenny had worked herself into such a frenzy that several of John's papers stuck to her forearms as she raised them from his messy desktop.

John wondered what Justina would think of this remarkable revelation. Smart, straight as an arrow and now, present at ground zero of the nuclear explosion called "a merger," Paul Dahl would make an excellent witness. "What was Paul's take on the whole thing?" John asked, knowing the answer.

"What do you think?" Jenny said, with confirming sarcasm. "He said he was so disgusted he was tempted to go straight to the SEC."

"Why didn't he?" John said. His eyes were now as big as Jenny's.

"Because it's like any other merger, and the chances of anyone listening to him—a peon—were slim to none, so why throw himself on a giant letter opener? But you know Paul, John—normally cool, calm and collected?—well, not when he was telling me the story. The deeper he got into it, the madder he got, till his face turned red and his voice cracked. I never thought the guy could get upset about anything, but he sure was upset over what he'd seen those few days before the merger announcement."

John hesitated. He and Jenny had confided much in each other during their tenure in the department, but some things you don't blab to anyone. On the other hand, for all he knew, Jenny was engaged in as much subterfuge as he was, and in the current environment, who the hell cared? If everything was up in the air anyway, why not throw some spice into it?

"I met with a lawyer yesterday, Jenny, about a shareholder suit against the bank."

"You what?" John wasn't sure if he saw surprise or fear in Jenny's face. He regretted that he had mentioned it.

"I saw a lawyer about the merger."

"John, do you realize . . ." Jenny's voice trailed off, and she covered her mouth, as if he had confessed to some terrible crime. It rattled him.

"What?" he asked, fearful that he had tripped all sorts of land mines that were about to explode in his face.

"Do you realize what they'd do to you if they found out?" She said, implying that a lawsuit would never get off the ground. He was miffed by her skepticism, but it gave him an idea.

"What can they do to me, Jenny? Fire me? They'd have to give me a severance package, and under the circumstances, they'd have to give me a pretty damned good one." In light of Jenny's reaction to his consultation with Justina, something told him not to disclose that this wasn't the first time he'd thought about a severance package. But he found a glimmer of hope in the notion that if he became a thorn of some sort, it might hasten his way to a severance package.

"No way, John. If they did that, people would line up to sue so they could be bought off." What did either one of them know about the strength and length of the lawsuit lever? Nevertheless, maybe she was right. Maybe the corporate hide was too thick for a guy like him to become a thorn of any kind. Maybe he was playing with fire, but now Jenny knew, and though he knew she shared his views on the merger—hell, three fourths of the people at HeartBank did—could he trust her not to tell someone carelessly about what he had told her?

"Jenny," he said earnestly, "I hope you'll keep this absolutely confidential."

She hesitated, which worried him. "Of course. I won't breathe a word." Angry over his own carelessness, John lectured himself to keep his mouth shut from then on. "So what do you think of the meeting next week with the bozos from Loan Star?" Jenny changed the subject. No one in the department had met any of the bozos from Texas, yet they were already bozos, the enemy, the despised.

"What? Who's meeting? Where?" John said. He hadn't heard a thing about it.

"John, you've got to start reading your e-mail," she kidded him. To carry through on her friendly ribbing, she walked boldly around to John's computer on the credenza behind his desk and looked at the list of e-mail messages that crowded the screen. Half of them were in boldface type—unread. "Holy shit, John! You have 795 messages sitting in your 'in box' and—my God, John—102 are unread. When are you going to delete a few hundred? Your mailbox must be at full capacity virtually all the time."

"I just make sure I get rid of the memory hogs—anything over fifty megabytes—on a regular basis so I can send stuff," he said sheepishly.

"Well anyway, Vohlmann sent out an e-mail this morning about the meeting. A bunch of our counterparts from Loan Star are coming up here next Tuesday to talk about transition issues—market overlaps, systems conversions, approval standards, organizational stuff. Blowhard said he was down in Dallas on Monday and ran into a couple of people from their national real estate group and said they were real assholes. The head of the department is supposed to be a big jerk besides—thinks he's in line to run our department after it's merged with his. Also, there's a rumor that we'll be converting to their loan accounting system, but someone in our operations told me that Loan Star's systems are nowhere close to being scrub-certified for Halloween Virus." John liked Jenny's use of the politically incorrect term for the potentially catastrophic computer bug. "Even if we started today, it would take close to a year to be virus-free."

"I wonder what Vohlmann's doing to position himself, position us," said John.

"Something tells me that the biggest asshole wins," Jenny said, "and despite all his shortcomings and as much as we make fun of him, Vohlmann is no asshole. If he doesn't get his act together pretty soon and become a flaming asshole, then I'd say we're all in a certain amount of trouble." John knew she was only half kidding. "Probably the biggest thing we have going for us is our long, cold winters. If the bozos from Dallas wind up running the show, at least they won't want to come up here and bother us between October and April."

"What's the format of the meeting?" John asked.

"Each of Vohlmann's directs is supposed to give a five-minute spiel about what we do, and kind of a profile of our groups." Jenny's eyebrows rose mischievously as she smiled. "Then we're supposed to spit tacks in their faces and tell them 'You might mistake us for Minnesota nice, but we can out asshole you cowboys any day of the week, so look out!'"

By now, John had pulled up Vohlmann's e-mail message regarding the Loan Star visit. As soon as Jenny left his office, he thought, he'd spend a few minutes deleting all the garbage messages that made his e-mail boxes look like his desktop. But first, Vohlmann's message, in his usual butchered style.

> Everyone –
>
> Next Tuesday we will host the senior management team of Loan Star CRE (Commercial Real Estate). All directs should plan to attend and give 5–10 minutes background on your self and your group. Lets look real sharp. Well talk about extent to which our markets overlap and what we can do to leverage off of each other going forward. Also we should be prepared to talk about systems

conversion issues and how our teams will be impacted by Fall Festifal virus and loan approval procedures. Any questions, let me know.

FV

Jenny was right. Vohlmann wasn't a big enough asshole.

◆ CHAPTER THIRTY-TWO ◆

Merger Music

JOHN ARRIVED HOME AND CHANGED into comfortable clothes for dinner *al fresco* and the outdoor concert at the pavilion on the north side of Lake Harriet. According to plan, Justina would stop by his apartment as soon as she herself could slip into something suitable after her late afternoon hearing in downtown St. Paul. While he was restoring his suit to a hanger in the closet, he heard her knock at the door of his basement apartment. "Come on in, Justina," John shouted from his bedroom at the end of a short hallway.

"Hi John," her voice sang out.

"I'll be right there," he said with his chin holding his suitcoat against his chest while he put the slacks on the hanger. "Make yourself at home. I'll be right out." Moments later, he checked himself in the mirror, combed his hair and walked to the front of the apartment to greet his new beloved. But when he saw her, he stopped dead in his tracks. A crushing wave of embarrassment crested over him and threatened to sweep Justina out of the room and away forever.

There in her hand was the book, the big yellow book, the *Classical Music for Dummies* book that he had bought the day before and read voraciously long into the night and again, early that morning. Now she knew what a hopeless dummy he was. The scene then progressed in a painfully slow series of freeze frames, in which John noticed every change in what had to be the expression of ridicule. First she lifted one corner of her mouth, then her lips parted as she narrowed her eyes and blinked. A smile formed; her chin rose and her teeth met to form the J sound. He was about to be clobbered with a laugh of contempt, but he deserved it for being so careless as to have left *Classical Music for Dummies* on the one chair in his sparsely furnished apartment.

"John, *what* are you reading *this* for?" Justina's words struck like a volley of poisoned darts. In her other hand were the CDs—*Bach's Greatest Hits* and *Mozart's Greatest Hits.* It's over, he thought, in the awkward pause that followed. She and I are finished, unless . . . unless . . . unless what? I have no explanation but to confess my ignorance. His jaws began to move but without sound at first.

"I tried to tell you . . ." he said, haltingly. "I don't know a damned thing about classical music, but Justina, when I heard that music in your office the other day, it . . .it was something I liked. I mean, I really did, and I could tell it was really important to you so I wanted to learn more about it, and well, I didn't know where to start, so I got the *Dummies* book, because that's what I am, Justina, when it comes to music, and well, I'm sorry, that's all. I'm sorry. I'm not what you thought I was, and I tried to tell you, but it was hard, and well . . ." John's voice trailed off, and he realized his face was flushed with embarrassment.

When Justina released the book and the CDs from her hands, like garbage into a barrel, they landed smack flat on the wood floor, and the resultant *'kphlank'* reverberated off the bare plaster walls. She threw her arms around John's neck and looked into his embarrassed face. "John," she said. "I love you." She kissed him lightly on the lips and slid her hands across his shoulders and down his arms to his hands. Her dark eyes peered into his heart as much as into his eyes. "I had no idea you didn't . . . I'm touched, John. That's all there is to it." She solicited another kiss and he obliged her with a dry brush of his lips on hers. "But John, you don't need the *Dummies* book and you don't need the *Greatest Hits* CDs, either. I'll teach you. I'll introduce you to the great music of the world, to composers who will become as much your friends as they are mine."

He wanted to wipe the perspiration from his forehead, but she clung firmly to his hands. "So you don't think I'm just totally ignorant?" he said.

"You're totally wonderful." She pulled him close to her, and he responded with a nearly crushing embrace.

Over dinner in the outdoor courtyard of Rigoletto's, near Calhoun Square, comfortable walking distance from Lake Harriet on the west side of

Minneapolis, John received his first lesson in music history. He wondered if somewhere along the line he would have discovered classical music if he had been allowed to continue college at St. Olaf. As he recalled for Justina, it seemed there had been a number of music people on campus. At the "U," it had been quite a different story, especially over on the West Bank, where the business school was located. "So you see, if my dad hadn't been laid off by the bank during my first semester of college, I would have continued at St. Olaf, and who knows, I probably would have discovered music a lot sooner. It was the bank's fault," John said, only half in jest.

His statement prompted questions about Marv and the circumstances surrounding his dismissal from First Metropolitan. Before long, the conversation turned to HeartBank, and for the first time since Justina had shot down the idea of a shareholder derivative suit, John brought the subject to life again. "Incidentally, Justina, a friend of mine, another of my boss's direct reports, told me something quite interesting yesterday." John retold the story of Fill-in-the-Blank as it had been recounted to Jenny.

"That's amazing," Justina said, in a way that told John he might now have something for a shareholder derivative suit. She laid her fork back into the pasta, took a sip of water and tapped her lovely lips with her napkin. "The corporation really is the plaything of the people—or in this case, it seems, the person—at the pinnacle." She picked up her fork to resume eating. "I spoke to one of my friends today, John, who has handled some derivative actions. He said they're really hard to win unless you have good, direct evidence that the officers or directors of the corporation have breached their fiduciary duties."

"What exactly does that mean?" John said. Justina's inquiry had surprised him, pleasantly, but it sounded as if she had only received confirmation of her original skepticism.

"Well," Justina said, with her tongue literally in her cheek and the corner of her mouth upturned, "there's this fascist, capitalist-pig, management-oriented legal concept called the Business Judgment Rule. It says that courts won't second-guess the decisions of a corporation's officers and directors unless they've breached their fiduciary duties to the shareholders. To show a breach of fiduciary duties is substantially more problematic than to show simply that the officers and directors did something dumb."

"But from a legal standpoint, how do you distinguish between a decision that's really big and stupid and a breach of fiduciary duty?" John said, with his fists on the edge of the table, his knife in one and his fork in the other.

"Well, let me give you an example. If all you can show is that the CEO—what's his name again?"

"Brinkman. Maximilian Brinkman."

"I love that name—*Maximilian*—or Maxi-milli-*on,* I suppose." Justina smiled at her own pun. "If all you can show is that Maximilian thought bigger was better and that based on the combination of HeartBank and the bank you're merging with—what is it again?"

"Loan Star."

"Loan Star? What kind of name is that? Anyway, if he can obtain what's called a fairness opinion that is based on reasonable assumptions, he wins in any kind of derivative action."

"But what's reasonable?" John said. He realized his emotions had driven up his volume, but he glanced around and decided the surrounding noise was more than enough to cover his conversation with Justina.

"That's going to be a fact question, and that's where you're looking at very expensive and protracted discovery."

"But can't you start with the investment banking firm's rendering the fairness opinion? I mean, how could they possibly give an opinion that the merger is fair to the shareholders, when they put it together in no time flat? And don't you point out to judge and jury that the investment bankers get an obscene fee for doing so? And Justina," John said, earnestly, "how the hell can Brinkman, or Brinkman and four other guys—forty, for that matter—reasonably conclude in the course of a week and in secret, that the merger is a good deal for shareholders?"

"John, look. You're not going to find anyone who hates big corporations more than I do. They're exploitative, wasteful and evil, as far as I'm concerned. And your questions are all exactly the right ones, but I'm just telling you from a practical standpoint, that unless you have direct evidence in hand that your Maximilian guy did something specifically and obviously in breach of his duty to the shareholders—some evidence, for example, that he knows it's a bad deal but went ahead anyway—you're going to have a very tough time proving your case or even getting sufficient leverage for a meaningful settlement. I have no doubt, John, that in the end, you're absolutely right. The HeartBank merger, and just about any bank merger these days, is a bad deal, all the way around. However, you're going to have to find evidence that would allow us to short circuit the normally cost-prohibitive discovery."

"I'll keep looking," said John. "If you had access to certain quarters, snooped around and talked to the right people, I'll bet you'd stumble across all kinds of juicy evidence. Take my friend in Finance, for example. The guy is a low-key, middle-mucker like me, but he sometimes finds himself in the most interesting places in the bank."

"Actually, John," said Justina, as she chased the last of her penne pasta around her bowl, "if there's evidence to be found, that's exactly how you find it. The discovery process in litigation is designed to uncover the truth, and often it does, but all too often the defense can hide behind the formalities and play a shell game with the truth until the plaintiffs quit. However, with your contacts inside the bank, you might well be able to sleuth your way around in a way an outside lawyer can't."

"Are you actually encouraging me, Justina?" John smiled.

"Hmmm. Maybe I am," she said, "but it doesn't seem that you need it, necessarily."

"You know, for the longest time, I viewed the bank as a decent place to work, a job that paid the bills, allowed me a few luxuries and gave the promise of more luxuries, or at least, greater financial security, if I held in there, did my duty and paid my dues. But eventually, I realized I'd plateaued. I felt like I was surrounded for the most part by tyrants, idiots, fools, money grabbers and powermongers. I tried not to be like them, which is hard sometimes, if you want to succeed. In time, I sank into the swamp, thinking I'd never escape, until this friend of mine, Steve Torseth—you've got to meet him someday—gave me the idea of going for a severance package. That was about ten months ago. After a series of diversions, you might say, I thought the merger might be my salvation, but so far, I'm no closer to a package than I was when I decided that was what I wanted."

"What would you do if you left the bank?" Justina asked.

"I don't know, Justina. It's really short-sighted of me, isn't it? To be thinking of how I can get kicked out—with a severance package, of course—without figuring out first what I'm going to do once I land in the street."

Justina pushed her dishes forward, propped her elbows on the edge of the table and rested her chin on the backs of her hands. Even with his eyes trained on hers, he could see her Ojibwa necklace—a gift, she had said, from an Indian woman whose runaway daughter Justina had helped several years ago—against the bare, beautiful skin across the top of her chest.

A small, polished, triangular agate pointed toward the area between her breasts, and John imagined them bare and beautiful. He ordered himself to continue talking.

"But you know what, Justina? As the merger unfolds, I've come to view the bank as a bad place for lots of people, not just me. I guess maybe you'd call it a place of injustice, all the way around, only most people have been beaten down, bamboozled, hoodwinked—whatever you want to call it—into thinking it's one big happy family, or more accurately, one big happy team, where everyone is supposed to be a team player, and if you're a happy, follow-the-leader kind of team member, you'll be rewarded with a button, a twenty-five-dollar gift certificate and potential career advancement. When in fact, it's a giant chess game, and the main team players are a few guys at the top, who are playing the rest of us like pawns. Truth is, if you want to become a chess player, you have to adopt the chess player's mentality and engage in behavior that is pretty much the exact opposite of what we're told we need to show if we want to get ahead. So you see, whether it's intentional or not, the few at the top issue two sets of rules for the game—the official rules, which have the imprint of HR all over them—and the unofficial rules, which are set by way of example. Only if you follow the unofficial rules will you get ahead—but then, only if they don't kick you out first for not having followed the official rules."

Justina looked at him admiringly. "I always looked at big corporations as exploitative, but primarily from an external perspective. Although, as you know, I've sued corporations for discrimination, I never really focused on their broad-based exploitation of employees." She leaned forward so the agate swung free, and extended her arms across the table toward John. He laid his hands on her forearms and absorbed her gaze. "John," she said. "I'm really proud of you for seeing injustice and wanting to do something about it. I'll do everything I can to help. Not just for you, John, but for all the people who are exploited, abused and manipulated and don't even realize it."

"You know," he said, "I'm destined never to be well off, but for the first time in my life, I don't care about financial security. I care about a little happiness, that's all." Justina's lips parted to reveal her perfect, white teeth, and John wondered how a man could be so lucky as to be seated with a woman like her at a small table for two.

The concert was a first for John, indoors or out. As he and Justina found seats in front of the pavilion, toward the center and about twelve rows back, where Justina thought the sound would be best, John marveled at how pleasant the weather could be in a place like Minnesota. The temperature seemed as pleasant as it could possibly be, and the sky contained not a hint of clouds. Behind them, the sun slid toward the horizon but with nearly an hour to go before it disappeared. Roseate rays of the declining sun struck the eastern shore of Lake Harriet and highlighted every detail along the water's edge, every leaf of the trees that lined the walking path, every runner, every biker, every couple who walked hand in hand.

Judging by his initial review of the program, John found no apparent connection between the St. Paul Chamber of Commerce and the Saint Paul Chamber Orchestra. When he finally came across the brief paragraph about the history of the "SPCO," as it was called, and the definition of a chamber orchestra, he was relieved he had followed his instincts and not asked Justina about an orchestra sponsored by the St. Paul Chamber of Commerce.

"This first piece," Justina said of Beethoven's *Overture to Prometheus,* "is something you'll really like, I think. I'll bet you'll recognize it. If you've never heard it, John, you'll certainly recognize it the next time you hear it. The next piece, from Mozart's *Jupiter* Symphony, is another one that's easy to recognize." As she drew her finger slowly down the program, John admired her hand. He doubted he had ever seen a woman's hand of such perfect proportions, with such beautiful skin. "Oh!" she said with delight. "The concertmaster is doing some Kreisler pieces. John you'll really love these. Elsa Swedborg, the concertmaster, is the sister of a lawyer I know. She's performing *Rosmarin, Liebesleid* and *Liebesfreud.*" John worried about the foreign sounding names. Learning classical music could get a little tricky if you had to learn a foreign language to remember the names of the songs.

"How many songs do they typically play in a concert?" John asked.

Justina looked at him with a glint in her eye. "First of all, John, they're generally called 'pieces,' not songs. Songs, like Schubert's *Lieder,* for example, are called 'songs' but virtually all other compositions are called 'pieces.' How many depends entirely on length. An overture, for example, might last only two or three minutes. A symphony can take thirty minutes or more, and there are all kinds of pieces in between. Generally, though, a classical concert will last around two hours, including intermission."

John loved the way Justina explained things. She didn't make him feel the least bit uncomfortable about it, though he realized he was light years behind her. Her instruction encouraged him to ask more questions, and their waiting time passed all too quickly. He was so engrossed in the process that he didn't join the automatic applause that occurred when the conductor took to the stage. Justina was absolutely right—John liked *Prometheus,* and he was sure he had heard parts of the *Jupiter* somewhere, sometime in his past. The Kreisler "pieces" were fun to hear as well, and he loved the way they made Justina smile.

They held hands for nearly the entire concert, and by the end, Justina had both her arms and hands wrapped inextricably around John's right forearm. After the final applause dissipated into the evening air and as the moonlight danced on the waters of Lake Harriet, John and Justina strolled along the shoreline path. In the shadows at the south end of the lake, they slowed their pace to a standstill, and there, John gathered her into his embrace.

Later that evening, with Chopin preludes and nocturnes wafting softly from the CD player next to the bed in Justina's apartment, they made love, and John realized that their love was a prize infinitely greater than any severance package ever granted in the history of the world. With one arm behind his head and the other around Justina's deliciously bare, sensuous shoulders, he felt her breasts pressed warmly against his ribs. Her head rested against his chest, just below his chin, and her perfume filled every breath with sweet pleasantness. John savored his bliss.

♦ CHAPTER THIRTY-THREE ♦

Loan Sharks

"THEY'RE A BUNCH OF ASSES," Jenny said from the doorway of John's office. "Their bank might be Loan Star, but they themselves look like a bunch of loan *sharks.*"

"You've already met them?" John asked, as he searched his desk for a printout of his outline for the presentation to the Loan Star bankers.

"I just poked my head into the conference room long enough to hear them exchanging lewd comments while they wait for us to assemble."

"Lewd?" John asked, surprised.

Jenny laughed. "Well, let's put it this way. Their heavy Texan accents twang all around my inner ears as if they were being lewd. I can't stand the way they talk."

"You'd better get used to it, Jenny. We could wind up reporting to one of them."

"That's a distinct possibility. Except for one guy who's shorter and fatter than I am, they're a lot sharper-looking than we are. Also, they carry their guns on the outside—holsters, every one of them, including the cowgirl—can you believe that they brought a woman banker with them?—and their bowie knives are right out on the table top." With her arms folded, Jenny leaned against the door-frame and assumed a cynical smile.

"Are you suggesting we don't carry weapons?" said John.

"We have weapons, all right—just look at all the back-stabbing that goes on around here on a regular basis—but they're nearly always concealed. It just isn't Minnesota nice to expose the blade until you make the plunge into someone's back, and even then, you need to be careful no one actually sees you do it. I think these cowboys," said Jenny, as she pointed her head in the direction of the conference room, "are going to be more up front about it, and the knives are just for backup. They'd prefer to shoot us dead."

"Are any of our people in there yet?" asked John.

"Not when I checked, and I wasn't about to be the first and only one. That's why I came down to get you."

John finally found his outline. "I'm ready for show time," he said and rose from his desk. By the time he and Jenny reached the conference room, all their HeartBank colleagues were seated or pumping caffeine from the dispensers at the end of the room. It looked like a giant face-off—the Loan Sharks on one side and Vohlmann with his direct reports on the other.

"I'd like you to meet Jenny Jacobson, head of Loan Administration, and John Anchor, Collateral Control," Vohlmann said, as they entered the room. John and Jenny walked down the line and shook hands with the enemy. John wondered how he would keep Hernandez straight from Mirandez and how C.T., the oversized guy in a sweat, would hold up in a seventy below wind chill. The name of the one to worry about, the man in the middle, was Garth Borash.

Sure enough, before John and Jenny sat down, Borash—a guy in a dark blue suit with slick-backed hair, black eyes and creases across the forehead so deep for his age that John thought they might be scars from some freak accident—seized the initiative and launched the meeting. "I think what we're here for," he said with a drawl so pronounced it sounded affected, "is to see how you guys up here are going to fit into our organization."

Vohlmann looked shell-shocked. He twirled his pen nervously on his notepad until he accidentally spun it with such pent-up force it shot straight off the pad and into his styrofoam cup of caffeine. The liquid slopped against one side of the styrofoam, and the cup suddenly shifted about an inch and a half on the tabletop. John pictured Vohlmann as a prize-fighter on his back about three seconds after the beginning of round one, while the Loan Star slickster bobbed up and down, victorious fists in the air.

Just then, the high-tech, metallic ring of a cell phone split the uneasy silence that followed the Loan Star's opening salvo. Never in John's career at HeartBank had he heard a cell phone ring during a meeting—at least while he was paying attention. "Excuse me," the Loan Star bully said, as he pulled his phone from the inside pocket of his suitcoat. Judging by its almost miniature dimensions and credit card thinness, John assumed it was a state of the art device that hadn't yet found its way to the Midwest.

"Yeah," the bully said. John didn't know anyone who answered a phone that way, even one equipped with caller ID. For something to do, Vohlmann took a gulp from his cup so he could go for a refill. John sat in nervous silence, fearful of indictment, sentencing and execution if he whispered anything to Jenny. His colleagues seemed to be frozen by a similar fear. Meanwhile, their Loan Star counterparts huddled, then guffawed, then rose with a commotion and poured themselves more coffee. Imagine these greasy cowboys coming up to our turf, John thought, and moving in here like they owned the place. He couldn't remember there ever having been a time when he felt guys like Blowhard and Sycophant were his allies, but with jerks like these Texans on the other side of the table, just about anyone could be your ally.

"Right," Borash said to the anonymous caller. "Tell that sonofabitch he's toast if the system isn't up and running by the time my meeting's over. I'm in the middle of a meeting right now. . . huh?" Borash stood up, and with angry eyes, he shot holes in the wall behind Vohlmann while the caller talked. "I don't care if he said it was bound to happen—he's the asshole who runs it now, isn't he? Tell him if he doesn't have it running within an hour he'll be running a fruit stand outside Casa Piedra, not the IT group." John noticed that the enemy bankers had grown silent, but none looked surprised. "I'm working that out right now," Borash barked into the phone. "We're gonna hear from these folks in a moment. Yeah, that's right. Huh? I don't know yet. We just sat down a minute ago, but I gotta think there are gonna be a couple of keepers." Borash allowed a wicked smile and winked at Vohlmann, whose perspiring forehead glistened in the hostile light. Vohlmann must be wetting his pants by now, thought John. Loaded with caffeine, Vohlmann had to be feeling the pressure.

Borash returned the phone to his pocket and nodded to the guy next to him—was it Mirandez or Hernandez?—who prepared to take notes of the proceedings. Borash himself was the only one at the table who sat without a notepad or a Franklin planner to absorb streams of ink. "Why don't we go around the table and explain what each of us does, so we can get a better lasso around our systems, markets, MO, you know, that sort of thing," said Borash.

MO? thought John. He hadn't heard that term in quite awhile, and it made him smile. As far as he could tell, Vohlmann didn't have anything resembling a *modus operandi,* nor did guys like Blowhard and Sycophant. Hell, no one, including John, had an MO. This would be interesting to watch, he thought.

"Why don't we start with you, Mr. V," Borash said to Vohlmann. Poor Vohlmann. Vohlmann had been out-maneuvered and out-gunned before he could even grab for a weapon. The Loan Star-HeartBank merger might have been publicly billed as another "merger of equals," but in the case of John's department, clearly it was a Loan Star takeover, or at least, Borash was playing it that way. Vohlmann, who had been so gung-ho over the merger announcement back in April, was letting these Loan Star schmucks walk all over him, right from the start. John wondered how a guy like Borash would view the idea of a severance package. He seemed like a hard-nosed, incisive player, who wouldn't have time for people like John who treaded water and desperately wanted, needed a change of scenery, if only a severance package became available.

With something close to panic in his eyes, Vohlmann swallowed some caffeine and prepared his response. "We're, uh, a national commercial real estate lending group, and we're on plan for, uh, just over $25 million net earnings . . . uh . . . after tax," he said. John noticed that Vohlmann's shirt was growing a darker shade around the armpit. "We, uh, have our own direct sales force, but we also try to leverage the franchise as much as we can, you know, by referrals from commercial bankers across the organization. I, uh, think we'll find tremendous synergies with Loan Star," Vohlmann said, unconvincingly. "When it comes to, uh, systems, we use our own systems pretty much for loan accounting and collateral control, hardware, software applications and support, but we'll be interested in what you guys have." John noticed the beads of moisture on Vohlmann's bald pate and figured that Borash and all the other Loan Star cowboys noticed too. Vohlmann had a bad case of nerves, and they were showing. Bad sign, John told himself. These sharpies from the enemy camp are going to eat Vohlmann for lunch. They'll go back to Dallas convinced they own us. Vohlmann took another sip of caffeine and poured himself some more to try to hide the fact that he didn't have an MO—or had he simply forgotten that was part of Borash's question?

"Maybe now we could go one by one here," Vohlmann said. He turned to his left, then to his right, like a scared deer, thought John, who doesn't know which way to turn for its escape.

"Whatever," said Borash, with a touch of boredom mixed with a hint of sarcasm. Blowhard went next, followed by Sycophant. Between Blowhard's nervous twisting of his pen and his voice cracking, not once but twice, and Sycophant's continual throat-clearing and unintelligible corporate speak, replete with "synergy," "opportunities in the marketplace," "impactful strategic dialogue" and "optimization of shareholder value," Vohlmann's two most important direct reports did not cut an impressive image, at least in John's eyes. John glanced at the Loan Star people and thought he saw mild smirks at best.

Vohlmann's other direct reports performed no better, except for Jenny, who was as bright and articulate as John had expected. John cheered silently when she took the offensive. "We appreciate your coming up here," she said directly at Borash, "but frankly, I'm eager to make the trip to Dallas next week to meet the folks who'll be reporting to me." It surprised the smirk right off Borash's face, and John noticed C.T. shift his sweaty weight around in his chair, as if Jenny's directness had given him an instant hemorrhoid. Ironic, thought John, that the only person with any balls on the HeartBank side of the table was a woman.

John's turn came next. "Frankly, there's probably reducible redundancy in my role as collateral control manager," he said. A battered looking Vohlmann snapped his head in John's direction, and out of the corner of his eye, John sensed that Blowhard's jaw had dropped far enough to have doubled his usual number of chins. John gave an overview of his area, and he found hope in the fact that the Loan Sharks showed signs of boredom with his summary. There was a big difference between a redundant bore and a fool. A redundant bore like himself, John figured, was more apt to qualify for an attractive severance package than was an insufferable fool, like so many of the bumblers on the HeartBank side of the table, though after he thought about it for awhile, he couldn't explain exactly why that would be so. Maybe it was simply that he'd rather be boring than be a fool.

By the time the Loan Sharks left, Vohlmann had as much life in his face as a day-old plate of lefse. For the first time in John's memory, neither Blowhard nor Sycophant could utter a word, let alone a long-winded commentary about a meeting they had just attended. A sense of doom and surrender filled the conference room. The bad guys had stormed into Dodge, shot up the town and left the sheriff and his deputies bound and gagged at their posts. Only Jenny had returned their fire, but if she ever posed a threat, the Loan Sharks would return and finish her off as well. No one needed to say it: time to dust off the résumé. But John was the only one in Dodge who clung to the hope for a severance package.

♦ CHAPTER THIRTY-FOUR ♦

Merger Truth

JOHN CLEARED A SPOT ON THE CREDENZA for the new CD player he had purchased at Target over the weekend. It was a relatively inexpensive model, but he wasn't seeking high-fidelity sound. All he needed was something on which to play his new CDs, and thanks to the severance package Sandy had extracted from him as part of the divorce settlement, he didn't have lots of extra money to blow. He searched for the outlet and noticed that a number of papers had slipped off the back and into the void between the wall and the back of the credenza. With a ruler, he pushed them aside to provide access to the outlet. He plugged in the CD player and plopped in a disc that Justina had given him the day before—a recording by Pinchas Zukerman and the Saint Paul Chamber Orchestra, performing J.S. Bach's Violin Concertos in A minor and E Major. "Baroque and Classical music make the best music to work by," she had told him. "You can remember Bach is Baroque—the first two letters are the same." John hit the play button and Bach came alive.

Just then, the phone rang. Without checking the caller's identity, John lifted the receiver. "John Anchor," he said, as he adjusted the volume of the CD player.

"Hi John. This is Tom Kinder," said the amiable lawyer, whom John had barely heard from since the disastrous hearing a couple of months ago.

"Tom!" John said. Sufficient time had passed to mitigate his embarrassment over the courtroom humiliation John had brought upon himself. "How are you doing?"

"Fine, fine. How about you?"

"You mean work or life outside of work?" asked John.

"Both, of course," said Tom genuinely.

"To be honest, Tom, life at work really sucks, especially in the midst of this merger, but my love life is going great outside of work." John surprised himself with the reference to Justina. Until now, John had purposely not mentioned his romance with Justina to anyone at work. He just wasn't the sort who talked much about his personal life to anyone, even his friend Jenny, and moreover, he didn't want to contaminate his perfect love by mentioning it in a place overgrown with all the things he detested about people. But Tom was a different person. He sincerely cared about people, and John had been deeply touched by the handwritten note he had received from Tom the day after the "gum shoe" incident in Judge Kanker's courtroom. Tom had written,

> John,
>
> Don't worry about the gum. All of us have had truly embarrassing moments we'd like to forget and eventually we do forget, until we have a chance to tell a funny story over beers. You'll recover, just as I have from such events.
>
> TK

After a two- or three-minute chat, Tom got down to the reason for his call. "Blake Huntington asked me to attend a meeting early this afternoon up on the seventieth floor to discuss the Walden case," he said. "Apparently, Brinkman, the merger attorneys and others are getting together to go over the status of some merger issues, and given the magnitude of the claim in the Walden suit, they want to get my assessment of the case. I thought it would be helpful if you were there so they could get a feel for it from the horse's mouth. You present yourself well, John—when you're not chewing gum, that is," Tom laughed good-naturedly. "I think they would feel more comfortable with my assessment that it's a lot of nonsense if they could hear you tell your story."

"I'm flattered," said John. Tom was a certifiably nice guy. "But I thought we're screwed in the case."

"We're not going to get summary judgment, if that's what you mean," said Tom "at least, not yet, but in the long run, they simply have no case. Don't worry, we'll get it settled, though it might smart a little."

"Okay, sure," said John. If nothing else, it would be fascinating to watch the merger mavens in action, however briefly.

"Good. Now I have a more important question," Tom said. "What are you doing for lunch today?"

"Is that an invitation?"

"Sure is."

"You're on. When and where, Tom?"

"We'll meet at Dean's Steakboard at noon. Chuck Lindstrom from the law department is going to join us too."

After the conversation, John cranked up the Bach as loud as he dared and leaned back in his chair, hands behind his head. He closed his eyes and allowed a smile of immense satisfaction to cross his face. He wondered how many powermongers at Loan Star and how many fearmongers among his peers ever found in their offices the kind of satisfaction that he had finally achieved in his—and with the prospect of a steak lunch to boot.

Lunch remained about three hours away, however. John killed time by reviewing a batch of collateral reports, speculating with Jenny about the speed with which Borash would take over the department, reading *The Wall Street Journal* and checking no fewer than twenty-three e-mail messages, including one from finance, which requested all of Vohlmann's direct reports to "identify and quantify ways the merger will save your area expenses or enhance your revenues." Just goes to prove, John thought, that none of those high-priced investment bankers, not to mention Brinkman, figured out any real benefits before the merger announcement. John wondered what effect this bit of evidence would have in a shareholders' derivative suit.

At around half past eleven, John began to check his watch regularly. He was eager for lunch, but he didn't want to show up more than five minutes early. Any earlier and people might question whether he was sufficiently busy. Force of habit, he knew. Why should he worry about such a thing at this stage of the game, especially from the likes of Kinder and Lindstrom?

In its day, Dean's had been one of the finer restaurants in downtown Minneapolis. Still a draw for the fading tail of the old boys' network, it had become retro without really trying. Lately, Dean's had undergone a surprising revival among professionals of the younger crowd. Its faded green exterior panels gave it the look of a tile wall in a bathroom of an old discount motel room. Above the entry hung a forties-style aluminum sculpture consisting of a band about three feet high at the base, which sloped inward toward the bottom, and a dart-shaped piece about ten feet high, which rested against the front and back of the band. Off to the side of this bizarre sculpture was the name of the place—Dean's Steakboard—in oversized, cursive lettering also shaped from aluminum. Over *Steakboard*, a giant image of a tenderloin steak, oozing with juice on a platter, was bolted to the wall, and over the steak, smaller lettering identified Dean's as Home of the Buttersoft Sizzler. John felt the cholesterol clog his veins as he scanned the building front on his approach. He noticed a fat pigeon perched inside the *o* in *Steakboard* and wondered if the management knew how much pigeon guano had built up on the lower part of the letter.

Just inside, John stepped into a dim foyer and approached the podium of the maitre d'. It took a second for his eyes to adjust from the brightness outside and to see that behind the podium stood a thin woman in her late sixties with half glasses on a chain, a frilly blouse, a huge build-up of red lipstick and a large stack of silver-gray hair. "Good afternoon," she said in a smoker's voice.

"Hi. I'm meeting a party by the name of Kinder," he said.

"Tom Kinder?" she said with a tone that suggested he was a regular. "Right this way, please." She led John into the dining room and nearly lost him as he slowed his pace to view the surroundings. Covered with long, heavy, light pink linen, the tables looked like an exhibit of old-fashioned skirts. A carnation in a vase served as the centerpiece for each table, and wine and water glasses stood guard over four-piece silver flatware settings. At each occupied table, a bread basket the color of the green, exterior panels sat as another reminder that time had largely left Dean's alone. For the most part, the patrons looked white, male, in their fifties or older and well-fed. However, John saw a few smartly-attired yuppies, as well. Hidden fluorescent lights around the perimeter of the room provided illumination. Spaced every twelve feet or so on the walls, sets of three electric candles provided atmosphere, as their filaments flickered in synchronized spasms.

Tom and Chuck greeted John warmly, and with hearty handshakes, he returned the reception. As John pulled his chair up to the table, a waiter gracefully appeared and with one of his white-gloved hands, snatched the sculpted linen napkin off the table, snapped it open with an elegant flair and allowed it to float down upon John's lap. John wondered if Justina would get a kick out of the place or get kicked out for her politics.

"May I start you with a beverage, sir?" asked the waiter deferentially. Dressed in a tuxedo, which close up, John noticed, showed lots of wear, the straight-standing waiter looked like a man whose job had long been an obsession.

"How about an Arnie Palmer?" John said, thirsty for a combination of lemonade and iced tea.

"It shall be yours, sir," said the waiter.

"So do they allow Democrats into this place?" asked John affably.

Tom laughed. "Only if they order steak and baked potato with butter and sour cream. I like coming here every once in awhile. I can fill my arteries with fat and wallow unabashedly in male chauvinist pig heaven for an hour or so. If my esteemed women partners want to criticize me for my political incorrectness, I plead guilty. At my age, I'm tired of pretending I'm not offending anyone. I say, cut the bullshit and eat steak."

"I'm all for that," said John.

"Just don't report me to the Diversity Council," said Chuck.

"Did you know I'm on the Council?" John said, unable to hide a smile.

"No," said Chuck. Tom laughed so suddenly it turned into a cough. "Is it part of your compulsory sensitivity training?"

"It's a long story," said John. He told them part of it, fully confident that they were a completely sympathetic audience, and besides, at this juncture, who the hell cared. In fact, as the lawyers responsible for the Walden case, they should know John's motives in wishing for an early resolution, good or bad.

John finished just as the steaks arrived. In Dean's trademark fashion, each steak oozed in juice on a metal plate embedded in a slab of oak two inches thick. He hadn't touched his salad yet, and to catch up, he decided to shut up and eat the thick slice of a head of iceberg lettuce graced by a tomato slice, adorned with a giant carrot curl and bathed in French dressing.

"So how is the merger treating you fellas?" asked Tom.

"You want the official lie or the real story?" said Chuck. His unabashed bitterness surprised John, who had always viewed the serious, deliberative, in-house lawyer as one who kept a tight wrap on his non-legal opinions.

"You mean to tell me," said Tom, as he carved into his Buttersoft Sizzler, "that the press releases I'm reading in the papers aren't entirely true? Chuck, I'm shocked!"

"There's a lot that would shock you about this merger," said Chuck, through the half-chewed piece of Buttersoft Sizzler that hung in his cheek. Chuck's outspokenness slowed John's chewing to a standstill. Chuck Lindstrom simply wasn't the kind of person who would say such a thing in public, whatever he felt inside, and he certainly wasn't the sort who talked with his mouth full. It occurred to John that Justina might find it helpful to talk to Chuck about a shareholder derivative suit.

"I can attest to that," said John. He wanted to show his support for Chuck, but in the awkward pause after his words, John wondered if the in-house lawyer had regrets about venting in public.

"Guys, I'm your lawyer, and more importantly, I'm treating you to lunch at Dean's," said Tom. "You're not allowed to keep me in suspense. What the hell *is* going on over there?"

"I haven't had a chance to talk to you about this, John," said Chuck, "so I don't know what you're experiencing in your area, but I can tell you this: Of the people around the bank I have talked to, I'll bet only one in ten thinks the merger is a good idea."

"You think it's that high?" said John sarcastically. Chuck looked surprised by John's response.

"Why, what's going on in Vohlmann's world?" Chuck asked.

"A group of Loan Star bankers from their commercial real estate group came up to our shop last week. They wore spurs and ten-gallon hats, carried Colt .45s and generally, acted like real assholes," said John. "They acted like they had marching orders to eat us for lunch, and unfortunately, most people were afraid to challenge them. We were all caught off guard. We needed a game plan to defend ourselves against them, but our fearless leader crumbled on the spot. I don't know what Vohlmann thinks or what he has been told, but everyone at my level is convinced the Texans have taken us over."

"It would certainly appear that way from what you've described," said Tom.

"The truth is, no one knows who is really taking over whom," said Chuck. "I attended a meeting with Loan Star in-house lawyers last week down in Dallas, and they were convinced that we were taking them over. There was panic in the hallways, and someone said there's a rumor that even with the corporate headquarters moving to Dallas, the law department is going to stay in Minneapolis. Apparently, Loan Star's general counsel is leaving, which means Blake Huntington will be general counsel for the new company, and Blake doesn't want to move to Texas. Blake is a perfectly nice guy, but a Loan Star lawyer told me he'd heard that Blake hated Texans generally and Texas lawyers particularly. I was amazed. This guy was sure that Blake was out to get every lawyer in the Loan Star legal department. Nothing could be further from the truth.

"But then on the other hand, I've seen situations like you described, John, where Loan Star bankers have run roughshod over our people. Frankly, there's such a huge cultural gulf between the way Loan Star operates and the way we operate, I don't know how the two entities can ever merge effectively. They play fast and loose with credit, and with some notable exceptions at HeartBank, we're generally much more conservative. Loan Star management is very strict—break the rules and you're out. They fire first and aim second. At HeartBank, you just about have to commit first degree murder in the course of robbing a teller to get fired. Take your friend Dennis Heckler, for example, John." Chuck was uncharacteristically as red as his medium rare steak.

"Take me, for example," said John. "No matter how hard I try, I can't seem to get myself kicked out."

"Then there are the systems problems. There couldn't be two banks with so many different computer systems. We can't even manage our own as they exist today—despite what you hear about our technology's being so advanced. How the hell are we going to convert or merge all these systems without blowing half the circuits? And I guess Loan Star has done next to nothing to prepare for the Halloween Virus. I heard estimates that even if they launched a massive effort starting as of last month, they wouldn't even be halfway finished with debugging, testing and all that by Halloween. One person I talked to in Audit says they're concerned that on that basis alone, the regulators might not approve the merger until after October, and if Loan Star blows up because of the Halloween Virus, the merger, of course, won't happen at all."

"Sounds like you've got interesting times ahead," said Tom. "So interesting, in fact, I think that now's the time for every insider to sell his HeartBank stock—what do you think?" Tom said, as he brushed his napkin across his smile.

"There could be some real buying opportunities in the months ahead," said Chuck.

"So, what do you make of the decision to move corporate headquarters to Dallas?" asked Tom.

"I heard that Max Brinkman hates living in Minnesota," said John, cutting into his Buttersoft Sizzler, which was inexplicably tough. "That's why he's not even here half the time. Someone said he loves cowboy stuff, hates winter and can't wait to get out of here. The move has nothing to do with the so-called strategic direction of the new organization. I'll bet when they got to the question of re-locating the headquarters it wasn't the quote-unquote difficult decision that Brinkman claimed it was. I'll bet when they got to that question, Blusser said, 'Okay, if you get to be CEO, then headquarters are going be in Dallas,' and Brinkman said, 'Sure, fine. Next subject.'"

"Huh," said Tom, between chunks of steak.

With the remains of their baked potatoes, the men mopped up the last pools of Sizzler juice on their steak boards. The waiter cleared the boards, and with a gold scraper, graded crumbs off the table. He then tantalized with a dessert tray loaded with selections sure to plug any arterial openings that remained after the feast of Sizzler cholesterol. However, fear of post-lunch drowsiness dissuaded the men from partaking. They ordered coffee—fully caffeinated—instead.

Tom looked at his watch. "It's almost show time. Should we start back?" John and Chuck agreed. Tom took care of the check, and sucking on their mints, the three men headed back to the HeartBank Tower. Enroute, they talked about the Walden case, and Tom offered John some guidance on what to say about it.

$ $ $ $

The men stepped into the elevator, and Tom hit the white button over the number seventy. "I forgot to bring oxygen," he said.

"Maybe the people who occupy the floor could use some too," said John. He couldn't remember just when, but he had visited the executive floor once. The assistant for one of his bosses ages ago had moved on to become an executive secretary for someone in the rarefied air at the top of the tower. When she retired, a send-off party had been held in the boardroom, and John, along with dozens of other former colleagues, had attended.

The express elevator rose, slowly at first, then faster, until John felt enough g-force to remind him of astronauts, and then so fast all three men moved their jaws to open their ears. Toward the top, the elevator decelerated, then slowed for a gentle landing at the seventieth floor. The doors opened, and Tom Kinder motioned for Chuck and John to step out first. Awed by what lay before them, they hesitated for a moment.

"Now that gives new meaning to the word 'carpet,'" said Tom of the thick, rich blue, beige and burgundy oriental rug that stretched over an area probably twelve by twenty feet just outside the elevator bank. It covered plank flooring—maple, John thought—which was exposed in an area a couple of feet wide around the periphery of the rug. The wood looked so pristine that John wondered if it had ever been touched by a shoe.

Just beyond the elevator bank, off to the side, a security guard sat at his post outside two enormous brass doors of an art-deco style, each with a series of sculpted panels depicting highly idealized scenes of industrial, agricultural and commercial activity. The guard bore a plump baby-face, flushed, with a small mouth and a red protruding lower lip. He wore a white shirt with sleeve creases sharp enough to cut anyone who moved too close to him. An American flag graced one sleeve, in attempted fraternity with law enforcement officers and other keepers of order across the country. The HeartBank logo appeared on the other sleeve, as well as over his right breast pocket. A large gold badge was pinned on the other breast pocket.

"Can I help you gentlemen?" said the guard.

"Yeah, we're here at the request of Blake Huntington for a merger-related meeting," said Tom, both hands on the handle of his briefcase.

"Names?" the guard asked laconically.

John felt a twinge of indignation, but he noticed that Tom, a hundred times the man that guard could ever be, showed no sign of displeasure. Tom gave the names, and after the guard checked his list, the doors opened ponderously. "You may go in," said the guard, as if his words were necessary to unlock an invisible barrier in the open doorway. "Turn right and go down all the way to the end. The boardroom is down there." The three visitors walked forth lightly, as if to avoid detection, past walls adorned with oversized European exhibition posters from yesteryear, framed in gleaming metal. John wanted to stop and view them, but Tom and Chuck showed no signs of slowing the pace. Besides, thought John, it would be decidedly uncool to stop and gawk at wall hangings.

Beyond Exhibition Hall, the floor opened up, with executive lairs to the left and secretarial stations to the right. The executive offices looked like showcase living rooms of the rich and famous, with leather sofas, floor-to-ceiling bookcases, floor lamps, desks the size of most cubes elsewhere in the tower and a wide assortment of wall hangings. As to the other side of the corridor, John wondered what the cube dwellers in his department would think of the rare wood paneling, state-of-the-art computers, wide-open counter space, potted plants, ergonomic chairs and expensive clothes among the row of attractive but haughty-looking secretaries.

The men slowed their pace as they approached the sprawling board-room visible through glass panels at the end of the corridor. There ahead of them, in full gear, was the power room, where more was happening than in all the other corners of the HeartBank Tower combined, where power and influence were being wielded in such concentration, with such force, it made John feel like less than a nobody. Even the straight and noble Tom Kinder shrank to the size of a peon compared to the self-appointed gods gathered in the HeartBank boardroom. The three men stopped at the doorway and gazed upon the scene. A crowd of fifteen or twenty men and women, but mostly men, all white (a few being Hispanic types, thought John), with the exception of a couple of blacks, occupied the room. Some stood conversing in twos or threes and most of the others sat among the couple dozen high-backed leather chairs around a table so big its construction must have consumed half the rain forest of a Central American country. John noticed a man off in a corner, talking into his cell phone while he looked out the window across the Minneapolis skyline. Another man on a phone sat alone at one end of a cabinet that stretched across the width of the room at the far end. The powermongers at the table sat at various angles. Some appeared immersed in piles of documents, others stared into the screens of their electronic notebooks and others, seated at all angles in the throne-like chairs, jabbered with one another. Still others licked the residue of lunch from their fingers—a catered lunch, a power spread of shrimp, lobster tails, cold cuts, rolls and bread, pasta salads, four-tiered fruit trays, chicken wings and enough dense, high-powered chocolate brownies to launch a space shuttle. The pickings had spread to all corners of the boardroom.

Starched white shirts dominated, and it occurred to John that he hardly ever wore a white shirt. Nearly all of his were blue, and for a moment, he wondered how different his career might have been had he worn white shirts all these years. But white shirts showed the ring around the collar sooner than blue shirts did, and long ago, he had figured out that he could save substantial dry cleaning costs by wearing blue shirts a couple of times instead of white shirts only once before tossing them into the hamper.

No one seemed to notice Tom, Chuck and John at the doorway, until a tall, dapper, sandy-haired man, perhaps in his late fifties, acknowledged them from the far side of the table. "Ah," said Tom. "There's Blake." Chuck and Tom moved into the room, and with John in tow, they edged their way around the room to greet Blake Huntington, HeartBank's general counsel.

"Good to see you," Blake said, as he extended his hand to Tom. Chuck drew up next and introduced John. In the crowded quarters of their immediate vicinity and as a passerby jostled him, John shook hands with the chief lawyer at HeartBank. "Good to meet you, John," said Blake. He then faced Tom and said, "We're about to get to pending litigation. We're kind of running behind here, so you're probably only going to have five minutes or so. What the auditors are going to want to know, I think, are the basic facts of the Walden case, the basic claims and kind of your overall assessment of it—you know, settlement value, time lines for possible resolution, that sort of thing. I've given summaries of it, but they need to hear from litigation counsel, so I really appreciate your coming up here to do this."

"No problem," Tom said.

"Maybe when this is all over, we can catch up over lunch," said Blake.

"I'd like that," said Tom, spontaneously.

Just then a voice boomed, "Okay, everyone. Let's get underway. We have work to do." John looked around and saw Max Brinkman standing in the doorway where John and the two lawyers had stood just moments before. Max the Man, thought John. Chief among chiefs. Brinkman stood in his shirtsleeves, fists firmly planted on his hips. He looked like a sea captain appearing on the bridge to resume control of the helm. Conversation diminished rapidly and people immediately moved to their seats. John overheard the man on the phone behind him say, "I gotta go. Where can I reach you in another hour-and-a-half?"

Hurriedly but politely, Blake said to John and the lawyers, "Why don't you take the chairs over there?" He pointed to a line of chairs behind the throne chairs on the opposite side of the table. "We'll get you on as soon as we can. Thanks much," he said, as he shook Tom's hand once again.

John liked the genuineness in Blake Huntington's face. The man's eyes radiated sincerity, and it looked as though Blake and Tom knew and liked each other. John could see it in the way they greeted each other—a hearty handshake, a look of relaxed familiarity in their faces, in their voices—and John respected Tom to the point of respecting anyone Tom liked.

Tom, Chuck and John shifted past people around the table to three vacant chairs near the doorway. Brinkman, meanwhile, moved around the other end of the room and took his seat in the middle of the opposite side of the table. He picked up a table knife and struck the side of a water glass to bring the meeting to order.

"We have a full agenda for this afternoon, so we need to keep the ball rolling here, gentlemen," said the omnipotent CEO. John wondered if Brinkman's slight of the women in the room was intentional or just an ignorant oversight. "First we're going to have a regulatory update—where we stand with the OCC, the SEC, the FDIC and the DOJ. I'd like to finish that up by three o'clock. Then we'll get a litigation update—notice that we fed all you lawyers really well so that the litigation report won't make you hungry." Mild laughter rippled around the table. "Okay. Huntington, are we ready to hear how we're doing in Washington?"

As Blake Huntington went through an outline, John leaned toward Tom and asked in a low voice, "Who are all these people around the table?"

"For the most part," Tom whispered back, "they're lawyers with the firms representing HeartBank and Loan Star in the merger—Lauter & Schlicher and Hefte Bolder, both New York firms—accountants and the investment bankers."

"Why isn't Bakke & Fulsom representing HeartBank in the merger?" John asked innocently.

Tom blushed and took a few seconds to respond. "Oh, the New York firms generally get the nod for transactions of this magnitude," he said. John realized he had asked an embarrassing question.

For close to an hour, various people at the table, most of them with pronounced East Coast accents, droned on about unimaginably boring legal arcana pertaining to obscure rules and regulations promulgated and administered by oceans of nameless, faceless bureaucrats. The scene prompted John to imagine an office the size of the Mall of America filled with colorless cubes and hapless people. Extreme drowsiness overcame John, despite his consumption of caffeine at lunch.

As he fought to retain consciousness, he recalled the vacation his family had taken to the Rocky Mountains when he was a young boy. For days before their departure, John was so excited about the trip across "cowboy and Indian country," as his father had described it, that he had been unable to sleep at night. But within a few miles beyond the western fringes of the metro area, John had fallen fast asleep. For the entire two weeks, John hadn't been able to stay awake in the car for more than half an hour, it seemed, and his sleepiness fueled affectionate laughter whenever his parents recalled the trip. Here was another trip across cowboy and Indian country; a glimpse into the epicenter of one of the biggest mergers in the history of banking, and John could barely keep his eyes open. He noticed he wasn't the only one.

Finally the time came for the litigation report, and after some summary comments, Blake asked Tom to talk about the Walden case. Tom rose, and John thought it was ironic that because his favorite lawyer—who was probably twice the lawyer that any of the people from Lauter & Schlicher and Hefte Bolder would ever be—had been relegated to a back seat in the room, he, Tom Kinder, the real lawyer from Minnesota's own Bakke & Fulsom, got to stand up while everyone else, including Maximilian Brinkman, remained seated.

"Hello, everybody," Tom said, affably. "I'm Tom Kinder with Bakke & Fulsom here in Minneapolis, and I represent HeartBank in the Walden case. This case is in federal court here in the District of Minnesota. We think it's a sham case, really, but we haven't shaken it loose yet. We moved for summary judgment awhile back but it was denied, so now we're awaiting a trial date. Plaintiffs are claiming damages of over a hundred million, down from a billion in their original complaint, but frankly, we can't see how they get to anything close to that."

"What are the allegations?" someone asked.

"They're claiming that we committed to opening a certain kind of funding account and then reneged, causing them enormous consequential damages. Our position is that John Anchor here," Tom said, as he gestured toward John, "who was handling the plaintiffs' inquiry, never made any commitment of any kind, and in fact, treated plaintiffs very cautiously from the very outset. When John realized plaintiffs were trying to scam the bank, he turned down their business and they turned around and sued.

"What we think is going on here, actually, is a scam on top of the scam. The first scam consisted of this questionable plan to set up what they termed a 'real estate funding account,' through which they would run up to half a billion dollars on an ongoing business. They claimed to be a financial agent for a nameless trust out of Hawaii. From the get-go, we saw all kinds of evidence that it was nothing but a ploy to get us talking. You know, flash lots of money in front of a banker to hold uninvested. The banker would then get dollar signs in his eyes when he figured all the earnings the bank would make on the money, which would be included in the computation of the banker's bonus. Then, at the right moment, the scammers would twist facts so it looked as if the bank had made a commitment. Hopefully then, the bank would deny the commitment and presto, you have yourselves a lawsuit. But that's only the first scam.

"The second scam is actually perpetrated against some local, unsuspecting contingent fee lawyer who is starved for a big win—preferably someone who has a history of suing, not representing, banks and large corporations. The scammers do some research and find just such a lawyer. They say, 'We just got screwed by this big bad bank. The bank made a commitment and then reneged, probably because we're black or we're this or we're that.' We have it on pretty good evidence, by the way, that one of the scammers is a minority. The lawyer gets all riled up and thinks he's suing for justice and all that. However, his main motivation becomes the prospect of hitting the jackpot. Think about a guy who has done mostly two-bit consumer and personal injury cases and suddenly gets hired on what appears to be a claim for $100 million. He'll get a third of whatever it settles for. If the case settles for just a penny on the dollar, that works out to a settlement of $1 million, of which the lawyer would take home over three hundred thousand—not bad for a guy a couple of years out of law school who's never netted more than forty thousand in a whole year." The "forty thousand in a whole year" made John think of Justina. He couldn't wait to tell her about his hobnobbing with the merger mavens.

"So you see," Tom continued, "the plaintiffs' lawyer is scammed into taking the case and fighting like a bulldog."

"Jesus Christ," Brinkman said, disgustedly. "Who was it who said, 'Kill all the lawyers'? What'll it take to send the pipsqueak ambulance-chaser back into his hole?"

"You mean, what will it take to settle the case?" asked Tom.

"Or smash it, depending on your definition," said Brinkman.

"It depends a little on your timetable, I guess," said Tom. "If you need to get rid of it because of your merger timetable, I think we could do that if you're willing to pay what amounts to extortion money, as opposed to a legitimate settlement amount. A legitimate settlement amount would take into account the cost of positioning the case for trial, wearing the bulldog down with onerous discovery, motions, that sort of thing, and the trial risk, which is always there, no matter how good your case is. What I'm saying though, is that what I describe as a quote-unquote legitimate settlement amount would be substantially less, I think, than today's exit price."

John wondered if he would be asked to speak. He felt his lunch churning disagreeably inside his intestines, as he contemplated the prospect of addressing a roomful of high-powered New York lawyers and the head honchos of HeartBank and Loan Star, not the least of whom were Maximilian Brinkman himself and Blusser, whom Chuck had pointed out as the bald guy in his sixties sitting next to Brinkman. On the one hand, he thought, it would make for a great story to tell just about anyone—Justina, Steve, Jenny, his parents. On the other hand, the mere thought of having to talk to this crowd was producing a considerable build-up of bowel pressure.

"Can you give us two prices—today's and the one you think would be more favorable?" asked Blake.

"I'd say today, as ridiculous as this sounds, you're not going to get this lawyer's attention for under $10 million," said Tom. Huntington cringed visibly, and John heard Brinkman mutter a "Jesus" under his breath. "Tomorrow's exit price is considerably less—I'd say around a million to two million."

"Bastard lawyers," said Brinkman. "I can't wait until you're all dead." The CEO seemed to relish the chance to make the room's bar association squirm. "Okay. Huntington, why don't you get together with Mr. Kinder and work things out? I want that case off our list, but that sonofabitch lawyer on the other side isn't getting any three and a third million out of it. I want that case settled for less than five million and I don't want that lawyer getting anything more than Blusser's ten-gallon hat filled with cow shit, which is all that scumbag lawyer deserves."

With that, one of the investment bankers (John assumed, by the man's glittering watch and cufflinks) who stood in the corner pocketed his cell phone and strode over to Brinkman to whisper something in his ear.

"Okay, people, we're going to take ten," said Brinkman, and with permission granted, people moved about.

Tom stood up, and Chuck and John followed suit. It was over, and John had not been called upon to speak. However, the pressure in his bowels remained, or rather, it recurred in waves, manageable at first, but increasing with each repetition. No sooner had the three men moved toward the doorway, than a man about Tom's age, with reddish, gray-flecked hair, and gold-rimmed glasses pushed his way into their path. "Tom Kinder!" the man said, almost accusatorily, as he pointed at Tom. When Tom responded with a face filled with puzzlement, the stranger said, "Bowdoin College, Class of '68."

Tom's puzzlement gave way to joyous surprise. "Mark Oppenheim!" He almost shouted the name, as the two men shook hands so hard that John saw Tom's fingertips turn white. "Geez, I haven't seen you since when—our tenth-year reunion? Back then I think you were still with Latham & Watkins, weren't you?"

"That's right. I moved over to Lauter & Schlicher soon after that." The two classmates plunged into an animated conversation to revive their long-lost connection. When they had exhausted their own post-graduate histories, they started in on the whereabouts and well-being of other classmates and regressed to the nostalgia of their undergraduate days. In his excitement, Tom forgot to introduce John. Chuck, meanwhile, had already been nabbed by his boss, Blake Huntington, whisked away and lost in the crowd.

Not knowing another soul in the room, John stood by invisibly. He felt like a klutz, not knowing whether to feign interest in the talk of two alumni of a college he had never heard of, or, since he hadn't been introduced to the Lauter guy, to look away, uninterested, to show he wasn't intruding, or to walk away altogether. Bowdoin College? He repeated the name to himself. Where the hell was Bowdoin College? No doubt it was out East somewhere—that's where all the hoity-toity schools were located, he had learned over the years. Most of them he had never heard of, though of course, what was he but just another Minnesota bumpkin, anyway?

As he stood in his awkward indecision, he felt a big wave of pressure in his butt. It reminded him of Steve's joke about the sphincter being the smartest muscle in the body because it knows the difference between a gas, a solid and a liquid. It just knows, thought John, that what's in there now is a liquid, and with each minute, the hydraulic pressure is building. If I don't find a restroom soon, I'll be walking like I've got a clamp on my sphincter. At that moment, the Lauter lawyer sneezed once, then twice, and offered an "excuse me." Tom answered with a "gesundheit," and John seized the opportunity to excuse himself. Feeling slightly embarrassed at not having introduced John, Tom released him without commotion. "I'll catch you later," he said.

John felt like the pilot of a B-17 in one of those WW II movies, who struggles to return his badly crippled bird to its base on the safe side of the Channel. As he left the boardroom, he realized his sphincter would not be able to resist the ever-increasing pressure long enough for him to reach home base—the rest room on his floor. He would have to crash land in a field somewhere in the English countryside. But where was a good field? He made a pass along the row of executive secretaries and radioed the least attractive of the bunch. "Where are the rest rooms?" he asked, trying like the dickens to mask his near panic.

"Around there," she said and pointed back in the direction of the boardroom. "Turn right, go way down to the end of the hall, turn right again and you'll find it there."

"Thanks," John's voice cracked. Now the B-17 was down to one smoking, sputtering engine, and work as they might, the crew could only hand crank one landing wheel. It was not looking good. In his imagination, John gripped the wheel and nursed the wounded plane over the hedgerows by the boardroom, banked hard to starboard and walked down the hallway toward an emergency airstrip in the form of the executive restrooms. He was losing altitude at an alarming rate. "Hang in there, baby!" he shouted to his crew, including the tail gunner who had taken some flak and was badly wounded. "We're gonna make it. Yes, baby, we're gonna make it!" And we're never going to eat at Dean's again, he thought.

In a back corner, John found the beacon that would bring him in for a landing. It was a polished brass door, which bore the word *Gentlemen* in an elegant, cursive script. When you've got a bad case of the trots, he thought in a panic, there's nothing more important—not money, not a severance package—than having a place to *go.* He pushed the door open just as his bowels pushed him. On the other side of the door, a scent like after-shave lotion filled his nostrils and a blur of brass trim, gold faucets, marble basins, imported tiles, cut-glass mirrors, lamps with fancy shades and small stacks of linen overwhelmed his eyes. He had never landed in such an opulent restroom, but opulence didn't matter. A stall did, and it wasn't clear where they hid the stalls in an opulent restroom. By now, John had passed the point of no return, where his sphincter could no longer constrict on its own. It needed help from his glutei maximi, flexed with anaerobic intensity. With the biggest muscle helping the smartest one, John assumed a prosthetic-like gait in search of the stalls.

To his great relief, the thrones appeared around the corner. They seemed to be vacant, for the door to each looked as though it were open a few inches. John pushed on the first door, but when it didn't budge, he realized that in a closed position, the latch side of the door was set back from the frame. He heard the occupant clear his throat. Awash with panic, John tried the next stall. This time he was lucky. The door swung open against the force of his hand. Frantically, he loosened his belt and nearly tore off his waist button. He yanked down on his zipper, and his trousers fell fast to the tiles. At the same instant, he hooked his thumbs on his underwear and pulled down, just as he lowered his buttocks onto the polished black seat. Against all odds, he had landed safely.

John was all set to let fly, when the outer door to the restroom banged open and a loud voice and the sound of expensive shoe leather hard on the tiles filled the room. "You think I did this for the shareholder?" the words reverberated against the ceramic walls. John recognized the voice. It belonged to Maximilian Brinkman. "You got that entirely wrong, my friend. This has nothing to do with the shareholder. I did this on a bet, and I need to close on the merger by the end of the third quarter to win, don't you see? So do whatever the hell you have to do, just get it done."

"A bet?" another voice broke in, as shoe leather clicked toward the urinals on the wall opposite the stalls. John heard streams of pee hitting water, and to his amazement, the smartest muscle in his body outsmarted the nerves in his bowels that signaled URGENT! He scarcely breathed. "For Christ sake!" the second voice whispered fearfully. "You can't do something like this on a bet. With whom? Christ, I don't want to know."

"You're my lawyer. I thought anything I tell you is privileged," said Brinkman. His voice sounded closer, as if his head had turned to double check for ears in the stalls. John pulled his feet back quietly, as far as he could, and when he looked down to his right, he saw an expensive, burgundy wing tip doing the same.

"I'm the bank's lawyer," said the other voice at the urinals. "If word ever got out—I'm no litigator, but Jesus, Max, they're going to depose me and privilege won't stand for shit."

"Okay, okay, but just so you know, Jerry, I need to get this thing closed no later than September 30, you understand?" Brinkman said, urgently.

"I think we can manage it, Max."

"You do and I'll let you in on some nice action—IPOs I know about, deal?" said Brinkman.

"How much?"

"A million, guaranteed."

"Now that's my kind of deal. But what's the bet?"

"I thought I couldn't tell you."

"We'll make sure no one knows." John heard the streams of pee diminish to a short trickle.

"I bet this friend of mine in Texas, head of an oil-drilling supply company, an old buddy of mine back in our training days in New York, that I could close on a mega-merger by September 30. If I do, he owes me dinner at The Opulate in Vegas, two bottles of *Chateau Petrus* and the woman of my choice."

"And if you lose?"

"A million guaranteed says you're not going to let me lose, Jerry." John heard the urinals flush, followed by the sound of a hand hard on a back. A few footsteps, a swing of the restroom door and silence returned to the room.

At long last, John let loose, and a blast of diarrhea, gas and other converted forms of his lunch at Dean's issued forth. Almost in reaction to it, the burgundy wing tip, draped by the loose pant leg of a fine, gray-plaid suit, shifted, then disappeared. The adjoining toilet flushed, and the stall door opened. John lingered behind, shaken as much by what he had heard as by what he had eliminated from his system. As he washed his hands, he shook his head in disgust. Brinkman and his lawyer hadn't even bothered to wash their hands.

$ $ $ $

John rushed to his office, closed the door and called Justina. "Darn! Answer the phone," he said aloud, impatiently. The intervals between rings seemed interminable. Finally, she picked up her phone.

"Justina, I've got to talk to you right away," John said urgently.

"What is it, John?"

"You won't believe what I just heard with my own ears!"

"Tell me."

"I can't over the phone. I've got to tell you in person. What are you doing right now?" John breathed hard.

"I'm through for the day. Come on down as fast as you can," she said.

John felt another urge to go to the bathroom. He dashed out of his office again and flew to the men's room on his floor. It took him five minutes to assure himself there would be no need for further visits to a lavatory in the near term. He was beginning to feel better, lifted by sheer adrenaline.

Minutes later, John recounted the extraordinary conversation he had heard in the executive restroom of HeartBank. It left Justina's eyes and mouth agape. She reached for a writing tablet and a pen and sat down at her desk. "Tell me again, John, only you have to tell me exactly where you were—exactly where Brinkman was, what the lawyer looked like, everything, exactly as you saw and heard it. I need to know the precise circumstances of the conversation."

John blushed. "No you don't," he said.

Surprise overtook Justina. "What do you mean?" she said. It took awhile, but she coaxed it out of him, and when she had, she laughed.

They laughed hard together, until John gathered enough air to say, "I can't wait to hear Brinkman say, 'Oh shit!'" and they laughed even harder. When she finally recovered, Justina grasped her pen and tapped it against her lips.

"John, we need to know who the other witness was," she said.

"The guy in the stall or the lawyer? Why do we need them?" he said, as he wiped the tears of laughter from his cheeks.

"The guy in the stall. The lawyer, we can assume, will deny everything—just as Brinkman will. It would be your word against theirs, and as much as I hate to admit it, as much as I love you John, your voice will get drowned, beaten, threatened into oblivion by theirs. We need a corroborating witness, a witness with stature, with instant credibility, a witness with shiny burgundy wing tips."

◆ CHAPTER THIRTY-FIVE ◆

Burgundy Wing Tips

THANKS TO E-MAIL, THE NEWS HIT every corner of HeartBank at cyber-speed. Blake Huntington was throwing in the towel, effective in two weeks. According to the party line, he had intended to retire by year's end for health reasons, but with the announcement of the merger and the stress it created, he decided he would move up the date.

"Strange, if you ask me," said John to Justina over the phone. "Yesterday, he looked in perfectly good health to me."

"Are you thinking what I'm thinking?" asked Justina.

"I'm thinking Huntington is our man," said John.

"Precisely," she said. "And here's my theory: Huntington hears what you hear and decides to confront Brinkman with it. Brinkman then fires him to get him out of the way of the merger but gives him a nice severance package to shut him up."

"That's exactly right," said John. "But do we go with the theory or do we look for the burgundy wing tips?"

"It would be nice to have shoes to confirm the theory," said Justina. "But now that he's history, how can we put the shoes on his feet?"

"I have an idea," John said. "Can I call you back?"

"What is it?" Justina asked.

"I'll call you back."

$ $ $ $

It would not be easy to line up an appointment with general counsel of the nation's eleventh largest bank at a time when he was preparing to retire and the bank was preparing to close on a mega-merger. However, the Walden case was of sufficient magnitude to attract what little attention Blake Huntington had left.

"Tell him it's really urgent," John said over the phone to Huntington's secretary. "It concerns settlement of the Walden case." In fact, Tom Kinder had been trying hard with Blake Huntington to settle the Walden case, ever since Brinkman's directive the day before. Within an hour, Blake Huntington himself was on the phone with John.

"I need to talk to you right away about something I know about the Walden case that not even Tom knows," John said to bait the general counsel. It worked.

"How about this afternoon at 2:00? My office is on fifty-four," Huntington said. John readily accepted and phoned Justina.

"Are you ready to check out Huntington's wing tips?" John asked.

"Huh?" she said.

"At 2:00 this afternoon, we get to meet Huntington in his office. I say we got him."

$ $ $ $

Just before the appointed time, John met Justina in the lobby of HeartBank Tower, which was as stone cold and uninviting on a hot summer day as it was in the dead of winter. They took the elevator to Huntington's floor, entered the reception area and announced their arrival. "Please have a seat," said the receptionist, authoritatively. "I'll let Mr. Huntington know you're here."

"Thanks," said Justina, "but I like to stay on my toes." She winked at John.

A minute later, a secretary appeared and led John and Justina to Huntington's well-appointed corner office. The afternoon sun streamed in, and in the distance, John could see a Boeing 747 making its final approach into the airport on the south side of Minneapolis. It reminded him that Huntington was also making his final approach to early retirement. Silhouetted against the brightness behind him, Huntington rose from his chair to greet his visitors.

"I'd like you to meet my other lawyer," John said. Justina extended her hand, while John peered down at Huntington's shoes. Yes! He almost shouted aloud. There they were—the burgundy wing tips. When Huntington gestured toward the chairs in front of his desk, Justina stole a glance at the shoes.

"I think you'll want to close the door," Justina said. With surprise wrapped in puzzlement, Huntington followed her suggestion.

According to plan, Justina seized the initiative. "The reason we're here, Mr. Huntington, is that my client here, Mr. Anchor, is prepared to initiate a shareholders' derivative suit against HeartBank based on your CEO's unabashed acknowledgment that the entire merger with Loan Star rides on nothing more than a bet. We know that you heard the same declarations that Mr. Anchor heard in the men's room on the seventieth floor on June 19. We need your cooperation." John wondered if there existed anywhere another lawyer as beautiful and as scary as Justina. He watched the color drain from Blake Huntington's face as the general counsel searched for a response.

"I don't have the foggiest notion what you're talking about," he said at last.

"Oh, I think you do," Justina said, with supreme confidence. His denial had occurred just as Justina had predicted, and though they had no proof other than the circumstantial evidence of burgundy wing tips and his surprise retirement, John and Justina figured proof would appear if they called his bluff and appealed to his reputed honesty and good citizenship. According to Tom Kinder, Blake Huntington was a shining example of how good people could and did rise to the tops of large corporations. Justina continued. "We think you're probably as repelled by this whole merger business as we are, and we ask you, Mr. Huntington, to join us in a noble fight against ego and greed. This is a battle worth fighting, and you know as well as I, Mr. Huntington, that while we are bound to be zealous advocates for our clients, there exists a higher principle to which we must adhere, and that is—the truth. Not just for ourselves and our clients, but for all of society. I know you agree with me. I know what causes you and your wife have supported. I know that you are a man of faith, that you have served three terms as president of your congregation at Lakeside Episcopal Church in Wayzata. I know you aren't about to sell the interests of HeartBank shareholders and employees, customers and communities down the river to a man who has only one objective—his own wealth and power. I know you're not that kind of man, Mr. Huntington." Justina had done her homework, and John sat in awe of her self-assuredness. There was no doubt in his mind that she was the best damned lawyer in America. He felt enormously proud of her. He loved her.

Justina's appeal left Huntington white and dumbstruck. Suddenly, he didn't look so healthy after all. In a panic, he clung to his denial. "You're crazy," he gasped. "I don't know anything about this."

John knew Justina had another arrow in the quiver, and in anxious anticipation, he waited for her to draw it forth, notch it in her bowstring, pull it back and release it. "Like I said, Mr. Huntington, I think you do know. If you're not willing to play straight with us, we'll see how you do under oath, because the next time we talk, it will be at your deposition, when, as you know full well, Mr. Huntington, you will have made an oath to tell the truth, the whole truth and nothing but the truth, so help you God." Huntington pushed himself back from his desk, as if the added distance could protect him from the dead-on attack after the fact. While he gasped for air, Justina stood up and motioned for John to join her. Together, they walked out. John dared not look back. He feared the man was having a heart attack.

On the elevator, which they shared with two other passengers, Justina stood as cool as a feline after a satisfying meal of milk and tuna. John felt almost manic, and he breathed with nostrils flared. He had never committed a crime in his life, but it seemed as if he and Justina had just robbed a jewelry store. It was exhilarating, and John suppressed the mild shame that crept into his thoughts. Out on the street, he embraced her ferociously and pressed his lips against hers.

"You were absolutely stunning in there," he said excitedly, as he held her head between his hands.

"We'll see," she said, modestly.

"He'll surrender, Justina. I know it. I watched him. You pinned him to the wall." He couldn't understand why she didn't share his wild enthusiasm. "Just imagine him at the deposition!"

"But you're forgetting something," she said. Her hands pulled his arms down from her ears.

"What's that?"

"We can't subpoena him unless we start a lawsuit, and if we start a lawsuit, John, it means whatever you get will be a few thousand dollars, nothing more," said Justina.

John thought something had suddenly gone terribly awry. "I don't understand," he said, his eyebrows tight with worry.

"I mean, John, that if Huntington doesn't fold on his own, we'll have to sue to depose him. If we've sued him, it means that any judgment against HeartBank, its officers and directors—any settlement with them, will have to be approved by the court and shared with all the shareholders out there. As surely as I'm standing here, other lawyers will join in the fray and legal fees would be split a dozen ways. Your take and mine would be a pittance."

"But . . ." John didn't quite follow her, and he was slightly embarrassed to have to ask for more explanation. However, curiosity and confusion outweighed his initial reticence. "We can still sue and win, can't we? We can still bring Brinkman to his knees, can't we, assuming Huntington talks in the end? And in the end, surely a guy like that isn't going to lie under oath, is he?"

Justina's eyes widened and darkened in a way John had never seen before. For an instant, he feared her. "John, we could do much better than that," she said darkly.

"How's that?" He imagined that together they had robbed the jewelry store, but only Justina knew where the loot was hidden.

She glanced furtively up and down the abandoned sidewalk. "Remember, John, what the proxy statement said about what Brinkman and Blusser were getting personally out of the merger?"

"Brinkman gets forty million," said John. Earlier in the week, they had pored over the statement that had been sent to every HeartBank shareholder regarding the terms of the merger with Loan Star.

"Exactly," Justina the jewel thief said. "What we would need to do is get to him and his lawyer and to them alone. When they tell us we're crazy and they'll crush us like bugs, we'll tell them we have a corroborating witness—one Blake Huntington. We'll then threaten to take the story public, to sue, to blow Brinkman and his merger to kingdom come. Then, John, we'll settle—just we ourselves, just you and I, John, and we walk away with millions. No one else, none of the shareholders, not a court, not the press, no one knows. We just quietly walk away with millions."

John stepped back. Before him stood the best and most beautiful lawyer in the land—and maybe the most ruthless.

"So you see, John, we don't want to depose Huntington, and frankly, if I'm any judge of a potential witness, we don't have to depose him. He had 'lie' written all over his denial up there." She pointed toward Huntington's high perch in the Tower.

John's necktie suddenly felt uncomfortably tight, and he loosened the knot and unbuttoned the top button of his shirt. "But Justina, Brinkman and his lawyer are going to play hardball. Without a statement from Huntington, how are we going to call their bluff? They'll deny everything and treat the Huntington card as a joker, pure and simple."

Justina looked beautiful, and the slight breeze in her hair blew a few strands across her face. She also looked cunning and shrewd. "John, I can taste the victory. Those guys can deny all they want, but how do they know that we don't have Huntington boxed in a trap, no matter how they want to play this thing out? John, believe me, I've won many cases on hunches, on instinct, on my assessment of how—in the end—people will behave. And here, John, my instincts tell me to go for the jugular—to hold up the bank, the greed mongers, the hoarders at the top, once and for all. We can do it, John! For the love of Mozart, we can do it! And think of it, John, we can share in the wealth of the guy at the top of the pyramid."

"Or is it greed—our greed too?" John asked, painfully.

Justina's face fell. She looked distant and vulnerable. Fear filled her eyes. Her lips moved, but she had nothing to say. Then, without warning, she pressed herself into John. He wrapped his embrace around her and felt her sobbing. He knew he could say nothing more until they were beyond the shadow of the Tower. With his arm still around her shoulder, he initiated steps down the sidewalk. Neither of them spoke until they had crossed Nicollet Mall along Third Street.

Finally, she spoke. "I'm sorry, John. I feel so terribly confused right now. Confused and upset."

"It's okay," John said softly. "I love you no matter what."

"But it's not okay. You're right, greed has taken hold of me just as it's consumed Maximilian Brinkman."

"Are we leaving me out of this?" John said with a comforting chuckle. "After all this are you going to deny me a nice fat severance package? The severance package I've been working on for all these months?" Justina stopped and looked up at John. As she did, a glimmer of felicity appeared through her darkened visage. She smiled and laughed. "That's what I love about you. You make me laugh when I'm upset." They kissed, looked long into each other's eyes, then continued slowly down the sidewalk, his hand in hers.

They walked silently, each absorbed in thought for a minute or two, until they both spoke at once.

"How many million can we—" John asked, greedily.

"I have an idea—" said Justina, hopefully. "I'm sorry," she said. "What did you say?"

John felt heat in his ears. "I was going to ask how much you think we could get out of Brinkman."

"That's just it, John. What I was thinking is that we can create a win-win situation." Neither one noticed the red light and the Don't Walk signal until a late model BMW blasted its horn at them. John yanked Justina's arm as he leaped backward onto the curb. "My God!" she shrieked. When he embraced her in safety, he could feel her heart beating against his.

"That was way too close for a Scandinavian," said John.

He drew a laugh from Justina. "We Jews are used to close calls," she said.

"Now that we just avoided getting run over," John said, "what was your win-win idea?"

She pulled at the sides of her light blue dress, as if the close call had put it out of adjustment. "Brinkman is getting forty million out of the merger, right?" Justina said. John nodded. "Then here's what we do. We go to him and his lawyer personally, and we tell them we have Huntington in our pocket. Then we say, 'cough up twenty million—ten million for us and ten million for charity.' If they cooperate—which they'll have to, if they don't want to personally experience the dead center of a nuclear explosion—great. Everyone's happy and no one in the world has to know. We then can take our money in good conscience—those charities will get ten million they would never have gotten otherwise—and we can go listen to Mozart full-time, volunteer for your friend's charity and a bunch of other good causes and Brinkman gets to keep his job as CEO of Megabank. Plus, he gets to keep twenty million—not a bad take—and gets to play philanthropic nice guy. And I," Justina said, as she lowered her chin and raised her smiling eyes at John, "get to buy a Bösendorfer concert grand for our musical gazebo on the shores of our own Walden Pond, where we can make love without having to worry about getting up for work early the next morning."

Her win-win idea whisked John into a different universe. His vision narrowed so that all he saw was Justina, smiling like a sly, sleekly beautiful cat, whose paw rested firmly on the tail of a mouse oblivious to its predicament. The street noise disappeared altogether. He wrapped his arms around her and squeezed her as she tightened her arms around him. "I love you beyond eternity," he said, with his cheek pressed against hers.

"And I love you beyond that," she said into his ear.

◆ CHAPTER THIRTY-SIX ◆

A Setback

WHAT ELSE COULD HE HAVE DONE? After that fateful encounter in the men's room on the seventieth floor, Blake had confronted Brinkman. Still fuming about the merger decision—over which he had not been consulted—Blake thought he could tie up Brinkman but good over the Big Bet. However, it was Brinkman, not Blake, who held the ace-in-the-hole.

$ $ $ $

"Here are your choices, my friend." Brinkman began his counter-extortion. He stood defiantly by the windows facing the expanses beyond the Minneapolis skyline and forced Blake to squint to see his threatening silhouette against the late afternoon sun. "Choice number one: You learn about a serious health problem, you take early retirement, effective the end of the month, and you never ever breathe a word of this to anyone, ever. Choice number two: I go public with the picture."

"What picture?" Blake didn't know what Brinkman was talking about.

"You know damn well what picture," said Brinkman, as he moved toward a large walnut cabinet in the corner of his office.

It was enough to jog Blake's memory. Back in November, at Brinkman's insistence, Blake had reluctantly joined a group of lawyers and HeartBank executives at a dinner celebration to commemorate the closing on a small bank acquisition out in Nevada. Blake was not one to imbibe or revel, and occasions such as the one in Las Vegas were anathema to him. During the third round of post-dinner drinks (a Diet Pepsi for Blake), a member of the hotel staff had appeared inside the private dining room, approached Brinkman and whispered something into his ear. Brinkman had let out a big cloud of cigar smoke, turned his head and said something out of the corner of his mouth. The next thing Blake knew, four women with an abundance of make-up and hair, in attire much too revealing for his sensibilities, were being ushered into the room. The door closed behind them, and the men—except for Blake—had hooted like savages. Before the tabletop strip teases had begun, the women had randomly selected three hooting savages—and poor Blake—to arouse with a jump on the lap and a perfumed embrace around the neck. Blake had reacted with an outburst of anger and disgust, but not before the flash went off. It was Brinkman himself who had pulled the trigger, and he laughed raucously, wickedly, mercilessly at Blake.

"What picture?" Brinkman repeated, while he pulled a manila envelope from the cabinet drawer. "The picture of you and that prostitute—she was a prostitute, you know. And I think just about anyone who sees the picture in the paper will know she couldn't have been anything but a prostitute and that the lap she was sitting on was yours, you self-righteous, pompous ass." Blake gasped when Brinkman drew the eight-by-ten photo from the envelope. It was the darkest form of blackmail. Like a shark at the smell of blood, Brinkman circled for the kill. "You're not going to stop my merger," he said through his teeth. "If anything tumbles out of your mouth about what you heard while your pompous ass was on the crapper, I'll make sure you wish you hadn't been born, you understand? I'll parade before the press a nice line of well-scripted, well-compensated bankers and lawyers from two of the most prestigious firms in the US of A, witnesses, all of them, to your adulterous ways, Mr. Righteous, you hear me?" Brinkman sneered viciously.

The heat of fear shot down Blake's spine. He felt as if he were in the sauna at the club. Blake's jaws moved without any sound. It didn't matter that Brinkman would pay him a large severance package to retire early and shut up. All that mattered was that the photo must never see the light of day, ever. He loved his wife and kids more than anything in the world. His daughter was a successful surgeon and a fine woman, devoted wife and loving mother to boot. Blake's son was well on his way to making partner at the Simms & Whitney law firm in Minneapolis and engaged to the shining light of her generation of Baskings, a distinguished family with some of the oldest money in the Twin Cities. No, Blake couldn't bring the horror of scandal and dishonor to his family. He loved them more than he hated Brinkman. Thus, with great bitterness, Blake Huntington, devoted husband and father; Blake Huntington, respected elder statesman of HeartBank, esteemed member of the local legal community, well-regarded member of the church vestry and perennial leader of fund drives for charity, accepted the terms of extortion.

$ $ $ $

The day after the surprise meeting with John and Justina, Blake decided to call in sick. He had never called in sick, in over twenty-five years, but it was easy now. Hadn't the official statement declared that it was on account of poor health that he was taking early retirement? That afternoon, while he sat in his study and looked out over his lawn, which swept down to the waters of Minnetonka, Blake replayed what was seared into his memory—the encounter with that bold woman attorney, who had come crashing into his life without any warning whatsoever. It was she, not Brinkman, who had checkmated him. In a panic, he had lied to her and her client, the banker, John something or other. He had never told a lie in his entire adult life. What on earth had happened to his moral compass? It was Peter denying Christ when the pressure was on, he thought. No, it was worse than that. He was Judas, who, in a moment of weakness, combined with pressure from Lucifer himself, had accepted thirty pieces of silver to betray all he had followed and stood for as an upright, outstanding, Christian, family man and pillar of the community. For his inveracity before the lawyer, Blake could be forgiven, but after a court reporter administered the time-honored oath—"So help me God"—he would not be capable of perjury, irrespective of forgiveness. He simply would not be able to lie under oath. And then all hell would break loose. That bold attorney would create havoc with the merger, with Brinkman, the whole insane bank, and Blake would step outside one fine morning to pick up the *StarTribune* and find his color photo on the front page and his family would be disgraced, not to mention his own conscientious works in life. He would wish he were dead. No, he would wish he had been dead for some time, so that disgrace would not have wrecked the lives of his loved ones and utterly destroyed all that he had worked so hard to become.

Many people his age died of heart disease or cancer, and he knew some went very gracefully, with full dignity and honor. Why, then, couldn't he view this situation in the same light as a terminal disease? Life had treated him well. He had experienced more blessings than any man could request. He was at the summit, and it was now time, before all the glory and riches of this life were irredeemably tarnished, to dispatch himself to the afterworld, which is where he would one day wind up anyway.

The decision to draw the curtains was unavoidable, and while the sun danced over the waves of Lake Minnetonka, Blake stared into the blue and drew up plans for the final scenes of the last act of his life.

Even at the end, he was a perfectly decent man. He did not want to blow his brains out, the way some do it, and create a bloody mess for someone to discover. He did not want to be missing for an extended period, worry his dear family to death and produce a god-awful stench for whoever might discover his corpse a week or more after he died. After all, it was not only summer; it was an unusually hot one. Better to go cleanly, quietly and quickly. He would inhale carbon monoxide until nearly all consciousness had seeped from his brain before he dialed 9-1-1. That way the police could trace the call and find him before his body became, well, unpleasant.

$ $ $ $

When Jenny delivered the news at just after eight o'clock the next morning, John went white in horror. "Last night," she said, "in a mini-storage garage just off Highway 280 on the border of Minneapolis and St. Paul, Blake Huntington parked his car, left the engine running and closed the garage door. The police found his body at around eleven o'clock."

♦ CHAPTER THIRTY-SEVEN ♦

Severance Package

JOHN FOUND JUSTINA STANDING AT HER OFFICE WINDOW and peering down at the alley and at the back wall of the building opposite hers. Mired in residue of ages past, the dirty yellow brick and rusted fire escapes hid safely from renovation. He looked at his watch and limply chastised himself for being so late again for work. He was about to suggest he should make his way to his office, but Justina spoke first.

"Our case—my entire practice, for that matter—is trapped in an alley like the one down there, hidden from the light of success," she said bleakly. "Just like the brown, bashed-up dumpster that guards the pockmarked alleyway, our case against Brinkman, like so many of my files, is heading nowhere. The one witness who could have cinched our case, John, is dead and gone. No amount of lawyering could bring back his testimony." John noticed a ripple in the window glass and reached out to feel it with his finger. "That ripple will always be there," she said. "I'll never reach a point when I can afford an office with modern glass and a view."

She stepped away from John and continued to stare through the window. "I don't feel like working any more today," she said, more to herself than to John, "even though my other cases scream for attention, and my lack of cash flow forces me to resort to some collectible hourly billing." John worried that the gloom of her predicament had extinguished all desire, even for him.

The phone rang, but it failed to break Justina's despairing stare into the bleak alley. It rang twice, three times, before the answering machine kicked in. "Hello, you've reached the office of Justina Herz. I'm fighting for justice right now and can't come to the phone. Please leave a message, though, and I'll get back to you right away."

"Fighting for justice," Justina repeated, sarcastically. "Right. And starving because of it." The machine beeped.

"Justina? This is Kathryn Huntington. Blake Huntington's wife. We've never met, but I've heard of you, and I'd like to meet with you. I found something you should have." Justina turned sharply and lunged for the phone atop her desk.

"Hello? Hello? Mrs. Huntington! This is Justina."

John snapped to attention, and Justina's face lit up as she quietly returned the receiver to the cradle and pressed the speaker button.

"Hello, Justina," sounded the voice. "This is Kathryn Huntington. I'd like to meet. I found a tape and a note that Blake left and you're going to want them." Disbelief filled Justina's face. Was this the break they needed or was it a cruel hoax? John wondered, afraid to breathe. Time froze. Seconds passed. "Hello? Are you there?"

"Yes, I am, Mrs. Huntington," Justina said, "and in fact, so is my client, John Anchor. That's why I've put you on the speaker phone."

"Hello, John," the voice said.

"Hi," he said. It was all he could get out of his mouth.

Justina leaned over the phone. "Mrs. Huntington, we're available anytime, at your convenience. I mean, where are you? We can meet as fast as you can get here, or do you want us to meet you somewhere else? I'm flexible."

"You can call me Kathryn, and how about this afternoon at around two o'clock at your office?"

"That's fine, yes, of course, we'll expect you then, Kathryn. Do you know where I'm located?"

"No, actually, I don't. I know you're downtown, but where I don't know," said Mrs. Huntington. Her voice sounded firm, genuine, reliable. It gave John an extra measure of hope. Justina gave directions.

Meanwhile, John looked out at the drab yellow brick wall across the alley and watched splotches of sunlight appear. Justina hung up and shrieked with joy. "Yes!" John joined in her ecstatic shouts. Now, finally, clouds yielded to resplendent light. "Nice job, counselor," he said and embraced her. They kissed so hard that John felt his lips go numb.

$ $ $ $

Kathryn Huntington's appearance and attire didn't disappoint. She looked as one would expect of a woman in her mid-fifties with a Lakeshore

Drive address—and whose late husband had just come by Lord knows how fine a severance package on top of the millions he was already worth in HeartBank stock alone. A collection of gold necklaces hung elegantly on her black turtleneck sweater, and her black, smartly creased slacks revealed a figure that exercised at an expensive club and ate at the health drink bar after her daily workout. Justina greeted her cordially, expressed condolences over recent events and ushered her into the conference room, where she introduced Kathryn to John.

"Hello, Mrs. Huntington," he greeted her. "I'm John Anchor, Justina's client from HeartBank."

"Hello John. Where would you like me to sit?" As Justina gestured toward the end of the conference table, Kathryn sat down, drew her purse onto the table and crossed her hands over it.

"Before I show you what I have," said Kathryn, "I want to say something to the two of you."

"We're listening, " said Justina.

"Good. For the past couple of months, Blake was very unhappy about the whole merger. At home, at least, he told me how he'd been bullied by Max Brinkman and others. He really hated the whole situation, but I think he felt pretty helpless. When finally he was let go, he turned bitter and depressed, despite having received a respectable sum of money in connection with his departure. His outlook deteriorated sharply until he plunged into a deep depression, where he wouldn't talk to me, couldn't sleep and just all-around seemed rather worried and blue. I didn't know exactly what it was that troubled him, but now I have a pretty good idea. I think extreme doubt arose in his mind as to whether he had done the right thing. He received a lot of money, you know. Do you know how much he received?"

"No," said Justina, nonchalantly, though inside she was dying to know the amount.

"Two million dollars in cash, two in restricted stock and one million in vested options," came the answer.

"Now that's a severance package," said John. Despite their outward gestures, however, John and Justina felt the weight of their confrontation with the deceased. They shot a glance at each other and grimaced. Both thought the same thing at the same time: We're responsible for his untimely death, are we not? But why suicide? Wasn't that a bit extreme?

"Anyway, I know Blake really wanted you to have this note and tape," said Kathryn, as she drew them from her purse, "and all I ask is that you keep Blake's memory close to heart, however you're going to use them. I wish you all the luck in the world."

"Thanks, Kathryn," Justina answered, as she fought back tears. John pulled up alongside Justina as Kathryn presented Huntington's note. It consisted of one sheet of paper covered with scrawling blue ink.

Dear Kathryn,

In the end, greed and ego rule the world. In the end, greed and ego ruin the world. I did wrong and would have been destroyed, without dignity. This way, it's with dignity. I'm sorry to have caused you so much pain, as I'm sure this will, but it's much better this way, trust me.

In this envelope is a tape, which can bring some very powerful people to their knees. Please deliver it to Justina Herz, a lawyer who is trying to sue HeartBank. She'll know how to use it.

Love,

Blake

John wanted to grab Justina and lay a kiss on her lips, but Kathryn's solemn countenance told him the celebration must wait.

It took some doing, but Justina finally uncovered a hand-held dictaphone. She slipped the micro-cassette tape into the little machine and pushed the play button. With their heads so close to each other, their hair touched; John and Justina leaned over the device to hear the words of Blake Huntington.

"This is Blake Huntington, the former general counsel of HeartBank National Association. I am making this record so that if need be, the world will know the truth about Maximilian Brinkman and the merger between HeartBank and Loan Star Bank in Texas.

"Last June—the nineteenth; it was a Wednesday—I was in the men's room on the seventieth floor of the HeartBank Tower. I had just attended a merger-related meeting. In the men's room, I overheard Maximilian

Brinkman tell the bank's lawyer why he, Brinkman, had orchestrated the merger. I remember it well, because it was so startling. He said, almost verbatim, 'You know why I decided to merge? You think it was for the shareholders? No way! It was on a bet! I bet dinner at The Opulate in Las Vegas'—I remember, because I had eaten dinner at The Opulate back in November—'two bottles of *Chateau Petrus* and the woman of my choice.' The lawyer, Jerry Stanwick in the New York office of Lauter & Schlicher, said he didn't want to hear anything about it, until Brinkman offered him a bribe in effect—insider information regarding upcoming IPOs. Brinkman said, quote- unquote, 'I'll guarantee you a million bucks.'

"It was then I realized I had to do something to stop the nonsense. I had been skeptical of the merger all along. Despite my position and tenure with the company, Brinkman hadn't informed me about the merger decision—let alone consult with me about it—until exactly seven days before it was announced to the public. Now I had information that confirmed my doubts: The merger had no sensible, rational basis in fact; it rested on no well-considered strategy. It was based entirely on the whim, the greed and the ego of the company's CEO. With the information I had, I felt it was my obligation to stop Brinkman in his tracks.

"Unfortunately, I made a terrible mistake. I went straight to Brinkman and confronted him with the evidence. It was then that he blackmailed me.

"To protect my family, I had no choice but to do what I am doing. I am sorry for where this has led, but I want everyone to know two things about it. First, the blackmail was based strictly, wholly, utterly on appearances, not reality. However, if I did not do what I have to do, Brinkman would do everything within his considerable power to frame me. It would be very difficult to disprove his malicious allegations. Second, I love my wife Kathryn, my daughter Katy and my son Corydon. I have always been true to them.

"If it ever becomes necessary for the world to know, I hope this tape will allow truth and justice to prevail. That's all."

The tape went silent, and John and Justina began breathing again. John didn't need his lawyer to tell him how close they were to seizing the Prize.

After repeating their condolences to Kathryn and walking her slowly to the elevators, John and Justina immediately went to work. Justina grabbed a notepad from a drawer in her desk, snatched a pen and began to write. It was all in her head, John could tell, and her thoughts raced well-ahead of her ability to jot things down. "Number one," she said, determinedly. "We call the office of—what was his name, Sandwick or Standwick?"

"Stanwick, I think it was—the lawyer, you mean?" John jumped in.

"Stanwick," she repeated. "We call his office and find out when he is next in Minneapolis. He could be here right now, for all we know."

"And if he's not scheduled here in the near future?" John asked.

"Then, John, we do things in reverse. We find out when Brinkman is next going to New York," she said, with her usual confidence.

"How do we get through to find out?" John felt as if he were now part of a chase scene toward the end of a thriller movie.

"I'm very good at posing as a secretary," said Justina, proudly. "I've used the tactic many times to get through to people who have their calls screened. The most knowledgeable and most powerful people in large law firms and large corporations are the executive secretaries. You get through to them and you gain access to a wealth of information and privilege. Trust me, I can handle this without any problem." John had no doubt she could. "In any event," she continued, "the next step is to confront Brinkman and his lawyer with the facts—and the tape, a copy of which we'll have back here, of course. And then, John," she said, her eyes filled with glee, "we'll lay out our demands. We'll present an offer that even a megalomaniac, even a madman, even a man obsessed with power and greed, or rather, especially a man obsessed with power and greed, can't refuse."

"Justina, you're amazing, absolutely amazing," John said, transfixed by her power and confidence. However, a twinge of doubt undercut his own confidence, or maybe it was a hint of fear that bothered him. He had never personally commanded such power over anyone the way he and Justina now held it over Brinkman, and John felt uncomfortable holding this kind of a club. "Are you sure we're not going to get clobbered in the process here, Justina?"

"John, I'm not taking this lightly, if that's what you mean. I have to be perfectly frank with you that what I'm proposing violates the Rules of Professional Responsibility, to put it mildly. But John, my entire career, I've followed the rules when so many others out there have violated them with contempt. Now it's time for our own little revolution, if you will, against the power and greed of the establishment. It's time to win, and why not play to win when you can't lose?"

$ $ $ $

Exactly eighty-four days before the deadline for Brinkman's grand bet to be won, John and Justina stormed the gates. He wore his MVP suit. She wore the striking red suit she had worn on the day he would savor forever. Armed with the tape and a well-crafted script, they arrived at the guard's station on the seventieth floor at precisely 12:28 P.M.

"Tom Kinder," John said, using the agreed-upon alias. "And this is my associate, Kristina Granlund. We're here for a twelve-thirty with Mr. Brinkman."

"You were up here a few days ago, weren't you, Mr. Kinder?" the guard said cordially.

"Good memory," John said, just as affably as Tom Kinder himself would have responded. The security guard looked down at his list of expected visitors and made a check mark with his pen. "Right through the doorway and to your right," said the guard, as the big bronze doors opened ponderously. So far, so good.

With John in the lead, the two conspirators strode down the hallway with a deceptive air of confidence. Only one of the secretarial stations opposite the Senior offices was occupied. Presumably the other secretaries were at lunch. John greeted the woman holding down the fort and announced himself and his "associate." It was the same secretary whom he had asked for directions to the restroom when his B-17 was going down.

She was eating lunch at her desk, and John happened to catch her just after she had bitten off a big piece of her deli sandwich. With her fingers over her lips, she chewed hurriedly, swallowed hard and let out a giggle. "Sorry," she said. "I bit off more than I could chew, you might say."

Assuming the natural graces of Tom Kinder, John responded with a relaxed smile and said, "No, my apologies. We shouldn't have sneaked up on you like that."

"You're here to see Mr. Brinkman?" asked the secretary.

"Yes, as a matter of fact, at 12:30," said John.

"You must be Tom Kinder."

"That's correct."

"He and Mr. Stanwick are expecting you. Here," she said, as she wiped her mouth with a napkin and rose from her chair, "I'll show you in." She led them in the direction of the corner office adjacent to the boardroom at the end of the floor. The boardroom, John noticed through the glass, looked like a war zone, with papers strewn all over the conference table, suitcoats draped over chairs and electronic notebooks hooked up here and there. A handful of people munched on take-out as they pored over documents or stared at monitors, but most of the merger mavens presumably were at lunch somewhere else.

The secretary stopped in the doorway of Brinkman's commodious office and gestured for John and Justina to continue past her into the exclusive lair of HeartBank's CEO. "Your 12:30 appointment, sir," she said. She vanished without further commotion.

As soon as they were past the doorway, John closed the door and leaned against it.

"I'm Justina Herz, and this is my client, one of your employees, John Anchor," said Justina to Brinkman and Stanwick, who stood together in the center of the mahogany-paneled, leather-bound penthouse office. Heartbank's attorney held what appeared to be a legal pleading, and John assumed it was the Walden complaint.

"What the hell?!" Brinkman looked as surprised as a squirrel in a trap when the door snaps shut. Stanwick, a man about five-foot-seven with ears disproportionately large for his head, looked like a smaller, more nervous animal caught in the same cage. Justina had laid the bait the day before when posing as Tom Kinder's secretary; she had phoned Brinkman's secretary to "carve an hour or so out of their bosses' busy schedules" to discuss secret negotiations to settle the Walden case.

"We're here to make you an offer you can't refuse." Justina continued with her script, as John's pulse beat hard against his watchband. They weren't jewel thieves anymore. They were robbing a bank.

"Where is security when you need 'em," Brinkman said. He overcame his surprise and lunged toward the phone on his carved mahogany desk. Justina stood in his way, and he threatened to shove her aside.

"Hands off me," she hissed, like a cat in the path of a threatening dog, "or I'll sue you for sexual assault, not to mention a few more serious matters." He backed off, stunned by her defiance. She hadn't flinched and now stood firmly, with her fists on her hips.

"Both of you, sit down over there." With one fist still on her hip, she pointed with her other hand to the luxuriant leather sofa at the far end of the room. Like dogs stunned by an electric prod, Brinkman and Stanwick retreated as she had commanded.

"Next time you build a monument to your ego, Mr. Brinkman," she began her prepared speech, "you might want to direct more closely the design of the doors to the bathroom stalls so as to allow you to discern more easily whether any of those stalls is occupied when you divulge incriminating information to a confidant while standing in the relative privacy of the executive lavatory." Brinkman and Stanwick looked as though they were competing with each other to see whose lower jaw could fall the farthest. "You see, Mr. Brinkman," said Justina, "Mr. Anchor, here, as well as Mr. Huntington, overheard your statement to Mr. Stanwick to the effect that this whole merger business was prompted solely by a bet."

Her words catapulted Stanwick from the sofa. "Attorney-client privilege precludes you from using it as evidence," he said. His mouth looked like a shark's.

"Sorry, Mr. Stanwick. That argument apparently didn't preclude the need to muzzle Blake Huntington, and it won't work on me. The privilege doesn't apply, sorry. You did not achieve the requisite privacy, and besides, you're the bank's lawyer, not Brinkman's personal lawyer. When it comes to suing you personally, I'd slash through the privilege with less effort than it takes to say, 'no dice.' Now sit down and listen."

Next, Justina held up, between her right thumb and forefinger, the micro-cassette bearing Blake Huntington's testimony. "I have in my hand the testimony of Blake Huntington, which corroborates the testimony of my client, Mr. Anchor." Justina gestured toward John and looked briefly in his direction. She was definitely on a roll.

"Where did you . . ." Brinkman tried to talk, but it seemed he was too stunned to do so.

"We got it from Mrs. Huntington, who found it with her husband's suicide note. We will have no problem establishing its authenticity," said Justina, with a face that John thought could strike terror in the heart of any man, even a man from the East Coast. "Which brings me to our offer."

"This is preposterous!" Brinkman spoke, but he seemed unable or afraid to get up from the sofa.

Justina cut him off. "What's preposterous is that someone in your position can abuse his power as you have. Now listen up. What we want, and what I know you'll want to grant us, given your alternative, is a severance package of $20 million. And we want it this afternoon. That means now. It means before we leave this office." John looked at Brinkman and saw a pathetic creature, whose power and gall had left him high, dry and completely vulnerable, like a warrior caught bathing in the river, whose uniform, equipment, weaponry and ammunition have all been stolen away by an extortionist now standing high up the bank.

"Twenty million!" Brinkman wailed. "You're a couple of terrorists. You're out of your minds."

"That's exactly your problem, Mr. Brinkman. We're out of our minds, and if you can't see your way to preserving your self-interest, then my client and I will do a few things that prove we're out of our minds." Brinkman and Stanwick remained frozen with fear. "We'll launch the mother of all shareholder derivative suits or a securities fraud class action, take your pick. We'll play Huntington's tape for our friends at *The Wall Street Journal*, and you'll be barred forever from running a public company. Your name will be mud so many times over you won't be able to crawl out from under it. And you Mr. Stanwick, we suggest that instead of threatening us with silliness like the attorney-client privilege, you apply your persuasive abilities more constructively and advise Mr. Brinkman to follow what's in his best interest. Of course, that puts you in a conflict, since you're the bank's counsel, but the alternative is for us to sue the daylights out of you and all your partners for securities fraud if Brinkman blows us off. You yourself know the truth, just as Huntington did and just as my client does. You have an obligation to withdraw as counsel to HeartBank. If you don't cooperate, we'll report you to the SEC, not to mention the New York Board of Ethics or whatever the body is called that disbars crooked lawyers like you."

"Talk about disbarment! *You're* headed for disbarment, the way you're terrorizing, extorting us," said Stanwick.

"But think about it. When Mr. Money Bags here pays up, do you suppose I'm going to need to practice law anymore?" Justina fired back.

John noticed Stanwick was working his face, his jaws, his brain, for some kind of comeback. "Nothing we agree to is going to be enforceable," the New York lawyer said feebly.

"And how's that?" Justina asked.

"A contract entered into under duress is unenforceable, and I'd say any judge or jury in any jurisdiction in this country would find us under duress in the present circumstances. Besides," Stanwick said, "a payout of this nature would require board approval, and you know as well as I that the board of directors can't be assembled on such short notice."

"Get real," said Justina. "First of all, we're not dealing with contract law here. We're dealing with the law of the jungle—your client's kind of jungle—and you're in the jungle with all the rest of us. Second, my fellow counselor, you're wrong about this transaction's needing board approval, because we're expecting payment from Mr. Brinkman personally, not from HeartBank. As I recall, he personally stands to get forty million out of the merger. Our deal still leaves him with twenty million. Third, once we consummate our little deal here, each of us will be equally motivated to ensure that no one outside this room ever knows what happened."

Stanwick was speechless. Brinkman was almost speechless. "Can I say something?" he croaked.

"Be my guest," said Justina with the calmness that accompanies supreme dominance.

"I couldn't possibly pull twenty million together if I wanted to. It's not like I have it sitting in my checking account. I'd have to liquidate certain holdings, it would take time, I'd have to consult my tax man, my accountant, my lawyer. I couldn't just stash it in a bag and say, 'Here it is, twenty million in bills.' There are a lot of decisions to be made, a lot of people to consult."

"Just like you did before you decided to merge with Loan Star?" Justina asked rhetorically. "It seems to us that when it came to a decision affecting two behemoth banks with combined assets of nearly two hundred billion"—Justina placed special emphasis on the *b* in billion – "said decision being your merger with Loan Star, you didn't find it necessary to consult with a whole lot of people. In fact, according to my eminently reliable sources, you didn't find it necessary to consult with anyone prior to leaping off the edge of the merger cliff. Contrast the merger with the matter at hand. Here we have a meager twenty million to contend with, and sitting on the sofa with you is *a* lawyer, at least, who can probably offer you some advice." John hadn't thought Brinkman could turn any whiter, but the CEO was beyond white. He was a clammy phantom of his usual appearance, and he groaned as if he were seriously ill.

"Besides," Justina said, after watching her prey squirm in pain, "what we're really talking about to get us out of here is only ten million up front."

"Huh?" Brinkman looked dazed by the apparent change in her demand.

John and Justina had worked it all out in advance. "And not only will we make it that much easier on you," she said, "but we're going to make a regular hero out of you, as well. Here's how it works. When I direct you to, you'll go to your computer or your speaker phone and you'll call up your accounts and effectuate transfers of a total of ten million cash to an account I'll write down for you. How you pull together the cash and how you deal with capital gains taxes and whatever other taxes might be due is entirely your business. Surely this is chump change for you, yes?"

Brinkman reeled against the back of the sofa. "*Aargh,*" he groaned.

"Good, good," said Justina. "Then comes the fun part. John?" Justina looked toward John and extended her arm in his direction. It was his cue to dig into his briefcase for a collection of papers and envelopes. "Let's look at the press release first." John handed her the top sheet. "Gentlemen," she said, "I have in my hand a press release, which has already been sent to the *StarTribune* for publication in Sunday's main edition. It reads as follows:

(Minneapolis.) HeartBank CEO, Maximilian Brinkman, announced today his personal pledge of $10 million to local charities. The pledged funds will be paid immediately to 10 organizations, ranging from the recently founded Christian Community Enterprises to well-established entities like United Way. Each will receive a million dollars. "It's a way for me personally to pay back the Twin Cities community for having been such a terrific partner with HeartBank all these years," said Brinkman. "It's my way of saying 'thanks' to a place I've called home over the past six years and a place I'll miss when the headquarters of our new company, HeartStar, moves to Dallas." Brinkman said the funds will be unrestricted, so they can be put to use in a way that each recipient organization believes is best.

Responses from the designated organizations have brought overwhelming praise for Mr. Brinkman, who in the past has been conspicuously absent from the Twin Cities Charity Club, a loose coalition of wealthy area individuals who publicize their own giving as a way to challenge other people of means to follow suit.

Maximilian Brinkman is chairman and chief executive officer of HeartBank, which recently announced plans to merge with Loan Star Bank of Dallas, Texas to form HeartStar Bank. Brinkman will be CEO of the new entity, which will be headquartered in Dallas.

Undoubtedly, Mr. Brinkman, when my friends at the *StarTribune* receive the press release, they'll want to run a big story about your magnanimous gesture. If you want it, you'll get some wonderful press out of this." Brinkman turned ashen-faced.

"At the same time, we will be mailing a letter to each of our designated recipients, Mr. Brinkman. We have ten for you to sign. John?" John handed her the letters. "Just how and when you pay the additional ten million is up to you and your beneficiaries, Mr. Brinkman. Needless to say, however, they will be expecting payment rather soon. Each letter reads this way:

> Dear So-and-so:
>
> Please accept my pledge of $1 million to your organization, which I shall pay by the end of this month. You may apply the funds as your organization deems fitting and proper. There are no restrictions, as long as the funds are used in a manner consistent with your charter.
>
> This is my way of saying thanks for all your good works. God bless.
>
> Sincerely,
> Maximilian Brinkman

"Max, we should at least ask if the pledges could be in stock instead of cash. The tax advantages are considerable—you save huge capital gains taxes on appreciated stock values," Stanwick said with a thin voice.

"I know, I know," Brinkman said with a perturbed tone.

"That surprises me," said Justina. "I had the impression you've never given much to charity before this." There was a twinkle in her eye as she winked at John, but Brinkman only fumed. "In any event, it's your call, Mr. Brinkman. All Mr. Anchor and I know is that you'll be signing and we'll be sending the letters as we've drafted them, and they say you'll be paying a million bucks to each recipient by the end of the month. If transferring to each charity a million bucks worth of HeartBank stock or 3M stock or whatever kind of marketable stock or bonds you have meets the expectations of the recipients of these letters, then I guess you can do as you please. In any event, here's the list of recipients, Mr. Brinkman: The Sierra Club; The Nature Conservancy; Street Homes, a shelter in St. Paul for homeless people; Hennepin County Shelter for Abused Women and Children; ASH, which stands for Affordable Seniors Housing; Harriet Tubman center, an African American community center in St. Paul; the Jewish Community Center in St. Paul; the Jewish Community Center in St. Louis Park; the United Way of St. Paul and the United Way of Minneapolis; and Christian Community Enterprises, a combination housing, job-training, inner-city enterprise organization." Justina smiled with victory. John beamed as he thought of his friend, Steve Torseth, founder of Christian

Community Enterprises. Wouldn't Steve be in heaven when his organization received a million bucks!

At that crowning moment, John rocked back on his heels and said, "Justina, there's one more," said John.

"There is?" Justina said, startled by John's addition. He meant to surprise her.

"Yes," he said.

"What is it?" she asked, her face filled with puzzlement.

"The Saint Paul Chamber Orchestra," he said proudly. "Another million bucks, for a grand total of eleven million."

"Of course!" Justina beamed. "John, you truly are wonderful," she allowed. Uninhibited in the midst of their astounding victory, she threw her arms around him and purposely left a big smudge of lipstick on his cheek. He imagined the love-making session that seemed certain to follow their victory. Justina then turned quickly back to Brinkman. "Are you ready to get busy transferring funds?"

Brinkman rose slowly from the sofa. Stanwick remained sitting in shock and looked back and forth between Brinkman and the two conspirators. "How do I know you won't come back for more once I've paid out the twenty-one million?"

"As my client puts it, Mr. Brinkman, 'Pigs get fat, but hogs get slaughtered,' and I don't want to get slaughtered. Pay us ten million today and pay our designated charities eleven million and you'll never hear from us again. You'll have your merger, a phenomenal reputation for magnanimity and on a net basis, you'll still receive a whopping nineteen million after the merger. Just to help you sleep at night, we'll send you the tape of Huntington's testimony and our only copy of it once we know you've paid on your charitable pledges. In addition, I'll sign any kind of covenant not to sue that Mr. Contract Law over here," Justina said, as she nodded in the direction of Stanwick, "wants to draft up."

A half hour later, Maximilian Brinkman had completed the necessary transactions, and the $10 million dollars were in John and Justina's newly-opened account. Having won at last his severance package, John glanced at his Timex, picked up Brinkman's phone and placed a call to Vohlmann. The call went into voice mail, and after the beep, John spoke his message.

"Fred, this is John Anchor and it's exactly 1:14. I won't be back this afternoon, tomorrow, the next day or forever. Before you know it, I'll be on a beach or a mountaintop or a sailboat or at an Austrian music festival somewhere with someone I really care a lot about. Jenny Jacobson can have all my stuff that's worth having. Otherwise, you can just throw it away. Thanks and, by the way, don't sweat the small stuff. Life's too short. Goodbye and good luck."

THE END